L. J. McDonald

The Sylph Hunter

D1496287

ALSO BY L. J. McDONALD

The Battle Sylph
The Shattered Sylph
Queen of the Sylphs
A Midwinter Fantasy

L. J. McDonald

The Sylph Hunter

Published by Montlake Romance, Seattle

www.apub.com

ISBN-13: 9781477818091
ISBN-10: 147781809X

Cover design by Anne Cain Graphic Art and Design

Library of Congress Control Number: 2013917233

Printed in the United States of America

For Oliver
And for anyone who ever faced down their own fears

PROLOGUE

The sylphs were dancing.

There were hundreds of them, a storm of colors swirling around each other in a glorious celebration of life. Despite the fact it was once a place used to lure and trap their kind, the underground chamber they used was now a brilliantly lit place of joy. Air, earth, water, fire, healing, and battle, they whirled in a mad happiness that had no music.

Over by the far wall of the massive chamber, Gel sat on the floor with his arms across the tops of his knees and watched the sylphs play. They were ecstatic with the idea of being free, the joy of being allowed to do what they wanted and to interact as they never had before the queen came. Not in Meridal, where even human beings were once sold as slaves and sylphs had been nothing more than property.

In the center of the chamber, a circle of noncolor gleamed, floating a dozen feet above the ground. The sylphs danced around it, calling those on the other side to come through and join them.

He'd been told it was a small hive past the gate, one badly depleted by predators, though Gel couldn't imagine what kind of predator would threaten sylphs. He'd seen the battlers the day the queen had arrived. He'd seen how much they had destroyed, including all of the nobility and even the emperor himself.

Gel closed his eyes, not really wanting to remember that day any more than he did any of the days before it. He'd spent years locked in a cage not much larger than he was himself, his tongue chopped out to keep him from speaking to the earth sylph who had been bound to him. She was only supposed to feed from him after all, him and the four others caged with him.

Are you all right? he heard Shasha ask in his mind.

Gel opened his eyes. Before him stood what appeared to be a young girl, except her skin was formed of smooth marbled stone and her eyes were rubies. She looked at him critically, her hands clasped behind her back while the sylphs behind her continued their silent display. The only real sound in the chamber was the chanting of the priests, left alive for their skill with the gates, and the fearful chattering of the humans brought in—sometimes against their will—to become masters for the newest sylphs. Most of the more experienced masters were like Gel, sitting against the wall and watching. To them, none of this was truly real and it was easier to just stay out of the way.

His earth sylph kept watching him. Her official master had been killed by the battlers during the rebellion, for the newly established crime of having kept a sylph under control like a tool. Gel had been nothing more than a feeder, one of the five men kept caged for her to feed from, all of them tongueless to stop them giving commands. Of all of them, he was the one she'd chosen to be her only master after they were freed. Gel didn't know why, but he wasn't unhappy about it because he'd always liked the little creature. When he'd been in his cage, she was the only highlight of the day, coming as she did in the shape of a pillar of earth and somehow seeming both sad and kind to him. He'd loved her a little bit and had always wanted to set her free. Perhaps she'd sensed that in him.

"I'm okay," he said slowly. The feel of his regrown tongue in his mouth was still alien to him and his words slurred.

Behind Shasha, the gate continued to glow, the storm of sylphs happily flickering around it. It shimmered briefly, and a tendril dropped out of the hovering gate like a thread drawn across his vision. Gel blinked.

"Do you want to leave?" the earth sylph asked. Spoken aloud, her voice was gravelly.

Gel shrugged, hugging his knees. Where was there to go? At least it was cool in here and there were no expectations. "It's all right."

"Okay." Leaning forward, she kissed him quickly on the cheek and turned, stomping back toward the dance. Gel lifted a hand to his cheek and touched the skin where she'd kissed him with a trembling smile.

The line swished again, dragging across the floor. Gel blinked a second time, squinting to try and see it more clearly, but the sylphs were in the way. He wasn't even sure he was seeing anything at all, since it was almost invisible and no one else appeared to notice it at all. Gel blinked a third time and shook his head, but the thread didn't go away, though the sylphs continued to ignore it. If they didn't see it, it had to be imagined. Gel sighed, feeling odd and out of sorts. He had his freedom, but he didn't know what to do with it. Going in a heartbeat from slave to . . . what? What was he?

Shasha came back toward him, her expression concerned. Gel didn't know what to say to her or what she wanted from him. Not much it seemed, save his energy and his company. She certainly didn't expect him to work, though he accompanied her when she did. Gel didn't like the idea of being alone. This whole freedom concept was much easier on her than him, but then again, sylphs in Meridal were now the rulers. All of the old leaders and masters of the former regime were dead or being hunted down. Those who remained weren't allowed to give orders at all; they were just supposed to exist in harmony with their sylphs.

Gel didn't have any urge to order Shasha to do anything, but harmony wasn't something he was sure he could ever get his mind around.

Shasha hunkered down beside him, looking at him with worry he could feel as well as see. She put a cool stony hand on his shoulder and he just stared toward the swirling dance and the gate, not knowing what to say, or even what word to put to this tumult of emotions inside him. Being mute had been so much easier.

The gate was swirling now as well, in a mimicry of the sylphs around it. That distortion was one that everyone saw. Gel watched the sylphs stop their dance, many even becoming solid as they peered curiously at the gate, and the battlers started to move in. Everyone seemed puzzled; they still didn't see the thread that swayed down from it. No, threads. Gel saw dozens now, dropping out of the gate and swishing across his vision. Hundreds? Gel blinked, now seeing the entire opening of the gate bearded by them, though that was the only place where he saw them. If it was his vision gone strange, wouldn't they be everywhere? Some were thicker than mere threads, grown in width to the thickness of a man's arm, or even a man's body. Gel stared. Shasha looked at him, confused by his confusion, and turned to peer uncomprehendingly at the gate, seeing absolutely nothing.

A water sylph that looked like a rolling ball of liquid wandered into the forest of threads. Immediately, she turned translucent and vanished, flowing so swiftly up the length of the tendrils that she was gone before he even realized she'd been touched. Gel's breath caught.

The sylphs definitely couldn't help but notice that. Even as the water sylph's master started screaming from somewhere at the edge of the chamber, the battlers began to roar. They didn't have time for more than that.

Things exploded through the gate, and these weren't thin as the first threads had been, but tentacles that were thick and barbed. The sylphs still couldn't see them, and even to Gel they were clear as water, visible more as a distortion than an actual object. He drew

4

breath, forgetting he had a tongue to scream with, and saw them tear into the sylphs, lashing together dozens with a single tentacle and yanking them in, only there were hundreds to lash with. Ozone stank in the air as the sylphs vanished, turning strangely gray before they were sucked away and the tentacles reached farther, sweeping through the room where the only sounds were sylph wails and human screams.

Gel finally remembered how to scream then, forgotten after years in the cages. His voice came out shrill and inhuman and he clutched Shasha's arm tight, his fingers turning white and painful against her stone. She was staring around, terrified and not understanding even as everyone else died.

We should have left, was all Gel could get himself to think. *We should have left.*

Something forced itself through the gate, ripping it apart but still managing to hold it open while the priests died. Gel continued to stare in horror. Whimpering, Shasha threw herself at him and he felt her arms go around him as tentacles ripped through the air toward them both.

～

It had been a good feed, the best it had had in a long time, but one that would have been dangerously rich had it been in free air. If it hadn't been in this enclosed space, it could have made itself float much too high above the ground, with the risk of winds tearing it apart or pushing it to where there was no food. It had just been so hungry though. Already through the gateway before it realized the way back would close behind it, it swept through the chamber, looking and feeling with its tentacles for more food, but it had devoured everything.

It paused there for a moment, collecting itself, but it was pressing uncomfortably against the ceiling and the way it had come was gone. There was nothing left to do but go out through an opening in one wall. There was no other exit and it could smell more food that way. That was all in the world that mattered. Just the sky and the food.

Picking the only route out of this place where the food had drawn it, it lashed a thousand tentacles, some as thin as a human's hair, others as thick around as an oak, flashing them down a wide corridor, and anchored them into the walls. Sure of its grip, it pulled itself forward, sliding its way down the corridor. The way was tight, but the creature was malleable when it had to be. Still, it didn't like this feeling and it swept its tentacles farther, grabbing and pulling.

It found even more food during the process. When a human wandered around the corner, drawn by the noise, it wrapped a dozen tentacles around him and sucked him in to feed. The taste was strange, different from anything else it had ever tried, but it was food and the food was all. It chewed, swallowed, absorbed, and nothing but a splatter of blood was left as it pulled itself forward again, making its way into a huge area of abandoned, shattered cages and catwalks. There it let itself float, squeezing its way upward to the ceiling and then across to another, smaller corridor. That was harder to get into, but it managed, pulling itself through and to an even smaller staircase that led up. It was almost trapped there, but it exhaled some of the gases inside it, forced itself out, and finally was free, letting its tentacles hang below it as it floated up, giving itself wearily to the winds and wherever they decided to take it.

Anything it saw on the way, it ate.

CHAPTER ONE

The *Racing Dawn* flew above the ocean, rising so high that it was clouds that buffeted her hull instead of waves. The massive air sylph who bore the ship kept the cold air from assaulting her passengers, as well as ensuring that no one was at risk of falling over the side.

Airi hovered right at the tip of the ship's bow, riding on the edge of the bigger sylph's nose so that she could feel the wind. She'd never try to do this herself and could never have traveled this fast for so long. She was young still, less than a hundred years old, and small, but she loved the feel of the winds blowing through her pattern. It was almost like music, all the winds of the world singing to her.

Happy, she shimmered farther forward, reaching past the bow of the ship, and felt a limb formed of air wrap around her, pulling her back.

Careful, the older sylph warned. *You might get sucked away.*

Airi settled down, resting against her grip. In a way, it still felt odd. They were both from separate hives, with different queens. Still, they weren't silly like battlers, to think that anyone alien was an enemy, so she rested there for a while with her friend, just loving the view.

Still, there was another friend she wanted to enjoy this with more. Airi squirmed free and fled back toward the main part of the ship, flickering invisibly past the crew out on the deck. She could take on a form and even become solid, but invisible was easier and the sylphs always knew where she was anyway. So did the only human who really mattered to her.

She went down the stairs to the rooms below deck. In the largest stateroom at the stern, she found her master sitting in a corner with his eyes closed, his hands gripping the arms of his chair. Airi flew over and swirled through his hair, kept just long enough for her to play with. She ruffled it up, bringing it into spikes before smoothing it down again.

Come up and see, she begged. *It's so beautiful.*

"That's okay," he swallowed. "I'm all right."

Are you afraid of heights? she giggled.

Devon nodded slowly, his bangs falling forward over his face with each nod. "Absolutely. Definitely."

She giggled again, whirling his hair into a jagged peak that reminded her of the mountains in the world where she had hatched. *You're afraid of everything.*

"No," he promised. "I'm only afraid of the things that can kill me."

Airi erupted into a storm of giggling at that, playing with his hair and his shirt until he looked as though he was in the middle of a wind storm. Devon sat tolerantly through it and finally sighed, reaching over to a dresser bolted to the wall next to him. Opening one drawer, he pulled out a small flute.

Airi immediately stopped teasing him, her breath catching as she settled down, hovering invisible in the air before him. Devon lifted the flute to his lips, tested the sound, and then launched into a merry jig full of eighth notes that had her dancing madly around the cabin.

Like every air sylph she'd ever known, Airi loved music. The world was full of it, from the sound of a breeze through the grass to the staccato hoofbeats of a horse cantering down a road. But the music that humans could make . . . Her world didn't have that kind of magic, and it reached through her, making her pattern sing from joy. All of her masters had played music for her, from Devon's grandfather to his father to Devon himself, and the pleasure of it was more than enough to make her forget the restrictive rules she used to live under, before they traveled to find the freedom of the Valley, where humans and sylphs were equal. Don't speak, don't take human form. Obey every command of her master until he handed her down to his son, just like every other sylph outside the Valley. She'd lived that way through two generations of men until she'd been given to Devon. All of them had rewarded her with the music, but Devon had done so much more. He'd allowed her to talk, allowed her to have an opinion, and once they reached the Valley, he'd given her full freedom. Perhaps that inclination was what made his music sweetest of all, and Airi danced to it, not caring about anything that had happened or still awaited them in the days ahead, once they arrived in Meridal to do the duty they'd been sent for, and help the newly risen human queen be the best leader she could to a kingdom she'd never expected to have.

∾

They'd made her a palace that floated in the sky.

Eapha stepped out onto an oval balcony that was twenty feet across, the edges protected by elegant railings. Plants had been brought up from somewhere and sat in stone boxes, their leaves healthy and damp thanks to a water sylph's attentions.

Dressed in a robe made of pearlescent pink silk, she belted the sash as she walked barefoot across the stone to look over the railing. A light breeze teased her rich black hair, blowing soft strands into her eyes that she brushed away with dark fingers.

Her palace wasn't nearly the size of the island that used to float over Meridal, now dropped into the ocean and lost, though water sylphs had salvaged many of the furnishings that now adorned her home. She'd been told that this little palace was only twelve thousand square feet in size. The *only* part had made her laugh with delight. The harem where she'd spent the last ten years of her life serving as a concubine with a hundred other women to placate the battlers wasn't that size. She used to sleep in a room crammed with bunk beds the concubines needed to share. Now her bedroom was fifty feet across and she shared it with only one person.

Eapha looked down. Far below her, the city itself stretched out, tan and brown in the morning light. There was a massive scar where the battle sylph arena used to stand, but otherwise the city looked serene and lovely from this height. She could even see people moving along the streets, tiny as insects from up here.

Easier to see were the sylphs. Water and earth sylphs didn't fly, of course, but she could see all the other types flying around, many of them swooping past the balcony as they saw she was there, calling their morning greetings to their queen. Eapha smiled and waved back at them. Their voices were so sweet in her mind. For all of them to have their freedom still felt like such a gift to her.

Eapha turned away from the beautiful view, raising her hands through her thick hair as she took a deep breath. The wind teased against her skin and she spun gently, moving her feet and legs into a dance. She'd always loved to dance in the harem, spending hours at a time perfecting the movement of legs, hips, and arms.

Eapha danced on the balcony, throwing her arms up as she swung her hips and belly, lifting up onto her toes and then down again, crossing the stone as though it were her own personal stage.

Only one pair of eyes watched her performance. Unblinking and the color of fire, they regarded her from within the bedroom, half hidden by the mass of sheets piled atop the bed. Unaware, Eapha continued dancing, her eyes closed and her lips wide in a smile as she moved her legs and arms, kicking them high and spinning more. The eyes continued to watch as she raised her arms back over her head, rotating her entire body from the waist.

Finally, the owner of the eyes got up and padded out onto the balcony. Four inches taller than Eapha's five foot six, his skin was even darker, his hair short with sideburns that reached down to his narrow beard. Lean with muscle, he padded nude to the side of the dancing woman, ducking in around her spin and catching her in his arms, her back against his chest and his hands soft against her breasts.

Eapha gasped as he caught her, her arms coming down as he caressed her breasts, his thumbs rubbing gently against her nipples. "Tooie," she breathed. The battle sylph who'd made her queen of Meridal mouthed his way down her neck, licking the curve of her shoulder as his hands continued massaging her breasts and then gripped her robe, yanking it open. Eapha leaned back against him, her eyes closed as her breath deepened with desire. Tooie's lust was flowing through her, making her damp for him, and he pulled the robe away, his body warm and hard against her back and buttocks. His hands left her breasts, moving down her bare skin and between her legs, where his fingers were gentler still.

"Didn't you get enough last night?" she whispered, turning her head to the side and up toward him. He kept her up late most nights as it was.

"Never," he breathed and kissed her.

As always since she'd become his master and then his queen, Eapha thought she'd never breathe again. She could feel his pleasure as his mouth covered hers, the touch of her skin against his body, all as clearly as she felt her own joys. More, she could feel how he felt them as well. Their combined pleasure created a cycle, always reinforcing itself, always growing, binding them soul to soul and making her cry out even before he lifted her enough to slide his silky length inside.

Eapha's back arched, her mouth gasping for breath as she leaned back against him, letting him do as he wished. Tooie lifted her up again, holding her beneath her thighs and against him as he thrust into her. It was perfection. Eapha rode the waves of pleasure, loving him, feeling him love her, and letting the core of that love grow until it overwhelmed them both, exploding through her.

Tooie set her gently down onto the stone, Eapha leaning against him for a moment while her legs trembled. Quickly, she belted her robe closed again and kissed him.

"Do you think any sylphs saw that?" she asked, only a little embarrassed at the possibility. Public sex had been something of an occupational hazard during her years as a concubine.

Tooie shrugged, his whole torso shifting with the motion, his red eyes—made that way since it was her favorite color—crinkling shut. "If they did, the elementals wouldn't care." They were all neuter anyway.

"And the battlers?" she teased.

"Ten seconds into that and they probably ran off to find their own masters."

Eapha laughed and he nuzzled her. It was most likely true. All battle sylphs were sensualists and loved sex, which was why the old emperor had ordered them kept docile by giving them beautiful women, and most of the nearly seven hundred of them in Meridal either had female masters or were looking for one. None of them were staying willingly with the strictly male feeders who'd been caged to provide them with energy, but they had no choice until they found a woman who was willing to take the place of each sylph's feeders. Of the men who'd once actually commanded the battlers, Eapha didn't think there were any left. Sylphs were bound to whoever named them when they first crossed the gate into the world. During the emperor's rule, those masters would then order their sylphs to obey the commands of dozens of other men in a complex hierarchy of control that made Eapha wonder how the sylphs could keep it all straight. The command of a master, however, was inviolate, trumped only by the word of Eapha, once she became queen. She could overrule the hierarchy, but the battlers weren't willing to take chances. If there were any men left who once gave orders, they wouldn't last long. The sylphs could track them through the same bond their masters used to make them obey.

Not that it mattered. Meridal was at peace, the emperor was gone, and the sylphs were in charge. Eapha kissed her lover again and preceded him back into the bedroom. He probably wouldn't let her get out of it for a while longer, but it didn't really matter.

She had nothing important to do today anyway.

~

Zalia woke long before the sun rose high enough to take the chill off the desert. Opening her eyes, she looked from her blankets to the other side of the small hovel she shared with her father. Xehm was lying on his own blanket, his mouth hanging lax as he snored. Grimacing, since sand didn't make a comfortable bed, she checked her blankets to make sure an asp or scorpion hadn't bedded down with her, and then rose and dressed. Her only dress was old and worn, but still serviceable enough given she would be wearing an apron over it once she got to work. Slipping it on, she put on her sandals and went outside, shivering in the cold air. For all the heat of the desert during the day, it froze at night and even the fires they burned weren't enough to keep them warm.

There were close to forty hovels just outside the city, built by the lee of a massive boulder where the winds weren't so bad. The hovels themselves were made of stone or whatever other materials they could find, all inhabited by people who were living on the edge of starvation, even in what was supposed to be Meridal's new golden age.

Leon Petrule had told them things would change with a human woman as queen of the sylphs. Zalia certainly didn't blame him for being wrong, but he'd left and nothing was really different. At least, not for her and her father, or any of their neighbors, and what had changed didn't seem to be for the better for anyone.

Zalia made her way through the darkness and climbed over the crumbling wall that marked the edge of the city itself. From there, she started down the narrow streets that would take her to its heart, going past tall, narrow buildings jammed in like too many teeth crowded into a mouth. Some were abandoned, surely had to be abandoned with all the people the battlers killed in the last weeks, but no one was really sure who owned what. There were people who had laid claim to entire neighborhoods, and if they had a sylph, the battlers took their word as truth. Those who didn't have a sylph were entitled to nothing. So no one lived in most of the houses and she and her father still had to scrape a living, surviving in the hovels that no one else wanted. It was a cruel thing, but she'd grown used to cruelty in her life.

Her arms wrapped around herself, Zalia trotted down the roads, trying to keep warm. Her shift started at daybreak and if she were late, there were hundreds of other hungry women who'd be willing to take her place for the few pennies she made. It was barely enough to buy food and water with, but it was better than the alternative. She couldn't arrive like this though. Presentable as her dress might have been, the rest of her wasn't.

She came at last to an extensive series of stables that had once housed the finest steeds in the city. Now the animals stood listlessly in their paddocks and stalls, tossing their tails at flies. All of them were looking thin from lack of proper care, though the sylphs were trying. There was no telling where most of their human tenders had gone, as hundreds of humans had abandoned the city in the first weeks after the queen's ascension, preferring the familiarity of human rule offered in other cities.

Zalia darted behind one of the stables. There was a barrel of tepid water there, good enough to drink and certainly decent enough to bathe in. Glancing around quickly, she filled her water bag and then pulled a bar of fatty soap out of her pocket and stripped her dress over her head, laying it carefully over a fence. Rapists she didn't worry about, not in a city of battlers, but if there were any supervisors left at the stable and they sent her away, she wouldn't have anywhere to bathe. That would cost her her job and her father only worked consistently during the fall slaughtering of the livestock. There was no guarantee that would even happen this year either, given how things were going.

She bathed as quickly as she could, rubbing wet soap over her body and gasping at how cold it was. The sun was still down and she jumped up and down to keep warm, her teeth chattering furiously. Her hair at least was good enough for her to get away with just a thorough brushing. The days she had to wash it were truly hellish. Splashing the water over herself, she gasped again, shuddering violently.

"Pretty," a voice said.

Zalia spun with a shriek, her hands up to cover herself. Standing by the side of the stable was a tall, muscular man dressed in a white shirt and pants that went to his knees. He was barefoot and he smiled at her, his teeth gleaming white in the darkness.

"Very pretty," he told her.

Zalia jumped for her dress, dropping the soap. She grabbed it up, but he caught her, his hand closing around her wrist as his warmth pressed against her cold back. "Don't," he purred. "I like you bare."

Zalia screamed, shoving back against him as hard as she could. He was much stronger than her and his nose pressed against the side of her neck, sniffing. Where were the battlers? she thought in a panic. Even before everything changed, they would tear rapists apart.

There were no battlers in sight though, and something was happening to her. Zalia's cold body was becoming very warm where he blanketed her, his arm sliding around her. She clung to the fence with her fingers, frightened and not understanding, but she was becoming very aroused, almost painfully so. The arm he had around her slid up to cup her breast and she cried out softly, the shock of his touch arching through her entire body and down to her toes. He nibbled on her ear and she shuddered, the place between her legs tingling with need.

What was wrong with her? She'd never been with any man in her life, but here she was nude with a stranger, just standing there while he adjusted himself, preparing to take her against an old stable fence where anyone might come and see. She couldn't seem to get enough air and lust had swamped her brain.

Her attacker sighed happily, shifting behind her, and she felt something that was strong as steel but coated with velvet press against her. She almost wanted to let him, her belly screaming that she allow it to happen. One push and it would be done, but a tear trickled down her cheek from the eyes she squeezed shut.

"Don't," she whispered.

He hesitated, stopping against her. "What?"

"Don't," she repeated. "Please let me go."

"But," he protested. "You want it."

No, she didn't. This wasn't real, it couldn't be real. "No. Please!"

He huffed, sounding more confused and disappointed than angry, and stepped back, releasing her. At the same time, the lust that

16

had been all but consuming her vanished and she was left shivering and sick to her stomach. Grabbing her waterskins and the dress, close to tearing the cloth as she yanked it over her head, Zalia ran, looking back fearfully over her shoulder while she did.

He still stood where he'd been left, staring morosely after her. His shirt had pulled mostly open and his pants were undone, showing the part of him that had nearly taken what she hadn't been prepared to give. Yet it was the sight of the tattoo branded on the dark skin over his heart that made her gasp. 111. It was the marker brand of a battle sylph. A battle sylph had nearly taken her for his lover and what would have happened to her then?

Zalia ran on, afraid to look back again.

≈

One-Eleven, since he hadn't thought of a name for himself yet and had the romantic notion that his new master would choose it for him, watched her go. She'd been so beautiful when he saw her from above, bathing in the water with her lovely breasts bouncing, the dawn's light glimmering off the beads of water on her nipples.

It hadn't occurred to him that she might not want to make love with him. The women in the harem had always been willing and they were the only women he really had experience with.

Since the queen rose, everything had become confusing. There were close to seven hundred battle sylphs in the kingdom, but only a hundred concubines. None of them were available anymore. Most had already been bound as masters to battlers and, to his amazement, some had chosen not to have a battle sylph at all. They had all left the kingdom, not that he understood why. One-Eleven had been spending weeks trying to find a female master among the women in the city who made his heart sing.

It hadn't been as easy as he'd expected. His old orders had told him to leave women alone unless they were concubines. It hadn't occurred to him during those years that other women wouldn't be interested. Now they seemed to think he was some kind of monster and the idea of making love with him was repugnant to them. Empathic, he could feel it, and it hurt.

Finally though, he'd found this lovely creature. Seeing her nude and unafraid, he'd thought that she was different from the other women, more open with her love like the concubines. He'd gone to greet her and she'd turned away. Almost though, almost he'd had her.

It was too much to give up on. One-Eleven straightened his clothing and frowned, looking through the darkness in the direction she'd gone. He had her pattern now; if he got close enough, he could find her again. He'd convince her to be his master, he decided. She was frightened of him? He'd change that. He'd find a way to make her love him, and then everything would be perfect.

CHAPTER TWO

The *Racing Dawn* dropped gently toward its cradle in the biggest harbor Devon had ever seen. He'd heard how big Meridal's harbor was, but the reality was almost unbelievable. Wharfs that stretched out a mile or more into deep blue waters had oceangoing vessels of all kinds docked at them. Hundreds of people went back and forth along them, working around numerous piles of stacked goods. Devon's ship passed over all of them, and the young man looked nervously over the side while it did. Even more impressive than the wharves was the huge city that sat on the edge of the shore, framed by beige sand that seemed to go on forever.

"It's unbelievable," he murmured, feeling intimidated and utterly out of his depth.

I thought you were afraid of heights, Airi said to him.

"Don't remind me." He blew out a breath and watched the ship lower to the ground, settling into a wooden cradle beside the pier. It was close enough to the oceangoing ships to make moving cargo easier, but still above the waterline. The feel of the ship stopping sent a shock through his legs and Devon staggered a bit, grabbing the railing for balance.

We're here, Airi said.

So they were. Devon looked out over the city that he'd come to as Solie's ambassador. Just within the area around the ship's cradle, he could see a marketplace fifty times larger than the square in the Valley and streets flanked with tan buildings that led to an immense wall encircling the city. Beyond it, the city itself rose, tall buildings stepping back into the hazy distance. Looking at the far horizon, Devon wasn't sure when the land gave itself up to the sky. He'd never seen such a massive city before. The heat, once the ship's air sylph dropped her shields, was immense.

When Leon had briefed him on Meridal, he'd described how large the city was. Devon just hadn't been able to appreciate what he'd heard until he saw it for himself. The older man had also told him that the streets were crammed with people, so much so that it was hard to go anywhere without bumping into someone.

That part of the description didn't match. The harbor was indeed filled with ships and their crews, but the streets themselves were next to empty, with only a few dozen people that he could see. The men coming up from the wharves seemed confused, as if they were expecting the thronging crowds Leon had talked about as well.

Devon started looking more closely at the buildings at that point. There were a lot of them, yes, but when he paid attention, he could see they were worn down and in poor repair, their colors and edges dulled by sand and neglect. There were holes in the street as well, none patched, and garbage in every gutter. Animal waste was left to bake in the sun and lent to the overwhelming stink of poverty.

"It's a slum," he murmured.

The chancellor did say that most of the wealth had been kept by the nobles on a floating island, Airi said uncertainly.

"Yes . . ." He searched the skies for it, though of course, Leon had told him about the hundreds of battlers who bore the floating island out into the ocean and dropped it into the waters, along with the entire ruling class of the city. The only thing Devon saw in the sky now was what might have been a tiny floating building, though it was so far away it was hard to tell.

Kadmiel, the master to the air sylph who brought them, wandered up as the rest of the crew disembarked and headed toward the city. The captain looked as if he'd glued a wildly overgrown thicket to his face and head, and his skin was so wrinkled it resembled a dried-out riverbed. He looked angry as well, his brows just as thick as his hair and drawn together, but Devon had learned over the days they spent traveling that Kadmiel was actually a very quiet man, spending most of his time sitting with his air sylph and watching the waves pass. He had been what Leon called a feeder, but with the queen's ascension, he'd been freed and Ocean Breeze chose to stay with him. Devon figured that said a lot about the man and he nodded respectfully as Kadmiel stopped beside him, though Airi playing with his hair probably ruined the effect.

"Are you going to meet anyone?" Kadmiel asked.

Devon felt his heart sink. Wasn't he? He didn't actually know what was supposed to happen when he arrived. Vague visions during the travel of parades of well-wishers and a carriage made of gold were obviously wrong, but he'd thought there would at least be someone. He looked at the nearly empty streets nervously, not sure what to do. Not even the arrival of Airi in a foreign hive seemed to have attracted any attention.

"No one's coming?" Kadmiel asked.

"I don't know," Devon whispered. He gripped the railing so tightly his fingers turned white. "I'm supposed to be an ambassador." It sounded so stupid saying it. He wasn't anything.

"Oh." Kadmiel thought for a moment. "I was just told to take the others back and bring you." He turned and looked back toward the stern of the ship for a long moment. "I asked Ocean Breeze to tell them you're here."

Devon looked at him hopefully. "Then they're coming?"

"I don't think so."

Devon sagged. Now what were they going to do? He was supposed to be here in Leon's place, helping Queen Eapha learn how to
rule her kingdom. He could guarantee that if it were *Leon* arriving,
there would be someone waiting for him, and if not, Leon would
march straight into that city and find them.

Maybe we should do that, Airi suggested.

Devon blinked. "What? How?"

Kadmiel looked at him in puzzlement and then up at his wildly
waving hair. Shrugging, he went back to Ocean Breeze, and Devon
sagged. "I don't want to go in there if they don't want me." He wasn't
a brave man. To just walk in was terrifying.

We can't go back either, she pointed out. *What other choice do
we have?*

Devon sagged even more. She was right. There was a battle sylph
back in the Valley who'd made it abundantly clear that he'd take it as
a personal favor if Devon never set foot in the same kingdom as him
again. It wasn't as though he had much to go back to anyway. His
father had passed away a few years after Devon moved to the Valley
and he was single, though he was going to be a father. He shoved
that thought away abruptly. The fact that he *wasn't* going to be the
father had also been made clear to him. He wasn't certain how he
felt about that. Sure, he liked Solie, but not enough to be a parent
with her. Especially not with a battle sylph already determined to
do the job himself.

"I guess it couldn't hurt," he admitted at last.

The *Racing Dawn* had no plans to go anywhere. In fact, Kadmiel seemed to not have any more direction than Devon, though he
was content to merely sit and wait. After being in a cage for years,
Devon supposed, it had to be nirvana just to sit on the deck and
watch the waves come in. He did agree to watch the bulk of Devon's
possessions, and Devon only gathered a few essentials, in case he

didn't find the queen immediately and wasn't able to get back to the ship by nightfall.

Airi invisibly hugging his neck, Devon walked down the gangplank brought up to the side of the ship and started inland, following the wide road that led away from the harbor. The farther he went, the worse the heat got, leaving him glad of the thin shirt he wore, but regretting the long pants and boots that were common back home. Around him, the men he saw wore billowy shirts and pants that reached to their knees, with sandals on their bare feet. Resolving to get himself a set as soon as he could, he fanned himself with his hand and kept going. Airi struggled to send a cooling breeze over him, though the best she could manage was to fan his sweat. As sylphs went, she was hardly powerful, but she took the edge off and Devon made his way gradually up from the harbor and into the city itself. He thought that once he stepped into the shade of the buildings the heat would lessen, but the air didn't move and the temperature didn't change, though he did wonder if it was actually getting hotter.

"I think I might just hate it here already," he remarked, and Airi started giggling.

The road continued on, straight enough that Devon didn't worry about getting lost. The number of people grew more numerous in the city, but they didn't turn into the crushing crowds that Leon had warned him about. That was probably a good thing, given how they stared as he passed. And that really wasn't surprising, since next to them, Devon figured he had to look as though he'd been dipped in bleach. They stared, but the men didn't speak to him, continuing on their own business while the women he passed ducked their heads and scurried away. That reaction was the strangest; he'd grown used to the Valley, where women had the same rights and strength of opinion as men. These women almost looked as if they were afraid he'd contaminate them.

You make them nervous, Airi told him. *I don't know why.*

Neither did Devon. Ahead of them, the wall he'd seen from the air ship towered over everything. The road led straight through it, passing under an arch where the gate had been ripped completely away, leaving strips of jagged metal sticking outward, stretched like taffy where they'd been pulled. Devon could only think of one kind of sylph that had the strength and violence to rip metal apart like candy, and he shuddered.

He walked through the arch and into the main city. This close, he could see chunks blown out of the thick stone walls of the buildings and from the cobblestone streets. Scorch marks were everywhere, and some of the buildings he passed were gutted, the remains vaporized or blown to who knew where. There was still a fair amount of rubble in the streets, but the people made no attempt to clear it away. They just edged around and sometimes over it, ignoring the mess as completely as the garbage. In the city proper, there was more rubbish than at the harbor, and without the ocean scent to mask it, the smell was even worse.

"Why doesn't anyone clean it up?" he wondered.

I don't know. No one feels like they care.

How could they not care? Devon wondered. They were the ones who had to live in it. He didn't see anyone who looked to be in charge; even in Eferem they had city guards to keep the peace. Here, there didn't seem to be anyone, though of course, Leon had briefed him about that as well, hadn't he? Meridal had battle sylphs.

A shadow fell across him, and Airi screamed in fear, pressing against his neck. Devon started and looked up to see a black cloud descending toward him, lightning crashing in mad silence within it. Two red eyes formed from ball lightning glared at him above a mouth of jagged, electrical teeth.

Many years before, when Devon had been a small child and Airi still belonged to his father, everyone in Eferem City had been ordered to attend an execution. Three men had been tied to stakes on the rise of a hill outside the city, and Devon had been in the front row when a battle sylph in the shape of a giant cat was set loose on them.

The creature had toyed with them at first, drawing blood with vicious swipes while the men howled. It had even freed them, cutting their bonds and playing with them more as they tried to run. It had tossed them in the air, and then just their body parts as it tore their limbs off. It ripped the men apart slowly and when it was finally done with them, it blew the entire hill to dust, leaving nothing behind.

The entire time the creature was torturing those men, Devon had been able to feel its hate, solid and unrelenting. Underneath, he could also feel its glee, and its sick pleasure.

Since that time, though intellectually he knew that not all battlers were the same, Devon had only been capable of one reaction when faced with them.

Devon's heart pounded in terror and he bolted, running down the street with his sylph pressed close to his neck and other people running around him. Everyone was trying to get away, whipped by the hate aura from the battler that speared into all of them.

It was obvious immediately who the creature was after. Devon felt the battler coming after him, and seconds later, something tripped up his feet. He crashed to the ground, rolling over to try and get Airi behind him. She wasn't part of the battler's hive. She was young and small, though, not a threat. Leon had told him she'd be safe!

Devon stared up into one of the most handsome faces he'd ever seen. That was normal. Battle sylphs could shape-shift into any kind of creature, but when they were human, they were always gorgeous, their beauty a lure and a reward for any woman who saw them. Even men were caught by that attraction, and Devon felt an old resentment that he'd never be that striking.

"Don't hurt us!" he blurted instead, one hand held out before him as though that would ward the battler off. He could turn Devon into a red mist coating the bottom of a crater if he wanted to. "We're here from Sylph Valley, as ambassadors. We're here to help your queen!"

Perfect hands on perfect hips, the battle sylph regarded them both. Beside him, Devon felt his air sylph shift and take on solid form, something she rarely did. Devon turned his head and saw her, in the shape of a young girl, still translucent but visible as she threw herself to the ground and cowered before the battler.

"Don't hurt my master," she pleaded. "I beg you!"

"Don't hurt her!" Devon yelped, more afraid for her in that second than he was for himself. What was he even doing here? He must have gone mad to think he could do this.

The battle sylph studied them both for a long moment. The rest of the street was empty now, no one left to witness anything as the creature stepped forward and hunkered down, glaring at them both through blazing eyes. He studied them, reading their emotions and probably their souls, and finally snorted.

"Pathetic little thing," he said at last to Airi, who just pressed herself farther down, as submissive as Devon had ever seen her. It might even have been the only thing saving her life. "The queen said someone was coming." Straightening up, the battler leaped into the air and changed, becoming again a black cloud streaked with lightning, and lifted away.

Devon lay where he'd been left, gasping for air. Beside him, Airi lifted her head and looked at him before shifting back to her usual, invisible form. He felt her press against his neck and back. *I guess he decided to leave us alone.*

"I guess." He moved slowly into a seated position. He was covered in sweat, most of it, he was sure, not due to the heat.

Too bad he didn't tell us where the queen was.

Devon shook his head. The less contact one of those monsters had with them, the better. Still, he thought as he climbed to his feet, it would have been nice. He looked down the length of the street they were on. With the heat haze in the distance and the turns, it was impossible to tell how long it was, or even if they were going in the right direction. With a sigh, he continued on.

~

Zalia found her thoughts turning back to the battle sylph.

Business was slow. Even back when the emperor ruled and the city was full, most people preferred to avoid the greatest heat of the day, and that had only become worse since the queen arrived. No one seemed to have money anymore, including those who'd been wealthy before the revolution. There weren't many of them left either. The battle sylphs had killed hundreds, if not thousands, of people in purges after they were freed. They'd destroyed a great many homes and lands as well, leaving most of the kingdom's wealth in ruins. Slavery was illegal, punished by the battlers' rage, but at least a slave in the old Meridal was fed.

Zalia cleaned one of the tables on the covered patio, wondering if anyone would come and what she would do if the restaurant closed and she lost her job. Likely, she and her father would have to join the exodus of those who were following the coastline to the next kingdom. There was no guarantee of salvation there and probably no fate better than becoming a serf or a slave, but it was better than no hope at all. Meridal was falling apart.

Maybe she should have taken that battler up on his offer, she thought furiously, and then blushed a vivid red. What kind of life was it to be a sylph's woman anyway? Her father's heart would have shattered. One-Eleven had been so warm though, his touch so exciting. She shivered for a moment and felt her toes curl in her sandals just the tiniest bit from remembered sensations.

"What's wrong?" Ilaja asked, and Zalia jumped, almost dropping her rag as she turned her still furiously blushing face to her fellow waitress. "Are you sick?"

"I'm fine," Zalia managed to squeak. "Just a little light-headed is all."

Ilaja looked somewhat dubious, but finally she shrugged. "Maybe you should drink some water."

Zalia shook her head. She was thirsty, but good drinking water was expensive and she'd spilled what she'd taken from the stable when she ran that morning. She'd wait until later and fill her skin again from one of the troughs back at the stable, provided she could manage it without being seen. She thought of the battle sylph again, ducking her head.

"Look at him," Ilaja said suddenly.

Zalia's head snapped up, her cheeks burning even more hotly as she expected to see the battle sylph coming back to try his luck again. Instead, she watched a man walking down the empty street, making his way in full sunshine during the worst heat of the day. He wore a heavy linen shirt and pants, as well as boots his feet had to be baking in. Zalia's eyes widened, wondering if it was Leon Petrule come back from whatever frozen land he'd gone to. It wasn't, of course. Leon couldn't come back because his battler wasn't part of Eapha's hive. The other battlers would have killed him. Besides, Leon had learned before he left how to dress properly for the heat and this was a much younger man, his hair sticking out everywhere in sweaty spikes and his face red from sunburn.

"He's so pale," Ilaja gasped.

Zalia nodded absently. Of course, Ilaja hadn't seen Leon close up when he'd come to the restaurant and he'd been trying to hide his identity at the time. He hadn't really done a good job of it, since the heavy cloak he'd worn only made him stand out when Zalia first saw him. It was the boots that had really made her wonder though, even before she'd seen his blue eyes. No one else in Meridal had blue eyes.

This man's eyes were as brown as a local's, even if his skin was shades lighter than anyone born to Meridal. He walked up the steps and into the shaded interior of the patio, heading wearily toward them. He must have no water on him, Zalia thought. Pale people like Leon didn't seem to handle the heat well. Ilaja backed away, afraid of him, and ran to the kitchens while Zalia stepped forward, wondering, with no small degree of fright, whether this would mean that more changes were coming to Meridal.

"Can I get you some water, sir?" she asked as she held a chair out for him.

He didn't so much sit in it as fall. "Yeah," he croaked, and, as she turned away, asked, "Is it always so hot here?"

Zalia smiled at him over her shoulder. "It's much hotter in the summer, sir."

His groan followed her toward the kitchen.

She got him a cool clay jug of water and a mug. While Ilaja watched her suspiciously and the cooks sat as far from the stoves as they could, fanning themselves, she put the water on a tray and carried it back out. The stranger was sitting slumped back in his chair, his head hanging over the back while he fanned himself with one hand. Zalia giggled but managed to hide her smile before she reached him.

"Your water, sir."

She set it all before him, carefully filling the mug with some of the water before she placed the jug in the center of the table. The man lurched forward, wiped sweat off his forehead, and grabbed the mug, draining it as fast as he could. His hand shaking a bit, he filled it again and drank a little more slowly.

"Thank you," he gasped at last, pressing the mug against his forehead.

"You're welcome, sir. Will there be anything else?"

He shook his head slowly. "I don't know how anyone can eat in this heat." He looked at her, his brown eyes shadowed and his face patchy from the burn. His hair was waving softly, though Zalia didn't feel a breeze. "Can you tell me where I can get some better clothes for here?"

"Of course, sir." She hesitated, wondering if she dared ask him anything. The staff weren't supposed to socialize with the customers, but if he did come here like Leon had . . . she hadn't seen the man much after the queen ascended, and once he had left, she hadn't seen anyone from that day at all.

"Do you know Leon Petrule, sir?" she asked.

He looked up at her again, his expression incredulous. His hair suddenly swept upward in a mohawk and she blinked.

"You know Leon?" he blurted.

Zalia nodded, holding her tray flat against her belly. "Yes, sir. He stayed with my father and myself while he was here. He's a very noble man."

The man stared at her for a moment and then squeezed his eyes shut, snapping his fingers repeatedly while he thought. "You're . . . you're . . . give me a minute . . . you're . . . Zalia! And your father's Xed? Xel?"

"Xehm," she corrected, smiling.

"Right. Sorry." He opened his eyes, looking at her again, and Zalia blushed a bit. He was rather cute under the sunburn and the soaked, wild hair. It swayed suddenly and she squinted at it, puzzled.

He looked upward, his eyes crossing. "Oh! Zalia, meet Airi. Airi, meet Zalia."

Out of nothingness, a girl formed from the sand swirling up off the ground. The fine granules made her outline as she looked up at Zalia and smiled. Before Zalia could do more than gape at her, the girl let go of the sand and it scattered across the floor again.

"Airi's my air sylph," the man told Zalia and carefully filled his mug again. "She's very pleased to meet you. She's shy about talking to anyone she doesn't know though." He sipped the water and exhaled heavily. "I didn't know water could taste so good." He paused for a moment, blinking, and then turned back to her, his face even redder than it had been before as he blushed. "I didn't tell you my name!"

"That's not necessary, sir."

He stood up. "It is. Leon told me how helpful you and your father were to him. He wanted me to find you." Before she could stop him, he took her hand and shook it. "My name is Devon Chole. Leon sent me to be the ambassador in Meridal for our queen."

Zalia yanked her hand back before anyone saw them. Ilaja alone would declare it a scandal, if only so she could take Zalia's place in the restaurant. "That's very good, sir. Our kingdom is very honored to have you here." She bowed.

Devon looked sheepish. "Yes, well, um, thanks. The problem is, no one showed up to meet me when I got here. I was kind of wondering, do you know where I can find the queen?"

CHAPTER THREE

Glutted by its feed, it let itself float with the winds out over the ocean.

It hadn't ever seen an ocean before and had no idea at first what it was, but some of the food spoke about it. It could hear them here as easily as on the hunting grounds it came from, and it mused on the word as it floated across the waters, past the wall that encircled the other new word it had learned of—*city*. It only snatched up a few morsels of food that wandered into its tendrils as it went, dissolving them in its belly as it drifted over the ocean, tendrils playing with the waves.

A few hours later, it realized its mistake. The winds kept pushing it away from the city and the water wasn't as rich with food as it would have liked. There was food, certainly, if it dipped deeply enough, but it was quick and small, tasteless and poor. Food was so much better when it thought, as so many things did in the place where it came from.

It floated for hours, the land dwindling in the distance until it couldn't even hear the food on the land anymore. It lifted its heaviest tendrils so that it could look more clearly, debating. Continue to float and come to another city with more food, or make itself hungry and return now? The food had believed that the ocean was very big though. It might not make it before the hunger made it sink.

At the edge of its tendrils, it felt motion in the water that wasn't just from currents. Something bigger than the tiny things it had been eating swam in its direction, filled with alien speech. Patient, as it was ever patient, it waited, watching as dozens of the great blue things came toward it as blindly as food ever did, great fins moving through the water while they blew streams of spray every time they surfaced. Unaware of it, they came closer, and it spread its tendrils outward, knowing that at least some of them would stumble through them.

They did. The first of the creatures, as large as an ancient breeding battler, swam through the rain of its tendrils, both thick and thin. Immediately, it plunged them deep, hooking them through its skin and blubber, intending to draw it in to feed.

It was a mistake. The creature was too large for it to dissolve and it bellowed, its wails sounding of danger, of pain, of escape.

The blue whales dived, fleeing in terror, and the one that it held went with them. The Hunter shuddered as it was suddenly yanked downward, its eyes blinded as its tendrils were pulled into the water. The salt stung them and it had an image of being pulled under entirely, to be left floating in all that water, unable to get airborne again before it sank and died. Terrified, it ripped its tendrils free, letting go with its barbs as fast as it could while the food kept diving, trailing blood behind while it went for the depths, holding its breath in a way that its attacker never could.

The Hunter got the last of its tendrils free as its underbelly and mouth slammed into the ocean's surface. The water was shockingly cold and it stopped, afraid to move and risk going under. Instead, while it was still, the waves lapped against its underside; and after a time, it slowly started to rise again. It didn't try to fight or speed the process. It just let itself ascend, lifting until only the tips of its tendrils touched the ocean, and even those it pulled up, not wanting to feel the water again.

This was an evil place, a horrible, hideous world. It looked toward the distant land and the dusty city with the food and made its decision. It would go back. Most of the time it drifted, finding food as fate found it, but it didn't have to be that way, not when matters grew desperate enough for it to risk the hunger that could keep it from floating.

It pulled its tendrils in, rolling over until its underbelly and mouth faced opposite from the way it wanted to go, and then it released that which let it float, expelling it behind in a wave as strong as any ocean current while it blew back toward the land, sinking ever lower as it did, and hoping its feed earlier had been enough to get it back in time.

Then it would feed again.

~

Zalia finished her shift long after dark and made her way home, her shawl pulled around her now that it was cold out again. Mr. Chole had gone on his way hours before, still looking for the queen. Zalia was sorry she hadn't been able to help him; he was a nice man and she liked him. She just didn't know where the queen was. She wasn't sure anyone did, not really.

Ahead of her, the streets were empty. Even with everything that had changed, a part of Zalia was still amazed at how many people had left. If they kept leaving, soon there wouldn't be anyone left in Meridal at all. The battle sylphs didn't care who left. As long as no one broke their rules, they left people alone. No one Zalia knew felt safe though, since no one knew what the rules were anymore.

"Hello."

Zalia jumped, looking around in surprise. The street had been empty, and who would talk to a lower-class woman after dark? An attacker wouldn't bother, and no other man would want to demean themselves, unless they thought her a whore for hire.

Sitting on a stone wall around one of the many empty houses, the battle sylph she'd seen just that morning smiled at her. He was wearing the same clothes as before, his hands clasped around one drawn-up knee. He really had a beautiful smile, she thought, and blushed wildly, remembering. He'd seen her naked! He'd touched her!

Zalia turned and ran, not knowing what to say to him, afraid of what he might do, afraid that someone would see her with a battler and think . . . what?

He was after her in an instant with a whoop of glee and she wondered suddenly if he thought they were playing. Weren't sylphs supposed to know what people were feeling? How could he mistake this for a game? What *was* she feeling? Confusion. Shyness. Fear.

Desire.

Zalia gulped and ran down a side alley, aware of the battler so close behind her that he could have reached out and touched the trailing end of her shawl if he'd wanted. Ahead of her, the alley opened out into a square and she almost flew out into it, panting but exhilarated at the same time and not really understanding why. All Zalia really knew was that she was running through a beautiful, moonlit night, a battle sylph laughing in unabashed delight behind her, and the only thing she could think of clearly was how warm he was. And how, for all his strength, if he caught her now, it was because she let him.

It was wonderful. It was sinful. It was freedom. It was too much. Zalia's unexplainable exhilaration turned into real fright and she heard him sigh.

Something rushed over her. Skidding to a gasping halt, Zalia looked up to see a black cloud streaked with lightning lifting into the sky above her. There was something almost happy about the way the lightning flashed through him, and One-Eleven formed a tentacle of black smoke, waving down at her as he flew away.

He was letting her go? He really was. Maybe they actually could tell what a person was feeling. Shifting her shawl back around her shoulders and gasping in the cold air, Zalia looked around at the empty square, seeing he'd chased her into a place where no one would ever have seen them, and smiled a bit as she continued on home.

~

Devon, to his utmost relief, didn't get chased by any battle sylphs after his departure from the restaurant. After the first one, they must have decided that he was harmless. Certainly they'd communicated about him. Devon knew that, for he'd seen the battle sylphs back home do it all the time. A threat one had encountered was shared among them all. It only took them seconds to talk to each other, Airi told him once. Likely, they were ignoring the two of them now.

I like being ignored by battlers, Airi said.

"You and me both," he muttered.

It had been a long, useless day. He'd thought he had a real break when he found Zalia, but she hadn't been able to help him. She didn't know where the queen was. No one did, or at least no one they could ask did. Devon certainly wasn't going to be demanding answers from a battler, and the other kinds of sylphs didn't seem to congregate on the streets at all. He tried seeing if Airi could ask, but she'd been against the idea. The battlers were treating them as harmless right now. That could change if a foreign sylph started asking about the location of the hive's queen. Devon figured she had a point and didn't press.

It was frustrating though. He'd been sent to represent Solie and to help Eapha sort through the problems a new leader would inevitably have. Devon had no idea what those problems would turn out to be, but Leon had felt that Devon had enough experience with seeing Solie go through it to be able to give some kind of assistance. Devon had been doubtful, but with Heyou vehemently wanting him gone, he hadn't argued as much as he could have.

Now he wished he had. Places such as the restaurant where Zalia worked were still functioning, but they were unusual and in the long run, this kingdom was falling apart. People were leaving at a rate that was alarming, given they had no real place to go, and no one seemed to be in charge of anything. If something didn't change soon, everyone would have to leave, just to try and survive.

Someone had to take charge. Devon gazed up at the beautiful colors that tossed across the sky while the sun set. Taking charge was supposed to be the queen's job; at least it was back home. It would have to be the same here; the battlers had killed everyone else who could have kept the infrastructure going. Granted, it was an infrastructure based on slavery, but still . . . He looked at a child huddled in a doorway, his face gaunt from starvation, but when he tried to approach, the boy ran off, vanishing around a corner. Meridal was going to die at this rate, along with everyone in it. Die or be conquered by someone else.

Devon sighed and kept walking, headed back toward the harbor, his feet aching and his mood depressed. He'd spend the night on the *Racing Dawn* with Kadmiel and Ocean Breeze and try again in the morning to find the queen.

Suddenly, he stopped in the center of the road, feeling Airi ruffle the hair on the back of his neck while he slapped a hand over his face. *What is it?* she asked.

"I'm an idiot," he moaned.

Really? Why?

Devon dropped the hand and started trudging again. "Ocean Breeze. I bet she can take us straight to the queen."

Airi thought about that for a moment and started giggling again.

~

Kadmiel sat on the deck of the *Racing Dawn*, watching the sun set behind the ocean. He sat cross-legged as he always had in his cage, his hands resting lightly on his knees. No one had come by to tell him what to do, but that was fine. He didn't know if he was supposed to turn the *Racing Dawn* over to someone or if he should leave her or even if she belonged to him now. That didn't matter either. There was food below deck, water by the barrel, and he had nothing to bother him.

Ocean Breeze hummed behind him, her winds keeping him cool as they had all day. He'd sung for her earlier, but right now he was comfortable. He'd watch the sun go down. When he became hungry, he'd get food. When he became tired, he'd sleep.

Will you sing to me again? Ocean Breeze asked.

Of course, he thought, and did so, his tenor echoing across the deck, down to a few workmen still doing their duty and unloading an oceangoing ship. His father had taught him to sing many years ago, in order to bring a better price on the block. Kadmiel's voice had been so high and sweet then, and so quickly lost when he reached puberty. His voice wouldn't entertain the halls it once did, but Ocean Breeze liked it and he still remembered the old songs.

> *Lady alone, silent in solitude,*
> *gown drained to white like the stone.*
> *Shadow behind her, light in her eyes,*
> *Her thoughts all inside and unknown.*

Ocean Breeze sighed behind him and started to dance, swirling around the deck while he sat under her, his voice carrying across the wharf as he watched the sunset.

We question, we wonder,
what this lady does feel.
Within her soft skin
is she real?

Or just an illusion
before a bare wall.
A picture of beauty,
not a woman at all?

The harbor was quiet, the people he'd seen on the docks before the *Racing Dawn* gone now, though he hadn't watched them leave. The sunset shone in his eyes, making afterimages like threads drift across his vision.

Lady alone, is she a person?
Someone who hates and who loves?
Free like a bird or trapped in a painting,
watching yet never involved.

The song ended, the last echoes lingering. Kadmiel heard Ocean Breeze sigh again, happy.

Then he heard her scream.

Her pain was there and gone in an instant, gone so fast he wasn't sure he'd felt it. Her *absence* though was ongoing and he turned in shock, reeling from the realization that she was *dead*. How could she be dead so fast?

He couldn't see her, not that he ever could, since she liked to be invisible most of the time. He saw a shimmering rain cross the deck instead, except this rain was more like dangling strings that flowed independently from each other, feeling across the wood toward him and so clear that he couldn't even be sure he saw them at all.

Kadmiel ran in terror. It was a twenty-foot drop over the side to the wharf. He'd break his leg if he went that way and the tendrils hung there as well. He was in a forest of them, all of them next to invisible but still making the world beyond hazy and hard to see. He could see through them though, enough for him to bolt for the hatch down into the ship, his heart pounding from fear and from grief as well. Ocean Breeze . . .

Kadmiel reached the door, ducking around a dangling tendril and feeling it brush against his arm as he ran inside and slammed the door. He backed up, staring at the thick door, and stopped, not by choice. Something held him and he stared down at his arm. The skin was dimpled, something shimmering and nearly invisible lying across it. He gasped.

The tendril wrapped around his arm, something sharp biting deep, and it pulled. Kadmiel howled as he was yanked off of his feet. He struggled, but then he slammed into the door so hard that it shattered and, of course, Kadmiel shattered as well.

The tendril pulled him upward, dissolving him with unimaginable speed until he was just a pool of energy, the same way it had Ocean Breeze. His killer sucked him in and ate him slowly, relieved that it had reached the shore after all, and floated back toward the city, using its tendrils to pull itself forward when the wind threatened to push it the wrong way. It was hungry and heavy, hanging far lower than it would have liked, but there was plenty of food here, just waiting to stumble across it, as it always had.

~

Once known as battle sylph 417, he'd been assigned to patrol the streets of Meridal and keep the peace. Now called Yahe, he did the same thing, though now he did so properly. He soared over the city as a cloud filled with lightning, scanning the people below him for any sign of danger.

Yahe didn't find any. No one was feeling the kind of malice that would have him diving down to destroy them before they threatened the hive. He felt a great deal of discontent though, which made no sense to him. They were free, they had no reason to be unhappy. He felt hunger and thirst as well, but didn't bother to wonder why they didn't just eat and drink something. Humans were strange creatures and only two of them had any real importance to him. Kiala, who was his master, and the queen.

He continued on his rounds, sweeping past other battlers following their own routes as he flew around the city toward the ocean. Where the battlers had all hated one another before, now they were hive mates and he dived around his brothers playfully, exchanging news of what they'd seen during their guard duty, or of how their masters were doing. Not all of them had female masters yet, but all were working toward it, and Yahe felt immensely grateful that he had Kiala. The thought that she might have chosen another battler, or even turned away from them entirely, wasn't something he let himself dwell on. It was just too horrifying to contemplate. He was lucky; that was all he let himself know.

From the harbor area, he felt a sudden surge of terror, quickly gone. Yahe paused, stretching his senses out, but the fear didn't return and after a moment, he continued on his way. Humans were like sylphs in that they felt brief little surges of terror from time to time, and he wasn't going to waste his energy running to attack because someone saw a scorpion. He continued on his usual route and when he passed over the harbor a half hour later, there was no one there. It was late so he didn't worry about that. Humans had homes, didn't they?

He continued on.

~

Devon reached the harbor past dark, and after almost getting lost more than once. To his surprise, it had become quite cold once the sun went down and he hugged himself tightly as he walked. Airi wasn't much help with cold, though she did keep any cool breezes away from him.

He was relieved to finally see the *Racing Dawn* still docked in her cradle. There weren't any lights left on for him and in fact there weren't any lights at the harbor at all. It was just more of a sign of how badly Meridal was falling apart, he thought grumpily. He hoped he wouldn't wake Kadmiel. Right now, he just wanted to lie down and get some sleep. The queen could wait until tomorrow.

Maybe in the morning he'd get Kadmiel to take him home instead.

A vision of Leon's and Solie's disappointed faces filled his mind, along with Heyou's snarl as the battler reminded Devon he had no home in the Valley, not if he wanted to keep all his limbs attached. Devon shuddered and climbed onto the ship, his boots echoing almost eerily on the gangplank and then even more eerily on the wooden deck. He still had to buy some sandals, but right now he was glad to be wearing the boots.

"The temperatures in this kingdom are insane," he grumbled.

Are we going to stay here tonight? Airi asked. *Ocean Breeze isn't here.*

Lovely, Devon thought, just lovely. So much for his great plan to have her take them to the queen.

"Well, do you have any idea where she went—" He stopped. Right before him was the doorway that led down into the interior of the ship. It wasn't just open; the door had been broken out of its frame and the deck was covered in wooden shrapnel.

There's blood in there, Airi whimpered in a tiny voice.

Devon could smell it too: a copper scent that was unmistakable. He backed away, suddenly terrified, and felt Airi press against the back of his neck, not playing with his hair for once. Suddenly, Devon was aware of just how *silent* the harbor was. Slowly, he looked over his shoulder and across the dark length of the wharves to the darker color of the water. Nothing. No voices, no footsteps, not even the sound of birds.

This place is dead, Airi whined.

That was more than enough for Devon. Turning, he pounded across the deck and down the gangplank, sprinting back across the stone toward the city he'd just left, Airi pressing fearfully against him. Not since that battler on the hill had Devon been this terrified. Instinct spurred him through and he ran, almost slipping several times on wet, filthy cobblestones. There were no people. He smelled the strong sea air, but in his mind, it turned to a copper reek and he felt Airi crying, as frightened as he was.

Attracted by his terror, a black cloud filled with lightning dropped down before him, looking at him with ball-lightning eyes. Devon screamed and ran in another direction, heart pounding. Another one cut him off and he darted another way, only to find a third there. There seemed to be hundreds of the creatures, but in reality there were only six. Six was more than enough to drive him into a sputtering panic.

Tell them! Airi squealed. *Tell them what we saw!*

Devon stumbled, crashing to the ground next to a building and cowering, his arms up over his head. "The harbor!" he screamed. "Blood at the harbor! There's no one there! They're all dead, we found blood!"

The battlers looked at each other, communicating in silence, and lifted away, vanishing into the night. Devon leaped to his feet and ran on. No one stopped him or Airi this time and he ran until he was exhausted.

~

Six battle sylphs swept over the harbor in close formation, looking for the threat. The human's terror had been undeniable and they moved quickly, ready to destroy whatever had sent the man running.

The harbor was empty. With a quick, silent word, they spread out, searching, but there were no people there; no sylphs; there weren't even any rats or cockroaches. Just crates of goods left sitting, some things spilled, and at one air ship, blood around a doorframe where the door had been torn completely out. That and blood randomly spread over the docks were the only signs of violence they found.

They gathered then above the harbor, massing into a single cloud while they discussed it. *What do you think happened here?* one of them asked.

The rest swirled. *I don't know.*

Should we hunt that human down and ask him more?

How would we find him?

He's probably still running in a panic.

He has that air sylph from another hive with him.

Why did we let her live?

Tooie said to leave her alone.

Get Tooie.

Most of them fell silent then, one of them concentrating his voice and calling out.

Tooie came a short while later, dropping down from the dark sky to join them. He already knew what happened from listening to their reports while he approached, but seeing was better than hearing secondhand and he floated over the empty docks, the others following respectfully. He was of an age with most of them, but he was the lead battler, the lover of the queen, and with her support his word was only secondary to her own.

Tooie spent the longest time at the *Racing Dawn,* examining the blood on the deck, walls, and the shattered door. Shifting to the human form Eapha liked, he ran a gentle hand down the wood, barely touching the splinters left behind.

"Humans aren't strong enough to do this," he noted. "Someone was pulled out."

None of us did it, one of the battlers said.

"No." If one of them had, it wouldn't be a problem because there would have been a reason for it. He looked out over the empty harbor. People had been leaving the city, for reasons he didn't understand, but this emptiness was eerie. As he stood there, a faint whistling tune sounded and all of them turned to see a man walk out from between two buildings and down to the harbor, swinging a waterskin as though nothing at all was wrong. Unaware of the battlers, he kept whistling, happy and relaxed.

Tooie turned away, walking to the railing of the ship and looking down past the cradle she sat in at the dark ocean waters lapping against the seawall only a few feet beyond. The water was dark and impenetrable. "Are there things in these waters that would hunt creatures on land?" he wondered aloud.

The battlers shifted uncertainly. *I've never heard of that happening before,* one said.

"Everything has to happen for the first time," Tooie replied, still watching the waters, so dark and unfathomable. Anything could be under there.

Do we tell the queen about this? the same battler asked.

Tooie thought about that for a moment. "No," he said at last. "She doesn't need to know."

~

Zalia returned to the hovel she shared with her father to find he had a fire going and was sitting beside it, carefully toasting a piece of bread at the end of a stick. He smiled at Zalia as she came up and handed him a full water canteen, along with her day's wages.

"How was your day?" he asked.

She didn't tell him about the battle sylph. She didn't think she'd have the courage to tell anyone that, let alone her father. Instead she told him about meeting Devon Chole and what he'd come for. He'd been a nice man, she thought, and far more approachable than Leon Petrule, who had been intimidating beyond belief, even when he was being kind.

Xehm listened in stunned silence, his mouth hanging open and his eyes huge. "He's here to see the queen," he gasped at last, "and you didn't help him?"

Zalia blinked, surprised at her father's reaction. "What was I supposed to do? I don't know where she is."

"He needs help." Xehm abruptly stood up, almost losing his bread in the fire before Zalia rescued it. "We have to help him."

"What are you talking about?"

Xehm waved around at the hovels and their neighbors, all sitting destitute and hungry around their own fires. "This isn't what was supposed to happen. We weren't supposed to still be here, living like this. I talked to Leon many times; I talked to him after that . . . woman . . . became queen. He told me what it was supposed to be like, and all the gods help me, I can't stop dreaming of it. Things have only grown worse though. Had Leon never left, it wouldn't be like this. If he'd had to turn that foolish woman over his knee and spank her, he would have. Now his replacement is here. We *must* help him get to her."

Zalia gaped at him. She hadn't seen her father so passionate in years. In fact, she didn't think she'd ever seen him so determined about anything, except for when her little sister had been sick while Zalia herself was still a child. With their mother long since taken to be a concubine in the harems, she'd thought he'd move the world to save her little sister.

Now she tried not to think about how he'd ultimately failed.

"What do we do, Father?" she asked, sitting nervously by the fire that was their only warmth, burning out of a bed of dried animal dung. "I don't know where to find him. He could be at her side already."

Xehm sagged, sighing before he sat down again. Zalia passed him the bread. "I don't think so. The gods wouldn't be that kind." He took a bite and started chewing before handing her another chunk to toast for herself. Zalia took it gratefully. She hadn't eaten in hours. "If he comes back to the restaurant," he decided, "bring him to me. Understood?"

"Yes, Father." Not that she knew what they'd be able to do. It was good to see her father fiery about something though, and good to think again that things could get better, as she'd believed when Eapha first became queen. She sighed and turned her toast over in the fire, daydreaming of better things.

～

One-Eleven watched the girl, his form hunched to the ground in the shape of one of the lizards that ran across the desert in search of food. In his natural form, his lightning would be too easy to see in the dark and he didn't want his human appearance to make her feel frightened again.

She was a beautiful woman, but not at all like those in the harems. She didn't just give what he wanted. He'd been surprised by that at first, but now he reveled in it. To have her, he'd have to prove himself worthy and win her, just like a suitor to a queen. Then she'd give him his name, as a queen would, and the world would be wonderful.

One-Eleven studied her with his reptile eyes, the night air cold against his leathery skin. This wasn't a nice place to be living, but he'd give her palaces if that was what she wanted.

Distantly, he heard a call, the head battler summoning all of the battle sylphs to a conclave. One-Eleven kept his belly low to the ground, not wanting to leave, but not able to stay. He drank in the shadowed sight of Zalia, committing it to memory, and backed away, sashaying in an odd, reptile walk across the sand until he was away from all the odd little human buildings. There he took on his cloud form again and rose into the air, heading across the city to where the battlers had been called to meet. His thoughts never strayed far from his new love, even when Tooie told them about the suspected sea creature that attacked the harbor and sent out scouting parties to find it. One-Eleven ended up in one of those parties, skimming the surface of the ocean while scanning as deeply into it as he could and destroying anything he sensed that was larger than a human child. They left the waters behind them thick with dead risen to float at the surface, but still he thought about Zalia, and how he'd win her heart.

⌒

Yahe had now been on duty for more than a day and was ready to start killing people if he wasn't relieved soon.

He was done sweeping overhead through the city. Now, as he had for decades while a slave, Yahe walked the streets of the city, looking for rule breakers. He was a beautifully handsome man, as flawless as his shape-shifting ability could make him.

Not that it was doing him much good out here. He didn't want to impress the humans in this pathetically shrunken marketplace and he certainly didn't have to impress the elemental sylphs he saw. The one he wore this shape for wasn't around to see him.

Disgusted, he looked up at the palace floating in the night sky, lights shining like stars in a few of the windows. Kiala was up there, waiting for him and growing so increasingly impatient that he could clearly feel it. She had reason to be. He was supposed to have been relieved six hours ago, but the idiot battle sylph who was to take over for him tonight hadn't shown. Yahe knew they were all brothers now that they were in the same hive, but that didn't mean he was required to like everyone and at the moment, he rather hated Bift.

Bift! he bellowed along the hive lines, as he had for the last hour. *Where in the chasms are you? BIFT!*

A few complaints came along the line back to him, from elementals as well as battlers, but no response from Bift. Yahe fumed, planning what he'd do to the miserable wretch when he found him. At this rate, he wouldn't be relieved until Bift's replacement showed up.

Bift obviously didn't understand duty. He'd been planning to take his master to the ongoing party at the gate to the hive world and had been bragging about it the last time Yahe saw him. Well, he wasn't the only one who wanted to go there.

In the back of his mind, Kiala's impatience started to turn to outright anger. Yahe miserably looked up toward her again. He wanted to be with her too, but he couldn't leave, not without someone taking over. Nothing was going to happen, he knew she'd say. No one would care if he were there or not. Yahe wanted to listen to that kind of logic, but obviously Bift had as well and where did that leave Yahe himself?

Grumbling under his breath and making the few people still cleaning their stalls very nervous, Yahe continued on his rounds, planning his revenge on a battler he didn't know he was never going to see again.

~

The winds still wanted to push it out to the ocean.

It had been tired after it reached the shore, its tendrils pulled up close to its body and still almost touching the water. It had never fallen so low, so it gorged itself on the life it found, devouring everything as quickly as it could.

That almost resulted in it blowing back out over the ocean again. The more it ate, the more the gases that kept it in the air increased, lifting it higher. Too high and it wouldn't be able to reach the ground unless it let some of the gas go or waited to grow hungry again. If a strong enough wind caught it before then, it could end up just about anywhere.

Mostly, it was a self-correcting problem, since if it started to rise too high, it wouldn't be able to reach the food on the ground. It glutted itself though, snatching up the food and devouring it as fast as it could, and rose high with food still in its tendrils, waiting to be swallowed.

It barely managed to grab the edge of one of the things the food called *buildings* before the winds took it back out again. Satisfied, it wrapped some of its strongest tentacles around the building, digging its hooks into the soft stone, and ate the rest of the food it had. It couldn't rely on the winds here, it decided. They would only drive it back out to the ocean, and as it hung there, it saw that it didn't matter if they blew in the other direction anyway. The word *city* was surrounded by the word *desert* and there was no food out there at all. It would have to stay in this unprotected hive and hope it learned from the food where to go next before it ate all of them.

For now, as always, the food didn't know it was there, which would make the hunting easier, at least until the battlers realized what was happening. Sometimes that made the hunting even better if they didn't just hide in their hive, and there was no hiding here. It dug its tentacle deeper into the stone. It could tear this city apart to reach the food if it needed to.

Crumbled stone fell to the street below and it wrapped another of its largest tentacles around a second building, watching with interest as battle sylphs arrived below, searching. The rest of its tentacles it pulled up. If one of the battle sylphs blundered into one, it wouldn't matter how much it didn't want to rise any higher. It would eat them anyway.

It got the tentacles out of the way just in time as one of the battlers swept through where they'd been, hundreds of feet below its actual body. The battler didn't react at all, but of course, he couldn't see it. None of the food could ever see a Hunter and it listened with sleepy interest as they searched the harbor and discussed what might have happened. None of them suspected it, which was good. The food tasted better when it was just newly frightened and not worn out by terror.

Floating in the air above the harbor, hanging on to one of the watchtowers that framed the main gate to the city, the Hunter slept, and listened, and consumed.

CHAPTER FOUR

Zalia was back at the restaurant before dawn, after a nervous bath at the back of the stable where she was half afraid and half hoping that One-Eleven would return. He didn't, or if he did, he just watched her in secrecy, and she tried to keep him out of her mind while she wiped down the tables and served water and cheese to the customers.

"He's coming back," Ilaja said, sounding annoyed.

Her heart suddenly pounding in her chest, Zalia spun around. It wasn't One-Eleven, she saw with something that might have been relief and something else that was probably regret. Of course it wasn't him. He'd never been to the restaurant and Ilaja didn't know anything about him.

Instead, Devon Chole was walking down the street, the dawn light shining on his face and fluttering hair. He was wearing the same clothes and boots as the day before and he looked as if he hadn't slept all night, or even stopped walking.

Zalia gaped at him in surprise, her daydreams about One-Eleven blowing out of her mind as she took in how tired and stressed he looked. Her heart surged for the poor man and she ran forward, meeting him at the edge of the patio.

"I didn't think I'd ever find this place again," he sighed. "This whole city is a maze."

"What happened, Mr. Chole?" she gasped, daringly reaching out toward him before snatching her arm back.

He didn't seem to notice her unseemly forwardness, stomping up onto the patio as though he barely had the energy to do so. His hair was still fluffing around, but not so much as the day before. Zalia thought about what her father said about wanting to meet him, but discarded the idea for now. He didn't look as if he had it in him to do anything other than fall down. His skin was badly sunburned from the previous day and he moved slowly as she led him to a seat away from the other customers. Ilaja sniffed noticeably from across the patio, but Zalia's heart clenched again at how much he needed her help, and how sweet the lines around his eyes were when he still found it in himself to smile at her.

"It's been a long night," he told her and slumped into his seat. "I've been walking since dusk."

"Whatever for?" she gasped. If she'd known he'd get so lost, she'd have guided him back to the harbor herself, though of course, she couldn't if she wanted to keep her job.

"I didn't have anywhere to go." He ran his hand through his hair wearily and looked around. "Can I stay here for a while? I mean if I keep ordering water or something? And food. I'm really hungry."

Zalia looked around at the nearly empty patio. "I think it'll be okay," she assured him with a smile and hurried off to fill his order.

$\approx$

Devon was nearly at the end of his endurance when he found the restaurant again and actually saw someone he recognized. In that instant, Zalia was the most beautiful woman he'd ever seen in his life, and when she returned his smile, probably without realizing it, a lot of the tension that kept him walking all night eased. He was still exhausted though and he slumped into a chair, not wanting to go anywhere for as long as he could manage it. His sword scabbard banged him painfully in the leg and he shoved it out of his way with a sigh. When Zalia returned with a bowl of something that looked like brown paste, flat pieces of bread, and a pitcher of water, her second smile made him want to put his head down on the table and sleep, safe at last. If he hadn't been so tired, he would have wondered about that.

Zalia set the food before him and poured the water, smiling at him again as she did so. "The hummus is fresh," she told him. "I hope you like it."

"Thank you," Devon said, wondering what hummus was and what he was supposed to do without a spoon.

"You scoop it with the bread," she added as he stared at it.

"Oh." Picking up one of the pie-shaped pieces of bread, he spooned up some of the paste and put it in his mouth. The taste was smooth with a bit of tang but delicious.

"Do you like it?" she asked hopefully.

"It's really good," Devon said, chewing hurriedly and grabbing his water for a drink. It really was, though he didn't recognize the taste at all. "What is it?"

"Pita and hummus."

Another woman stepped over to them, touching Zalia's arm with a distrustful look at Devon. It said *different* to him as clearly as if she'd shouted it. She whispered something to Zalia and hurried away toward the other customers, most of whom were staring at Devon.

Zalia smiled at him again, and this time her smile was a little sad, as though she were reluctant to go. "Please let me know if you want something else," she told him and hurried away. Stopping a few feet away, she looked back at him. "Oh, please see me before you go." She blushed. "My father wants to meet you. I'll explain later."

Devon watched her go, his food and water forgotten despite his hunger. She really was a nice-looking girl, he thought.

She likes you, Airi giggled in his mind.

Devon started at Airi's voice, realized he was staring after Zalia, and returned to his food. "She's just being nice," he murmured before shoving more pita and hummus into his mouth. He wasn't sure which was which, but he liked them.

No, she likes you. Her pattern flows around yours.

Devon almost gagged and had to take a quick swallow of the water. It wasn't very cold, but it still tasted wonderful, even better than wine.

"You're crazy," he told Airi, barely remembering to keep his voice down. He hated talking to her just in his head, always afraid he'd start thinking something he didn't want to say and have her hear it by accident, but he didn't want anyone overhearing him either.

Am not, she retorted, a little miffed. *Her pattern meshes with yours. It's pretty. She likes you too.*

"I don't like her," Devon spurted, loud enough that the people at the nearest table turned to stare at him.

Yes, you do, Airi informed him smugly. *I can feel emotions, remember? You like her, she likes you. It's fun.*

"I'm too tired to like anybody," Devon muttered, though he didn't really feel that way at the moment. Airi had never said this about any woman to him, though according to his own father, she'd done so once with him. That had been with actions then instead of words and had been when the man first met Devon's mother. Airi had no interest in romance, but she definitely understood love.

Devon watched Zalia come out of the kitchens with another pitcher of water for another table. She was demure and quiet, her skin darker than any woman's he'd ever seen and her hair a wave of solid black that reached to the small of her back. Her nose was long and her cheekbones high. She looked underfed and almost scrawny, and now that he thought about it, she was the most beautiful thing he'd ever seen.

See? Airi said.

It wasn't fair! He didn't have time to run into some potential love of his life. Not in a city he didn't know on the other side of the world from everything he'd ever known. Not when he was all alone except for an air sylph in an alien hive where his only allies had vanished, leaving blood trails and broken doors behind. He was supposed to go home in a year, only he couldn't. Not when Heyou was waiting to tear his guts out, just in case he developed some sort of interest in his own biological child. The child he hadn't wanted to help father. How could *this* get added to all of *that*?

Because something had to go right? Airi asked reasonably.

Devon almost snorted the pita, or perhaps it was the hummus, out his nose.

~

Zalia's shift was unbelievably long, even for someone born in Eferem, where there was no such thing as workers' rights. Devon watched her serve water and food, clear tables, and clean dishes from when he arrived before dawn to well after dark. He stayed in the corner where she'd put him, paying a penny each hour for the privilege and to keep the water flowing, and probably slept in his seat for a portion of the day. At the very least, he seemed to lose track of a few hours.

Finally though, it was night again and the oppressive heat fled. Zalia's coworker, who'd glared at Devon periodically during the day—when she wasn't ignoring him—wandered away into the darkness with the cooks from the kitchen, and Zalia came over to him.

"Did you enjoy your nap, sir?" she asked him with a smile.

Devon jerked upright. "Urg . . . wha—?" he managed. Airi started giggling and ruffled all the hair on his head straight up. Zalia started giggling as well.

Normally, Devon would have been terribly embarrassed to have two females laughing at him, but something about Zalia made him feel too comfortable for that, and of course, he was used to Airi's sense of humor.

Without his realizing she was about to, Airi appeared at his side, solidifying into a young girl with hair as long as Zalia's, though she was almost colorless. It was something she did extremely rarely; usually when Airi wanted a human to see her, she just pulled bits of fluff and detritus into her pattern and used them to form the outline of her shape. Going solid didn't come as naturally to air sylphs as it did the other elementals. Devon stared at her in surprise while Zalia gasped with shock and, to Devon's relief, delight.

"Thank you for letting us sit here all day," Airi said to Zalia.

Zalia clasped her hands together. "Oh, you're so beautiful! You're really a sylph?"

Airi nodded and beamed at the young woman, her hair blowing in a breeze that wasn't there for the two humans. "I am."

Zalia looked toward Devon. "I don't think I've ever really seen a sylph," she admitted. "Not up close." A sudden blush covered her face. "Well, just a few times."

Devon blinked, rubbing his stubbled cheek and really regretting what he was sure his breath smelled like right now. Through the fuzz and heat of the day, he'd noticed there weren't any sylphs passing by. He'd hoped there would be, so he could ask one of them where the queen was. Perhaps they didn't mingle with humans who weren't their masters here. "Do you know where the sylphs are?" he asked Zalia. Airi couldn't sense any, but it was a huge city and they weren't from her hive. She'd sense them if they were close enough, but until then they were lost.

Actually, she'd sensed many battle sylphs during the day, but neither of them were prepared to go near that kind of sylph if they didn't absolutely have to. Being surrounded last night had been bad enough.

Devon shuddered at the memory, but Zalia didn't notice, thinking. "I'm not sure," she finally said. "I've heard rumors, but I'm not positive where to look. We should go and talk to my father. He wants to meet you."

So she'd said before. Devon stood, content with the idea of spending more time with her. "Lead the way," he told her and saw her blush prettily and look down, a tiny smile on her lips. Devon's heart gave a great thump and he offered his arm, wanting nothing more than for her to take it. She looked puzzled for a moment, but put her arm timidly around his and walked with him, Devon letting her take the lead through the darkened streets. Airi giggled happily and played with both their hair, tangling it together in the air behind them.

～

The little arrangement of hovels was a dim shape in the darkness, intermingled with the warm glow of small fires lit for warmth and to cook food. Devon gaped, not able to make out many details but appalled by the poverty of it. Leon had told him about the place, of course, but Devon hadn't really grasped how poor it really was, nor had he expected it to still be here. The city was huge. Why couldn't they move there?

Beside him, Zalia's stomach rumbled loudly as the smell of food wafted to them.

"Sorry," she apologized.

Devon stared at her. "When was the last time you ate?"

"Before work this morning."

Devon stopped. "You haven't eaten all day? They make you serve people food and don't let you eat?" Guilt filled him. No wonder she was so thin. "Why didn't you say something? I would have bought you something to eat!"

Zalia stared at him for a moment, her mouth moving as she obviously tried to think of something to say. Finally, she dropped her hands away from her stomach and shrugged. "I would have been fired. I'm there to work, not to eat. A lot of people have left this place, but there are still hundreds of women who'd like to have my job."

Devon frowned. "Do you get any days off?"

"No. I work every day."

He blew out a breath in exasperation. Zalia was no better than a slave and that was the sort of thing supposed to change with a queen. He had to make sure it changed.

"Things will get better," he promised her. "I mean it."

She shrugged, neither agreeing or disagreeing, and led him over to one of the fires where an older, gaunt man with thinning white hair stood to greet them.

"This is my father, Xehm," Zalia told him. "Father, this is Devon Chole."

"It's good to meet you," Devon told him, shaking a hand where the fingers were thin as bird bones.

Xehm grinned at him, showing a lot of missing teeth. "It's a pleasure meeting you," Xehm enthused. "Mr. Petrule sent you then?"

"He did, sir. Myself and my air sylph, Airi." Airi swirled his hair, but didn't make herself visible.

They sat around the campfire, Zalia passing her father her wages and a waterskin. A pot of what looked like porridge was bubbling over the fire and Devon kicked himself. It hadn't occurred to him to buy food to bring with him. Stupid, he told himself. He had to stop being stupid.

You're not stupid, Airi told him.

The porridge was passed around. Devon tried to refuse, claiming he wasn't hungry, but his stomach growled and Xehm gave him a hurt look. He accepted then, hating that he was taking any of their food. It wasn't even very good and it certainly couldn't be nutritious, but it must have been all they had. Zalia and Xehm shared it easily though and it finally occurred to him that it was part of the way they survived. They shared. Well, he'd have something to donate to the pot himself, he promised. He had a lot of money on him. It wouldn't last forever, but surely it would feed these people for a good amount of time.

"It's wonderful to meet you," Xehm told him. "Mr. Petrule said that he was going to send someone."

"Yes." Devon looked around a little uncertainly. "I have to say, this isn't quite what I expected." He turned back to the old man, not sure how to phrase this. "I thought it would be different."

The old man's eyes turned sad. "So did we."

Devon shot a look at Zalia and turned back to her father, feeling Airi's presence against the back of his neck. She wasn't playing with his hair anymore, instead listening intently. "What happened?"

Xehm shrugged, staring down at the small fire that was their only source of warmth in the now frigid night. "What happened? Suddenly there was a queen, right here. Every sylph in the city rose up and hundreds died. Literally hundreds. They tore handlers apart in the streets and swallowed up the entire arena. The island that used to float over the city was hauled out to sea and dropped. Every sylph here gathered around this place." He looked toward one particular hovel that seemed no different than any other. "Then a few days passed, your friend left to go home, and we found that the only thing that really changed was that no one was in charge of anything anymore."

"Didn't the queen do anything?" Devon asked.

"I don't know. I never spoke to her. None of us did. The sylphs wouldn't let any of us near her and then she went away with them. Most of the people in this city don't even know there's a queen, though I assume she's still alive."

"So you don't know where she is then."

"No. Only the sylphs do."

Devon looked away, shivering a bit in his clothes as he thought. He didn't know what Eapha thought she was doing, but it obviously wasn't any of the things Leon had told her. Solie never would have done what it seemed this woman was doing and this entire place would die if she didn't smarten up. He thought of the blood on the *Racing Dawn* and shuddered.

"Do you know any sylphs?" he asked. "Someone who could take us to her? I really need to talk to her."

Xehm shook his head. "Not personally. None of the sylphs come near us lowly people. And their masters . . . I haven't seen anyone who is a master to a sylph. If they aren't also kept separate, they hide what they are. I don't blame them. I imagine there are a lot of people who would find it easy to blame them for what's happened." Devon sagged in disappointment and Xehm added, "But I have heard rumors of where they like to gather."

"Really?"

"It's said they get together at the gate to the world they came from," Xehm told him. "It's supposedly an endless celebration where they call new sylphs into this world and haul people off the street to be their masters, whether they're willing or not. Here, the sylphs have all the rights to choose who will be their master." Beside him, Zalia looked away.

Devon noticed her reaction and noticed also his own response to the thought of her upset. His stomach flipped over and he cleared his throat, even as Airi giggled knowingly into his mind. "Do you know where this gate is?" he asked.

At that question, Xehm grinned at him with his gap-toothed smile. "Oh, yes. That I do know. We'll go there in the morning and see what help we can find."

~

Zalia guided Devon over to one of the huts, one abandoned by its previous owners when they'd joined the exodus. Well aware of her father's eyes on them and of her own shyness, she kept her gaze locked on the sand under her feet, not aware of how Devon looked at her, though her father was.

"I'm sorry I won't be able to go with you to the gate tomorrow," she said.

"So am I." There was something so wistful in his tone that she looked up at him despite herself and saw him start, turning away with an embarrassed cough. "I mean, um, that is . . ."

A translucent girl appeared on his other side. "He likes you," she said.

"Airi!" Devon barked and the sylph vanished.

Zalia felt as if she had to be blushing to her toes and was glad that he couldn't see it through the darkness. She just felt so silly, and excited at the same time.

"I like you too," she said, really hoping he didn't hear her and wishing he would at the same time.

He did. Even in the darkness, she saw him duck his head and smile. She'd never felt attracted to anyone like this and she found that something about Devon Chole, despite the fact that this was only the second time she'd met him, made her feel complete. That was really strange, since she hadn't been aware that anything was missing in her life, but she liked it. She really did wish she could go with them in the morning to find the sylphs and beg them to take them to see the queen. She hoped even more that once he spoke with the queen, he'd stay, and perhaps take an interest in her. Zalia blushed and gestured at the tiny hovel. It wasn't useful for much more than keeping the sand off, but all the hovels were like that.

"You can sleep here tonight," she assured him. "No one will bother you."

"Thank you," he said. He hesitated for a moment as though he were about to say something else, and then vanished inside.

Airi's shimmering shape appeared beside Zalia. "He really does like you," she whispered. "He's just shy."

Zalia blushed even hotter, though inside she was delighted. "Why are you telling me this?" she asked. "Why do you want us together?"

"Isn't it fate?" the little sylph asked reasonably and vanished again. Zalia felt a small gust of wind in the otherwise still air as Airi swept into the hovel to join her master.

Still blushing furiously, Zalia made her way to her own hovel and lay there for a long time before she was finally able to sleep.

CHAPTER FIVE

In the harems, the worst possible crime for a concubine was to cause a battle sylph to fall in love with her. They could play with her, or have sex with her, or even kill her if they so wanted, but they couldn't love her. Love took their attention away from their duties, from their masters, and so it was forbidden. To have a battle sylph in love with only her was the next worst thing to a death sentence for a woman. She would be dragged from the harem the instant it was found out, her battler lover under orders not to follow, and her tongue would be cut out so that she could become a feeder for an elemental sylph instead. She would spend the rest of her life sitting in a cage like an animal, feeding a sylph, and waiting to die.

One woman had been living out that fate in the feeder cells when Eapha became queen. While the rest of the battle sylphs had been gathering around the queen or killing the men who'd once owned them, the battle sylph once known as Five-Eighty, now called Haru, had gone smashing his way into the deepest levels of the feeder cages, looking for a woman he hadn't seen in thirty years.

Fareeda was a tiny thing, her face gaunt and heavily wrinkled, her hair gray and coarse. She'd long since lost all her beauty and hadn't spoken once since she was carried out, her eyes glazed with madness. She didn't seem aware of anything, but if her battle sylph tried to leave her, her scrawny little hands would grasp his arm with a strength it wouldn't have seemed possible she still had.

Haru doted on her. He brushed her hair and kept her clean, held her glass to her mouth and fed her by hand with great patience. He carried her from her bed to her toilet to her couch by the windows, never leaving her and rarely saying anything either. To see them, they looked bizarre, Haru being so beautiful while Fareeda was such an ancient wreck, but Eapha had an empathic ability beyond normal compassion, forced on her by her queen status. She could feel people and whenever Haru was more than a few feet away from her, Fareeda's emotions turned into an endless sort of screaming inside of her. However, when he was at her side, they calmed. Not quite to happiness, since Eapha had the feeling that emotion was forever gone from the woman, but certainly to something of peace, and he loved her. Absolutely loved her.

Not everyone felt comfortable around the woman though and Kiala leaned over toward Eapha, sitting beside her in the palace's great room on a silken cushion. "Why do you let her stay here?" Kiala whispered. "She's so creepy."

A few of the other women there nodded, but Eapha shook her head. "That could have been any of us," she reminded them. Fareeda wasn't hurting anyone and she deserved to have this. Eapha hadn't let just anyone into the palace with her. Except for Fareeda, they were all members of the Circle that had worked together to hide from the handlers the fact that they'd each taken a single battler for a lover. Without it, they all would have ended up like Fareeda.

Kiala's lips firmed. She'd come closer than anyone else in the Circle to being a feeder. She'd been dragged out of the harem along with Lizzy Petrule, and she would have ended up in a cage with no tongue herself if Eapha hadn't become queen that very night. She didn't look understanding now, but then Kiala wasn't a woman known for her compassion. A few of the other women looked contrite though.

Sorry, one of them gestured, using the sign language that had let them form the Circle and had allowed their battlers to communicate with them despite their orders to never speak. *She is a little scary though.*

We would be too, Eapha signed back. *Just leave her be. Maybe she'll get better.*

I doubt it, Kiala added, her gestures rough with annoyance. *She'll die that way.*

Probably, Eapha thought, though she didn't say it aloud. Haru didn't know sign language and he wasn't looking at them anyway, though he had to know what they were feeling. He didn't care though. He was with his love and her mental state meant nothing to him. Eapha sighed, missing Tooie.

She hadn't thought Tooie would be so busy. She'd imagined he'd be more like Haru, never leaving her side. There were other sylphs around who could run things; it didn't have to be him. Still, he seemed to enjoy it and the other sylphs appeared to expect it of him, so she didn't say anything. Still, seeing Haru with Fareeda made her miss him again and she hoped he finished up with whatever it was he was doing and came home soon. He was supposed to be at her side; everything else would take care of itself, or at least so her friends kept assuring her.

Eapha lounged on her pillows with her friends and watched Haru feed Fareeda some porridge, patiently spooning it into her mouth and scooping up the excess from her chin. She ate mechanically, staring at nothing. Fareeda was lucky she had him, Eapha thought. How many other former feeders were out there? She shuddered at the thought, but the sylphs would be taking care of them, wouldn't they?

While her friends started gossiping, Eapha wondered about that. What was being done about the feeders? Were they just dumped out on the street or were the sylphs taking care of them? She honestly wasn't sure, but after a minute, and before the others could notice her introspection and start teasing her again, she pushed the thought away. It wasn't her place to be poking her nose into anything. The sylphs in Meridal had spent centuries as slaves and the city was theirs now. They were fully capable of making all the decisions themselves and they didn't need someone like her second-guessing them. Who was she anyway? The sylphs called her their queen, but she was really just a concubine at heart, with no education or prospects. All she was good for was sex, not running a city.

Eapha sighed and turned her mind back to her friends and their suggestion about starting a card game. That she was good at, and soon enough, her mood was back to normal, happy and content with whatever life was able to give her.

~

Zalia was gone by the time Devon managed to stumble his way out of the already overheated hovel and into the even worse heat outside.

"I'm never going to get used to this," he groaned while Airi tried to cool him down, though all she really succeeded in was to move the already hot air around.

Maybe we should get you a hat, she suggested uncertainly.

Devon put a hand to his sunburned, peeling face. "I think it's too late for that," he sighed and made his way over to where Xehm sat by the fire pit they'd used the night before. Devon's feet were sweltering in his boots again and he didn't even want to consider what he smelled like.

Xehm handed him a waterskin, beaming at him. "Good morning, young sir."

"Morning," Devon grumbled, barely able to stop himself from guzzling down all of the water. His lips were so dry and cracked that they were painful and his skin burned. He was undoubtedly red on every inch of exposed skin and he'd never been so filthy in his life. Xehm just continued to happily smile at him.

He thinks you might marry his daughter, Airi told him.

Devon managed not to spit the water out at that revelation. Marriage? He'd only met the woman twice. Marriage wasn't something that entered into his thoughts, especially not with everything else that was going on.

Still, he thought almost without realizing it, he did miss having Zalia there, even after only a few hours. Dirty, sweaty, and hideous though he was, he wanted her there.

"Let's get going," was all he said.

"Of course, sir," Xehm agreed.

They walked to the place where the gate was rumored to be. There were some men trotting along the streets and towing small carts that passengers could ride in, but Xehm didn't pay any attention to them and Devon didn't want to know how much they would cost.

At first, he'd had the impression that Xehm just sat at the hovels all day, leaving his daughter to work her insane hours bringing in money. In actuality, the old man went into the city every day, looking for any sort of temporary work he could find and haggling for food and other necessities with the money Zalia brought. They did some of that as they made their way along, Xehm putting the bread and porridge he bought into a sack he carried on his back, and Devon was shocked at some of the prices the staples were going for. There was no regulation of costs at all and corruption was rampant.

There were battlers in the markets they passed, watching for threats, but they did nothing for any customers being cheated. Instead they descended on anyone who became irate about it, which actually served to protect the merchants and help keep the prices high. Devon was disgusted to see it, but not too surprised. Battle sylphs generally weren't any good at comprehending things like money. Devon knew that Leon had spent years getting Ril to grasp the intricacies of the concept—thanks to the battler's indifference, not his intelligence—but Ril still didn't care and the other sylphs were just as bad. Humans had to be in charge of things such as finances and infrastructure, which was why there was only one sylph on the Valley council. Devon sighed. He supposed it was two now, since Ril had taken Devon's old position as Solie's majordomo.

If Eapha had turned over the running of Meridal to the sylphs, and he was strongly suspecting that she had, then she was a fool.

By the time they got where they were going, the morning sun had risen high in the sky and it was witheringly hot. This time though, Devon took the opportunity while Xehm was buying his groceries to purchase an overpriced linen shirt that was much lighter than the one he had been wearing, knee-length pants, sandals that felt strange on his feet, and at Xehm's suggestion, a thin cloth to wrap around his head and part of his face to keep the sun off. The rest of his body he covered with an exorbitantly expensive healing cream that made him sigh so deeply in relief that Airi started giggling again. His old clothes he carried in a sack, remembering how cold it got once the sun went down. His sword he left on his hip. Few men around him carried their own, seeming to prefer knives instead, but no one did more than glance at it either.

The entrance to the place where the sylphs had their gate was a small building the size of a shed in the center of an otherwise empty square, one with openings in the roof that were shaped like mouths. No one was guarding it and the door was not only open but long since ripped off its hinges.

Xehm and Devon walked up to the doorway and looked in at a dim staircase. Both men were silent for a moment, studying it.

"Perhaps we should ask the battle sylphs at the market for help?" Xehm suggested at last, a little nervously.

"No," Devon said and went in first, Airi flowing past him to lead the way down the stairs. After a moment, Xehm followed.

The stairwell came out in the middle of a corridor that stretched to either side of the steps. To their right, they could see a shattered door leading to a chamber with broken furniture in it, and beyond that, more broken doors leading into another, seemingly larger room. To their left, it ended much closer at another broken door through which cages could be seen. The floors were already starting to become obscured with sand, the stone beneath stained black. It smelled faintly of copper.

"Which way?" Devon wondered.

"The stories say the gate is below where they keep the feeder cages." Xehm nodded to the left. "They must be that way." He looked to the right. "That must be the way to the concubine harem for the battlers." His voice turned sad. "They took my wife to be a concubine."

Devon was stunned. "What? That's awful! Didn't she come back when the queen rose?"

"Oh no. I suspect she died in there many years ago. She always was delicate." He sighed. "My Zalia is much stronger than her mother."

"Yes," Devon murmured and led the way to the left. He didn't want to see the harem.

Once he entered the area where the feeder pens were kept, he realized he didn't want to see them either. There were thousands of cages, layered upward and outward in a chamber so large it boggled his mind, all connected by catwalks and stairways, each enclosure hardly big enough for a single man to move around in. All of the doors were destroyed and the cages in the center of

70

the great chamber were torn completely away, forming a massive well. Devon walked down the black-stained catwalks, remembering Leon's brief about Ril's battle to get to Lizzy, and had to shudder at the thought of what all the dark stains and the faint copper smell had to be. Ril wasn't powerful enough to have destroyed the center of the pens though. Devon could only guess that a group of battlers did that.

They'd done a pretty thorough job of it as well. After a few minutes of walking, making their way over or around the wreckage, Devon and Xehm came at last to a place where the catwalk and all of the cages were simply gone. There was nothing but fifty feet or more of air between them and where the catwalk resumed on the other side.

Xehm looked nervously over the side, hanging on to part of a cage as he did. Devon didn't blame him. He was hanging on to the closest intact cage himself. "I didn't realize it would be like this," the old man said, his voice echoing a bit in the emptiness. "Can there be anyone down there?"

"This wouldn't stop a sylph," Devon said. "There could be hundreds of them."

"Are you sure? I know I suggested coming here, but perhaps we should go back."

And ask a battle sylph to introduce them to his queen? Not a chance. "We go down," Devon said, even as he wondered if it was possible. There didn't look to be any way to climb safely.

I can carry you, Airi said.

Devon shuddered at the thought. Airi was strong enough to lift him and could even manage two people for short distances, but the experience was terrifying. Devon loved Airi and trusted her with his life, but his dread of heights . . . His dread of battle sylphs was worse.

"Okay," he gulped. He turned to Xehm. "Airi will get us down."

The old man looked puzzled, staring at him in confusion. Devon just took a deep breath, stepped to the edge of the catwalk, and raised his arms over his head.

Airi wrapped her winds around his arms, getting a good hold, and lifted him off the ground. Xehm yelped at the sight, but Devon had his eyes squeezed tightly shut, afraid to look as she carried him forward and then lowered him, dropping him down quickly as his shirt hunched up and air much cooler than that on the surface chilled his sweaty skin.

I'm going to set you down, she told him.

Devon opened his eyes. He was near a stone floor, only a few inches above it as she waited for him to prepare himself. He braced himself and she lowered him that last little bit, setting him on his feet.

"Thanks," he told her and her winds swirled around him, hugging him warmly before sweeping his head wrap off and spiking his hair into a single ridge from front to back. Giggling, she left to get Xehm.

Devon took the time to get his racing heart rate under control and look around. He seemed to be at the lowest level of the pens, the metal cages torn to shreds around him. A minute later he heard a nervous yelp from above and looked up.

Xehm was falling slowly toward him, though he seemed instead to be racing down an invisible hill as his legs churned madly, running in place while he kept his arms above his head in what looked like a victory salute. Devon had to hide a smile. It looked silly, but he knew how terrifying the experience was. It appeared that Xehm wasn't any braver than he was.

Airi set Xehm down and he dropped to his hands and knees, panting. Devon hunkered down beside him, putting one hand on the old man's bony shoulder. "Sorry about that," he apologized. "It's easier if you keep your eyes shut."

"I was afraid she'd drop me!" Xehm gasped.

Never.

"Airi would never drop you. She hasn't dropped me yet anyway."

I dropped your grandfather once, Airi admitted. *I was very young though and he was very drunk. He kept squirming. Your grandmother was unimpressed when he crashed through her roof. Then again, she wasn't your grandmother yet.*

Devon blinked and finally decided he really didn't want to know. "Come on," he said, standing again. "I think they must be this way."

They walked across the scrapped remains where the cages had originally been bolted into the floor, heading toward a corridor clear of the wreckage on the other side. A dim light glowed down it, but Devon wasn't entirely sure that meant there was a sylph down that way. A fire sylph in a central location could light up miles of tunnel using carefully placed mirrors.

"I'm not sure we're going the right way anymore," Xehm said uncertainly behind him.

Devon shook his head, not completely sure himself, but too curious not to look now. They'd come too far to turn back. "What do you think, Airi?" he asked.

I can feel a sylph, she said. *I think.*

"Airi says there's someone down there," Devon said and walked into the corridor, small and nearly claustrophobic after the huge area where the cages used to be. The corridor was square and squat, with sharp man-made angles, but there were periodic areas of destruction along the walls and floor, spots no more than a few feet wide where the smooth stone was pockmarked. Devon walked around the strange holes, not sure what they were. Xehm just followed after him, his lips firm, and Devon wondered suddenly if the old man was frightened by the closed-in spaces.

Before he could suggest that they go back, despite his own personal curiosity, the passageway opened up again into another room. It wasn't anywhere near the size of the cage room, but somehow, it was far more grandiose. The walls were covered in frescos of colored stone, showing hundreds of years of the subjugation of sylphs by the people of Meridal. The pictures didn't present it that way, all of the sylphs depicted instead as being blissful with the chance to serve, but the rest of the room proved the lie to that.

In the center of the circular room's marbled floor, an altar stood, the top flat and unadorned, though even from where they stood, they could see the surface was black from dried blood. Most sylphs were drawn through the gate by offerings of skill, but hundreds of women had been sacrificed on that altar to trap the battlers. Devon stood in the entrance, staring at the altar and the great circle imbedded in the floor around it, and felt as though the deaths of all those people were soaked into the place, reaching out to draw him in. The room even reeked of it, the acrid smell of copper strong in his nose. Airi pressed against Devon's back, cold.

"This place is horrible," Xehm whispered. "It's nothing but death."

This was where the sylphs were supposed to be gathered to celebrate their victory? In this place? Devon didn't see any sylphs. He saw the same large pockmarks on the floor and walls as in the corridor, and something else that he didn't recognize until he forced himself to walk forward and take a closer look.

What he saw made him jump back in horror. The blood wasn't just on the altar. There were pools of it scattered everywhere on the floor, so thick in spots that it still looked to be tacky, and when he moved close, his stomach roiled at the stench of it. Devon stared at the blood and felt his gorge rise, even as Xehm stepped up beside him and gasped. Suddenly, he wished he still had his boots on, so that his bare toes wouldn't be so close to it.

"What did this?" Xehm gasped. "The battlers?"

Not the battle sylphs, Devon thought. They could destroy things, but they blew up their target and everything around it. If they'd done this, the blood would have been splattered, not pooled, and there would have been a lot more damage to the room itself than the odd hole. Something inside of him screamed that this was done by something else entirely and he had a suddenly incongruous wish that Zalia was there with him, just so he could assure himself that she was all right.

"Airi?" he whispered. "Are there any sylphs here?"

The little sylph pressed against his back, easily as terrified as her master. She didn't flee though. Not even though she could have grabbed him and raced back the way they'd come, out into the fresh air of the city. Neither of them knew if it was any safer up there anymore, not after what they'd seen only the night before last at the harbor.

"Airi?" he repeated.

Yes, she said at last, shivering against his back. *I can feel one. She's hurt and so frightened. She's hiding. I wouldn't have felt her at all if I weren't so close.*

Devon frowned. Why would an elemental sylph hide? Back home, any of them who were in danger screamed for the battlers. They certainly hadn't seemed too concerned outside. Perhaps they'd already dealt with the problem, though if they had, why was she still hiding? Why would she hide at all if the battle sylphs were the cause of all this blood?

"There's a sylph here," Devon told Xehm. "Airi says she's hurt somehow. Maybe she can tell us what happened."

"I don't think I want to know," Xehm whimpered. The old man was pale, his brown skin tinged with gray, and he shivered where he stood. Devon didn't blame him. He also didn't agree.

"I don't want to have whatever did this do it again," Devon argued and turned completely to face his sylph. He couldn't see her, but he could feel little kisses of air on his face. "Can you talk to the sylph?" he asked her.

Yes, she said and flitted away.

"Make sure we can see you," Devon called after her. He didn't want any more surprises.

Sand on the floor, blown even to these depths from the surface, suddenly lifted, caught in a tiny whirlwind, and formed the outline of a skinny human girl. It was easier for Airi to make those kinds of shapes than to actually become solid, and right now, probably felt safer for the little creature as well, even if that safety was an illusion. She crossed the floor to a corner far from the corridor they'd come in by, to where a gouge in the floor was nearly five feet deep, though only two feet across. Airi hovered on the edge of the pit, looking down. *She's down there.*

"Did she do this?" Devon asked, indicating the pit as he walked up to the edge.

No. I think something tried to dig her out. Oh, Devon, I'm scared.

"So am I," he murmured.

"What is it?" Xehm asked, stopping beside him.

"I don't know yet. Airi, do you?"

I don't want to know. I'm scared. She dived down, fading back to invisibility as the grains of sand that made her up splattered against the ground beside the dark circle of what looked like a much smaller hole, right in the center of the pit. Left on the rim, Devon had the sudden feeling that Airi did know what was going on.

~

Airi did indeed have a suspicion of what was happening, though the thought of it made her want to grab her master and fly for home, fly until her pattern gave out on her. It wasn't anything she'd ever encountered herself, but her home hive had stories. Stories of disappearances and deaths, and the scars of outright attacks still marred the outer layers of her birth hive itself, even after centuries, left as a reminder of what could happen to even the most prosperous of hives.

Airi shuddered and made her way down the narrow airhole that the earth sylph had left. If she was right in her suspicions, then an earth sylph was the only type of elemental with any hope of surviving it. It was only their walls that could hold the monsters out and she'd taken an incredible risk leaving even such a tiny way in.

The reason why she'd done it became apparent a moment later, as Airi flowed into a hollow in solid stone, bored nearly fifty feet below the chamber. The edges were rough, the entire thing obviously formed in a few bare instants of strength and panic, leaving the sylph herself too weak to get back out. Or rather, too weak to get her master back out.

A man lay insensate on his side in the hollow, the marbled form of his sylph lying embraced with him, though the stone of her couldn't have been warm for him and the hollow itself was very cold. Airi cautiously fluttered down, afraid of what the older sylph would do, but her pattern was hurt as well as exhausted. She'd been just fast enough to live, but not to keep from injury.

Go away, the earth sylph breathed, unmoving.

I can't, Airi told her. *I have to help.*

She drifted closer, studying the earth sylph's pattern. She was from a different hive, but unlike Ocean Breeze, she wasn't even an air sylph. Airi didn't feel as though she had any way to relate to the other sylph except for in the one similarity they both shared.

My master is above, she told the sylph. *He wants me to help you. My name is Airi. My master is Devon. What's your name?* The earth sylph was silent. *What's your master's name?*

There was a long pause. *Gel,* the sylph said at last. *I'm Shasha. I . . . can't get him out.*

Encouraged by the answer but still nervous, Airi moved closer, seeing how Shasha was injured. She'd lost part of her pattern and was leaking energy even as she lay there. She didn't have the strength to tell if there was still danger outside her hiding place, let alone to get out of it.

Except for the masters they were bound to, the energy of this world was poisonous to them; to try to consume it was to die. The energy within themselves was natural to them though, no matter its source.

Airi eased up to Shasha's side, afraid the older sylph would interpret her actions as a threat and lash out. Shasha just lay there and Airi stretched out beside her, delicately linking her pattern to the injured sylph so that she could feed her some of her own energy.

It felt strange. Shasha wasn't from her hive and was an earth sylph. Even back home, air sylphs and earth sylphs didn't interact much. Their jobs were very different and they didn't have much need to actively work together. Besides, what Airi was doing now was a very rare thing. Usually, a healer would be sent for a wounded sylph or the queen would order them abandoned if they couldn't make it back to the hive themselves. For two elementals to share their energy was almost never done, but it wasn't unheard of.

Airi fed Shasha some of the energy that she'd taken from Devon that morning, now changed within her to something edible for all sylphs. It wasn't the most nourishing—Airi wasn't a food sylph and wasn't designed to produce energy for others to eat—but it was enough for Shasha to regain some small amount of her strength, if not to heal herself. Airi didn't have enough power in her entire pattern for that.

It was intimate though. Airi felt her pattern blend up against the earth sylph's, and felt some of Shasha's pain and desperate fear for her master, even as Shasha experienced Airi's terror and uncertainty at being in the heart of an alien hive. That need for someone else to be there for them echoed through both sylphs and Airi felt her energy pour into Shasha's damaged pattern, the flow controlled by the other sylph.

I won't take too much, Shasha promised.

I know, Airi answered, knowing that was the truth.

A moment later, it was done. Shasha rose from beside her unconscious master, a slim creature of marble and gems. Beautiful, she raised her arms and Airi felt the stone around them move, shifting around the earth sylph as easily as the air did around Airi. Gently, the chamber she'd made rose, lifting up through the ground.

What happened? Airi asked her finally, though she knew the only reason Shasha would have run the way she did was from a predator, and that there was only one predator in existence where calling the battlers wouldn't make a difference.

Gleaming ruby eyes turned toward her, glistening in the sparse light coming through the airhole Shasha had left to give her master a way to breathe, despite what must have been a very real terror that the thing which drove her into the ground to begin with would be able to find it and use it to reach them.

A Hunter, Shasha told Airi, to her unsurprised horror. *A Hunter has come through the gate.*

CHAPTER SIX

On the same morning that Devon and Xehm went to the gate and found Gel and Shasha—and for the first time since she had started working at the restaurant, landing a job that saved her and her father from starvation and probable slavery—Zalia woke after dawn.

For a moment, she just stared up at the cracks in the roof of her hovel in confusion, not understanding what she was seeing. She hadn't seen the sun shining down on her and her blankets in almost five years. Every morning, she'd already been at work by the time the sun rose.

Suddenly, Zalia realized where she was and rolled out of her blankets, scrambling to her feet in a panic. Unaware of how his own morning would fare, her father was still sleeping in his bed, snoring, and he didn't wake as Zalia bolted out of the hut, running toward the city. She passed Devon's hut with only a miserable glance. She'd stayed awake until long into the night, thinking about him. Even the realization that she might lose her job because of it couldn't cool her warm thoughts toward the man and she hoped that he'd have a better day than she looked to as she ran to the restaurant. She didn't stop to bathe first. She would only be later and there would be too many people around the stables to risk it now. As she ran, she worked her fingers through her hair, getting the knots out as she tamed it into something that wouldn't get her fired on the spot. Her clothes she could do nothing about, but at least her apron would mostly hide how worn and old they were.

Ilaja saw her coming up the street, panting as she ran, and the other woman's eyes widened as Zalia hurried to the edge of the patio. There were already customers in the restaurant, drinking and eating in the cool air of early morning.

"Where have you been?" Ilaja demanded. "You'll be fired for this!"

Zalia ran up and stopped before her, panting desperately. Ilaja looked at her in disgust. "I'm sorry," she gasped. "I'm sorry."

"Don't tell me," Ilaja sniffed. "The cook's already sent word to the owner. He's not going to care why you were whoring around."

Zalia stared at her in shock. She and Ilaja had never been friends, but she'd never expected this kind of response from the woman. "I wasn't whoring!"

"I saw you leave with a man," Ilaja snapped. "This is supposed to be a wholesome place."

Zalia's world reeled. "I wasn't whoring!" was all she could manage to repeat. The customers were starting to look in their direction with what seemed to Zalia to be delight. "What did you say to them?"

"I just told them what I saw," Ilaja said and turned away, returning to her customers with a smile.

Zalia felt sick. Ilaja hadn't been joking when she said Orlil would fire her, and from the way she was smiling, Ilaja didn't care. There wasn't nearly the business there had been in past years and being the only waitress would mean more tips for her. Trying not to cry, Zalia went to get her apron and work her tables. If he stayed true to past history, the owner wouldn't be around until midmorning. Perhaps if she made a good enough impression on her customers before then, she wouldn't lose her job.

It wasn't easy. Zalia was so stressed, she messed up several orders and even flubbed a pitcher of water, almost dousing a customer who mercilessly berated her for her mistake. Ilaja's smirks didn't help either as the woman passed her several times, beaming at her own customers. All of them seemed to take a perverse pleasure in Zalia's misery. Zalia tried to tell herself she was just imaging things and no one was against her, but her fear was too great. She couldn't afford to lose this job. There wasn't much left for a woman of her station in Meridal, save to become the whore Ilaja had already called her.

No one would want her then, she thought desperately. Her father would be so ashamed; only what else could she do?

It was close to midmorning; more customers were taking seats in the restaurant. It looked as if she'd lose her job on one of the busiest days they'd had in months. Zalia put a pitcher on one table and turned to the next to set down their pita and hummus, the same dish she'd served to Devon the previous day. None of this was his fault. He'd done nothing but treat her with respect, and Ilaja had disliked him from the start.

Someone sat down at the table behind her, the chair scraping against the stone. Zalia finished setting out the meal and turned around.

"Hi," One-Eleven said.

Zalia gaped at him, her heart hammering. He was as unbelievably handsome as before, his carriage utterly different from Devon's as he sat there grinning. He was wearing simple clothes, but he was so beautiful that everyone looked at him. Even Ilaja was gaping. No one recognized him for what he was, Zalia realized. Then again, how could they? He wasn't behaving like a battle sylph and there was no reason for one to come and sit at their restaurant. Well, there was, she thought after a moment, wasn't there?

As if he could read her thoughts, and some of the stories said the battlers could, One-Eleven grinned even wider, lounging in the chair as if it were a throne. He didn't seem to care at all that everyone was staring at him, or perhaps he felt in some fashion that it was his due. Either way, he was confident and strong, everything she didn't feel she could be, standing there with her tray clutched to her breast and not knowing if she'd still have a job in the next hour.

"What are you doing here?" she whispered a little frantically. Ilaja was serving another of her tables nearby, glaring jealously at Zalia.

One-Eleven's grin didn't even flicker. "I finished the job I was assigned and I wanted to see you. So I came by. You don't mind, do you?"

What was she supposed to say to that? Zalia didn't know what to even think. She just knew there was a warmth puddling in her belly at the sight of him and suddenly the memory of Devon was far away. She felt guilt at that, but One-Eleven was just so suddenly and overwhelmingly *there* that she couldn't think of anything else except him and how he was making her breasts tingle. At that thought, she remembered how he'd found her bathing at the stable and the warmth of him against her back and buttocks as he cupped her breast and prepared to take her virginity.

She'd never keep her job acting this way, she realized frantically, suddenly angry at him for adding this stress on top of the fears she already had. "You can't be here," she hissed at him. He blinked. "You'll ruin everything!"

"How?" he asked, sounding reasonably and, unfortunately, loud. "I just wanted to see you."

Zalia's voice had been quiet, only carrying to One-Eleven, but his still came out at a normal volume and Zalia flushed as she realized what it looked like—her snubbing a customer right in the restaurant. Ilaja sniffed and stepped up beside her, shouldering her aside. "Well, if you can't at least be nice to a valued customer," she said, "I'll have to help him." She turned her smile on One-Eleven. "How can I help you . . ."

Her voice trailed off. One-Eleven was glaring at her in silence, his body language suddenly tense and angry. The very way he held himself was both a threat and a promise. He looked straight into Ilaja's eyes without blinking and she squeaked, suddenly backing away.

What did he make her feel? Zalia wondered in amazement and looked back at him. One-Eleven still glared at Ilaja, but when Zalia turned to him, he flickered his eyes at her for a moment and gave her a brief smile that started all the warmth up inside her again.

She sagged. "You have to order something to stay here," she told him.

"Oh, okay. I can do that."

A sudden thought occurred to her. "Do you have any money?" she asked.

"No."

Zalia hugged her tray tighter, trying to think. Maybe she could convince him to meet her later, after her shift ended, if she still had a job. But if she did that, what was to prevent him from trying to seduce her? Did she even have the strength to stop him again? Just the thought of it had her throbbing with needs that didn't care how ready for it all she might actually be. Part of her wanted him inside her and it didn't care about anything else.

One-Eleven studied her, tilting his beautiful head to one side to regard her while his smile continued to play around his lips. Oh yes, she thought with something that might have been excitement as much as it was despair. He'd have her if he came on her alone again.

Ilaja tapped her shoulder and she jumped. Zalia hadn't been

aware of the woman leaving or coming back, but she'd regained her composure. "Orlil wants to see you inside," she said with a smirk.

Zalia's heart sank. Of course Orlil would show up now; he couldn't have possibly seen her in a worse light than standing in the middle of the patio, ignoring all her customers while she stared at one man as though she wanted to tear his clothes off.

"What's wrong?" One-Eleven asked, his smile gone.

"Wait here," Zalia murmured, waving him down when he started to stand. She was so frightened that all of her ardor was gone. She was so terrified she could even think about Devon again, and wondered a little guiltily if, when he did find the queen, he'd be able to ask her to give Zalia a new job.

She walked across the patio toward the kitchen, her tray still held against her breasts like a shield. Probably sensing what was coming, the other customers laughed as she passed, though a few had the dignity to look sorry for her. No one said anything; there wasn't anything for anyone to say. There wasn't even anything Zalia could say to defend her case, not without looking like a harlot, and that would still get her fired anyway.

She walked through the wide doorway and into the kitchen. It was swelteringly hot inside, the heat of the day's sun combined with the roaring fires of the cookstove. Pots bubbled on the stoves and cooks shouted at each other, somehow producing food out of the chaos. The cool water she served was kept below, deep underground where the heat didn't reach.

That was where Orlil had his office. Zalia made her way down the steep steps in the dark, one hand on the dry wall as she made her way. Orlil carried his own lamp down with him and didn't want to waste money lighting the stairs. Anyone else who came down here for the water always risked a broken leg or neck. At the bottom of the stairs was a large cistern that held their water, the liquid dark inside the well. Zalia saw something move in the shadows that might have been a rat and crossed the room toward the office on the other side. The cellar was at least ten degrees colder than the patio outside and she shivered, though that might have been from fear.

Orlil's office was small, the battered desk covered with the abacus and wax tablets he used to keep track of the restaurant's sales, as well as those of the other businesses he owned, most of which she didn't know anything about. Zalia suspected that, even with the chaos in the city, Orlil was still a very wealthy man.

Unfortunately, he wasn't a kind one. Orlil was bitter, scrawny to the point of looking starved, and his head was shaved to show his free status, not that it mattered anymore. Theoretically, everyone was free now, but Orlil had enough authority over Zalia that he may as well have owned her. He directed what hours she worked, what money she kept from her tips, what she could wear, and how she was to behave whenever she was at the restaurant. Zalia had always suspected that he would have been raping and beating his waitresses if it weren't for the battlers. Any violence against women resulted in an instant response from them, though they'd always couched it under the rules against disturbing the peace before and taken the transgressor to die in the arena. Now they'd probably just kill the man. That reminded her of One-Eleven upstairs and she bowed deeply to hide her sudden blush.

"You wanted to see me, sir?" she said.

Her head down, she couldn't see him, but she imagined Orlil frowning and lacing his long fingers together on top of the desk. "I don't want whores working in my restaurant," he said flatly.

Zalia's head came up, her heart hammering though she'd known this was coming. "I'm not a whore!" she protested.

Orlil's frown deepened, glaring at her through the light of the oil lamp. "Ilaja saw you whoring with a man last night and I saw you with that man when I came this morning. I don't want women selling themselves here and ruining my reputation."

Her heart sank further. "I haven't been selling myself," she promised. "Please, sir. I haven't done a thing."

He looked away. "All women are whores. I don't want to see you here again."

Zalia fell to her knees, tears in her eyes. She'd starve. Her father would starve. There weren't any jobs in Meridal anymore, not with so many people leaving and so much confusion. Her father was too old and frail for this to happen to them. "Please, sir!" she begged. "I can't lose this job! I've never been late before. I've never failed you!"

"You failed me this time and I'm not in business to deal with failure." He regarded her for a moment, his gaze making her feel slimy even through the terror. "Perhaps I can use you at one of my other businesses."

Zalia clasped her hands together before her breasts. "Sir?" she asked hopefully.

"I have a massage parlor down near the docks," Orlil told her. "I can use another girl there."

Zalia's heart fell. He was firing her for being a whore and offering her a job in a massage parlor instead? "But I'm not a whore," she repeated in a whisper.

"All women are whores," he said again. "Take it or find someone else to sell yourself to."

Zalia started to cry.

Orlil glared at her in disgust. "Stop crying, you stupid little—" He looked up. "Who are you?"

Zalia looked around. One-Eleven was standing in the doorway, one hand resting on the frame and the other a fist against his hip as he looked in, so much in shadow that he was hard to see. The shadow of his face turned toward her and she felt something from him. Not lust this time, she felt comfort instead, covering her as though it were a blanket. How could he affect so deeply what she felt? she wondered. She clung to the comfort, suddenly wanting to go to him.

"Please go upstairs, sir," Orlil said, obviously mistaking the battler for a customer. He rose to his feet. "Someone will be there to serve you."

One-Eleven's face turned toward him, indistinct in the darkness. "You made her cry," he said.

"Oh, yes, well, just a little discipline for—"

"You frightened her and made her cry." One-Eleven walked into the room, his face emerging into the light as he came in, his inhuman beauty revealing itself as he stopped beside Zalia, one hand trailing down to lovingly touch her hair. He never took his gaze off of Orlil. "You called her a whore."

"Well, I'm sorry if you misheard, sir—"

One-Eleven's eyes suddenly changed, swirling to red ball lightning as his mouth filled with flame. "I don't like the way you talked to her."

Orlil screamed, throwing himself backward in terror, his eyes huge. There was nowhere for him to go in the small office and his back slammed into one of the wooden file cabinets he kept there. One-Eleven was on him an instant later, one hand holding him down by the throat while the other drew back, fingers changed to vicious claws.

Zalia shrieked and threw herself at him, grabbing that arm and trying to hold it back with all her strength. Orlil was gibbering in terror, scrabbling at the hand that held him by the throat while urine stained the front of his pants. Even in the poor light, she could see how terrified he was.

"Stop!" she wailed. "Please stop! Don't kill him!"

One-Eleven looked down at her, his expression puzzled. "He hurt you," he pointed out.

Zalia shook her head frantically, pulling on the arm while she pressed her side against him, trying to move him away. He let her, stepping back and releasing Orlil. The scrawny man dropped to his knees, choking.

"Don't hurt him," Zalia told him. "Please. I just want my job back, my job *here*. That's all."

"That's all?" One-Eleven looked at Orlil. "So?"

The man looked up in terror. "Yes, yes! She has a job as long as she wants!"

One-Eleven's nose lifted. "For more money. I hear that stuff's useful. And better hours. I want time to play with her every day."

"Yes!" Orlil agreed, nodding frantically. "She can work half days for twice the money!"

"Good," he nodded. "Double that." He gestured to the door. "Get out."

Orlil fled, his sandals slapping against the floor as he fled to the stairs.

Zalia gaped after him, not really grasping yet what just happened. She just stood there, staring at the doorway with her mouth hanging open, too numb after everything to even think yet. Orlil would want to kill her for this humiliation, but if he did, One-Eleven would kill him. She was safe.

Or not. Desire spread through her again, flooding her despite her stress. "Zalia," the battler breathed, standing behind her as his fingers touched her shoulder and traced down her arm. His warmth moved against her back and his mouth pressed against the side of her neck, his lips burning hot. "Zalia," he whispered again.

Zalia shuddered, lust she wasn't sure was her own flooding through her, making her nipples perk and her belly tighten almost painfully as she stood there, head tilted back with eyes closed and gasping for breath. The cold of the room suddenly didn't seem to be cool enough as he reached around, fingers carefully undoing the buttons of her dress.

She should stop him right now, tell him no and get out. She didn't want to be the lover to a battle sylph and she was falling in love with Devon Chole, she was sure of it. She didn't want to be taken by a sylph in a place where anyone could walk in, without even agreeing to it, without even knowing anything about him other than that he wasn't human. The pleasure of his touch had her though and she only managed to gasp again as he fully undid the dress and pulled it back over her shoulders, letting it slip to the ground.

Zalia wasn't wearing a wrap for her chest, her small breasts brown and quivering. One-Eleven stroked them, cupping them in his hands and swirling his hands around them, his fingers touching her nipples and pinching them gently. She jumped with a tiny squeal, afraid to make too loud a sound, afraid to do anything. She wasn't participating, she told herself. This was all being done to her and oh, it felt so good. It wasn't her fault though and she wasn't a whore. She could say stop at any time, no matter how badly her body wanted it.

One-Eleven stood behind her, kissing her neck on each side while his hands massaged her breasts. Trailing his kisses around to the back of her neck, he worked his way down, bringing his hands down to the tie of her undergarment and undoing it. She drew in a breath to stop him then, but the fabric dropped to the floor along with her dress, and his hand cupped her mound, his long fingers curled around to sink into her dampness.

Zalia's sudden orgasm bucked through her, making her shake with pleasure, even as her knees gave out. One-Eleven caught her and lifted her up, and she found herself suddenly lying on her back on Orlil's desk, staring hazily up at the battler as he stripped off his shirt and dropped his trousers, his eyes never leaving hers. She looked down nervously to see the erect length of him and he leaned forward, kissing her aching nipples again before he looked at her.

"I'm going to make love to you," he whispered.

Zalia gasped, the core of her clenching, screaming for him. Her hands tangled in his hair, lost, even as he spread her legs wide to either side of him and kissed his way back down to the untouched land between them.

"You smell so good," he breathed and dropped his head to taste her deeply.

Zalia almost choked holding in her scream, her head thrown back over the edge of the desk as her back arched with a second orgasm, every muscle inside her tightening with pleasure. One-Eleven was nuzzling her, licking her with her legs up over his shoulders, and in seconds, yet another orgasm flooded through her, making her fingers grab his hair while her legs clenched on either side of his head. She shuddered uncontrollably, but he held her hips still, slowly licking her and gently pressing his warm soft tongue against a small hard knob of flesh above her opening until a fourth orgasm rocked her, making her buck on the desk until her back hurt.

This last rush of pleasure also drained her, clearing her head enough to think again as he pulled back and kissed her inner thighs, sending more tingles through her. Still, a flush rose to her cheeks at seeing herself lying nude and wanton there, ready to let him do whatever he wanted to her, and she had been, hadn't she? All while just lying there and giving the responsibility all to him. It wasn't *her* fault, then. Only it was, wasn't it? She was just as much a participant as the battle sylph and she was lying to herself to think otherwise.

The only problem was, she didn't know if she really wanted this at all. The pleasure was overwhelming, but how much of it was her and how much was what he was making her feel? She didn't know anything about him at all and she was interested in Devon as well.

Was it fair to him for her to make love to a battle sylph? Was it fair to One-Eleven to suddenly back out now, after he'd already made her feel so good, and after he'd saved her job?

She did know, however, that she definitely didn't want to lose her virginity lying across her boss's desk while everyone she worked with was upstairs, possibly talking about the two of them. She didn't want to feel ashamed later either. One-Eleven definitely didn't deserve that.

Zalia took a deep breath, her fingers tightening over the edge of the desk as she braced herself to tell him, even while the pleasure grew inside her again. Ultimately, she didn't need to say anything as the battler lifted his head, looking at her for a moment in exasperation before he sighed.

"I should have spent less time on foreplay," he said ruefully and straightened up. Leaning over her, he pulled her up until she was sitting on the desk and kissed her. It was the first time he'd actually kissed her mouth and Zalia relaxed into it after a startled moment. It was definitely easier than what he'd been doing before and her arms looped around his neck, her chilled body enjoying the warmth of him as he moved his lips against hers, his tongue gently touching hers. She was still sitting on the desk with him standing nude between her bare legs, but the lust was eased, One-Eleven backing down. Ultimately, Zalia felt a lot of gratitude at that.

"I'm sorry," she whispered at last, when he finally pulled away. "I just . . ." Her lip twisted. "I just don't know anything about you! I mean, what do you like?" He grinned and she blushed. "That's not what I meant. I just . . . I can't make . . . love to someone I'm not in love with."

"You don't love me?" he asked.

"I don't know you!" she cried. "I'm so grateful for what you just did about my job, but I don't know you. I'm not like this."

"Okay," he sighed and kissed her forehead gently before running the back of one finger down her cheek. "I want to get to know you too. I just figured I'd really get to know you first."

She blushed again. It felt as though she'd never stop. She wasn't really too embarrassed to be sitting there with him though, not after what they'd just been doing and how he'd made her feel. "I'm sorry," she said again. He raised an eyebrow. "You . . . I mean you made me feel fantastic and I didn't . . . I mean . . ."

He smiled. "I can feel what you do. Trust me, I enjoyed it." He kissed her forehead again. "I can feel you're getting cold too."

She was. One-Eleven stepped back and Zalia hopped down, grabbing up her dress and undergarment and dressing as quickly as she could. One-Eleven ducked in to kiss her neck again and she touched his cheek for a moment, still not sure how she felt about their intimacy. "I have to go back to work."

"I got you shorter hours," he pointed out.

"I know . . ." She looked down. "I have to think."

"Okay." He kissed her forehead again and her eyes fluttered closed. "I have to go on guard duty in a little while anyway." He walked her out, following her up the stairs. Once there, Ilaja looked over at her in amazement while Orlil hurried over, his face still pale, and counted out more money into Zalia's hand than she'd ever seen before. One-Eleven watched critically while he did.

"Your shift is until the noon hour," Orlil told her, looking at One-Eleven for confirmation. The battler thought it over and nodded.

"Plus she gets every third day off," he added.

Orlil winced. "Every third day," he repeated.

"Starting tomorrow," One-Eleven smirked and walked away. Orlil bleakly watched him go and then looked at Zalia for a moment, his expression blank. Turning, he went away, leaving her standing there holding a handful of gold and wondering if she should feel bad about finally being paid enough to live on. She could pay for a real home with this, and afford good food for herself and her father, as well as clean clothes and actual baths.

Ilaja edged up to her, her voice laced with contempt. "And you said you weren't a whore," she growled and walked away.

Zalia gripped the gold so tightly that her hand started to hurt and it was a while before she went to re-collect her tray.

CHAPTER SEVEN

It took them a long time to get back to the surface. Gel, Shasha's master, didn't fully regain consciousness, only staring numbly at them for a moment while Devon and Xehm put his arms over their shoulders before his head dropped down again, sagging limply. Devon wasn't sure if he was injured or just deep in shock.

At least Shasha didn't need help. Devon wasn't sure he could have moved the other sylph at all if she hadn't been able to walk. She trudged slowly ahead of them, obviously tired, but determined to keep going. He hoped she could get herself to the surface since he doubted that Airi would be strong enough to carry her. She'd have enough trouble just getting the humans up there.

She pressed against his neck, cool against his spine. *I don't like it down here,* she said.

"Neither do I," Devon muttered. Xehm looked toward him and he jerked his chin over his shoulder. "Just talking to my sylph," he explained. The old man nodded and returned to his thoughts, which from the tightness of his jaw didn't seem to be peaceful. "You can get us up there?" Devon asked Airi.

Yes. I'll need to feed though. It's hard work.

Devon nodded. He'd expected that. Airi fed off his life energy, but it was rare she took enough that he was aware of it. He suspected he would this time. He looked at Shasha's back as she stomped heavily along ahead of them. It was beautiful and bare, but the color and consistency of marble. "Why didn't she call the battlers?" he asked

Airi. Xehm shot another look in his direction, though of course, he wouldn't be able to hear the answer.

Airi's answer was long and hesitant in coming. *Because no matter what they would say, they can't help,* she said. *They would have died too.*

Devon frowned, the thought of a battler being helpless too alien a concept for him to comprehend. "How can that be?" He'd seen battlers fight, far too many times. They were unstoppable, unless they were killed by another of their kind.

Hunters are the invisible death, Airi told him. She sounded stressed. *No one's ever seen one. All we know is, if one comes, we die. No warning, no yelling for help, no trace. We just die. All the rest of us can do is hide in the hive and hope the food lasts long enough for the Hunter to go. It's said even battlers can't kill them.*

"So that's why Shasha didn't call them," Devon murmured, watching the earth sylph lead the way.

No. They come to where groups of us are. Worse, it hears us if we yell for help. It would have found Shasha if she called them. Killed them and found her.

Devon closed his eyes for a moment, wishing he wasn't here, that he hadn't come, and most of all, that Zalia was with her father at his side so that he could make sure she was safe. "Where is the Hunter now?" he asked.

I don't know. Maybe it went back through the gate? She sounded hopeful.

Devon thought of the harbor and that blood on the *Racing Dawn,* far away on the ocean side of the city. "Do you really think that?"

No, she whimpered. *I want to though.*

So did he. "It'll be okay," he murmured.

Promise?

"I promise."

They reached the end of the passageway then, the ruin of the cages beyond even more ominous now that Devon knew what sort of creature actually destroyed them. After whatever damage the battlers did, something huge had drilled its way up through the racks of cages. Shasha stopped at the edge, fidgeting as she looked out and upward.

Devon could guess what had her so nervous. "It's not there," he assured her. "We went through earlier. It's safe."

Shasha turned and looked at Devon over her shoulder, her oddly beautiful face expressionless. "Nowhere is safe," she said to him, her voice earthy and deep. "We have nowhere to retreat."

Xehm frowned at the earth sylph, having only heard Devon's half of his conversation with Airi. "The battle sylphs will destroy this thing," he assured her. "Whatever it is."

Shasha turned her ruby gaze on to the old man. "A Hunter came to my home hive. So many battle sylphs died that another hive came. My queen died. I went through the gate." She looked back into the great chamber and steeled her shoulders, striding forward. Making her way over to the tangle of caging, she started to climb as easily as if she were walking up a flight of stairs.

Devon looked over at Xehm to find the old man staring back at him, his eyes fearful. "What can kill battlers?" Xehm mourned.

Devon just shook his head helplessly, not knowing how to answer that.

~

It was past noon when they got out of the tunnels, the air outside scorching hot but a relief after the silence and death of the underground. Shasha led the way out, again moving uncertainly at the exit, obviously fearful of being attacked, but then walking with more

confidence when she saw a human moving around outside the small
building that held the entrance.

Devon was pleasantly surprised when that person turned out
to be Zalia.

"Zalia!" her father gasped, rushing forward to embrace his
daughter and leaving Devon with Gel. Gel had recovered some of
his senses while Airi lifted them up to the surface and he pushed
away a bit to stand on his own, shivering and silent. Shasha walked
over to pat his hand reassuringly. Airi pressed against Devon's back,
mostly asleep from the effort of lifting them so high on top of helping Shasha.

Zalia hugged her father, saying things to him in a low tone that
he exclaimed at in surprise. Devon saw her flush red at one point,
shaking her head, and hand her father a small pouch that he took
with an expression of wonder.

"We need to hurry," Devon called to them. Nice as it was to
see Zalia, they had to get moving. Shasha didn't have direct access
to the queen; earth sylphs couldn't fly, but she could take them to
those who did. Devon looked up at the small palace floating over the
city. It should have occurred to him sooner that she'd be up there.

For now, they'd be traveling on the ground, and for once in his
life, Devon was unnerved at the thought of doing so. Suddenly, the
wide-open air and shadows of the city were frightening, knowing as
he did that there was something invisible out there that would kill
all of them too quickly to even give a warning. He squinted, trying
to peer through the blistering noon sunshine, but all he could see
was the haze that shimmered the buildings and some sort of weird
desert mirage like a giant egg off toward the ocean. Just looking at
them made his eyes ache and he closed them for a moment, pinching
the bridge of his nose.

"Let me help him," Xehm said suddenly, having returned. He took Gel's arms, gently speaking to the dazed man as he led him away. Shasha walked ahead of them. Devon found himself standing with Zalia and flushed nervously, looking at the ground when he found himself unwittingly staring into her deep black eyes. Airi pressed against his shoulders, mumbling something that might have been encouragement if she'd been completely awake.

"I thought you had to work today," he said, painfully aware of how pathetic he sounded, as well as the fact that her father had taken everyone else ahead to give them some privacy. At least he wasn't worrying about the Hunter killing them in the next breath anymore. Devon was so focused on Zalia that the possibility wasn't even in his thoughts.

Zalia ducked her head, shyly wringing her hands together before herself. "I . . . I have the rest of the day off. I only work mornings now, with tomorrow and then every third day off."

Devon blinked and looked directly at her again. "How'd you manage that?" he asked. He'd thought there weren't any rules giving workers rights in Meridal, unlike back at home.

She turned bright red, the color of it barely showing through her hanging hair. "My employer . . . he was yelling at me for being late . . . and a battle sylph came."

"Oh," Devon breathed. That was one thing the creatures were good for. No woman in Sylph Valley had to worry about being abused. In fact, it was unusual for the battler to go so easy on the man. Devon doubted there were any orders from the queen containing their behavior here. "I'm surprised he didn't kill him," he admitted.

Zalia looked up again, her eyes tired and her blush already fading. "I begged him not to. I didn't want anyone dying because of me."

Devon smiled and reached out to touch his fingertips to the edge of her soft jaw before he could think about it. "Good for you," he told her.

Zalia smiled at him and reached up with her small brown hand to lay it over his pale, sunburned one. Devon's heart started hammering again. "Thank you," she said.

They both stared at each other, shy and speechless, but it was hot out and the roads weren't completely deserted. Finally they had to return their attention to their surroundings or risk being left behind. Xehm was already a few hundred feet away with both Gel and Shasha and the two of them hurried after them until they were only a dozen or so feet behind.

"Do you like having more free time?" Devon asked her.

She put both her palms against her cheeks, her eyes wide. "I don't know what to do with myself! I feel so decadent."

He laughed. "I'm sure you'll think of something to do."

She looked at him and flushed prettily again, dropping her eyes. "He got me better wages too. The battle sylph, I mean. I have so much money now."

"Yeah, well, battlers do like women to be comfortable," he admitted.

Zalia peered at him, studying the tension around his eyes. "You're afraid of them, aren't you?" she asked.

Devon winced, not wanting to admit that to her, but what was he supposed to do? She'd be able to see how badly they frightened him the minute he came near one and they would definitely be guarding the queen. He couldn't imagine them not doing so. "I'm scared stiff by them," he admitted. Her eyes widened. "I always have been."

"Oh." She frowned. It was a very pretty frown, he thought. "Why?"

Devon hesitated, not sure he really wanted to talk about it. She peeked at him through the cover of her hair and suddenly he couldn't keep silent, if that was what she wanted.

"When I was a boy, a battle sylph was used to execute some prisoners. I think it was the king's idea of an object lesson to the rest of us, since we had to watch." He shuddered, remembering the blood and the screams of the men. He remembered the evil, toothy grin of the battler and felt the old terror.

"He did more than kill them," Devon said softly. "He tore them apart, and he kept them alive for as long as he could while he did."

Zalia stared at him, her face troubled. "That is so awful. They're not . . . they're not all like that, are they?"

Devon managed a small smile. "No," he admitted, "but that was my first impression of one and I never was able to forget it. I've never had a good interaction with a battle sylph."

"Not ever?" she asked, reaching out to touch his bare hand with the tips of her fingers. Immediately that bare patch of skin felt as though it was burning, he focused so much attention on it.

"Not really," he breathed. Yes, they'd saved the Valley, yes, they kept everyone safe, but the only major interaction he'd had with a battler since the Valley was established was Heyou demanding his seed and then telling him to leave. "I can't go back," he said. He stared into nothing. "The queen's battler said I could never go back." Now he was stuck here, with another queen who wouldn't see him and a monster even the battlers couldn't stop.

"Why?" Zalia gasped.

Devon shook himself and looked down at her, thinking that there was something good about being banished to Meridal. "The queen wanted a baby, but the only way her battler could get her pregnant was with a man's seed. He demanded mine and then told me to leave. I can't go back."

Zalia gasped again, her eyes wide. Her fingers had moved until she was holding his hand with both her own and now she squeezed it tightly. "That's awful."

Devon shrugged, not sure what else to do. "I'm numb to it. I never would have wanted to have children though. At least, not with Solie." He realized what he'd just implied with that last statement and ducked his head at the same time she did, both of them blushing.

They were quiet for a time and Devon realized belatedly that they'd stopped walking. Xehm, Gel, and Shasha were nearly out of sight and they were standing together in the shadow of a building, holding hands.

Zalia finally rubbed her thumb over Devon's knuckles, making his heart skip a beat. "Do you think battlers are evil?" she asked.

"Evil?" He thought about it for a moment and finally shrugged, almost dislodging Airi from where she'd wrapped her vaguely solid self around his neck to sleep. "No. Amoral definitely, but not evil."

"Amoral?" she questioned.

Devon dragged the hand she wasn't holding through his hair. Without Airi fluffing it around, it was heavy and soaked with sweat, reminding him of how thirsty he was. "Um, uncaring of consequences. Not even that." He paused thinking. "They don't think of consequences. Sometimes I doubt they think at all. Most of them just react based on what their instinct tells them to do."

"Oh." She was quiet for a moment. Their pace had slowed to a crawl but they'd followed the others into a part of the city Devon hadn't seen yet. It was more affluent than anything else he'd encountered so far, with the exception of one massive building that looked as though it had once been oval in shape before it was reduced to rubble.

"Do you think they can love?" Zalia asked.

Devon forgot about the circular building and flushed red again, wondering if she was trying to tell him something with that question.

Airi stirred against his neck and giggled. "Um." He tried to think honestly. "They do. Sometimes I think a lot of them can't tell the difference between lust and love, but most of them do."

"Oh." That might just be her favorite word, he thought. "Then they feel things like love the way a man would?"

Devon's heart nearly exploded in his chest it was hammering so loud and Airi squealed in his mind, wide awake now and excited. "Yes," he said as casually as he could, running a hand through his hair again. "They do."

"Oh."

Devon allowed his arm to drop back by his side again as Zalia let go. By some coincidence or a puff of wind from Airi, it brushed against Zalia's for a moment and then away. A moment passed and her hand brushed against his again, for no particular reason. They both walked along, looking forward as their hands brushed together a third time and then, with neither saying anything, entwined a second time, despite how miserably hot out it was. Neither of them really noticed the heat. Zalia was used to it and Devon was walking so far outside of himself that he didn't care.

～

Zalia walked along holding Devon's hand, happy with the situation but confused. Her father obviously approved of the thought of her union with Devon Chole, the ambassador from Sylph Valley, but Zalia was torn.

Not about her feelings for Devon. Quickly as they'd come upon her, she was sure about them. Devon made her feel like no other man ever had and what else was this happiness and the fluttering in her belly if not the start of love for him?

It was One-Eleven that caused her confusion. He also made

her feel like no man ever could, taking her and making the pleasure explode through her until it was all consuming. She remembered just that morning, the feel of him tasting her and how it made her entire body spasm with ecstasy, and her hand tightened involuntarily around Devon's. He looked down at her and tightened his own grip for a moment, returning hers. Zalia had to blush and look down.

No woman should have to make this kind of choice! Both of them were so different, so utterly opposite from each other, and she didn't really know anything about either. She couldn't have both of them—that thought wasn't worth dwelling on even if she thought either of them would be willing to contemplate it. Nor did she want to be shared.

She had to make a choice, before things went any further, before either of them learned about the other and perhaps something horrible happened. She had to.

"Tell me more about yourself," she said to Devon, looking up at him nervously. "Not about battlers. About you."

He blinked, rubbing his thumb along the outside of her hand for a moment while he thought. "Me? Um, I was born in Eferem, in Eferem City, where the king lives. It's a kingdom way far away, to the south of Sylph Valley. My family have been air-sylph masters for three generations. Airi belonged to my father and grandfather before me."

"They just gave her to you?" she asked.

"Yeah." He reached up to nothing she could see on his shoulders. "Sylphs have no rights in Eferem. Airi wasn't even allowed to talk, so I don't think Dad and Granddad ever realized how smart she is. I did let her talk though, which was illegal. I could have been executed for it." His hair ruffled madly. "She only talked to me, until we went to the Valley. Sylphs are free there."

"How did you happen to go there?" Zalia asked. She liked the sound of his voice. "Was it because of Airi?"

"Oh, gods, no," he laughed. "I like to think I would have, but the Valley didn't exist when I left Eferem. It really was all a big mistake. Not that I regret it, but it was terrifying at the time."

He went on to tell her about how he'd seen the battle sylph Heyou escape the castle with Solie and impulsively sent Airi to follow them. That led to him trying to get to the village they had escaped to before his retired father was hurt, the battle between Ril and Heyou, and Devon himself ending up as a fugitive along with Solie when Airi rescued her from Leon's sword.

"Mr. Petrule was the enemy?" Zalia gasped, stunned. He'd seemed the noblest man she'd ever met, not someone who would try to assassinate a girl.

"Yeah. Luckily, he switched sides." Devon shrugged. "Solie just has this way about her. Mostly he did it for Ril. It was become a good guy or lose him, I guess. I never really understood what was going on between those two. They don't have any sort of master-and-sylph relationship that I've ever even heard of before." He looked at her again. "I just happened to be in the right place at the right time, I think. I ended up as Solie's majordomo."

"What's a majordomo?"

"Her chief steward," he said. "Basically, I was her secretary. I arranged who could see her when, her appointments, that kind of thing. Plus I took notes at any meetings so we'd have a record of everything. There weren't a whole lot of people in the Valley when we started who could read or write."

She couldn't read, Zalia thought. She'd never had the need, even if her status hadn't been too low for it to be allowed. "And now you're her ambassador."

"Yeah." He looked sheepish. "Not that I'm doing that good a job of it so far."

Zalia smiled at him, not looking down this time when he met her gaze and smiled back. "We'll find the queen," she told him and was happy at her use of the word *we* when his smile widened.

If they couldn't find someone to take them to the queen where they were going, she thought, then she could ask One-Eleven to take them instead. Her smile faltered a moment later at the image of One-Eleven meeting Devon, as well as the consideration of just what the battler would want in return for his help, as well as how, deep inside, the very thought was as exciting as it was terrifying.

~

Exhausted from all of her efforts, Airi hugged her master's neck. She'd drunk some of his energy, but she didn't want to drain him until he was also tired, not in this heat, so was now sipping despite her need, and trying her best to keep the back of his neck a little bit cooler than the rest of him.

She did listen to his conversation with Zalia. She was asexual herself, with no interest in her own physical pleasure, but she liked to see her master happy and more, Zalia matched him. The thought of them getting together and having children that might be her masters in the next generation excited her. Zalia made Devon's pattern sing and that translated to her as the most beautiful music she could imagine.

Zalia, she knew, felt the same link to Devon. There was no way she couldn't, and that only excited Airi more. She pressed against her master's neck, wanting to encourage him, but not wanting to frighten him again. Devon hadn't had many relationships in his life and certainly none had ever had the potential of this one. To Airi, this felt so much more important than foreign queens and Hunters and she pressed close, watching them link hands with all the happiness her kind could feel.

~

The favorite meeting spot of the battle sylphs was in the ruins of the arena where they'd once fought for the amusement of the emperor. It was a bit ironic for them to meet there, but it was a familiar place to most of them. All of them knew where the ruins were and they were central in the city. It made sense to go there.

They did so when they wanted to rest and commune with their own kind, floating together above the rubble as a massive black cloud filled with lightning. They also met there to exchange news and to start guard shifts, taking turns so that each of them would have time for their women.

The middle of the day was one of their shift changes, when the humans were sluggish from the heat and less likely to cause trouble. An hour after Devon and his companions passed by, they descended, some shifting to human form, most staying clouds, and a few even changing back to the mouthless, green, backward-legged creatures they'd been while slaves of the emperor.

"I've found her!"

His hands clasped behind his back, Tooie stood atop a shattered piece of wall and looked down at one of his hive mates. "You have?"

One-Eleven grinned at him happily, three times Tooie's age but as excitable as a juvenile. "I have. She's absolutely beautiful. I've never seen anyone like her, not even in the harem." His smile faded. "But she hasn't slept with me yet. I know she wants to, but she keeps stopping me. It's frustrating."

Tooie's smile widened. It was almost funny to think of himself as the voice of experience. "Of course she wants to sleep with you. You could make a half-dead rat want to sleep with you."

One-Eleven blinked and looked a little nauseous at the thought.

Tooie reached down and tapped the battler's nose, making him start. "If you want something real and lasting, you need to do more than just make her want to sleep with you," he told him seriously. He'd known One-Eleven since his own enslavement started and he knew the older sylph was one of the worst of them when it came to single-mindedness. "Remember Ap?"

One-Eleven's eyes darkened. All of them remembered Ap. She'd been the most popular concubine in the harem and all of them had had her many times. She'd been addicted to sex, wanton and hot. When Eapha gave them all their freedom though, Ap had been the first to leave, setting sail on the first ship that would take her. When one battle sylph asked her why she'd want to leave, her answer had been that she wanted more.

Tooie saw what might have been the faint look of comprehension in One-Eleven's eyes and nodded. "I didn't sleep with my Eapha the first time I met her. Most concubines I did, but with her, I became her friend first and she's still with me."

One-Eleven frowned. "So what do I do? I really want her."

"Get to know her. Try talking to her. Human women aren't like queens."

One-Eleven looked dubious, but Tooie didn't have time to wonder if he'd actually listen instead of giving in to his instincts and just taking the woman. She'd surely enjoy it, but it was harder for them to form a real bond that way, especially with these desert women who were all so afraid of their own bodies and what they could feel. Yahe swept down, yelling for Tooie's attention even as he shifted to human and stormed toward him, his fists clenched at his sides. Tooie didn't need to be an empath to tell how furious the other battler was. One-Eleven took one look at him and retreated to think about his woman.

"Tooie!" Yahe bellowed. "You better do something! Bift has skipped out on his shift twice! I've been walking back and forth in that stupid marketplace and circling this damn city for more than a day! Kiala is going to kill me!"

That was unusual, even for Bift. Tooie frowned as the other battlers close by looked on, whispering amongst themselves. Yahe ignored them all, glaring up at the lead battler in absolute fury. Tooie didn't blame him. He'd heard Kiala cursing about her battler standing her up not long ago. "Did you try and call him?" he asked.

"Yes! The bastard is ignoring me!"

Bift should have at least answered. He certainly should have showed up for his shift and Tooie would be talking to him about that. In fact, he'd take a few other battlers and slam the lazy creature around a few times as a reminder about duty. It was unnatural for a battle sylph to ignore the urge to guard, but it did happen from time to time.

Tooie closed his eyes. As lead battler and lover of the queen, his senses had actually grown more sensitive and he reached out to Bift, searching for the battler's unique pattern among the thousands in the city.

He didn't find it.

Tooie's eyes snapped open. "Do you know where he went?" he asked, staring over Yahe's head at the distant hills of sand beyond the city. They were as wide as the ocean and in their own way just as deadly.

"He was going to the gate," Yahe sulked. "I wanted to take Kiala to see it."

Tooie looked over his shoulder at the other battlers of the Circle, the secret group that hid their monogamous affairs in the harem by pretending to sleep with each other's women. When Eapha became queen with Tooie as her lead battler, they'd become his closest confidants. Yahe was one of them, if one of the more temperamental, but the others looked back at him with the same sudden concern.

Raanan, Laik, Kadin, Ogden, Xenos, Baback, Banner, Edom, and Gaetan. All of them handsome beyond human limitations for their women's sake. All of them with names given by those women, now that they didn't have to be designated solely by numbers. They'd worked together to protect their women from the handlers who would have taken them away, even though they were from different hives and hated each other. They got over that hate because they'd needed to and learned to communicate when they were forbidden to speak, whether aloud or mind to mind. Turning to them instead of any of the others felt natural, especially given how their new shared hive pattern made them brothers, even beyond their shared history.

He should have answered me, Tooie signed, making the gestures with his hands that they'd all learned years ago, taught by Baback's lover Ulani, who'd come to the harem knowing how to sign thanks to a deaf brother. It had become their lifeline to each other and to the women they loved. Other battlers looked at them curiously, but most turned back to their own conversations while the eleven of them gathered around, even Yahe spotting the hand gestures and widening his eyes with sudden surprise.

He wouldn't have left Meridal, Laik signed.

Banner nodded in agreement. *Definitely not. His master would never let him, even if he thought of it. Taini would never want to leave.* None of the women who were masters to battlers would, not when it was a death sentence everywhere else. A woman in control of a battle sylph was considered an abomination in most of the world.

Besides, outside Meridal, women were little better than property at the best of times. In Meridal, they were loved as dearly as the queen.

Come, Tooie decided and changed shape, lifting off the ground as a cloud of black and lightning. The other ten members of the Circle rose with him, all of them abandoning their human forms so they could take to the sky.

It wasn't a long trip. They arced over the city, scanning the ground for danger from pure instinct as they headed to the same small building that held the stairs Devon and his friends had used. They didn't take the stairs to the corridor that led one way to the harem and the other to the feeder holding cells. Instead, they swept into vents in the building's roof, bypassing the harem and the feeder chambers entirely as they flashed straight down a shaft that led deep underground, and emptied out in the corridor to the summoning chamber itself.

Tooie saw the damage immediately, the chunks taken out of the walls and floor and the destruction in the chamber itself, along with the dried pools of blood.

The eleven battle sylphs spread out, their energy patterns high and their hate spreading. To others it would cause fear, undermine courage. To them, it was reassuring as well as a warning to their enemy.

Delicately, Kadin reached down with a length of smoke to touch one of the blood pools. *This is human,* he said silently to them.

Tooie floated over to join him, as did the others. Only humans left traces of their death. When sylphs died, there was nothing but drifting sparkles and the stench of ozone, then nothing at all.

What can do this? Edom asked.

Tooie looked toward the altar where the gate would have opened. It had been kept open for a long time, he thought. There would have been a lot of sylphs and humans here to celebrate it. Bift wouldn't have been the only battle sylph in attendance either.

I know of only one thing that can kill a battler before he can send out a warning, he said in grim understanding.

≈

The Hunter woke to the sudden roaring of battle sylphs through the city. Its tentacles were tucked up underneath its body, except for the one it used to secure itself to one of the buildings, and it stretched and sighed, peaceful after its sleep.

Through the city, it could hear the battle sylphs shouting out the warning, calling out its presence to every sylph there, as well as the growing panic of the smaller sylphs. Anchored, it listened to their conversations, careful for any sign of a real threat to itself, not that there ever was. The creatures were as helpless against it here as they were in the old world. It could continue to eat with impunity, it seemed. It tucked its tentacles closer to itself. Once it had finished sleeping, at any rate.

CHAPTER EIGHT

The neighborhoods of the city grew progressively wealthier the farther the group progressed, the streets wider and cleaner. They started to pass more opulent homes, all of them surrounded by courtyards and tall stone walls that hid most of the buildings and anyone who might be using them. The garbage that had been strewn all over the rest of the city was less as well and there were even a few desert trees on the sidewalks, still alive in the blistering heat. They didn't see any people, which, given the temperature, didn't surprise Devon.

Zalia looked up as he panted and swallowed with a parched throat, and she smiled, patting his hand with her own.

"I must look like a roasted tomato," he told her.

"You're cute," she disagreed and blushed, looking down.

Devon grinned at her, squeezing her hand despite the heat and his general, sweaty misery. She made him not care how his body felt in this place. She made him not think about the horrible things they were going to have to deal with. With Zalia at his side, it seemed, he could do anything.

Ahead of him, he heard Xehm exclaim. Devon looked forward again to see the road curved. As he and Zalia came around the corner, he spotted Xehm and Gel standing with Shasha before a huge wall that crossed the road and vanished between buildings to either side. He could tell it was sylph-made. It stood nearly as high as the buildings, and though it was made of stone, it was all one piece and had an organic flow to it that reminded him with a sudden pang of the sylph buildings back home. Sylphs had built almost all of Sylph Valley and the entire town had that same organic feel.

"It's beautiful," Zalia said.

"They always are." Devon looked up at the top, nearly thirty feet or more above their heads. It wasn't entirely consistent in height. There was no gate either. Devon was just wondering how far they'd have to walk to get to one when Shasha stepped forward and pressed her hand against the wall.

The stone rippled, wavering like a pool of water through which someone had swept an oar. From Shasha's hand outward, the wall swept away, the stone bulging into a frozen wave that left an opening both wide and tall enough for all of them to pass.

"That's amazing," Zalia gasped.

It was, but Devon could see how tired it made Shasha. The earth sylph swayed slightly for a moment before she stomped forward, leading the way with Xehm right behind her, the old man still more than half carrying Gel.

Devon and Zalia followed, walking through the arch in the wall and looking around curiously. Shasha waited just inside, and the moment they passed, she closed the wall again, rippling the stone back down into place. That done, she looked up at the sky and the top of the wall that cut off the sky above them.

"What is it?" Zalia asked her.

The earth sylph turned those eerily beautiful ruby eyes on her. "The wall isn't enough," she said. "A dome would be better." She looked upward again. "Yes. A hundred feet high and ten feet thick." She sighed. "I like the sun though and my master is afraid of being closed in again." She turned those eyes on them again. "I never should have taken him to the gate. I just wanted to see it and he didn't want to be alone."

Her voice sounded like gravel rolling in a wooden barrel. Devon frowned, feeling Airi press against his neck again. "A dome. Against the Hunter?"

"Yes. A proper hive. I'll still miss the sun though."

Devon and Zalia looked at each other as Shasha walked heavily away, moving after her master. What would life be like in a stone dome, he wondered, and saw the same question on Zalia's face. Neither of them spoke it aloud and they continued after the others, still holding hands.

It was radically different on this side of the wall. The architecture didn't change much, though it did become richer the farther they went, obviously being a neighborhood for the wealthy who hadn't lived on the floating island the sylphs destroyed. What was different was the number of people around, as well as the number of sylphs.

They were everywhere. Even standing by the wall, Devon could see sylphs of every type and in every shape imaginable, scattered everywhere and doing, he supposed, what sylphs do. No wonder he hadn't seen any of them anywhere else in the city. More, there were humans as well, in even greater numbers than the sylphs, though there was something wrong with many of them. Devon's skin actually crawled as he saw how many of them were just sitting on the road or wandering aimlessly, most of them with a blank look on their faces. A few looked insane. More looked terrified.

"What's wrong with them?" he whispered. Zalia shook her head in mute confusion, nervously pressing against his side until he put his arm around her shoulder and held her to him. Even with the heat, it felt right. She smelled good, like some kind of desert flower.

They're feeders, Airi told him. *A lot of them are really messed up in the head.*

Devon swore softly, Zalia looking up at him in confusion. "Feeders," he explained. They were the men and women who'd been less than slaves in Meridal when the emperor ruled. They'd been the ones living in the cages he'd seen, closed-in places so small there was barely room to stand and turn around, all of them with their tongues cut out so that there was no risk of them giving their sylphs orders. He looked ahead at Gel, who was mostly walking on his own now, though Xehm kept a reassuring hand on his shoulder. The man shuddered occasionally, though there was no way for Devon to know if that was from the horror his life had been in the cages or this latest trauma.

Zalia looked around in amazement and a bit of fear at the people they passed. Many of them stared at the newcomers, though no one approached and no one spoke. They didn't seem to interact with each other either, or with the sylphs who moved among them. The sylphs were just as silent, though with their ability to speak mind to mind amongst themselves, there could be thousands of conversations going on and Devon would never know it. It was eerie, and terribly sad. These people were wounded in a way he couldn't comprehend, hurt down to the core of their very souls. Kadmiel had at least been functional and mostly normal, though quiet, and Gel had been interested enough to go with Shasha to the gate. These had to be the most broken of the feeders. Devon really hoped that they were in the minority, since he didn't want to think that there could be thousands of them wandering around in here with dead eyes.

"I didn't know they'd stayed," Zalia whispered. "I never saw any on the streets, so I just thought they'd left, like so many others had."

"Where would they go?" Devon wondered. They had no possessions, no money. Many of them were wearing the shifts they must have had in the cages and not a few were completely naked. The sylphs might not even have been willing to let them go. Sylphs were loyal to their masters and they needed them, even if they only officially kept one now, which would be typical. Sylphs were also monogamous in their affections. Still, there were five human feeders for every sylph in Meridal. There were five thousand sylphs in total, leaving up to twenty-five thousand people here behind this wall, if the sylphs kept them all.

Devon felt a great wave of compassion for them, remembering what Shasha said about raising a dome. They had to protect these people. They'd been through too much to have to deal with an invisible Hunter on top of it. Not now that they had their freedom at last.

"We have to keep them safe," he said, looking at the numb men and women walking on the street. In a doorway, one huddled against the jamb, her arms around her bony knees as she endlessly rocked back and forth, a small spark of flame dancing around her as a fire sylph tried to console her. "We can't let them die."

Zalia looked at him and her gaze hardened as she nodded in agreement.

We will, Airi promised him.

"We will," Zalia unknowingly echoed.

They just had to reach the queen and find out what she thought she was doing. These people needed more than to be left on the street, even one with a sylph wall around it. Where were the healers?

Ahead, the street continued through the expensive neighborhood. The six of them kept going, making their way through the crowds in silence themselves, Shasha leading the way, Xehm helping Gel, who was definitely recovering now that he found himself on familiar ground, and Devon following with his arm around Zalia, Airi dozing against his neck. He was sure he still stank, but Zalia didn't seem to care at all and even here, he was happy to be with her.

She's good for you, Airi told him again.

Devon just smiled a bit, despite the depressing scenery. He wasn't in the mood to argue with his sylph. Especially not when he knew she was right.

After a few blocks, they started to hear music, happy and melodious and coming from up ahead, dozens of instruments playing together enthusiastically if not terribly well. Devon and Zalia shared a look and kept going, even as Airi perked up on Devon's shoulders. She loved any kind of music, after all.

Apparently, so did the Meridal air sylphs. They came to a large square where the street opened up and stopped. It seemed not everyone who'd been a feeder was as damaged as the poor souls who haunted the outer streets of this refuge.

Hundreds of human beings were crowded into the square, most dressed in fine silks of so many colors that it looked as though a rainbow were moving in there. Many of them were playing instruments, dozens of them banging away on makeshift drums, others playing flutes or recorders or other instruments Devon didn't recognize. Some were even slamming rocks together, or bits of steel, and everyone without an instrument was clapping. At least, everyone who wasn't dancing.

Men and women spun and twisted wildly, dancing together with a sensual abandon that made Zalia blush and turn her face into Devon's shoulder until she realized whom she was doing that to. Her blush deepened even more and she hesitantly pressed her side even closer against him. Devon caught his breath, his finger gently stroking her cheek as his heart hammered inside of him.

Airi squealed against his neck. *It's wonderful!* she cheered and suddenly left him, flashing away. Devon blinked, looking up, and narrowed his eyes, staring for a moment before he laughed.

"Look," he told Zalia, pointing with the hand he didn't have around her.

She looked up, squinting. "I don't see . . ." Her voice trailed off. "Oh!"

There were air sylphs above the dancers, all dancing themselves and nearly invisible, as Airi preferred to be. There were so many of them though that they moved the hot air, creating a shimmer that wasn't like any heat haze he'd ever seen before. They danced wildly to the music that the humans below were creating, twirling in ecstasy.

"It's beautiful!" Zalia laughed in delight.

It was and Airi was up there, dancing along with them. Suddenly, Devon itched to pull out his flute.

Xehm appeared at their side, catching Devon's arm with an expression on his face that could have been either excitement or horror. "You have to see this," he said, not seeming to take any notice of how close his daughter and Devon were standing. He just turned and pushed his way through the dancers.

Devon and Zalia followed, having to almost force their way through the exuberant crowd in order to not lose sight of the old man. He didn't lead them far.

They came to a fountain, the base nearly fifty feet across and filled with water that flowed up through a statue of a woman with outstretched hands and poured over again into the pool below. Devon had seen fountains in Eferem and the Valley before and didn't think anything of it until he heard Zalia gasp in shock beside him. Then he realized: this was a desert kingdom, a place of aridity where water cost as much as wine back home. Zalia must never have seen this much unprotected fresh water in one place in her life. There wasn't even a covering to protect it from the sun's drying heat. A water sylph waded through the pool, her legs merging with the liquid she moved through, her blue, watery hair trailing down her back to join the flow.

People were gathered all around the fountain, making it take a while to reach the edge as they used dippers left on the rim of the basin to drink. Remembering again how thirsty he was, Devon made his way forward until he was able to get hold of a dipper and fill it, feeling as he did how cool the water was.

He held it up to Zalia first. "Help yourself," he told her. She looked at him with wide eyes and then touched her fingertips to the underside of the ladle's bowl, holding it steady while he brought it to her lips, and she drank, her eyes closing with pleasure.

It was the most erotic thing Devon had ever seen.

Finally, she finished and looked up at him with sparkling eyes. "Thank you," she told him.

"You're welcome," he said hoarsely and drank the rest of the water in the dipper. He was sure it was all in his mind, but he could swear that it tasted better for having touched her lips.

"This is incredible," Xehm exulted, looking around like a child while he drank from a dipper of his own. Even with the mass of people there, there seemed to be enough for all and no one tried to jostle them for space. Having all of this water available, no one seemed to worry about it and Devon remembered bitterly how much Zalia's restaurant charged for even a single carafe.

"It is," Devon admitted. Gel was sitting on the rim of the basin, one hand stroking the stone ripples that formed Shasha's hair while she held a dipper for him. When he finished it, she refilled it and held it up again, dipping her fingers in and stroking them lightly across his brow before urging him to drink more.

Airi returned to Devon's side. *She loves him,* she said. *He must have been kind to her, even while he was a feeder.*

He must have, Devon mused and wondered where the other four feeders that had been assigned to her were.

That reminded him of everything they had to do. Happy or not, these people were nothing but targets now and even if they weren't, everyone outside these walls was living in poverty. Meridal hadn't changed with the addition of a queen. It had only shifted who was poor and who wasn't.

"Shasha," he called and the earth sylph looked up at him, her ruby eyes shiny enough to be mirrors. Devon stared at his own reflection, dark and shadowy. "Talk to the air sylphs," he told her. "We need to get to the queen."

Shasha hesitated, looking at her silent master and then at the sky she wanted to cover with a dome, though with Gel so weak she didn't have the strength. Finally she nodded and turned toward the maelstrom of nearly invisible dancers above the crowded human celebration. Devon looked up at them as well, hoping there would be someone willing to help them, and even more, that the queen would listen.

∼

Airi pressed against her favorite spot on Devon's back, right between his shoulder blades, where she could sense the impulses flickering through his spine and feel his heart beating. She could sense the blood and air flowing through him as well, all of it making up part of the pattern that was so uniquely him.

Looking at the hundreds of dancing air sylphs, she could see them where her master couldn't. They were beautiful, all of them happy as they danced to the music that the humans produced, many of whom were masters and most of whom were just as happy as the sylphs. It didn't matter to any of them that the composition wasn't very good. Air sylphs loved music. It was as fundamental to them as their ability to control the element of air.

Shasha looked up toward them as well, speaking along the hive line, and Airi listened to her asking them to send someone who could bring them to the queen. If it had been Airi and her own hive, she would have wanted to scream out a warning about the Hunter instead. She was happy to see all the dancing and hear the music, but still she felt the uneasiness of the open air above them.

Airi had never suffered a Hunter attack on her home hive before she crossed the gate, but she'd heard about them. She'd heard that not even battle sylphs could stop them, no matter how much they complained that wasn't true. Only earth sylphs could, with the hive walls they raised. Airi looked at Shasha, who was tired and sad, but still older and stronger than she. Back home, the slightest hint of a Hunter would have everyone in the hive, the earth sylphs sealing it so they could wait the Hunter out. Queens rarely sent battlers out to fight the Hunters, not if the hive wanted to survive beyond it.

Airi sighed, ruffling her master's hair, though it was so heavy with sweat she couldn't move it much. Shasha was exhausted, but she had to want to get to the queen herself to warn her, and get those walls started. This was an air sylph party, though, and Airi knew her own kind. She wanted to panic at the thought of the Hunter. This many air sylphs without any protection likely would. That wouldn't help any of them, and because this was a place for air sylphs, there were no earth sylphs around. Once the earth sylphs did hear about the Hunter, those walls would be rising. Airi shot another nervous look at the sky. Shasha couldn't shout a warning without a panic, or she would have done so already. Airi understood that intellectually, but she doubted she would have had the same courage as Shasha. If she'd been there when the Hunter came through the gate, she would have started screaming for help, instead of hiding the way Shasha had, and she would have died for it.

Shasha turned to look at her, and Airi started as she sent a silent whisper of explanation to her mind. It was more than the lack of earth sylphs that made Shasha wait. It was more than the panic of air sylphs and likely water and fire as well. The walls wouldn't be made at all until Shasha saw the queen and she ordered it.

After all, the queen was the only one who could stop the battle sylphs from rising.

CHAPTER NINE

The flight to the palace was the strangest experience in Zalia's life, next to the day all of the sylphs had risen and taken over the city. After they had their fill at the fountain, Shasha spoke with something in the air that Zalia couldn't really see, and then she and the others were lifted off the ground. Devon cursed while her father started praying, and Gel just shuddered, hanging on to Shasha for dear life. The feeling of suddenly being in the air startled Zalia, but catching sight of the consternation on Devon's face started her giggling uncontrollably.

"Oh, thanks," he groused, though he did have a faintly ill-looking smile on his face as he rotated in midair. "At least you're not afraid of heights."

Zalia peered down at the ground below, already shrinking rapidly away. She could see people staring up at them and pointing, though the music continued. It was fascinating. "I guess not."

"You're lucky." He gagged slightly and closed his eyes.

He was so sweet, so different from One-Eleven. Zalia reached out to pat Devon's hand and turned to her father, who looked extremely ill. "It'll be fine, Father," she promised him.

"Just get me down," he moaned. Gel wasn't looking around at all and Shasha stroked his hair, her face expressionless as always.

A little to Zalia's regret, the journey was quick, the palace growing in appearance with tremendous speed as they flew toward it. It was a building from the city itself, she saw. The entire underside of it was sand and rubble, a bulbous blob of it showing how the building had been scooped right out of the ground before being lifted into the air. Zalia couldn't see the air sylphs who had to be holding it aloft, but she could see the holes of caves where they must have been and did see balls of flame indicating fire sylphs darting around and inside the building.

The palace was all archways and great windows designed to let in the breezes, the stone of the walls a pale gold that shimmered in the sunlight. Balconies and patios were everywhere around the exterior and there was a lot of vegetation as well, plants carefully tended by water sylphs and thriving despite the heat.

Their bearer brought them to a wide courtyard that started at the front doors of the palace but ended abruptly behind them at nothing. The invisible sylph set them down and Zalia stepped well away from the edge. She wasn't afraid of heights, but without someone actively holding her the way the air sylph had, she didn't trust the winds there. The men moved even faster, except for Gel. He still trudged slowly, but at least he was walking under his own power, his eyes dull and tired, but aware. Zalia wasn't sure why Shasha brought him, though she supposed the sylph didn't want him out of her sight. Gel looked like he needed a full meal and a good long sleep. That reminded her with a blush of the money she'd given to her father, and the fact that tonight, they'd all be able to have a full meal and sleep in a place that was a real home.

Because of One-Eleven. Zalia closed her eyes, not wanting to think about his kindness and what else he'd done to her, along with saving her job and giving her more freedom than she'd imagined in her life. She didn't want to think about what she felt for him, or what she felt for Devon, or what it said about her that after a lifetime of nothing but work and sleep, she suddenly felt desire for two men. Not that One-Eleven was a man . . . not that it was supposed to matter.

Zalia shook her head and followed the men toward the palace. Ultimately, any thoughts about her own love life were going to have to wait until more important things were dealt with. With that in mind, she followed the others inside.

~

Devon looked around with a bit of trepidation as they went inside the palace. It was obviously just plucked out of the ground and converted for this purpose, and he peered uncertainly at the cracks along the base of the walls. He really didn't want the foundation to fall off while they were there.

It was still a beautiful building, the walls made from marble with silks hanging everywhere. The windows were high and arched, letting in breezes that were cooler than what he'd felt in the courtyard, and Devon wondered what fire sylph got the lucky job of keeping the place cool for the queen. From what he knew about fire sylphs, it was easier to pump heat into the air, and they had to be at least a certain age to be able to draw it out. Back in Sylph Valley, they took turns heating a central furnace in winter so the air sylphs could pipe that heat through all the buildings in the town. In summer, it was easier to just open a window. Sylph Valley didn't even hope to get as hot as Meridal, though.

Along with the marble walls and silks, delicate wood furniture that must have been imported a phenomenally long way stood against the walls of the wide corridor, inlaid with shiny pieces of stone or shell that gleamed in the sunlight. Weapons hung on the walls as well, crossed swords and lances placed next to paintings that were different from any Devon had ever seen before, not that he considered himself an artist. It was the masters of fire sylphs who tended to have the artistic talents. Earth sylphs preferred masters who could make things. He looked at Gel, wondering what sort of talent for invention he had. The man walked with them, holding one of Shasha's hands in his own and staring at the floor. He seemed to be coming out of the shock he'd been in, but he was far from recovered yet and Devon wasn't sure he ever would be. They needed to get him food and a place to rest soon, provided they could find one. Devon huffed out a breath at the thought. It was just another burden. Ultimately, he didn't have the time to worry about one ex-feeder. He had to make sure that *everyone* was safe and that all the mistakes this miserable city was making were corrected. Just do what Leon would do, he told himself, steeling his shoulders firmly and tightening his grip around Zalia's hand just a bit as he did. His heart hammered. Do what Leon would do. He didn't know what Leon would do.

They walked around a corner, leaving the corridor they'd been following and entering a new one. It was just as wide as the first but short, ending at a set of double doors so heavily carved they were nearly hypnotic. Not that Devon saw them. A man beautiful beyond human limitations stood before the door, dressed in plain pants and a white shirt that should have been too hot for him. He was completely unarmed as he turned toward them.

Hatred washed over them, making Devon freeze in his steps with terror, all his thoughts gone. Xehm gasped aloud, the color washing out of the old man's face while Gel jerked upright, his eyes wild. Shasha spun and grabbed hold of him, holding him up as his knees weakened, and probably keeping him from bolting as well. Airi whimpered in Devon's ears, but Shasha only looked concerned. Of course, the earth sylph was from the same hive as the battle sylph guarding the door. He wouldn't bother to flash her with his hatred.

Zalia looked in confusion at Devon's face. She wasn't terrified either. Of course, Devon thought with an anger that didn't get through his fear. She was a woman. No battle sylph would casually make a woman feel as if she were about to lose control of her bowels and run screaming, just for daring to come close. Men, however, were an easy target and one no bully would pass up. After all, they weren't a threat to the battler and he was empathic. He could already tell they meant no harm to the queen he was guarding.

Devon forced himself to step forward. He wasn't sure how he did it, except it must have had something to do with not wanting to fail at this, not wanting to have to go home and face Leon's disappointment or Heyou's anger. Maybe it had to do with his own sense of responsibility toward these people, little as he knew them. After all, there was a very good chance that if someone didn't act quickly, they would all soon be dead. Mostly, he suspected it had to do with the small, dark hand he held in his own and the woman who stepped forward beside him. He did it for her. It was still unbelievably hard. The battle sylph was glaring now and the hate was growing stronger. These creatures didn't have Solie's order not to kill whoever annoyed them. They didn't have her order not to use their hate aura. He could destroy them in an instant if he chose, though he probably wouldn't for fear of upsetting Zalia. Maybe.

Somehow, Devon found the strength somewhere deep inside of himself to take another step.

"My name is Devon Chole," he managed to say after clearing his throat several times. Airi was still whimpering against the back of his neck, as frightened as he was. "I am the ambassador for Queen Solie from Sylph Valley. I'm here to see Queen Eapha."

The battler stared at him, his eyes narrowed and angry. With a step taken toward them, he leaned forward and sniffed imperiously, studying Devon.

"Why would she want to see a coward like you?"

Devon felt his stomach drop out from under him as he heard Zalia gasp. He shouldn't have come, he should never have come; Leon made a mistake sending him. The man should have stayed here himself. They had respect for Leon. He'd freed Eapha from slavery and told her and her battler how to make her a queen.

"Leon Petrule sent me," he gulped, hoping this battler had heard the chancellor's name before.

Apparently he had. The battler's lip curled and he spun away, returning to the doors. As he did, the hate aura dropped and the men behind Devon gasped in relief. Humans weren't designed to handle a battle sylph's hate and Devon had never been able to understand how the men who were masters to bound battlers could stand it. In places like Eferem, battlers never dropped their hatred. At least this one had, though that didn't allay Devon's fear any and he wiped sweat off his brow that had nothing to do with the heat. Knowing that the battle sylph could feel his terror didn't help either.

The battle sylph paused while facing the door, his head tilted a bit to one side, and then grabbed the handles and threw both doors open.

"The queen will see you, coward."

Past the battler was a chamber that must have been some sort of sitting room. It was large, the ceiling at least two dozen feet high with chandeliers holding hundreds of slim candles that could be lowered for the candles to be lit. None were glowing at the moment, thanks to the sunlight that shone through the floor-length windows. There were eight windows, their glass forming the back wall of the sitting room, and overlooking what had once been a garden. Now the garden ended only a half-dozen feet beyond a series of rosebushes, dropping off into nothingness without warning. The floor was more of the polished marble, covered by intricate carpets that were worth thousands back home. More silk, artwork, and weapons hung on the walls, while the carpet was covered by beautiful, delicate furniture like that in the halls, all of it inlaid with the ornate, detailed shell and stonework he'd seen before.

The rest of the floor had pillows of every color scattered over it; lounging on these were women. Startled, Devon counted nearly a dozen, all young and beautiful, before one of them stood up and made her way toward them, nearly tripping over the multitude of pillows and her friends. They laughed at her, shouting out that she shouldn't be so clumsy.

She was only a few years older than Zalia, with the same dark hair and brown skin. Where Zalia was growing more beautiful to Devon every day, this woman was almost heart-stoppingly so, and would be worth taking a second look. Devon very carefully didn't take one. She had a battle sylph for a lover and they were nothing if not fiercely jealous.

"Queen Eapha?" he asked with a deep bow, well aware of the guard watching him. The women lounging on the pillows giggled, watching avidly.

The woman smiled. "Yes, I am. Did Leon send you?"

Devon straightened up. Her eyes were kind, if distracted. "Yes, ma'am. I'm here as the ambassador for my queen and to offer you all the assistance I can." He hesitated, his mind flashing through the many things he had to talk to her about. The poverty, the economy, the Hunter as well. There was so much. This entire country was falling apart and Eapha stood before him, no interest lighting her eyes.

She actually shrugged at him. "I'm not sure what you can help with, to be honest. The sylphs have everything under control. I just try not to get in their way."

Devon gaped at her. Was she insane or just stupid? Realization of what was happening flashed before his horror—and disgust—set off the battle sylph. Queen Eapha was lounging on pillows in a floating palace—whether it was her idea or not. Devon knew the battle sylphs back home would love to isolate and protect Solie this way, if only she would allow it. Here Eapha had and because of that isolation, she had no way of knowing how bad things in her kingdom were. She'd never see it and the only reports she must have been getting were all coming through sylph biases.

"I really need to talk to you," he told Eapha earnestly and this time saw a flicker deep in her eyes, something of doubt at her own words. "There are a lot of things I need you to know."

"She knows everything she needs to know," one of the women lounging on the pillows called, waving languidly with a hand holding a fan of cards. "Come on, Eapha, it's your turn."

Eapha opened her mouth to say something, but before she could, the battler roared in anger. Airi shrieked and grabbed her master, yanking Devon straight off the ground and into the air, away from the battle sylph that was turning to smoke and lightning and wrapping himself around Eapha despite her startled screech. He still roared his warnings. The other women were also screaming now, scrambling up from the pillows while Xehm grabbed his daughter, pulling her in terror toward the exit. Gel stood frozen, shaking as Shasha braced herself at his side, not willing to run if he wasn't.

Clouds of battle sylphs appeared at the massive windows that overlooked the city, the depth of them blocking the sun and turning the interior to sudden night.

Twenty feet above the floor in his sylph's embrace, Devon felt his chest grow tight as he forgot to breathe. The battle sylphs were pouring into the room itself now, coming in through one of the windows. Some of them converged on the women lounging amongst the pillows, the rest shifting to human as they circled the queen. Exhausted, Airi finally dropped Devon down beside Xehm, Zalia, and Gel, but retreat was impossible. Battle sylphs were between them and the doors now, looking at them more with curiosity than malice. Devon was a little bit relieved by that realization, but horrified as well to see one standing far too close to Zalia, smiling at her. She stared back at him, her face bright red. Her father appeared scandalized to see him, but also too afraid to say anything.

Devon was pretty sure there weren't as many battle sylphs in the entire Valley as there were crowding into this room right now.

One battler held Eapha's hands, looking down at her. He was tall and dark, his eyes a glistening red color. Eapha smiled up at him, love in her eyes.

"My king," she said, her tone laughing.

The stern face he'd been looking down with lightened and he smiled, the skin around his eyes crinkling. "My queen," he answered her. The smile didn't last long, fading in the next instant. "We have a problem," he told her. "There's a Hunter in the city."

Airi groaned against Devon's neck, reminding him what she'd said about not wanting the battlers to fight the Hunter. It still felt like an alien concept to him. Fighting was what battlers were born for.

Eapha looked baffled. "What's a Hunter?"

The battler nodded shortly, his face hard. He was as aware as Airi of how dangerous these things were, Devon realized. The rest of them were grinning, their excitement palpable, even as Shasha shook her head sadly and Airi moaned again against his neck. Whatever it was the elementals thought about the Hunter, the battlers were obviously in disagreement.

"Hunters are predators from the hive world," the battler said. Most of the women had wormed their way through the crowd to see what was going on and each of them stood with a battler close by, usually with his arm around them or holding their hand. They watched curiously, a few picking up on the glee of their battlers and smiling. At least Eapha wasn't smiling, not while she looked up into her own battler's face.

"How did it get here?" she asked.

"It came through the gate. It killed everyone there. I don't know how long ago, since no one was able to send a warning."

She looked alarmed; Devon shared her feelings. "How can it do that?"

"They're unbelievably fast," one of the battlers laughed with a cocky grin.

"Then no one survived?" Eapha asked.

"We did," a gravelly voice answered before the lead battler could.

Eapha turned toward them, as did the rest of the battle sylphs and their women. Nervous all over again, Devon looked over his shoulder at Shasha. The earth sylph gazed at her queen without expression, both hands holding one of Gel's while he stood beside her. He was white with fear, but at least he looked to be interacting with the world again.

"What happened?" Eapha asked her.

The earth sylph looked down. "Everyone was celebrating. The gate had opened onto a hive where there were many willing to come through. We were pulling humans off the street to become masters. There were hundreds." She looked away from them, obviously unhappy with the memories but not willing to be silent. The battlers and women stared at her, as did Gel. He reached out with his free hand and laid it on Shasha's stone head. She smiled at him. "I lived because I was far from the gate. It came through and everyone . . . died. I'd seen a Hunter attack before and I knew . . . I dove for my master and buried us both. I still barely made it."

"Why didn't you call for help?" one battler furiously demanded.

She looked at him. "You know why."

He glared. "You know nothing," he snapped.

Devon took a deep breath. He didn't like the thought of speaking near so many battle sylphs who were already angry at having their abilities questioned, but that was what he'd been sent here for. "Your Majesty?" he called, noting that it took a moment for Eapha to realize he was speaking to her and turn his way. She looked uncertain and pale, as she should be.

"I saw the gate," he told her. "The place was devastated." He shivered. "And the cages that were used to hold the feeders were destroyed, as if something huge had pushed its way to the surface."

Eapha's jaw dropped, alarm flickering across her eyes. Devon didn't like to see anyone frightened, but this woman needed to be worried. "How big are these things, Tooie?" she demanded, turning back to the lead battler.

Tooie hesitated for a moment and then shrugged. He actually looked a bit sheepish.

"The same thing happened at the harbor," Devon continued, partly to cover Tooie's lack of an answer, but mostly because he had to. He didn't know for sure if the battlers reached the same conclusion he had about what happened there. He knew they were aware something went on, thanks to his own panicked flight, but not if they'd equated it with the Hunter. Eapha gaped at him. "Two nights ago. Everyone was gone, including some friends of mine. All I found was their blood."

Eapha stared at him, looking horrified, and spun toward Tooie again. "Why haven't you killed it?" she demanded.

He shrugged again. "It's invisible."

"What?"

"It's invisible. We can't see it. We know it's out there, but we can't find it yet." The rest of the battlers grumbled agreement, none of them looking happy.

"You sylphs are in charge. What can you do?" Eapha asked, still looking up at Tooie.

"Kill it!" the other battlers shouted, more taking up the roar until the room resounded and the humans had to put their hands over their ears. In the midst of all that sound, Shasha stepped forward.

"Raise the hive," she told the queen, who blinked and lifted a hand so she could hear. Instantly, every battler was silent. "Surround the hive with walls ten feet thick, and let no one out," Shasha concluded. "That will protect us."

"Ten feet?" Eapha gagged.

"Anything thinner and the Hunter will be able to pull them apart."

Devon felt ill at the very thought. So, apparently, did Eapha. She paled and looked back at the women she'd been sitting with, all of whom were shouting suggestions, most of which seemed to involve the battlers throwing explosions around until they caught the Hunter in one. Eapha even looked at Devon for a moment, but before he could think of what to say, she returned her gaze to Tooie.

"She'll make that hive, but you can find it and kill it," she told him. "Right?"

"Right," he agreed.

Wrong, Devon started to say, but Tooie looked out over the heads of the others and they roared again, most of them immediately shifting to cloud form and rising into the air, darkening the room as they flew out the window, Tooie with them. Devon ducked, his arms up protectively around his head as they went past him, close enough that he was brushed by the warm edges of their mantles. "Wait," he tried to shout at them, but none of them seemed to hear, and in all the noise, he wasn't even sure he'd spoken aloud.

They'll die, Airi mourned. *They'll all die.*

A moment later, the majority of the battle sylphs were gone out the window again and the women were looking at each other, some a little uncertainly, the rest with the beginnings of amusement. Eapha hugged herself, rubbing her arms, and her friends surrounded her, reassuring her that the battle sylphs could fix any problem, that they would be safe and she didn't have to worry about them.

That just wasn't true. Devon took another deep breath and stepped forward. "Your Majesty?"

One of the other women turned toward him, her expression angry. "Can't you see she's upset?" she snapped. "She'll talk to you some other time." She made a languid gesture with one hand.

"Your Majesty, I have to talk to you. It's important."

Something stronger than stone grabbed Devon's shoulder and he froze, his breath catching in his throat as the hand dug in hard enough to hurt and another clamped over his mouth before he could speak.

Despite Devon's muffled protests, the battle sylph had no problem hustling him and the others out.

CHAPTER TEN

Eapha sat heavily on one of the few chairs in the room, this one a chaise covered with embroidered fabric. She and the other women were too used to only having pillows to really be comfortable sitting on harder surfaces, but right now she wanted something solid underneath her.

Ten-foot stone walls were all that could stop this thing? Plus it was invisible? She remembered having nightmares as a child, horrible dreams where she was being chased by something she couldn't see. She'd run down the streets of her neighborhood and always it would be after her, following her around every turn, and no matter what she tried to say to anyone, no one would believe her. Not a little slave girl like her.

Over in his corner, Haru looked up from Fareeda and over at Eapha, a frown on his face as the battle sylph studied her and then sniffed the air. Was he trying to sniff out the Hunter? she wondered. Haru just turned back to his lover, still frowning.

Kiala bent down in front of her, the woman's face skeptical and a little annoyed. "What's wrong?" she demanded. "You're not worried, are you? The battlers will find that thing and destroy it and we're safe up here until they do. Yahe says that Hunters attack along the ground, not this high up. This place is completely safe for us, and that dome will protect everyone else." The other women nodded in agreement.

"It won't be able to hide from them for long," Abra added, "even if it is invisible. Did you feel how excited they were? They finally get to do something important."

The women laughed, all of them bragging about how their own battle sylph would be the one to kill it. Eapha's shoulders sagged. They were right, of course. There wasn't anything to worry about, was there? She couldn't quite shake the feeling that Tooie had hoped for something else out of her though.

She frowned for a moment. Was she imagining that? With all the emotions going on in the room, it had been hard to separate any of them out. She'd been overwhelmed by the excitement of all the battlers and her own friends, familiar with them as she was. She hadn't even been able to pick out Leon Petrule's representative. He hadn't been all that impressive; he looked even younger than her and terribly frightened. She looked around, but he'd already gone. She sighed. He must have been as unimpressed with her as she was with him. She knew her friends were. Their indifference for Eapha's position was like a burn on her soul that she flinched from. Devon must have felt the same about her. No wonder he left.

"Someone suggested a card game?" she asked at last, straightening her shoulders and looking up at her friends. Pleased at that, they all went back to their pillows. Eapha joined them, their happiness a balm to her, despite her own doubts.

In the corner, Haru watched them from where he knelt before his lover, just as he always had. Nothing of what he was thinking crossed his face, but he studied his queen for a long moment and then looked at his sweet Fareeda. Her mind was broken, but her soul was still there and she was vulnerable, so frighteningly at risk. Haru flicked his gaze to the huge, airy windows that made up the majority of the palace and touched his lover's face, whispering silently to her for a moment before he rose and went to look out those windows, leaving her whimpering in fear behind him.

He didn't look for the Hunter; that would have been a waste of time. Instead he looked for signs of the earth sylph who'd just left, and the walls of the hive she and her kind would raise. When it was ready, he and Fareeda would go there and wait it out. After all, pride and bravado were nothing compared to the safety of the woman he loved.

~

"Damn!" Devon swore. "Damnit, damnit, damnit! I am such a failure!"

No, you're not, Airi told him.

"Devon!" Zalia gasped and blushed, looking embarrassed at actually having called him by his first name; then she firmed herself and said it again. "You did nothing wrong, Devon."

Xehm nodded in agreement. "She knows of the danger now. The Hunter will be found and killed, and until then, we'll be safe in Shasha's hive." He nodded again decisively. "You've done very well."

Devon tore his hands through his hair, Airi squeaking as he disrupted her careful mess of it. "I didn't do anything! She didn't even hear me. Airi *said* that the battlers couldn't hunt the Hunter. Shasha said it too! And who gets to go into this hive they're going to make? Is everyone going to agree to it? Or will it be just the sylph masters and to the grave with everyone else? And that's just the most immediate problem. This whole city is falling apart and no one's taking responsibility for it." He glared up at the palace, floating so far over their heads that he couldn't make out any detail. Was Eapha safe up there? Devon had no way of knowing. He just knew the rest of them weren't and he had to force away a very real shudder at the thought that the Hunter could be right in front of him and he wouldn't see it.

Xehm looked uncomfortable at his outburst. "She said that the sylphs were in charge," he started to argue.

"That's the whole problem!" Devon wailed, aware that he was starting to sound hysterical. They were back in the master section of the city, behind the great wall, though not in the crowded square they'd been in before. Still, people passing on the street looked at them curiously, those who weren't huddled in doorways or walking in a mindless daze. "Sylphs can't be in charge of anything!" He dipped his hands over his shoulders, into Airi's pattern. *I'm sorry,* he whispered to her silently. *I'm sorry.* "People don't get this. Sylphs are hive animals. They're like godsdamned *bees*. They do what they're told, they don't think independently. In the whole damn Valley, *Heyou* is the only sylph who does anything without direction. Even Ril has to have the threat of Leon's boot up his ass to do something without a handbook, and gods forbid that Mace do anything that's not for the good of the hive."

I'd be offended if I didn't agree with you, Airi said, giggling.

They gaped at him. "That stupid idiot," he continued, pointing up in the direction of the palace, "is supposed to be giving the orders and she isn't!"

Even Gel and Shasha were staring now. The earth sylph had been rubbing her master's hands, kissing them gently every once in a while as he looked down at her. He was definitely awake now and he stared at Devon, his jaw hanging open.

"Maybe you should have told her that," Zalia said hesitantly.

Devon spun on her and sagged. She was so beautiful and kind. He really did love her, he decided, even if he had just met her and the whole idea was crazy. It didn't matter. He loved her anyway. "I really don't think that would have gone over well. They tossed me out for disobeying one of those useless women there. How would they react to 'Hi, Your Majesty. You're a dolt.' The battle sylphs probably would have torn my head off."

A faint smile tugged at Zalia's lips.

"Maybe I should just rip your head off now," a gleeful voice said from behind him.

Airi shrieked in Devon's ear, turning into a visible swirl of screaming sand as the surprise of it jerked him forward and he tripped over Xehm's feet, stumbling against him. The old man staggered under his weight and they both fell over, landing painfully on the stone ground.

A beautifully chiseled battle sylph stood where Devon had been standing, his hands on his hips as he grinned down at them. He laughed and looked at Zalia.

"That was fun!" he cheered. "He's easier to scare than most people!"

Zalia blinked at him, her huge eyes filled with an expression Devon couldn't quite recognize. "Don't scare them," she whispered, her hands trembling slightly.

Immediately, the battler's full attention was on her. "But it's fun!"

She shook her head. "You could have hurt my father!"

"Okay, Zalia," he sighed.

"You know him?" Xehm managed as he and Devon untangled themselves from each other. He looked understandably horrified at the thought.

Zalia ducked her head as the battler walked over to stand beside her, pausing a moment to sniff her hair as he did so. Xehm's breath caught in his throat. Devon wasn't breathing at all.

"His name is One-Eleven," she admitted. "He's the one who defended me against Orlil, and got me better working hours at the restaurant."

Xehm hesitated for a long moment and then stepped forward, his hand outstretched. "Thank you for helping my daughter," he said.

One-Eleven looked at the hand for a moment and then finally shook it with what was probably more gentleness than his norm. "Welcome," he muttered.

"Why are you here?" Zalia asked. "I thought you were all sent out to hunt for that thing?"

One-Eleven grinned at her in a way that made Zalia blush and Devon start to feel very uncomfortable. Finally the battler's face sobered. "I'm supposed to make sure the earth sylph doesn't have problems getting the wall set up."

With everything that had happened, Devon managed to forget that Shasha was supposed to be raising a ten-foot-thick wall to protect everyone. Standing up, he looked back at her.

She still seemed tired—Gel was utterly exhausted—but that didn't matter. While the rest of them had been interacting with One-Eleven, she'd obviously put out a call. Hundreds of earth sylphs were trudging heavily down the street toward them, some little more than stumpy pillars of mud, others as delicate and finely formed as Shasha herself. She turned toward them, drawing herself up to her full height, and Devon could only imagine what she was telling them in that silent mind speech the sylphs used.

It was obvious what it had to be. The earth sylphs looked at her and then at each other, their expressions—those who had them—nervous. Finally, they reached out to hold hands, the entire mass of them.

The earth shook.

Zalia screamed, One-Eleven catching her when she stumbled. Devon just fell down again. The ground heaved, rumbling so loudly that he could barely hear the screams of people caught in the quake all around them.

A wall erupted out of the ground. The leading edge of it was only fifty feet beyond the group of them and Devon stared at the hugely thick stretch of stone as it blasted upward, easily ten feet thick and dozens high in seconds. He could only see the edge closest to them for the first few seconds, but it grew fast, the earth continuing to rumble and groan as it fed the growth, the swirling patterns of different types of stone rippling as they fled past to their right. The entire thing was rotating as it grew from the ground, he realized, corkscrewing itself into the sky. Deafened by the sound, he felt Airi clinging to him and wanted to hold Zalia, only she had her face buried against One-Eleven's chest while he held her, looking calmly up at the wall. Devon felt a sudden surge of jealousy and the battler turned to him, his eyebrow lifting. Terror flooded through Devon.

The roar of the growing wall became even louder, the length of it suddenly rising high enough that it blew past the height of the buildings, casting its shadows over the city as it continued to corkscrew upward, starting to curve inward now, far over their heads. It had to be dozens of blocks across, Devon thought in horrified amazement. The energy of it had the hair on the back of his neck rising and Airi was shivering against his neck, frightened by it all. Surely it could keep the Hunter out. Even a battle sylph wouldn't just be able to blow through that much rock.

How many people were still outside? Everyone who hadn't been a feeder? How were the rest of them going to survive in here? How much food was there? Water? Sanitation? How much planning had gone into any of this beyond "put up a wall"? Devon lay sprawled on the ground, watching that massively thick stone wind upward, the ground growling and shaking like a live thing as it was birthed under the control of the earth sylphs, and felt a great deal of trepidation. Perhaps even worse, he felt relief as well, that he and Airi and Zalia and the others were safe, even if no one else outside that wall was.

The shadows deepened, unnatural night falling across the buildings. The screams of people in the sudden silence that fell once the stone closed overhead echoed with horrific loudness, until a dozen or more glowing dots shot upward, gathering at the peak of the dome. They swirled together, flaring into light, and Devon squinted at the tiny sun provided by the fire sylphs.

He let his breath out in a long, shaky sigh. There was even a breeze starting in the enclosed air, keeping the air moving.

We're safe now, Airi said quietly.

Devon rolled over and sat cross-legged, his hands dangling in his lap and his head hanging. "Yeah, we are," he mumbled and closed his eyes, trying not to think of anything for a while, especially not about how many people weren't safe at all.

~

The Hunter roused as it saw the dome closing over part of the city.

It wasn't surprised, but it was irritated as it saw a large percentage of its food supply wall itself away. That annoyance was tempered by all the rest of the food still walking around.

It had dropped in altitude during its doze, lowering fifty feet or more back toward the ground. It was still high enough that it would need to unravel its tentacles to almost their full length to reach the ground. That was fine. It was still tired despite its sleep and didn't want to hunt. Nor did it want battlers stumbling across it just yet. They were hunting for it, spreading over the city in their hundreds, but none were high enough to be any sort of threat, not that they ever were. They'd always hunted for it close to the ground, since that was where it fed from. Even the heavy tentacle it used for an anchor was wrapped around the roof of a building above the level where they searched.

The Hunter twined its tentacles closer to its core and settled down to watch them complete the hive. The walls looked thick and solid, stronger than it could smash through. Still, it had found its way into more than one sylph hive in the past. For the time being, it would concentrate on the food still wandering around unprotected. The solid human creatures weren't as nourishing as the sylphs, but they had a certain flavor to them that was almost addictive. If only it had known that human energy held it in the world, the same way a master held a sylph.

It would need to husband its feeding, it knew. It still didn't like the look of those great deserts as something to cross and it had no good memories of those oceans. If it ate all of the food here, then it would have no choice but to try the deserts and had no great hopes for how successful it would be. And then what? Another city if it was lucky, followed by another quest for food? This world was much sparser than its home had been.

Below it, battlers ranged through the city, searching for it and calling out to each other. The only way they could find it was by having one of them stumble into its tentacles and the others realize that he'd been eaten when he stopped calling. It was an inexpert science, but they had no other choice. Finding it wouldn't do them much good, since they wouldn't be able to do much damage to the tentacles they always targeted, but fear of a lucky strike to its body had driven it away from more than one hive. It watched a battler fly directly below it, passing obliviously within only a dozen feet of its anchoring tentacle, and let the creature pass unmolested. It was only starting to get hungry and wasn't in the mood for the taste of angry battlers anyway. It wanted some of these funny-tasting humans instead. Too bad none of them were close. It could sense them though, and there were more of them outside that protective dome than within. It cast a hundred eyes upward at the floating palace, hovering high enough that the Hunter's crest was actually even with it. There were humans there as well, all tasty, helpless, and conveniently easy to reach.

CHAPTER ELEVEN

They owed a great deal to the battle sylph One-Eleven.

Zalia wandered across the floor of her new home to look out the window at the artificial sky. To simulate nighttime, or perhaps just to take a break, only a few fire sylphs were up there and the sky was a lot like the normal night sky, except with only a few, larger than normal stars lighting it. Or perhaps it was better to compare the sylphs to small moons. They gave just enough illumination for those on the streets to see by, but not to interrupt anyone's sleep, and the air wasn't as cold as it usually was either. It wasn't anywhere near as hot as during the day, but it wasn't frigid either. She felt comfortable standing there at the window with her arms wrapped around herself.

It was more a tremendous sense of uncertainty that had her hugging herself. In her entire life, she'd never lived in any place larger than the hovel she and her father used to share. Now she was alone in a suite so large that it took her a dozen steps just to cross the living room she was in. Her father had one just like it all to himself across the hall and Devon was two floors down. Whoever once owned this place, they were gone now, leaving more opulence in the apartment than she would ever have imagined. It had everything she ever could have dreamed of, and she didn't have to share it with anyone. All because One-Eleven brought her and the others here and essentially gave them the apartments.

Zalia rubbed her arms, her skin covered in goosebumps even though she wasn't actually cold. Perhaps she wasn't going to be living here alone. She couldn't imagine just being given a home like this for nothing and she already knew what One-Eleven wanted. She'd seen it in the smile on his face and the twinkle in his eye, along with the anguish in her father's when he'd looked at her for a moment before accepting the apartment. It meant that he wouldn't be sleeping in the cold sand hoping a snake or scorpion didn't try to curl up with him for warmth. It also meant his daughter wouldn't be living her life out in abject poverty and that they could stay in this safe place that was apparently only for sylphs and their masters.

She hadn't looked at Devon's face. She hadn't dared.

Now she stood at the window and waited, not sure if she was waiting at all, or what exactly she was waiting for, though she had her suspicions.

Those suspicions made her tingle, her nipples hard against the arms she had crossed over them, and she swallowed, remembering the sensations that One-Eleven was able to invoke in her. What he'd done to her in her employer's office, how he'd made her feel when he found her bathing at the stable . . . She was still a virgin, she told herself. She wasn't sure that what they'd done was anything less than sex, but her maidenhead was still intact.

How much longer would she be able to say that, she wondered with something that might have been despair, or could have been excitement.

Zalia closed her eyes, not sure what kind of decision she was making and if she had any choice in it. Then again, what kind of choice did a woman in Meridal ever have? All the freedom she had now was due to One-Eleven. She had a debt there, even if the sight of him didn't make her toes curl and her breathing speed up.

She was falling in love with Devon Chole, she had no doubt of that, but part of her loved One-Eleven as well, with all the fiery passion within her, and she knew already she couldn't be shared. Even if either of them were inclined that way, she didn't want to be that kind of woman. Did she? She thought of Devon's warm brown eyes, his nervous determination, and his smile, and sighed. If she was going to be completely mercenary, and she wasn't sure that was the best way to look at affairs of the heart, what could he give her that One-Eleven couldn't? Devon had nothing except the coins in his purse and his air sylph. He couldn't even gain an audience with the queen to do what he'd come for and eventually he'd have no choice but to go home. He might even leave sooner, to warn his own people of this Hunter. He had no reason to stay, she thought miserably, while One-Eleven had no reason to leave.

Was every woman faced with this sort of choice? she wondered and wished for the first time in a long while that her mother was there to talk to. Her mother had been beautiful, so achingly beautiful, and when she hadn't been able to pay her debts, she'd ended up sold to the harems. She would have understood what it felt like to have the attentions of a battle sylph, Zalia thought bitterly, and how nearly impossible it was to say no.

Her mother was long gone though, and when the slaves were freed, she hadn't returned. Zalia didn't expect her to anymore.

Would One-Eleven remember her mother? she wondered. Would he remember a single beautiful woman among all the hundreds he'd had access to?

None of whom he was with now, she thought with a sudden blush. Out of everyone in the harem, out of everyone in the city, he'd chosen her.

"You're blushing."

Even though she'd been expecting him, Zalia jumped. Outside her window was a ledge only about a foot wide that circled the entire building. Elaborate architectural details she had no name for were sticking out from them at intervals and One-Eleven stood on the end of one, leaning on one foot with most of his weight. Zalia's first thought was that he'd fall, but that was silly. He'd just change shape if he did, though she doubted he'd fall. He was far too graceful for that.

One-Eleven's smile widened into a grin and her blush deepened. "Can you hear what I'm thinking?" she blurted.

"No," he told her, shifting his weight onto both feet and gesturing for her to move back. She did and he leaped forward, landing on the windowsill for a moment before he hopped down into the room. Zalia stared at him, her heart pounding furiously again.

"I only feel what you're feeling," he explained. "That's it. But I can usually guess what it means." The grin flashed over his face. "Or what I'd like it to mean."

Zalia ducked her head, blushing furiously, even as she felt her nipples hardening even more than before and the muscles between her legs tightening to the edge of pleasure. He hadn't even touched her! she thought.

A moment later, he did. Zalia felt his rough hand stroke her cheek and slide down to cup her chin, gently forcing her face up. She found herself staring into his beautiful brown eyes, gazing down at her with so much desire that she trembled.

"Tooie says I should talk to you," he whispered. "I think talking's overrated."

He kissed her. Zalia gasped as his mouth pressed against her own and his tongue flicked past her lips, brushing lightly against the end of her own tongue. The feel of it shot right through her, straight to her toes, and she had to put her arms around his neck before she fell. His strong hands closed around her ribs, just firm enough to not be ticklish, and his thumbs brushed upward against the lower swell of her breasts.

She'd never thought she'd be so sensitive. Her entire body felt charged and every part of it that he touched ached. She tightened her grip around his neck, not resisting as he kissed her, and the lust and desire were so strong it was as though he was inside her head. Maybe he was, admonitions that he couldn't read her mind aside. He could certainly control what she felt and she was as helpless against what he was doing to her as she had been before. She could stop him, she told herself. She'd stopped him twice now. She could trust him to stop again.

It was just, at this exact moment, Zalia didn't want him to. She couldn't even quite remember why she'd been so resistant.

One-Eleven sighed happily against her mouth, his hands sliding around from her ribs to cup the side of her breasts, his thumbs stretching farther to circle her areolas. Zalia rose up onto her toes, aching for him to touch her nipples, but he just kept circling them, his soft lips working ever so softly against her own, the tip of his tongue flicking out occasionally to taste.

It was wonderful, if only she could breathe, if only he'd *touch* her. He seemed content just to circle her nipples and run his hands along the swell of the rest of her breasts, his body strong and warm against the length of her own.

Gently, One-Eleven's hands moved, sweeping under the curve of her breasts, still without touching her nipples, and up between them to undo the topmost of her dress's buttons. He kept kissing her and she let him, her eyes closed in a haze of desire. One-Eleven undid the button and pulled the pieces of fabric wide, caressing the patch of bared skin between them for a moment before he moved down to the next one. She had six on the front of her dress in all and he undid all of them before he pushed her dress open, his hands returning to their position cupping her breasts, rough against the bared skin and so incredibly warm.

Finally, he touched her nipples, pressing them into her, and she cried out into his mouth, pleasure sparking through her. It felt as though he'd touched lightning to those two points and she was weak from it.

"Good," he whispered against her lips, reaching his hands up for a moment, just long enough to pull her arms from around his neck and down by her sides. Her loosened dress slid over her shoulders and pooled by her feet, leaving her naked from the waist up. One-Eleven leaned back to take a long, appreciative look. "My gorgeous girl," he said and stroked one hand down from her breast to the top of the undergarment she wore.

How could she be so calm with him, she wondered, though *calm* was perhaps the wrong word for the fire within her. Any other man seeing her this way would have sent her diving for cover, even Devon, but One-Eleven had buried her shyness underneath his overpowering need. All she had to do was go along with it and he'd . . . oh he'd . . .

The battle sylph grabbed the bottom of his shirt and pulled it off to expose his own chest. She gaped at it, her mouth hanging open in desire until he bent forward to roughly kiss her lips and dropped to one knee, fingers undoing the tie of her undergarment. Hooking his fingers in the fabric, he pulled it down to her feet in one move. Zalia squeaked at that, but he buried his face in the hair of her mound and gave her core a soft lick that made her screech instead as her knees buckled. One-Eleven rose instantly, shedding his own pants as he did, and caught her before she could fall. His body was hard and perfect against hers, his gaze catching hers and never leaving it, his smile grabbing her breath and causing her to hold it without thinking as he held her with one arm and reached down with the other to the source of the heat that was burning her.

Zalia bucked, pleasure exploding through her with the force of her orgasm. One-Eleven chuckled against her mouth and his hands moved down, grasping her buttocks and abruptly lifting her up against him as he strode forward, his erection pressing almost painfully against her belly, though it felt tantalizingly erotic as well. Zalia tried to get enough breath into her gasping lungs to ask him where he was taking

her, but he only took a few steps before he lowered her, and her buttocks and back came down on the rough fabric of a chaise that stood in
the center of the room. She'd been sitting on it before walking to look
pensively out the window. Now she lay on her back and One-Eleven
came down on top of her, his knees wedging her legs wide apart, his
mouth crushing down on her own. She was in a haze, burning inside,
and in one motion, he pressed the tip of his erection against the part
of her that burned the hottest and pushed his entire length inside.

Zalia gasped, her eyes flying wide open. She hadn't thought . . .
she hadn't expected him to just . . . A moment later, she threw her head
back as she wailed in the throes of the strongest orgasm she'd had yet,
just from the feel of him inside of her.

One-Eleven sighed in true happiness, his hand caressing her
cheek as he started to move, pumping his hips back and forth as he
slid in and out of her. Zalia lay with her legs spread wide for him on
the rough fabric of the chaise, her breasts jostling back and forth as he
rocked her. Seeing them move, he purred appreciatively and ducked
his head to take one of her nipples in his mouth, never slowing the
speed of his thrusts. Zalia gasped again, helpless against what was
building inside her yet once more. The feel of him was uncontrollable
and all she could do was gasp for breath, hanging on to the edges of
the chaise for support as he moved against her, his passion bringing
her to ecstasy again and again, until she had nothing left in her and
he finally hugged her close to him, holding her tight as he finished
with a sigh that said that everything was finally right with the world.

~

They'd moved to the bed.

Rather, One-Eleven had carried Zalia's sleeping body to the bed
and tucked her in. He lay beside her now, watching her. He didn't

normally sleep and hadn't since long before he left his own world. He didn't really understand why humans needed to do it so much, but he'd figured out the necessity. Zalia wouldn't be too happy to have him wake her up now, no matter how badly he wanted to sink into her warmth and love her again. And again and again and again. He never wanted to stop.

For now, he was content to watch her sleep and feel her exhaustion and satiation. When she woke, he'd take her to the queen and have her become his master. Then he'd never be alone and could get rid of the five feeble men who were his feeders right now. All of them were half-crazed things wandering the alleyways of the city, never getting far enough that he'd have to worry about something happening to them, not that he cared beyond their necessity as a food source. As with a lot of the battlers, he'd stopped the healers from growing their tongues back, and once he had a true master, he could get any of his brothers to destroy them for him. The only orders he wanted coming his way would be from sweet Zalia.

He watched her sleep, her long hair falling over her face with dark strands that he kept brushing back so he could see her. She'd been resistant for so long, but he could tell she'd enjoyed herself. How could she not? He'd given her every ounce of pleasure he could, flooded her with it to the point where she had to be exhausted now. Tooie had said to talk to her, but what was there to talk about? He didn't care about her past or her future, beyond how it would be with him. He loved her; that was all he needed to know, and now he'd been with her. They had a lifetime of lovemaking ahead of them. What else could they possibly need?

Another strand fell across her face as she shifted in her sleep and One-Eleven brushed it away, wondering what her name for him would be once she was his master. Whatever it was, it would be perfect, just as she was perfect.

In the back of his mind, a call came, a summons warning about an incoming storm. One-Eleven looked down at his sleeping lover, not needing to sleep himself but not wanting to leave her. Still, duty was an absolute for his kind and she would be waiting. As soon as he could, he would be back for her.

Careful not to wake her, One-Eleven slipped out of the bed and away, gathering up the clothes he used when in human form. He didn't put them on, instead stowing them inside his mantle as he changed to his natural shape and slipped out the window. Hovering outside, he looked in at her for a moment, his lightning flickering in happiness, and then flew away, leaving her behind and alone.

～

Airi was feeling much better. She'd snoozed, perhaps even sleeping a bit from time to time, and sipped at her master's energy all day, slowly replenishing herself without exhausting him. She'd never been so tired before, what with navigating that chaos of twisted metal while carrying people and especially with feeding so much energy to Shasha.

Now she was lying on Devon's chest while he lay on his bed, partially trying to play his flute in the prone position but mostly drifting toward sleep himself. She nestled against him, feeling his emotions as he floated away. He was tired, hating this place with its heat and dangers, and loathing himself for his own failure to make any kind of difference. She felt bad for him for that, though she wasn't surprised. Nobody had ever been able to make a queen do anything. That was just the nature of queens. At least they were safe now in this new hive, and the tension she'd been carrying flowed out of her. She felt happy and light again.

Devon's attempt at music petered out entirely and his hand, still holding the flute, relaxed down against his chest, settling through her. Carefully, she squirmed free and rose up above him, looking to see if she'd woken him. Devon just rolled onto his side and started to snore, the flute tumbling out of his hand and over the side of the bed to the floor.

Airi looked at it. It was really one of the few things they owned here. Devon hated this city, but he did love Zalia. Airi could feel it in him and feel it in the woman as well. She wasn't jealous of either of them. Airi wanted her master to be happy, to live long and well and have children who would become her future masters, since no matter how much she loved him, she couldn't make him live forever. She wanted Zalia to make him smile.

The temperature in the room was dropping; not as badly as outside the hive, but still more than would be comfortable for him. Airi flew over to an ornate cabinet against the wall and solidified, becoming a translucent girl that, though Devon didn't know it, looked just like his grandfather's youngest sister had when Airi first came across the gate. She could open the door in her usual form, but she was still young, even after decades in this world, and the likeliness that she'd wake Devon was high. So she opened the door the way a human would have and lifted out a blanket from inside. Bringing it back to the bed, she covered her master with it and picked his flute up off the floor, setting it on the bedside table. Devon mumbled something meaningless and continued to sleep.

Now she had the rest of the night to entertain herself without him. Back home, Airi would have visited her sister sylphs, gone to the classes they took to learn to read and write, or just socialized. Here, she was a little unsure of her place or her welcome. Shasha seemed to like her well enough, but she was undoubtedly still recovering from her own exhausting day and Airi didn't know where to find her anyway. It was so much more difficult when she wasn't part of the hive pattern.

Perhaps Zalia was still awake. Airi liked the young woman, from the texture of her pattern to how she made Devon feel. He'd always been a little stupid around women, but Zalia was made for him. Airi could sense it.

She flitted across the room and out the open window. Zalia's apartment was on the other end of the building and a floor up. Airi didn't know if they'd get to keep these rooms, but they were certainly better than anything they'd ever stayed in before.

Airi floated upward and along the length of the building, scanning carefully for Zalia's energy pattern. She could find Devon anywhere in the world, but he was her master. Until his death, she could find his father as well, even though he'd given her away, and she'd been able to feel his grandfather even after he did the same. Devon, she was confident, would never give her away, not without her consent.

Zalia wasn't obvious to her at all, except by the natural ties of interest and affection that were already binding the young woman to Devon. As with all humans and sylphs, her pattern was unique and the little air sylph only took a minute to find her.

She could tell the instant she did that something was wrong. The woman was awake, frightened, angry, regretful, and filled with a morass of despair, desire, and fear that was hard to sort through. Airi hesitated for a moment. As with all sylphs, she was empathic, but her compassion was usually limited only to her master and hive mates. For a moment, she wanted nothing to do with Zalia's confusion, but then she remembered. This was the woman that Devon was falling in love with and her pattern perfectly fit with his own.

Airi flitted up to the open window letting into the woman's apartment and inside. Zalia was sitting on an ornate chaise in the center of the room, nude but wrapped in an embroidered sheet. Her hair was a mess framing her face and tears were streaming down her cheeks. Her lips quivered as she tried without success to hold in intermittent sobs. Her hands shook as well, holding the sheet closed over her breasts. Invisible, Airi went unnoticed.

This was very wrong. Airi thought for a moment, wondering if she should go and wake Devon to come and deal with this, but somehow she doubted he'd know what to do any more than she did. This might even scare him away and she didn't want that to happen.

With a little sigh that was no more than a whisper of wind, Airi took on solid form. She wasn't good at it—only healers and battlers were naturally good at changing shape—and she never could make herself stop being transparent, but she did look human and even had a semblance of clothing, as translucent and wispy as the rest of her. It wasn't comfortable for her. She felt terribly vulnerable around anyone but her master and forced herself to not show it as she took a step toward the young woman, her hand outstretched.

"Zalia?" she called. "Zalia, please don't cry."

Zalia jumped, turning with a gasp to gape at her and nearly losing her grip on the sheet in the process. Her tear-blotched face turned white, red flaring high on the cheeks. "Who are you?" she gasped, desperately wiping at her eyes with the back of her hand as if she could hide what she'd been doing that way.

"I'm Airi," Airi reminded her. "I heard you crying."

Zalia's eyes widened. "Is Devon with you?" she asked in horror.

Apparently waking him would have been a bad idea after all. "He's asleep. I came to visit."

"Visit?" Zalia repeated stupidly. "Me? Why?"

Airi shrugged, her head tilting from side to side. "I like you."

To her surprise, Zalia's eyes filled up with tears again. "You like me? Well, I guess that makes sense since not being liked isn't my problem."

Airi gaped at her, knowing exactly what the woman was feeling but not understanding any of it. Hesitantly, she moved closer, reaching out a gossamer hand to tentatively pat Zalia's knee. "What is your problem?" she whispered.

Zalia's lip twisted. "Your kind like me too much and now I'm ruined."

She was liked by an air sylph and that ruined her? "I . . . don't understand?"

Zalia gave a bitter laugh and rubbed her face again, smearing the fresh tears everywhere before she took an edge of her sheet and dried her face. She tried to drag her fingers through her tangled hair and gave up with a wince. "I'm surprised he hasn't shouted it to the whole world. He left fast enough."

"He . . . who?"

The woman sagged, tugging the sheet even closer around herself. "One-Eleven. His name is One-Eleven. He was here and . . . when I woke up he was gone. I feel like such a fool." She buried her face in her hands.

Airi felt a chill that should have been alien in such a hot climate. Human men weren't the ones with numbers instead of names in this place. It's not fair! she wanted to scream. Devon loved Zalia. Airi could feel it. Why did a battle sylph have to come interfering with that? Devon was shy and silly when it came to women. A battler could make Zalia orgasm with a look. How was Devon supposed to compete? How was any man supposed to compete?

Unaware of Airi's emotions, Zalia dug her fingers into her brow, her eyes and nose still hidden by her hands. "I don't know why I did it," she wailed. "I'm a good girl! How could I do *that*? I barely know him! And he didn't even stay around!"

Likely the battler was called away for duty, Airi thought as she realized what Zalia was saying. "I . . . I don't think I've ever heard of any woman saying no to a battler," she admitted. "I don't think you can."

Zalia raised her face to look at her. Airi felt her continuing confusion, as well as a hope that she had a reason for this not being her fault, and below it all, a guilty desire to do it all again.

"They make you feel what they want you to," Airi told her. "You don't have any choice. If they hate you, they'll fill you with the terror of that. If they want you, well . . ."

"Can all sylphs do that?" Zalia asked.

"Well, yes," Airi admitted. "Us elementals don't really bother." Nor were they as good at it. Even when she'd been a slave in Eferem, Airi hadn't thought of trying to influence the emotions of her masters. That was for battle sylphs and especially queens to do. The queens to control their hives; and the battlers, she supposed, in the hope of gaining a queen. Given the competition for one queen and the skill they needed to stand out from their brothers, it was no wonder a human woman was so helpless.

"Why would he?" Zalia whimpered.

"Would you have slept with him if he hadn't?" Airi asked a lot more bluntly than she'd meant to. Zalia's eyes turned impossibly big and the little air sylph raised the hands she hadn't become used to yet, waving them frantically. "That's not what I meant!"

What she said now could change Zalia's future, she realized. If she told Zalia that the battler was just using her, manipulating her emotions to get what he wanted, she would believe her. She'd never want anything to do with One-Eleven again, leaving her open for Devon. Only there was no guarantee she'd be interested in Devon after this. Airi could feel the young woman's deepest emotions, and she'd seen over a number of years how stupid humans were about a woman's chastity. Zalia would be devastated by this and Airi didn't want to see her hurt. More, Devon probably wouldn't want to take the risk of poaching on what a battle sylph considered his territory. Worst of all, that battle sylph would very likely see Airi's interference as a direct threat.

No, that wasn't the worst part. Airi looked at Zalia, feeling all of her hopes for her own master dwindling. The worst of it all was she just couldn't do it. No matter what it might mean for her master's happiness, and her own, she couldn't lie to Zalia.

"He loves you," Airi admitted. Zalia blinked. "It's what battlers are made for. He'll love you forever, with all of his heart. If he's not here now, it's because he had to go. He'll be back."

"Oh," Zalia said in a very tiny voice. Airi couldn't tell through the morass of emotions inside her whether she was happy about that or not. Not wanting to be there anymore, since she would have been so happy if things had gone differently, Airi let herself become intangible again, her pattern returning to invisibility as she flew back out the window, wanting nothing more than to return to her master's side and try to think of a way to tell him about this.

∽

Zalia watched the air sylph vanish in front of her and felt the faint winds of her leaving. She was almost glad of it, for while she appreciated Airi's explanation, she wanted to be alone to think.

Ilaja would call her a whore. Right now, Zalia didn't care what the other woman thought. She didn't feel like a whore, even if she wasn't really all that sure what she did feel like. Physically, except for a bit of soreness between her legs, she didn't feel any different. The virginity she'd preserved for her entire life didn't feel to be worth much now that she'd lost it. She hadn't suddenly become a new person and she didn't feel any more or less confused than she had before One-Eleven came into her room. Did she love him? She didn't know. She'd always told herself that she'd only make love to a man she loved, who was her husband, and she didn't know that she loved One-Eleven. He hadn't said more than a few dozen words to her. How could she love him?

Zalia closed her eyes, shivering despite the warm air that still came through the window, even with the darkness outside. It didn't cool down as much in this hive as it had at the hovels.

Airi said that One-Eleven loved her. He'd certainly told her he loved her, but according to Airi, he had no choice. Zalia took a deep breath and wiped her eyes, rising with the sheet still wrapped around herself so she could go to the bedroom at the back of the suite. Well, she'd done it now, but she refused to keep pretending. She'd love One-Eleven if she could, but she wouldn't pretend.

She just hoped that it would be that easy.

CHAPTER TWELVE

There was a thunderstorm high in the air of the desert, far on the horizon but stacked from the ground to the roof of the sky.

Still attached to the harbor gate by one of its thicker tentacles, the Hunter raised a few of the lighter ones and looked at the storm through a thousand eyes. It had seen storms before in the world it left, but nothing like this. There everything was jungles and grasslands that broke for the chaos of huge mountain ranges, full of jagged peaks and deep, twisting canyons. These clouds it saw on the horizon were as tall as a mountain, crackling with the kind of lightning that a battle sylph couldn't even dream of. Equipped with so many eyes, it could estimate exactly how far away those massive, angry clouds were, and shifted uncertainly as it felt the wind from them blow against its tendrils and tentacles. Storms could be lethal to the soft flesh of its main body and there were no deep canyons to hide in. Nor could it let the gentler leading winds of the storm blow it clear. There was no telling where it would be when the winds finally died. It was far too likely that it would end up back out in the middle of that ocean again.

There was also no way of knowing whether those storm clouds would stay on the horizon, so the Hunter took its cue from the food. As the storm clouds built up in the distance, the human food scrambled to take everything they owned inside, hurrying around with scarves tied over their faces as the winds increased, picking up particles of sand from the ground and tossing them around. The sand didn't rise high enough to touch even the lowest of its tucked-in tentacles, but the Hunter didn't trust that the fine grains wouldn't and it suspected it would be very vulnerable to being flayed alive.

It needed sanctuary. The Hunter looked toward the dome of the hive, risen up over the tallest building in the city and inviolate. That would be a good place to hide, if it could only get in. That wasn't going to happen unless it found some way to breach the outer shell and it doubted it had the strength, even if it had the time. It could hear the winds of the storm and hear the distant thunder, even as it listened to the fear in the voices of its food.

The harbor it had been dozing above had nowhere it could go to hide. The palace floating above it might be no safer, given how many windows were punched through the fragile thing. It had to find somewhere else to go.

The sand was already starting to flick against it, even with its body so high in the air, so it reached forward with one of its thicker tentacles and wrapped it around a building a block farther inland. Only when it had a secure hold did it release its grip on the gate it had been dozing above and pull itself forward. The building groaned, the strength of its tentacles compressing the clay bricks that made it, but it kept pulling and lashed out for the next one, careful to keep the rest of its tentacles tucked up underneath its body. It didn't want to waste any food that might wander into them now and it certainly didn't want to rise any higher.

It reached for the next building, swaying its way over a small square where humans were carrying barrels of oil into a building, chattering fearfully. In even the small amount of time since it had started moving, the winds had doubled and the horizon had turned black. The Hunter's delicate body was bulbous and heavy, hard to pull through the roaring air, but it didn't dare let go of any gas yet. Not until it found a place of safety, one with a food source for when this storm was done. Enough air sylphs could stop such a storm, but they were all hiding in their hive, ignoring the outside world.

The irony of that didn't escape it.

It kept crawling over the rooftops, dragging itself through the air as the wind continued to increase. The food couldn't see the storm from the ground, but they continued to retreat, all of them vanishing inside buildings and barricading the doors behind them. The Hunter could see though, floating above the buildings as it did, and what it saw only made it grab for safety and pull itself along faster.

In the distance, the storm, even as it became invisible in the setting sun, continued kicking up an increasing amount of sand. Each larger particle knocked loose other particles that knocked loose still others, and then the wind lifted them all up and ran with them. A wall of sand hundreds of feet high and dozens of miles wide raced across the desert, screaming its way forward as the storm continued to feed itself and grow, howling like a live thing. If the full force reached it, the Hunter's fragile body would be torn apart.

The Hunter searched desperately for a place to hide. The tunnels it had originally come from occurred to it, but they lay on the other side of the city, perhaps too far to reach. More, there was no food left in there and it would have to deplete itself almost entirely to get low enough to drag itself through that tiny opening. If this storm lasted too long, it could starve to death before it was free again. If it didn't find safety, it would die anyway. Its tentacles were strong enough to resist all but a direct hit from the most ancient battle sylph, but the core of it was next to helpless.

There were buildings around it, none perfect for its needs, though it would wedge itself into the closest in the next minute if it wasn't able to find anything better. The wall was rushing toward the city with incredible speed and the winds that preceded it forced the Hunter to dig its tentacles deep in order to keep from being blown away. They were hard on the fired clay, and one of the roofs crumpled away entirely as it gripped a little too hard. It saw a group of surprised faces look up at it before its tentacle, no longer gripping anything with the roof gone, swept involuntarily across them. Filled with their energy, the Hunter grabbed again more tightly before it could rise any higher into the storm and dragged itself farther, more buildings cracking now as it pulled itself along.

Ahead, it spotted a long, wide building with a series of empty paddocks around it, easily large enough to fit into. It could sense the food stirring restlessly inside, enough there to make up for the gasses it would have to expel.

The Hunter released most of its gas then, sinking lower to the ground and into the rush of blowing sand. That hurt, and the full wall of sand hadn't even reached the city yet, though it could see before it dropped that the danger was close. The wall of sand was only a few leagues away and moving nearly as fast as sound.

The stable doors were closed, barred against the storm. The Hunter pulled itself around to the front of the building, which fortunately faced away from the path of the storm, and slipped a dozen of its smaller tendrils in through the cracks under and around the door. It pulled carefully then, wanting the doors open but not broken. It would do no good to take sanctuary if the wind merely followed it in. It broke the doors open at the center, where a crossbar had been placed to hold them shut. The moment they opened, it started to force itself inside, letting even more gasses go in order to make itself small enough.

There were animals inside, glossy creatures with long noses and four legs. They started to whinny and rear as the Hunter entered, kicking at their stalls in a panic. Could they see it? it wondered. That wasn't supposed to happen; only one of its own kind had ever been able to see it before. To be seen by food was disconcerting and it had to resist the impulse to lash its tendrils out and devour them all to protect itself. That would only swell it to a size that wouldn't fit in this small space.

The sandstorm lashed against the half of it still outside the stable, abrading it painfully, and it wrapped its tendrils around the heavy supports for the stable's roof, forcefully pulling itself in. The horses screamed louder and from the back, a human came, bearing a pitchfork and with a frightened look on his face. He clearly saw the Hunter wedging into the stable's main aisle, its tentacles mostly tucked underneath it and leaving it nearly blind save for the ones it used to pull itself in, and he dropped his pitchfork, his mouth hanging open in shock. The Hunter was almost as shocked itself at the realization that the human could see it.

The Hunter forced the last of itself into the stable, pressing against both the floor and ceiling, as well as the doors of the stalls on either side. Looping two thin tendrils around the door handles behind it, it pulled them closed and wrapped a dozen more around them, holding them closed despite the rising winds outside. The storm was screaming even louder than the animals and the stable shook, the door fighting to tear itself back open. Fortunately, it wasn't so hard to hold it closed, not when it had the strength to tear apart all but the strongest stone.

Finally regaining his wits, the human food bent over to grab his pitchfork and ran back for the door that he'd come through. The Hunter lashed out, careful not to hit him, and slammed the rear door closed, holding it shut.

The man skidded to a halt before he ran into the tendril, which saved him from being absorbed and proved absolutely that he could see it. The Hunter shifted uncomfortably, not liking this situation, but knowing it didn't really matter. This food would fulfill his purpose soon enough and the chance that he would draw the attention of the battlers was minuscule. Not in this storm, and even if the storm were over, the battlers would never bother to save a man.

The Hunter settled down to wait out the storm, ignoring the screaming of the food inside the stable as much as it did the shrieking of the wind without. No one was going to hear any of them anyway. It used the time instead to test how well the human could see it, learning eventually that the man could only see it very imperfectly indeed. It wasn't ideal, but better than it could have been. Overall, it was a peaceful wait.

~

Yahe searched for any women not able to find sanctuary in the storm. It wasn't easy at all, not with the massive winds that threatened to throw him into the buildings around him, provided they didn't tear him apart first. He'd certainly experienced storms hitting the city during his time in this world, but he'd always been sent to the harems for the duration. The air sylphs would stop the storm instead, most of them going out to meet it while it was still weak, while the rest lifted the emperor's island high enough not to be threatened. They'd already done that for the queen and her entourage, including his beloved Kiala, but the air sylphs didn't dare emerge now, and that left no protection for the other women in Meridal other than what he and his brothers could give. He suspected that Kiala would have a few things to say about that—he could feel her irritation with him in the back of his mind—but he could also sense she was safe, and instinct demanded he do this. He loved Kiala dearly, but if she had her way, he'd never see another woman again in his life. It was silly; he'd never dream of betraying her. But it was easier to just do what he needed to right now and deal with her anger when the city was safe.

Unfortunately, doing what was needed meant Yahe wasn't safe at all. The battle sylph fought against the winds, fueling his flight with rage as he forced himself forward through the blasting sand. He was deafened and next to blind, but his other senses were still good. He couldn't detect the Hunter—no sylph could—but he doubted it was out in this nightmare. Instead he focused on finding any women who needed his help. He hoped on one level that the storm destroyed the Hunter, but in all honesty, he'd rather kill it himself. Any proper battler would.

The wind screamed all around him, blowing sand so fast that he had to stay partly intangible just to keep it from tearing him apart, even as he remained solid enough not to be sucked away. It was a hard balance to maintain.

Below him, he felt fear. No storm had been allowed to hit Meridal in centuries and the humans were all afraid of it. Yahe flew low to the ground, winding his way through the winds that filled the streets, and tried to find any women who would need him.

There were a lot of women in the city, holed up in different buildings, sometimes together, sometimes alone. He ignored any men that he sensed with them. After all, they didn't enter into his consciousness any more than frightened animals did.

A child was crying, a little girl child not yet to breeding age, and there was discomfort in her fear. Yahe dropped down, pressing against the side of a building. The sandstorm was so bad now that he couldn't see at all, but he reached out with a tentacle formed from his mantle and felt along the wall. There was a window badly boarded up and a door cracked with age. It was no wonder the child was hurting, he thought as he felt the place where the sand was coming in.

He squeezed in along with it. Inside, he found a small room with bare, cracked walls and old furniture. A man huddled there against the storm, shielding three small children with a tattered blanket.

Seeing Yahe, he gasped in terror, dropping the blanket to expose the three children.

Yahe ignored him. One of the children was a girl, so he shifted to the human form he'd adopted for Kiala when he gained his freedom. The girl, who couldn't have been more than five years old, gaped at him along with her brothers as Yahe stepped forward and knelt down.

"Hello, beautiful," he said to her and she gulped, her eyes huge.

"You're a battle sylph," one of her brothers said. Yahe ignored him, other than giving a glare to remind the boy what battlers thought of males. The two little boys shrank back against their father, who looked equally as terrified. That suited Yahe fine.

The sand still blowing in through the cracks in the slum didn't. The little girl was in danger here so long as the storm lasted. No, he thought as he looked into her innocent brown eyes. She was in danger as long as the Hunter was alive.

"Come here, sweetheart," he said as he slipped his hands under her arms and lifted her up. "I'm going to take you somewhere safe."

"No!" her father cried, reaching a hand toward him. Yahe glared at him and hit the man with a concentrated burst of hate, tightly focused so the girl wouldn't feel it. The man gasped in terror, cowering back against the wall and clutching his boys.

Yahe cradled the girl against his chest and turned away, sweeping the edge of his mantle up to protect her from the sand as he kicked the door open and went out into the storm. Shifting around her, he took her inside of himself and rose up, cooing to comfort her whimpers as he flew toward the dome of the hive. She'd be safest there. All of the women would be safest there.

Tooie, he called. *Can you hear me?*

I hear you, he heard after a long minute. *What's wrong?*

I have a girl I'm bringing to the hive. Yahe paused to dart across a square where the winds were doubled in strength, with nothing to slow them down. *I've been thinking. We have to bring all of the women to the hive. If the storm doesn't get them, the Hunter will.*

True enough, Tooie agreed. *We'll have to gather them.*

Yahe fought his way through the storm to the hive, tired and wanting to go see Kiala, whose growing anger was strengthening in the back of his mind; but he knew he had other work to do. First he had to get his precious cargo to safety; then he had to go back out to save the rest of her sisters.

~

Tooie stood on top of the highest peak of the palace, balanced on the tip while he looked down at the storm that raged below them.

The air sylphs had lifted the floating palace as high as they could while the storm rolled in, leaving them drifting above a roiling ocean of sand covering the city. The sand wasn't touching the palace, but they'd had to go up so high that frost was forming on the outside of the building and even he felt a touch chilled by it. The air was thinner as well, though nothing yet to be worried about.

Despite the cold, the women had gathered on one of the balconies, wrapped in warm lace shawls while they peered over the railing at the storm beneath them and giggled. Tooie gazed down at them all, though his attention was focused mostly on a single woman standing to one side, not in the center as she deserved to be.

He loved Eapha so much, loved her with a bond between their spirits that would last for eternity. She was everything to him, his purpose, his life, his soul, and his hope.

He just wished she'd live up to what she *could* be.

He closed his eyes, not wanting to even think it for fear she would know, but he couldn't stop. He loved Eapha and she'd given all of them their freedom, but she was letting them down now and she didn't even know it. Nor did he know how to tell her.

Tooie turned away, not wanting to see her since he still loved her so much and he couldn't tell her how terrible a queen she was. The hive could die and she'd still be sitting with her friends, afraid to defy them and as separated from her sylphs by her attitude as this storm now made her from the hive below.

He'd tried to make up the difference and lead the hive himself. He understood what was going through her mind after all, and how difficult her past made all of this for her. She wasn't born for this kind of destiny. She'd been birthed into the worst kind of poverty, sold by her parents into slavery, used as a whore. In the entirety of her life, she'd never been able to make any of her own choices, and now she was supposed to make them for everyone else? It was no wonder she was frozen, too terrified to act, and using her friends' apathy as her excuse. Maybe she'd come out of it and be what they needed, maybe she wouldn't. Until she did, he'd do his best without her.

It was just so hard to resist instinct, to make himself think of the repercussions to everything they did. That wasn't what a battle sylph was made to do. Tooie was exhausted and growing more so as the threat of the Hunter continued. He desperately needed Eapha, but he couldn't ask her to help more than she was willing, not when he loved her so. He wanted to protect her and care for her; keep her from facing all the dangers of the world. If she wanted to leave everything up to him, then he'd carry the weight for her and not complain.

Most of the women had gone back inside, not liking the cold and bored now by the swirling, impenetrable storm. Tooie continued looking down. Eapha still stood there, looking not at the storm but up at him with tremendous love in her eyes.

She'd been through so much already, so much that she hadn't asked for. Tooie smiled down at her, sending her his emotions of contentment and love, even as he held back his worry and doubt. He could deal with this; he had to.

Eapha continued to look up at him, smiling now, and his pattern surged. Just so long as she loved him, he could do anything. Beat anything. Be anything. They both continued to stand there, smiling at each other while the world roiled in mad chaos below them.

CHAPTER THIRTEEN

Devon knew something was wrong with Airi the moment he woke up. He could feel how unhappy and stressed she was, and see the knickknacks and toiletries she was tossing unthinkingly into the air as she thrashed above the surface of a dressing table. He rather suspected she had intended to wake him, even though there was light coming in through the windows as the fire sylphs mimicked the rising sun. Looking out through the tall arch, he could see the inner wall of the hive, beige-colored and close enough that he could tell how rough it still was.

Airi threw a set of hairbrushes he never intended to use into the air, lashing them back and forth in a tantrum. Her emotions were as close to furious as he'd ever felt them, and filled with despair as well. He had no idea why she felt that way. He couldn't read her mind any more than she could read his.

"Airi?" he called, running a hand through his hair while he sat up. It felt greasy and gritty. He'd been too tired the night before to try and bathe, instead going to bed as soon as he found his room. He'd thought about asking Zalia to join him, but even if her father hadn't been right there, he'd felt nervous about it, afraid she'd say no. Probably she would have said no. It was better to take things slow and let both of them get used to each other.

Devon shook his head, trying to clear it of sleep, and looked at his air sylph again. He could actually see her, though more as a distortion of the air than an actual shape.

"What's wrong, Airi?"

The plethora of items in the air, from brushes to emery boards to powder puffs for makeup, all abruptly stopped spinning and dropped. Devon blinked as they crashed with a tremendous mess all over the dressing table and floor. It really was a good thing he had no use for them, he thought.

Nothing, she sent.

In all his life, Devon had never had his air sylph lie so blatantly to him. He'd never had her even try to lie and for a moment he didn't have the faintest idea of what to do about it. Oddly, the first thing that popped into his mind was his father's instructions when he took Airi and Devon to the priests to have Airi's bond transferred to his son. He'd said to always be firm, always in control. Even then, Devon thought that was unkind. Airi had no choice but to obey and even though she preferred it that way, there was no point to reminding her of it.

He also remembered a sylph in the Valley who'd started acting nervously and lying, though it was to people other than her master. The chancellor and the queen both noticed it and forced the sylph to admit that her master had been abusing her.

A sylph who acts upset must have a reason, Leon had said. Don't leave them alone any more than a decent man would leave a suffering friend alone.

"Tell me what's wrong, Airi," he ordered.

The air stilled, Airi's emotions swirling toward panic for a second and then crashing down into a sudden resignation that actually felt relieved. No matter what she'd said, this wasn't a secret Airi wanted to keep.

Zalia has been seduced by a battle sylph, she admitted. *She was crying in her room.*

Devon stared at her, not even blinking while the air shimmered and Airi became visible, forming into the young girl she sometimes became. Standing there, she wrung her hands together, a change from her usual nervous gesture of juggling things in the air.

"Devon?" she asked aloud. "Are you okay?"

Devon realized that his mouth was hanging open and closed it. He felt absolutely nothing, he realized. That seemed strange, though he supposed it must mean he was in shock. That was normal. Really, how else was he supposed to react to learning the woman he loved had been crying because she'd been seduced by the one creature he was most terrified of in the entire world?

Airi moved closer, still somewhat visible, though she was fading again already. *Are you all right?*

No, he wasn't all right. Devon stared down at his hands and noticed they were trembling. He was starting to feel something as well, he thought, as his mind churned to a slow conclusion.

If he did the sensible, reasonable thing and backed away, following his usual trend of never getting between a battle sylph and what they wanted, he would lose any chance of being with Zalia forever. An entire life he'd just barely started to see for them would be *gone*. Was the battle sylph who'd seduced her the one who gave them these rooms? The one who made Zalia so nervous, though Devon had been so terrified himself that he didn't think it odd? Was this his price for such generosity?

He was outraged, Devon realized, absolutely furious, and he clung to that anger with the desperation of a man who knew he'd drown if he didn't. Zalia had no more choice but to feel desire from a battler's lust aura than Devon did fear from their hate. Sure, there were women who deeply loved battle sylphs in the Valley, but if that were true in this case, why had she been crying?

His hands were starting to hurt. Devon refocused his distracted gaze on them and saw he'd clenched them so tightly that his fingernails dug into the skin. Airi cooed, swirling up toward him with her gentle winds. He felt her concern, as well as her renewed hope.

You and Zalia are made for each other, she told him.

They were, weren't they? Devon had never felt so comfortable with another woman, never fallen in love so quickly. He'd never fallen in love at all, actually, which made perfect sense now. He'd just been waiting for Zalia.

He wanted to go up there right away, dry her tears, and tell her he didn't care what that creature had done. He wanted to take One-Eleven and beat him into a righteous heap, leave bruises on his perfect face and make him cower in fear of more pain.

He wanted to do all of the things he knew were impossible to do.

Devon let his hands fall by his sides, filled with a still certainty. He'd failed in his mission in Meridal. He hadn't brought assistance to Eapha. He hadn't forwarded the importance of the treaty with Sylph Valley. He hadn't been able to help Kadmiel and Ocean Breeze. He hadn't been able to do anything about the Hunter. He'd done nothing by coming here except make it easier for a battler back home to play daddy without any competition.

He'd told Zalia about that, he mused. Told her how Heyou took his seed for Solie and essentially banished him. He'd told her about Yanda, and how the mad battler terrified him so badly that he'd never stopped being afraid of them. He'd have to tell her even more. He'd have to tell her about his childhood in Eferem City, tossing balls for Airi to catch and throw back when his father wasn't working with her, learning to play the flute and letting her pick the music he'd learn, just so he'd be ready when she became his. How his father had wanted him to play the fiddle instead, the way he had, but how

176

Devon's fingers were useless on the strings. He wanted to tell Zalia how Airi would squeal and run in a rush of silent giggles every time he tried, until Devon's father relented and let him switch to the flute instead. He'd spent hours practicing with it, readying himself to be everything Airi would need to ensure she never regretted being with him. He wanted to tell Zalia about the day his father handed her over to him, and how sad Airi had felt to him, how tossed away, and how full of wonder she'd been when his first command to her had been that she speak to him and not be his slave.

He looked at his air sylph, not able to see her now but knowing where she was and that she was looking straight back at him. "I'm not afraid," he said, though he was. Oh, he was so terribly afraid, but the anger bolstered him, and the determination. And, most of all, the love did, for he did love Zalia. He reached out for Airi and felt her winds swirling around his fingers and arms, reaching up to tousle his hair. It was dawn, if those fire sylphs were paying any attention at all to the sun outside the dome, and surely Zalia would be hungry. He knew he was, despite it all.

"Let's go see if she wants some breakfast."

~

The storm was dying, barely an echo of the horror it had been when the sun first went down, but One-Eleven still tumbled gleefully in it, enjoying the feel of the winds as they threw him around without direction. It was how he felt after all. Excited and swept away. Soon he'd get to go back to Zalia. He'd be able to take her to the queen and have her made into his master. Then they'd be together forever, even when he was away from her, and he'd have a name, something perfect that she'd pick just for him.

Yahe passed below him, heading for the hive with a frightened cargo of five women. One-Eleven swept down toward him, flanking him excitedly. *Did you hear?* he crowed. *I'm going to have a master!*

Yahe flashed anger at him. *What are you doing? We have to get these women to safety.*

One-Eleven rolled indifferently over the smaller battler. *So? The storm is dying. Once it's over it'll be easier to move them without anyone getting hurt.*

Yahe growled, lashing a tentacle toward him that slapped painfully against the edge of One-Eleven's mantle. One-Eleven yelped, surprised by the attack. *What did you do that for?*

The Hunter will be back once the storm dies! They'll be in more danger then!

One-Eleven went quiet, realizing his stupidity. Of course, the storm was protection from it. Back in the hive world, storms were welcomed because they kept the predators away. Embarrassed, he flew off, looking for the energy patterns of women. He still wanted to go to Zalia's side, he really did, but duty had to come first.

Soon, he promised her, though he knew she couldn't hear him. She wouldn't until she was his master for real, just as he wouldn't be able to sense her from this far away until that moment.

He could feel women though. Ignoring any other fears or desperation he felt, he darted down past a large stable toward a small house where he sensed three female souls. There were half a dozen men there as well, but they didn't matter. It was only the women who were worth saving.

~

In the hive world, storms would come down out of the huge peaks from time to time. They would rush toward the lowland jungles and fill the canyons with winds that would batter any sylph to nothingness against the sharp rocks. Built on the flat mountain plateaus between the peaks and the lowlands, the hives did better, the winds there not quite as lethal as in the canyons, and their fields didn't grow high enough to be more than flattened by the winds and rains, though sometimes massive boulders were knocked loose and thrown down onto them. The sylphs themselves just holed up until it was over, which sometimes took even longer than this sandstorm promised.

While they'd still been slaves, they'd done much the same thing in Meridal when the sandstorms hit. At least, the battlers had, crowding into the harems and resisting the urge to rage at each other and frighten the women. Tooie had never stopped to think what the elemental sylphs used to do during storms, or what they would be doing now if they weren't in the hive, afraid to come out. They might have been able to stop the storm. They certainly would have been able to protect the crops.

Tooie stood on the edge of a vast field, one of many that framed the northern side of the city. Only there wasn't much left to the field at all. Where there had once been seemingly endless rows of crops, now there were just the torn remnants of plants nearly buried by sand. None of the elemental sylphs had been out during the storm; he hadn't even thought of sending them. When there was a Hunter around, elementals stayed in the hive to keep them safe.

Tooie groaned aloud, wondering how much food was actually stockpiled in the city. He'd have to ask the elementals; surely they knew. Then he'd have to send his battlers out to collect it. It was just more work on top of gathering the females together and searching for the Hunter, and he doubted there would be enough stored in the city itself to last long, not with all the women they had to feed. Not if they couldn't find and kill that Hunter.

He looked up toward the palace floating above the hive, brought lower again now that the storm was over. Eapha wouldn't want to hear about this. What would she say anyway? Collect the food and save the humans. He could figure that one out for himself without bothering her. He'd have to find out how much food there was and if there wasn't enough, they'd have to ration it, or reduce the number of humans they needed to feed. He couldn't in good conscience leave a single woman to starve or be eaten by the Hunter outside the hive.

Tooie sighed again and changed to a cloud, lifting up into the air as he planned the searches and the rescues and just how many men they could throw out of the hive and still make it possible for the women to have daughters.

~

After the storm ended, Eapha went down the hall to the great sitting room, kicking at the sand that had managed to get in despite the air sylphs' efforts. There, she found Haru bundling Fareeda into a large, ornate shawl. He was tremendously gentle with the old woman, smiling at her as he brushed her hair back over her shoulders, and lifted her into his arms, straightening up. She leaned her head against his collarbone, her eyes closed.

Eapha stared at them in surprise. She'd seen Haru move Fareeda around in the palace, since he neither bathed her nor expected her to relieve herself in the main sitting room, but this had the feeling of a more permanent leave-taking. Haru wasn't planning on bringing her back, Eapha could feel it.

Haru turned, seeing her, and stopped, his eyes wide. He stared at his queen, his brow suddenly wrinkling with both concern and protective instincts as he looked at her and then down at Fareeda, torn.

Eapha still wasn't used to these strange emotions she felt from the sylphs. It was bizarre enough to get them from Tooie, let alone everyone else. She even felt her friends' emotions whenever a sylph was near, as Haru so often was, and she was intimidated by their indifference for her position. Now she felt Haru's desperate need to get his master to the hive below them, coupled with his urgent instinct to protect his queen.

She could hear her friends coming down the hall, Kiala's voice rising above the others as she complained about the sand in the hall. Suddenly, Eapha didn't want them here while she tried to deal with Haru. There was nothing for her to waste her time with, they'd think, even if most of them wouldn't say it. Kiala would just argue that the world owed them for what they had been forced to go through in the harems. Certainly no one had any right to tell them what to do.

Eapha walked toward the battler and his master, her hands clasping underneath her full breasts. "Where are you going?" she asked softly.

Haru ducked his head, looking down at Fareeda again. "To the hive. I want her to be safe."

Eapha looked around at the huge windows, which showed a magnificent view of the city. They were so high up she could barely see the edge of the hive itself, looming below them as though it were some sort of monster's egg. She could even see shredded clouds passing by, and swirls of dust that looked like anything from a stretched-out puppy to the top of an immense jellyfish. She turned her attention back to Haru. "It's safe here," she promised him.

Haru drew into himself, holding Fareeda closer and refusing to look Eapha in the eye. "It doesn't feel like it," he whispered. "The walls aren't thick enough." He lifted his head to look at her. "Come with us, my queen?"

He couldn't possibly think they were in danger here, could he? Eapha saw Haru did, but she knew Tooie didn't agree. Hunters in the hive world took sylphs working in their crop fields, he'd told her. That was low to the ground, not hundreds of feet in the air. She was probably safer here than she would have been in the hive. Haru didn't look as though he was willing to believe it, but how could she blame him, after he'd been separated from Fareeda for so long?

Behind her, the rest of the women came into the sitting room, laughing and talking among themselves. Eapha put a hand on Haru's arm before they could notice and start teasing her about putting on airs again.

"Go," she told him. "I don't think it's necessary, but do what makes you happy. I'll be safe here."

"Are you sure?" he whispered back, his voice just as low as hers. "My queen, your place is in the hive."

She smiled at him sadly. "My place is out of everyone else's way. Go now."

Haru shook his head, his eyes sad, but he turned and carried the old woman toward one of the open windows, changing his shape to that of a lightning-filled cloud while he did. Fareeda held carefully within, he flew out the window and down over the edge of the palace. Eapha walked over to the window herself, watching him descend until she saw him make his way inside the hive, the wall rippling to let him through.

"Where's he going?" Kiala asked, walking up beside her.

"He wanted to take Fareeda to the hive," Eapha answered. "He didn't feel she was safe here." The other battlers did. Even Tooie did. Why didn't Haru?

Kiala snorted derisively, breaking Eapha's thoughts. "There's nowhere safer than here. I wouldn't want to be in that dark, cramped place. Too much like the harem again."

Perhaps, Eapha thought, but wondered as well what it really looked like in there. Tooie hadn't said much about it, or how it was maintained. In their limited time together, talking wasn't something they bothered with. He was down there somewhere right now, feeling stressed to her wondering mind, but determined as well. He seemed to have everything in hand, but maybe she could go and look at the hive herself, see what was going on there to find and destroy that Hunter. Maybe she could help as well.

Kiala glanced at her. "You've got that look on your face again," she noted.

Eapha blinked. "Look? What look?" She stared at her friend.

"The look where you're thinking of meddling again. Come on, come and have breakfast with the rest of us." Grabbing her hand, Kiala towed her toward the tables on the other side of the sitting room. Sylphs were bringing them plates of fruit and cheeses, just like they'd eaten in the harem. None of them were used to anything heavier.

They were her dearest friends, but Eapha looked back toward the window where Haru had vanished. Where was that young man Leon had sent? she wondered. He'd wanted her to do more than just sit around. She tried to remember how young and unimpressive the man had looked, how obviously terrified. He'd been just as confused as she was.

Still, he had been sent by Leon Petrule, who was the least confused and unimpressive man she'd ever met. If only Leon had stayed. She sighed as she watched platters of cheese and fruit fly invisibly into the room, the sylphs who carried them content. If Leon were here, it wouldn't matter what she thought or what her friends said. She'd be a queen for real; he wouldn't let her be anything less.

So why are you letting yourself be less? she asked herself.

Right at that moment, Eapha didn't have an answer.

CHAPTER FOURTEEN

Zalia came down the stairs that led from her apartment soon after dawn, wondering how it could be that she didn't feel completely different. She'd lost her virginity, sullied herself in a way that she couldn't ever be cleansed from, but other than a bit of soreness, she didn't physically *feel* any different. She'd always thought the world would be changed once she took that step. Certainly she'd been led to believe it would.

Emotionally, however, she felt completely different, as if the words I SLEPT WITH A BATTLE SYLPH were inscribed in glowing letters across her forehead. How could people not look at her and just know? How could her father not know? How could Devon?

Devon had to know, she'd realized in the earliest hours of the morning. Airi would have told him, and that just made her nervousness and uncertainty worse, because she still felt so much for him that she couldn't describe. Even after One-Eleven had taken her, she could see the possibility of a lifetime with Devon Chole, which was just foolishness. Men of her culture wanted their women pure and untouched. A single passionate tryst with One-Eleven had made her completely undesirable to any human man.

Even as the thought of that was terrifying to her, she tried to find hope in it. Battle sylphs were loyal to their women. One-Eleven would never abandon her, even as a part of her feared he already had. He wouldn't let anyone taunt her and call her *whore* or abuse her or threaten to fire her from her job. She closed her eyes for a moment, not sure if she'd have a job anymore, even with One-Eleven's threats to her employer. It wasn't as if she could go there to work now, not with the Hunter in the city. For all she knew, it had already gone through and devoured her employer and Ilaja. There might not even be anyone left at the restaurant, just as there might not be anyone still alive in the hovels she and her father had lived in.

They didn't know about the Hunter, she realized with a horror that made her forget any thought about the purity or lack thereof in her body. There were people she'd grown up with in those hovels, all of them too poor to find a home within the city, though some held jobs as she did, each of them trying to help the others survive another year. They weren't even considered citizens and were only a step above slaves. No one would be going to their rescue.

She ran down the stairs, ignoring her fear and uncertainty, just as she did her hunger and thirst. Her father wasn't down yet, probably still asleep in the first bed he'd had access to in decades, but Devon was in the foyer of the building, his hair lashing around despite the lack of wind as he looked up at her, his eyes calm and searching.

She ran right up to him. "My home, out on the city edge. No one there knows about the Hunter. We have to warn them!"

"Whatever you want," he said.

~

There was a large gathering of people at one place by the inner wall of the hive, where the stone had an arching half circle a darker shade than the rest rising fifty feet or more in the air. According to Airi, that was the entrance in and out of the hive.

Devon, Airi, and Zalia ran toward it, passing confused people on the street. Most of them were just standing there, staring up at the dome. Thanks to their sylphs, they knew what was happening, but

Devon doubted the reality of it had sunk in for these people, given how there wasn't a panic going on. Granted, if there was, there were more than enough battlers to stop it and these people had once been feeders. There was a broken fatalism in all of them, as if they couldn't quite muster up the courage to care. The dancers and musicians they'd seen the first day weren't in sight, so perhaps it was only the damaged that were out here now.

Devon felt a little damaged himself. What was he thinking? Defying a battle sylph's territory? Leaving the hive when he knew there was something out there that would kill him without his ever seeing it? Was he crazy? He looked at Zalia running beside him and decided that it wasn't insanity. It felt too right for that. Noticing his attention, Zalia looked at him sideways and blushed, smiling tentatively before ducking her head. Devon's heart surged.

When they arrived, they found the entrance was placed where the wall of the hive cut through the center of a large square, leaving plenty of room in front of it. Only there were a lot of people standing in that open space, making it as crowded as the party the night before.

These people weren't celebrating. They were all women and girls, most of them weeping or wailing outright, jostling in a near panic or clinging to each other as they crowded around sacks of grain and crates of dried meats and fish, all dumped wherever there was space.

Devon slowed to a walk, staring at them. "What's going on?" Zalia whispered in his ear, pressing close to him in a way that felt wonderful even as his own heart pounded with nervousness.

They've been evacuated here, Airi told him, *because of the Hunter.*

That made sense, Devon thought, since it was what he and Zalia had just been planning to do. Maybe they didn't have to go out there at all. There was something wrong though, something it took him a moment to see, though it was obvious once he did.

There were no men in the crowds, no little boys or even infants. He could hear women wailing for their sons while they clutched their daughters tight, other women crying for husbands and fathers who'd been left behind.

The archway in the hive wall swirled, the stone rippling and pulling away as if it were no more substantial than a set of curtains. The scent of sand came and a dozen battle sylphs swooped in through the opening, which closed behind them before the anxious women could escape.

The battlers settled into a hovering line, waiting patiently as each of them landed in the center of the square long enough to set down their cargo. Most of them carried women, all as stunned and horrified as the rest of the women in the square. The remainder carried crates of foodstuffs that earth and air sylphs Devon hadn't noticed before put into stacks or transported out of the square altogether.

"Why are they only bringing in women?" Zalia asked in a whisper, realizing the same as Devon.

"Because battle sylphs are cruel," he assured her and tried to ignore her flinch. Solie never would have allowed this in the Valley. Eapha never *should* have allowed it. Cursing himself again for his absolute failure with the queen, he grabbed Zalia's hand, feeling Airi tangled through his hair, and towed them both through the crowds toward the archway. He hoped they could get the sylphs to open it. Battle sylphs in their natural forms turned massive eyes on them as they passed, making Devon's balls curl up against his body with terror, but they had too many hysterical women pressing against them and pleading to bother with a single man and his alien air sylph. They let them by.

An earth sylph fifteen feet tall and shaped like a heavyset clay woman stood unmoving by the archway. Devon hesitated. Earth and fire sylphs tended to be the smallest in size of the elemental sylphs, but their size did still indicate age and he guessed this doorkeeper had to be very old indeed. She had no eyes or features on her face, but still she turned her rounded head toward them, looking down past massive dangling breasts at the three of them.

Devon swallowed. He wasn't afraid of elemental sylphs the way he was battlers, but she looked like she could step on him. Not that she would. Elementals were incapable of deliberately harming a living creature.

Still, she might *accidentally* step on him.

"We want to go outside," he told her. The earth sylph just continued to look at him, or rather, point her head in his direction. The stone of the arch didn't move. "Please?" he added, to no effect.

Let us through, he heard Airi plead. *We have something we need to do. We'll be right back, we promise.* The earth sylph was unmoved, finally lifting her bulbous head to continue staring without eyes across the square.

Devon swore softly, though he wasn't terribly surprised. Most sylphs weren't exactly independent thinkers. Beside him, Zalia bit her lip and stepped forward.

"Please open the gate," she said. "I'm with . . . I'm with the battle sylph One-Eleven. He wants us to go through the gate."

Devon stared at her, wondering with an absurd sort of pride how much courage it took a woman of this culture to say that in front of him. The earth sylph rotated her head down to look at the young woman for a moment and then the stone of the gate swirled, making an odd, sucking sound as a hole only a bit larger than a standard doorway opened.

They hurried through it before she could change her mind or the battle sylphs notice that a woman was leaving their forced sanctuary. On the other side, the opening led on to a tunnel several dozen feet long, the far end just as dark as the stone that closed behind them.

Zalia looked back at the archway as it sealed itself behind them, leaving the air heavy and oppressive. Once it did, the far end of the tunnel rippled open to show daylight.

Hurry, Airi cautioned. *She won't leave it open for long.*

Devon grabbed Zalia's hand and ran, her long legs letting her keep up as they sprinted for the exit. As they ran, he hoped that the Hunter wouldn't be waiting for them outside, but of course, if it was, the battlers wouldn't have been able to get in.

The earth sylph must have been able to tell that they were outside, for the moment they passed through the arch, it closed behind them again, becoming smooth and dark against the rest of the hive wall. It towered over them, sitting like an alien growth in the rest of the city.

Devon and Zalia stopped, Airi whimpering as she clung to her master's hair. The earth sylph hadn't left them much time, but it might not have just been because she was afraid of the Hunter getting in. There was sand everywhere, piled waist high in corners and spread across streets that were clear the day before. The air was cloudy from grit and in the outer half of the square, men were gathered, hundreds of angry men who were shouting at the hive to give them their women back.

How could they be brave enough to dare and anger the battlers, Devon wondered distantly, though of course that was just what he was daring with the woman whose hand he held. At the sight of them, the men grumbled and glowered, looking angrily at them.

"How did you get out?" one demanded in a fury. "They stole my wife!"

Devon swallowed, not wanting to antagonize the man more, but these were human men. He was scared, but not terrified. "I know. The battlers are evacuating the women. They want out as much as you want in. We can't do anything about it," he added.

"How did you get out?" another man demanded.

"I was in there when the hive went up," Devon told them. More men were watching them now, some devastated, most angry. "I don't think they cared if a man left."

"What about her!" the first man shouted, pointing at Zalia. She edged behind Devon, pressing against him in a way that made it a bit hard for him to think.

"I snuck her out," Devon said. The murmurs grew. "I could only get one out! You think they'd let me bring them all?" A few men looked disappointed, though most were still shocked at what happened and their own inability to do anything about it.

"Why did they take them?" one man wailed, forgetting his dignity in his pain. "Why did they take my Loresha?"

More murmurs and angry shouts rose at that, but most of the men watched Devon, wanting answers.

"They took them to protect them," he shouted, knowing only a fraction of the crowd could hear him but not knowing what else to say. The battle sylphs certainly wouldn't bother to explain. "There's a creature loose here somewhere, something from the place the sylphs came from that they can't find. It eats people. They're evacuating all the women and female children to keep them safe." He pointed at the hive.

For a long moment, the men close enough to have heard what he said gaped disbelievingly at him, but none of them could deny that the battle sylphs were grabbing their women and daughters and hauling them into a giant stone dome that hadn't existed two days before.

"Why didn't they take us?" one man finally gasped out.

Devon gave the man an almost apologetic look. "We're men. Why would they want to?"

There was silence at that, but Devon could feel the rage growing again and Airi was whimpering in his mind, whispering for him to go, just go. He started to back away, still holding Zalia's hand and pulling her with him. He couldn't just leave them without a warning though.

"Don't stay here!" he shouted. "Whatever the Hunter is, it's invisible and it's deadly! It kills everything!" He tried to remember how to survive it and could only think of needing walls ten feet thick. "Get out of the city if you can!"

The rumbling rose again, turning into a roar of rage and frustration, as well as fear, and Devon ran, Zalia flanking him as they sprinted for a side street that had been turned into a narrow alley thanks to the dome. He'd just barely reached it when he heard the battlers roar, attracted by the growing riot.

They couldn't see Zalia, he thought as he felt their hate, and his heart pounded with enough force it might burst. If they saw her, they'd take her and leave him and Airi here alone. That was unbearable and Devon ran harder, Zalia's voice panting in his ear as she matched him, both of them slowed by the drifts of sand as they raced down the road and along others, Devon with no idea where they were going.

The sand was worse on the main streets, slowing them to a crawl as they were forced to struggle through it. These streets were mostly deserted, except for crumbling footprints from people who'd already made their way through, undoubtedly on their way to the dome. The dome itself rose over everything, casting its shadow over them even when they were blocks away.

"Where did all this sand come from?" Devon gasped, moving through it despite how his sword tangled with his legs and his feet sank ankle deep or more in spots, still tugging Zalia along. Despite the shadow of the dome and the early morning, the temperature was rising steadily and Airi worked to keep them both at least a little bit cool. They should have brought water, he thought. He was such an unthinking fool.

"There must have been a sandstorm during the night," Zalia gasped, holding her skirts up as decorously as she could as she labored through the sand behind him. "They can blow in and out horribly fast and if the sylphs don't fight them, they can just about bury the city."

And of course, the sylphs had all been nice and safe in their hive. Devon realized that at the same moment he realized he was holding Zalia's hand hard enough that it had to hurt, though she wasn't complaining. In the middle of a sand dune that covered most of the street and all but the sign above a little silk shop, he stopped and let go of her, staring at her in embarrassment.

"I'm sorry I held your hand so tightly," he told her, though he felt like an idiot. Now was the chance to be brave and manly. To show her what a wonderful person he was, how much better he was than a battle sylph who could turn her insides upside down. All he could really think was that he'd been tired last night and he'd gone to bed before he bothered to bathe. He smelled, and he'd left his flute on the floor next to his bed.

Airi snorted in his ear at that and madly ruffled his hair.

Zalia smiled at the sight, her entire face lighting up for a moment that made her beyond beautiful to Devon. It faded quickly and she hugged herself despite the heat as she looked down and away.

"You must think I'm such a foolish woman," she whispered.

How could she think that, he wondered, though of course, he knew. She had to be thinking that Airi told him what she'd done, which she had. In Zalia's mind, he must have been thinking her to be loose and worthless, though that was in his mind only because of his realization that it was what *she* thought.

His fear of battle sylphs might have made him a coward, but her desire for them didn't make her a whore.

"Zalia," he whispered, his heart suddenly very calm as Airi squealed in excitement and lifted off his shoulders, leaving him alone for this one moment of truth. He barely noticed as he reached forward to cup Zalia's cheek just as she looked back up, her gaze wondering at his tone.

He kissed her, his mouth soft against her dry lips, his eyes slipping closed at the contact. Zalia stiffened for an instant, but whether she truly desired him or her affair with One-Eleven had scoured away some of her inhibitions—or even a combination of the two—she returned his kiss, her mouth moving as ardently as his while her arms wrapped tightly around his neck. Her mouth was soft, so dry and perfect, and her tongue darted out to flick against the tip of his own, leaving him to wonder if she'd learned that trick from her first lover. He put that thought away. Her past didn't matter any more than his right here and now.

He held her against him, her breasts and belly warm and sensual, sending his heartbeat racing again for reasons that finally didn't have to do with fear. He kissed her, each touch of his lips against her a gentle benediction about how he loved her. He'd never felt anything so right, so perfect, and her sheer response showed how deeply she felt the same. Most of the women he'd kissed—and there hadn't been many—had let him do most of the work. Zalia was as involved as he was, and her fingers tangled in his hair as his hands stroked up her sides, the base of his palm just lightly brushing against the edge of her breast. She gasped at that, rising up ever so slightly on her toes, and he felt a surge of gratitude that he'd been able to cause her pleasure.

Daringly, he turned his hands and flicked his thumbs slowly across the sides of her breasts again. She deepened their kiss and clasped her hands over his own, leaving him to decide he'd gone far enough. A moment later, she brought them around and pressed them fully against the swell of her breasts and nipples for a single moment as she tensed in obvious reaction. Then she pulled them away and moved her head to one side, breaking their kiss.

"We have to go," she breathed.

"Of course," he answered, even as he took a moment to remember what it was they had to do. Right. Now was not the time for this, no matter how badly he wanted to make love to her. He kissed her again instead, hugging her to him as tightly as he could, now that he knew how sensitive her nipples were, and finally let her go with a last stroke along her arm and a kiss against the back of her hand. Then he clasped his fingers with hers and pulled her past him, letting her take the lead since she was the only one of them who actually knew the way.

CHAPTER FIFTEEN

They saw no women while they crossed the city. They didn't see many men either, but those they did were almost all wandering in a shocked daze, or heading purposefully in the direction of the hive. They did see blood, splattered across the sandy ground in more than one place, though most of it was covered by sand, and they did see battle sylphs. They were all over the city and it was Airi who kept them from being discovered and Zalia rescued by the searching clouds.

"They're really taking all the food they can find, aren't they?" Devon noted, peering around the corner of an alley where they'd hidden after Airi's latest warning. Zalia stood out of sight of the road behind him, while Airi played with the ends of her long hair. All of them were trying to ignore the splash of dry blood on the wall beside her.

"The fields must have been destroyed," Zalia mused, rubbing her arms. Devon looked back at her questioningly. "There are crop fields north of the city," she told him. "We depend on them for a lot of our food."

"You can grow food in a desert?"

"The sylphs can." She looked toward the hive. "But none of them were there to protect them from the sandstorm, I don't think." They hadn't seen a single sylph who wasn't a battler.

They weren't, Airi confirmed. *None of them will come out while the Hunter is here.*

So the city had lost its largest source of food. Devon watched a battler swoop by, a half-dozen bleating goats held in tentacles below his belly. Goats who'd need to eat from the same crops that were now destroyed. "The bastards," he growled. "Not only are they leaving all the men to be killed, they're leaving them to starve." He turned back to his companions, one that he could see, and the other that he couldn't. "This city is doomed."

Zalia gaped at him in horror. "Is there anything we can do?"

"Not us. Certainly not me." He looked up toward the palace, still floating above the hive. "The queen could, if she wasn't more interested in sitting around with her friends." Zalia looked devastated. Devon took her hands, squeezing gently until she looked at him. "We do what we're trying to do now. Get as many of your friends into the hive as we can." He shuddered. "And try to convince the battlers that without men, there eventually won't be any women either."

"Do you think they'll listen to you?"

The very thought made his gut tighten. "Honestly, no. But if enough women got together yelling about it, they just might." He smiled at her. "Leading them in that will have to be your job."

Zalia's eyes were huge, her hands pulling away from his and clasping under her chin while she frantically shook her head. Oddly enough, she reminded Devon of himself when Leon had first asked him to come to Meridal. He stepped forward and reclaimed her hands with his own. "Don't be afraid. You're a brave woman, you can do this. And no battle sylph would ever hurt you. They love women."

She flushed red, obviously remembering the night before, and looked away. Devon leaned in and kissed her cheek. "I believe in you," he told her.

The look Zalia gave him at that was one of amazement.

Battle sylph! Airi suddenly warned.

Devon tightened his grip on Zalia's hands, tugging her with him deeper into the alley, which ended at a door into someone's dwelling. It was already broken open from the outside and they hid in a small room scattered with sand. The battle sylphs didn't have to see Zalia to recognize her as a woman. They could feel her pattern from a distance, though he hoped not so easily through walls. As Devon peeked out the door, his heart pounding with near panic, Airi wrapped her own pattern around Zalia, flaring it up. It made her more obvious to the battlers, but with any luck, they'd choose to continue ignoring a young, foreign air sylph.

As he looked down the alley, he saw a man run along the street it branched off. He was only visible for an instant as he ran past, but that was more than enough time for Devon's frightened mind to remember him, as well as the pregnant woman he towed by the hand behind him. He saw her hand cupping her swollen belly, her hair streaming behind her. Before he could do more than acknowledge that he saw them, a black cloud flecked by lightning flowed past, following them, and his gut clenched with sudden terror, his bladder threatening to empty itself. A horrified second later, he heard a scream of terror, followed by a wail of loss. The battler reappeared again, already gaining altitude as he carried his unwilling cargo away. Worst of all, the man reappeared only seconds after he passed, chasing them, his arms outstretched in a pleading gesture as that horrible sound continued to issue from his throat.

Devon? Airi whimpered.

Devon turned toward them both, his arms going around both sylph and woman while he tried to push the memory away. The pain in that man's voice . . . and there was nothing he could do. Nothing except hold on even tighter to the woman before him and know that if the battlers found her, there was nothing he could do about it at all.

"Devon?" Zalia whispered against his ear, her voice frightened.

Are you all right, Devon? Airi asked.

Right at that moment, he wasn't sure he'd ever be all right again. "Let's keep moving," he said at last.

They did, traveling slowly across the city, following back routes Zalia knew that were once used by the lower classes so they didn't have to be seen by their betters. There was a risk to using them. They hadn't been abandoned, being too twisty for most of the sand to fill and familiar to the majority of the men and women who were left, but there were a lot of nooks and corners that the main roads didn't have where they could hide from battle sylphs. The farther they traveled, the more obvious it became that those hiding places and Airi's efforts were the only reasons they weren't found, and increasing numbers of battlers rose up over the buildings and returned to the hive with men's voices following in outrage.

"There probably won't be any women left at the hovels when we get there," Zalia commented.

"No, but there will be men and they won't know what's happening." They'd warned as many men as they could, not that they were sure they were wholly believed. Still, it wasn't as hard to convince anyone that there was an invisible predator among them as Devon would have expected. Despite how ludicrous it sounded, a lot of the men believed them anyway, perhaps because they were superstitious by nature, maybe due to the fact that they needed to have a reason for what was happening, and an explanation for all the blood they'd seen. They were cowed by the storm that ravaged the city, something that was never allowed before, and Zalia wasn't the only one to realize that the food they needed was likely gone as well. The existence of the Hunter was just one more thing to deal with in a world filled with events they'd always believed to be impossible.

"Where are we supposed to go?" one man asked, standing with

his three boys, all of whom were weeping for their mother. "What's a safe place for us?"

"I don't know," Devon admitted. If every single man in the city went to the entrance to the sylph hive, the battlers still wouldn't let them in. "Just keep spreading the warning."

"Warnings won't be enough," the man groused. "Someone better think of a place to go. For me, we're going to the place what's got our women. Come on, boys." He left with them.

That was the final response of most of them, even those who believed. Whether they believed or not, all they could really deal with was the fact that the battle sylphs were stealing their women and their food, and most of the men were moving toward the hive, for whatever good it would do them.

Devon just hoped doing so wouldn't turn them into a target for the Hunter. The thought that it could be anywhere made his skin crawl. They didn't even know anything about it yet, other than that it killed. That was all Airi knew of the things. Hunters came and they killed and that killing drove battlers mad. Devon could believe that. For a creature designed to take direct action, an enemy such as the Hunter must be unbearable.

All the three of them could do was continue on, spreading their warning, and hope they didn't stumble across the thing themselves, even as they continued to pass the blood it left behind. Devon found he kept straining his eyes for any sight of it and suspected Zalia was doing the same. The sun played havoc with his vision though. The day was growing blisteringly hot and bright, making him squint constantly, and all the dust in the air was being twisted by the inconstant wind into bizarre shapes that his mind kept recognizing, just as it would clouds overhead. He saw a nightmarish two-legged cow, a giant with a narrow club over its shoulder, a flat-based ball with a hundred strings hanging from its underside, a massive puppy gamboling; all barely visible, all gone if he looked away at something else. Sweat that had nothing to do with the heat trickled down between his shoulder blades and he gripped Zalia's hand tightly, despite how warm it was. She didn't seem to mind; her grip was just as tight.

Thanks to their need to keep hiding, it took much longer than their original trip in before they reached the edge of the city. The number of women was already dropping hugely; with seven hundred battle sylphs who could pick up a dozen or more women each, it didn't take long to gather them. Not seeing any women left the sand-filled streets feeling morose and lifeless, except for the anger and confusion of the men who were left. Worse, the hotter the day became, the less any of them were willing to listen to Devon's warnings. Zalia's friends, he hoped, would. This was starting to feel as if it were a race, one where the goal was to save even one person from the Hunter, and unlike the battlers, Devon refused to define personhood by gender.

They paused for a long moment at the edge of the buildings, looking over the sandy expanse that led into the desert itself. The broken wall he'd seen before was now completely buried and many of the hovels were gone, taken by the wind. Those that remained were even more lopsided and half-buried as well. He still saw people, struggling to dig their pathetic little homes out of the sand.

He didn't see any women at all.

"They've already been here," Zalia mourned.

Devon gently squeezed her hand. "Your friends are safe," he reminded her. "No matter how crazy all of this is, remember they're in the safest place left. We just have to get the rest of these people to safety too." He'd been thinking about that. Ideally, they'd go to the hive. If all of the women demanded it at once, surely the battlers would let the men in. If their masters ordered them, they'd have to. So it was a matter of convincing the masters to order it. The only problem was, a lot of the battler masters were former harem slaves who likely didn't think highly of the average citizen of Meridal. This could get ugly very fast if half agreed and the other half decided the men were cutting into their limited food supplies. There might end up being a civil war in the hive over who was good enough to save.

If only the queen would get involved . . .

Standing in the questionable shade of a building, Devon thought to himself that there was only one place he could think of to evacuate the men, short of getting them to drop everything and travel without food or water to the next city, which would be a death sentence. The only place even close to resembling the hive for the thickness of its walls was the underground complex that led to the gate room they'd been in before. It once held thousands of feeders, and even with the tiers of cages that were destroyed, there was room for everyone there, if not comfortably. The Hunter came from there, but they could block the entrance and it was hundreds of feet underground. Now that he thought about it, not even the walls of the hive were so thick. To survive, they'd just have to find a source of water and collect enough of the food left before the battlers took it all. The men of Meridal would need to work together to manage it and Devon quailed at the thought of what kind of organizational and leadership skills this would take. More than horrified, he shared his epiphany with his air sylph.

Can we do this? Airi asked.

Could we live with ourselves if we didn't even try? he silently replied, realizing as he did that it truly was that simple. Knowing didn't stop his fear, but it did temper it with certainty. Leon would have been proud. Airi just sighed and he felt her press against his back and neck, lending her support.

Squeezing Zalia's hand, he walked with her out onto the sand to see if they could start with these people in working toward their own survival.

~

The winds were light once the storm passed. Well fed by everything in the stable, the Hunter floated along above the city, its tentacles grazing the ground. It watched the battlers gathering the breeding members of the local population, but they left a great deal of food for it and so it did nothing to stop them. Not particularly hungry or wanting to risk rising too high, it wandered along the periphery of the city itself, learning the layout and tugging itself along by grasping buildings with its tendrils. It tried not to cause too much damage to them; it wouldn't do to have the battle sylphs or the food notice.

The local food wasn't like the sylphs in many ways. The sylphs it could understand, hearing their mental voices quite easily and using that against them. The humans didn't have mental voices for it to listen to. If they thought about something strongly, it could sort of pick it up, but its information about this world so far came from the sylphs. It was good enough. The human food creatures were as easy to devour as anything else, even if they did seem more aware of its existence than a sylph. That was the only alarming factor about this new hunting ground. Its greatest weapon was its invisibility and if a human saw it and told a battle sylph, they could end it. Its tentacles were largely indestructible and easily replaced, but its actual body? If the humans pointed it out, the battlers *would* end it.

It became obvious pretty quickly that wasn't going to happen. The food in the stable clearly saw it, but no matter how the human screamed, no battle sylph had come through the storm for him. They ignored the food because it was male, it realized. It wasn't hard to do so. It would have been able to figure that out even if it didn't hear the battlers talk about only saving the females.

So it let them. It could distinguish between male and female patterns, so whenever it came across one during the day, with increasing rareness, the Hunter lifted its tendrils high and let them pass. Any male with them it also let pass. Soon enough, the battlers would gather them all together and then it could feed on the males left behind with impunity, for even if they managed to actually see it and realize what it was in time to react before it devoured them, the battlers would ignore their cries, at least until it occurred to them to use the humans to find it. Meanwhile, the males were gathering together into a single place, where feeding once the females were gone would be easy. It could graze for days or possibly even weeks before the food supply vanished, as long as it was careful to resist the urge to glut. Then, it could break into the hive and gorge on the females and sylphs the battlers thought they'd saved, afterward letting the winds carry it where they would in the hope they took it to more food.

Ten-foot-thick walls weren't something it could pull apart with just its own strength, but its kind was intelligent and it knew there were a great many ways to crack open an egg.

∽

The men of the hovels, all of them surviving by sharing their fires and their food, were understandably shocked. The battle sylphs had swept down on them only hours before, taking every female from infancy to old age. Left behind, the men and boys hadn't known what to do, and like so many others in the city, they'd been working themselves into a froth of useless anger over it when Devon and Zalia arrived.

The appearance of a woman after they'd lost so many—as well as being a woman they knew—had more of an effect on them than it did on the other men they'd passed. Devon suspected that in a day or more, Zalia would draw the attention of every man who saw her, which wouldn't necessarily be safe. These men were family though and they greeted her warmly.

"Zalia, dear Zalia!" one old man exclaimed, hugging her tightly. He was so thin Devon had to hide a wince, imagining his own elderly father that poor and gaunt. "We never expected to see you or your father again. Where is he?"

"My father is safe," she promised, hugging him chastely for a moment before she stepped back and looked at them all. "Please, all of you have to listen to us. Everyone's in great danger." They looked at her worriedly and she turned to Devon, suddenly too shy to speak.

Devon took a deep breath and started to talk. He told them about the Hunter, about the damage it did in the feeder pens and the harbor, and how it was invisible, with only pools of blood from its victims left behind. He told them about the creation of the hive and the battle sylphs' efforts to save what they considered the city's most important resource.

"So there's no room for any of us in this hive of theirs?" the old man who'd hugged Zalia asked.

"No, sir," Devon told them and they murmured fearfully among themselves. "We can try to convince them to let us in, but that will have to come from within, not from us standing outside shouting about how unfair it is." He looked at Zalia. "We need to assume that they aren't going to let us in, no matter how much we hope that changes. We need to go somewhere else."

"Where?" a younger man asked. He looked nervous, and as if he very badly wanted someone to tell him what to do. Devon knew just how he felt.

"We'll go to the place where they used to keep the feeders and concubines," Devon told them. "It's underground and big enough for everyone. We need to spread out and gather as many people as we can convince to come, and more, all of us need to get as much food and water as possible before the battle sylphs find it all. It's the only chance we have. If we don't, we'll either get eaten by the Hunter or starve to death."

There was more murmuring. "You said the thing came out of the gate under the feeder pens," the young man pointed out.

"I know," Devon admitted. He didn't like that little bit of reality either. "But the gate's closed now and at least in there, it only has one direction to come at us from and we can block the entrance. I think this is the only chance we have."

The men looked at each other uncertainly. Devon knew he was no great speaker, but in the end they agreed, because they had no other choice. Each of them would spread out, talk to as many other people as they could—who he hoped would have heard about the Hunter from the men Devon already talked to—and bring as much food and water as they could to the tunnels. If all went well, they'd be able to move from those tunnels to the hive itself before too much time passed.

As they headed out, bringing with them more food than Devon would have thought existed in the ramshackle little settlement, Zalia looked at him. "I wasn't sure you'd be able to convince them," she said. "Not to go to the feeder pens. They've always been considered foul by my people."

He shrugged. "They want to live." He reached out to take both her hands in his own again. It felt so nice to touch her and he didn't want to let her go. In fact, he wanted to run his hands up her arms to her face, and feel those soft lips and delicate cheekbones. "I've been thinking. Once we're set up in the tunnels, I think you're going to have to go back to the hive. You're the only one with a chance of convincing them to let us in." If he could come up with a way to get her there that wouldn't leave her exposed to the Hunter.

She bit her lip. "I can't imagine anyone listening to me."

He lifted one hand to cup her cheek. It was just as soft as he'd been hoping. "I can't imagine anyone ignoring you. You'll have those gates open while we're still trying to figure out who sleeps where in the tunnels."

Zalia shook her head, her eyes damp, and turned, pulling him to the hovel she'd shared with her father. Miraculously, it was still standing, its roof decidedly thinner and more battered than before. Devon wasn't quite able to let himself think about what she wanted him in there for, until she dropped to her knees in one corner and dug into the sand, uncovering a package wrapped in oilcloth. Unwrapping it, she exposed a box of dried fruits and meats, as well as a round, hard cheese.

"Here," she said, offering it to him. "You'll need this."

Devon lowered to his own knees beside her. "I don't want to take you and your father's food."

"Take it. You need it and I don't want the battlers to sniff it out."

She held it out to him again, and this time Devon took it, his hands closing over her own around the box. Zalia looked down at them for a moment and then up at him, and Devon's breath caught at the look of love in her eyes.

CHAPTER SIXTEEN

Zalia found all of her petty insecurities burned away by the stress of the day. Given the danger everyone faced, the hundreds who could starve or be devoured, her emotions over losing her virginity seemed pretty pointless. Something had to be done, and she was with the man who was actually doing it. Devon Chole made her notice him from the first moment she saw him. Now he made her want to shiver, and he *included* her. Her opinion mattered, her help was invaluable, and he needed her. She was terrified of what she had to do, but the desire she felt was stronger than her fear.

They could die, she thought as she leaned over the box of food toward him. They could die so very easily and she wanted to be alive instead, with him, by choice, and know that whatever she felt with him came from within her.

Devon blinked at her as she leaned toward him, his hair ruffling madly for the first instant, and Zalia saw a flash of Airi's gleeful face over his shoulder before the air sylph fled. Then Zalia was kissing him.

Devon's mouth was warm and dry, his lips chapped. He gasped in surprise and she deepened the kiss, moving her mouth gently against his own. A moment later, he got over his shock and grabbed her, yanking her forcefully against him. The box of food got between them for a moment and she shoved it out of the way before wrapping her arms around his neck.

Even inside the hut, it was the hottest part of the day and his body burned against her, but somehow it wasn't hot enough and she wanted more. She pressed her breasts and belly against his chest, and the pressure on her nipples was heavenly.

"Devon," she whispered, not sure what she wanted to say but liking the sound of his name on her tongue.

He didn't say anything in return, but his grip tightened around her, his hands working under the edge of her dress and pulling it up. She let him, lifting her arms above her head to make it easier for him to slip the shapeless thing off. For a moment he only looked at her, making her blush, but his eyes were wide with wonder at what he saw and when he lifted his gaze up to hers, her desire only burned hotter.

He stripped off his shirt and they reached for each other again, he dressed only in his pants and sandals, her only in the undergarment that was tied around her waist. His skin was far hotter bare and so pale, unlike anything she'd ever seen before. Her own skin stood out in marked contrast against it as she laid her hand on his chest and he covered it with his own before kissing her again. It didn't seem there could ever be enough kissing.

Still kneeling in the gathered sand, they were pressed together as close as they could, her nipples hard against his chest, his length harder against her belly. She wanted him, didn't think she'd ever wanted anything so much, and there was none of the overwhelming lust that One-Eleven filled her with. Just love, and desire, and trust.

"You're so beautiful," Devon whispered, his kisses moving to her ear as his hand stroked lightly down her ribs to the ties of her undergarment, which he tried to untie.

"No, I'm not," she said, reaching down to help him with that knot before moving her own hands over to undo the buttons of his trousers. She'd never felt so daring or in control.

His eyes opened, a rich shade of brown she'd never seen before she met him. "Yes, you are. Don't ever fool yourself into thinking that you aren't." He pushed her loosened undergarment down over her hips and sighed, his fingers caressing the curve of her buttocks. She sighed as well, sure he was wrong but not willing to argue it with him right now. Besides, at this moment she felt very beautiful indeed.

They lay together on the sand, kicking the rest of their undergarments off and never taking their gazes off each other, hands caressing each other's faces and throats, moving down the other's body to find the spots they liked.

"Devon," she whispered, "please make love to me."

"Yes," he breathed. He shifted his hips closer, his rough worker's hand stroking her hip and around it, encouraging her to lift her leg before he brought his hand back around and across her damp heat. Zalia cried out as he touched that soft, burning part of her, her stomach clenching and pleasure radiating outward through her. He kissed her then, swallowing the end of her cry, and angled himself, letting her feel the rounded head of his length before he held her hip more firmly and used it as leverage to push himself inside.

She cried out again, though this time there was no pain. Devon filled her, wonderfully, completely. He pulled out before pushing forward and deep inside her again. The length of him inside her felt as if it were the softest satin encasing the hardest steel, and she tentatively moved her own hips in counterpart to his own. She met each thrust, backed away from each sliding retreat, her own efforts taking him deeper than she could have imagined he would go, deep into a part of her that burned for more.

"Zalia," he whispered again.

He rolled over onto his back, pulling Zalia up to kneel over him, her thighs straddling his hips. For a moment she felt exposed, her entire body wantonly displayed for him, but there was so much love in his eyes that her momentary fear didn't last and her back arched in pleasure instead, her breasts jutting outward as her head tilted back, her hair trailing over his thighs as his slow thrusts reached even deeper into her, right against the part that burned the hottest, so deep within her she'd never known it existed before.

She flexed her hips, riding him there on the sand, and he reached up to caress her breasts, sending shocks of pleasure deep inside to where he strained to reach. Zalia cried out, the pleasure surging within her, and worked her thighs to ride him faster, wanting more, wanting this joy to keep increasing, even as it formed a knot inside her that begged to be released.

Below her, Devon gritted his teeth, his face twisted with pleasure. He squeezed her breasts and moved his hands to her hips, helping her to rise and drop, rise and drop, and force the storm within her to grow even more. Streamers of sweat were dripping off both of them and she didn't care, didn't care about anything but this joy that was building out of control and how she wanted to share it with him.

The pace increased. Devon had his feet braced against the ground now, lifting his hips and pumping them against her as hard as he could. She had her hands flat against his belly as well, pushing against him in counterpoint rhythm and the pleasure was so great it was almost pain. She whimpered endlessly and the sound of it made him groan in need, loving her even faster.

"I feel . . ." she gasped. "I feel you so deeply in me. It's overwhelming!"

"Let it overwhelm you," he managed. "Zalia, I love you so much!"

"I love you!" she cried and the pleasure became too much. It rose and crested and abruptly exploded throughout her, turning her voice into a shriek as every muscle in her body tightened, vibrating with utter joy. Devon cried out and she felt him stiffen as well, pushing up into her one last time and freezing in place, the length of him pulsing through her and sending her into another tumult of sheer ecstasy. A moment later, he collapsed back down again and she fell onto him, gasping against his shoulder while she listened to his deep breaths.

It took a long few minutes to get their breath back as they lay there, still entwined. Finally, Zalia lifted her head and looked at Devon, not knowing what to say to him but not regretting what they'd done. She felt alive and no matter what came later, she couldn't regret it.

He looked at her evenly, reaching up one hand to cup her cheek. "When this is over," he whispered to her, "will you be my wife?"

How could she be anything else? Zalia's eyes filled with tears. "Yes," she promised.

~

One-Eleven was starving and exhausted when he got back to the hive. He'd spent hours fighting his way through the storm, rescuing woman after woman, along with gathering all the food he could find. By the time the storm died and dawn came, he was close to shaking, but there was still so much to do. The women were frightened and hiding, running when they didn't need to, and it took until well past midday before the flight could be sure they found them all.

The only thing he wanted to do was go to Zalia and take her to the queen, have her made his master so he could lose himself in her. He was so tired though that he wasn't sure he had the strength to actually lift her that high, so he had to wait a little longer.

He carried his last rescued woman to the hive, bunching in the tight tunnel with several other battlers, and set her down in the great crowd that was gathered in the square just inside. There were a great deal of men just on the other side, not that he noticed them shouting, or noticed that many of them were starting to move away, following a call to their own safety. One-Eleven didn't really care.

The only males not of his hive line that he'd deal with at all were the ones he looked for now, leaving the woman behind with a loving pat on the head while he listened absently to the conversations of the battlers around him.

There'd been no sign of the Hunter during the storm, he heard. A few of them hoped that it was killed by the high winds and wouldn't bother them again.

Do you think that's likely? one of them asked.

Don't be stupid, another retorted. *It's still around. I saw some men shouting this morning about their friends vanishing.*

Did they see where it was? someone else asked excitedly.

No, unfortunately. They just knew the other men were supposed to be behind them and then they were gone. There was blood, they said. I've seen a lot of blood in the streets today.

One-Eleven didn't join in the conversation; spoken as it was down the hive lines, he didn't have to be with anyone to hear them talk and he continued on his way, following his instincts to where a certain group of men waited. Not that they'd moved much from where he'd left them.

I think the males have figured out what's going on. I saw them gathering.

Gathering? Gathering for what?

That pale man with the foreign sylph. He has them gathering in the feeder tunnels. It's the same idea as our hive, I guess.

He managed to convince them?

Well, I guess even men aren't so stupid that they won't notice their own kind getting eaten all around them.

One-Eleven dived down, headed for a small building well past the square where the masters had been dancing, near the far edge of the hive wall. He really should have made them move closer, he thought.

How much food have we gathered? Tooie asked over them all and a chorus of unsure answers came back. *Is it enough for everyone?* he pressed.

I don't know, someone admitted. *For a while. I don't know how long.*

We need to make the food last as long as we can. We have to reduce the number of people eating it.

There were shouts of protest at that, One-Eleven joining in as he swept through a window he'd broken before and into the building. In one of the inner rooms, five gaunt men sat in silence, their faces pinched and eyes stressed by old horrors. None of them reacted to his arrival, which was good. At least they still didn't have their tongues and couldn't give him orders. It was bad enough to be bound to the pathetic creatures in the first place, though that would change soon enough when Zalia was his master. Then he could see these ones killed.

A thought occurred to him. *How about we toss out all the men?* he sent along the hive lines to his fellow battlers.

There was some immediate agreement, but a lot of uncertainty at that. *Most of them are masters,* Tooie argued. *They're needed to feed us.*

So? It was the most brilliant idea One-Eleven ever had. *We just brought in thousands of women. Bind them to all the sylphs who have male masters. Throw the men outside for the Hunter and the women left in here will have enough food, as well as sylphs to love, even if they can't all have battlers.* Some would have to go to the elemental sylphs, he guessed. It wasn't the best solution, but it was better than having men around.

The roar of approval was immediate and One-Eleven beamed in their response. It really was a brilliant idea and after long moments of arguing that One-Eleven certainly didn't understand, Tooie was forced to go along with it.

～

Haru listened to his brothers plan their future without participating. He really hadn't spoken much since Fareeda was freed. She didn't have any need to speak, so he didn't feel any real urge to.

The urges he did have were a lot more direct. Standing at the window to the suite he'd taken, he looked out at his brothers swirling over the buildings in the hive, already zeroing in on the men below, and turned back to the wide bed behind him. Fareeda was asleep, her thin, gray hair spread out over the pillow.

She was weak and frail and beyond mad from abuse, but he didn't see her that way. He saw only the young woman he'd known and loved so long ago, and the pattern through her that resonated so deeply within him. It was as delicate and gossamer as a spiderweb, but so achingly beautiful as well. She needed special care and the best protection he could provide her.

He looked back out the window again, thinking over all the things he'd heard his brothers say. He hadn't gone out with them, but their descriptions were buoyed by visual images and he could see what they'd seen in the city as clearly as if he'd been there.

He bit the perfect lip he'd formed for Fareeda's appreciation, thinking. This was a queenless hive, hard to imagine but true. There was no leader here who could truly guide them, no one who would. The other battlers cheered about victories and selections, and how the hive was going to thrive.

All he saw was it falling apart.

Haru thought some more, dwelling on things he truly didn't like. This place felt safer than that target of a floating palace, but not by much, and not for much longer. Not with the internal hatred he saw coming. Not without a leader who actually took charge. The queen had told him to do what he thought was right, even if that included abandoning her. Perhaps it meant abandoning everyone else as well. He took a deep breath and looked at Fareeda. He'd promised her she'd always be safe. As safe as he could make her.

Haru crossed the room and gathered her up, blankets and all, the old woman barely stirring as he cradled her against his chest and carried her out of the room. With everything he knew and felt and heard, Haru believed there was only one place in Meridal right now where she would be safe.

∼

One-Eleven fed just enough from his quintet of masters to make himself feel flush again, and then he snatched them all up and carried them inside his cloud body to the square outside the hive. There he dumped them on the cobblestones, feeling a great weight lift off of him as he did so. Around him, other battlers did the same, tossing men out to join the crowds gathered there. One-Eleven didn't much care how loudly they shouted or what they said, though he did notice they were starting to withdraw from the rear, men yelling at the others to come with them, that there was somewhere safe. They'd be killed if they stayed.

He supposed they would. One-Eleven looked around at the crowds, thinking of a new idea. Apparently, the prospect of having a female master made him clever. He had to be, he thought. Strength alone wouldn't be enough to protect Zalia.

He flew upward, abandoning the men who'd fed him for so long as he searched out Tooie. He found him farther across the square, watching sadly while two battlers peeled a water sylph away from a scrawny, frightened-looking man. One-Eleven ignored her misplaced loyalty as he looked at the lead battler.

I have an idea, he told him.

Another idea? Tooie asked flatly. One-Eleven still preened at the recognition.

Watch the men here, One-Eleven suggested. *When the Hunter starts eating them, we can target it.*

Tooie turned toward him, his great, swirling lightning eyes regarding the older battle sylph. It was a bit strange to have the lead battler be younger than so many of them, but that was the queen's choice and it did make it so much easier to bully him into doing what the rest of them knew was right. *What?* Tooie said.

Other battlers nearby heard them and converged, the lightning flickering wildly inside them.

That's a great idea!

Do you think it'll come after them today? We could kill it today if it did.

Brilliant!

Their adulation washed over One-Eleven and the lightning in him increased in happiness. This was going so well. Years of inferiority were washing away from him and he knew it was because of Zalia. He never could have conceived of any of this if he hadn't known she was safe in the hive, waiting for him. A sudden, sobering thought occurred to him and he hoped Tooie wouldn't put him on guard duty today. He still needed to go back to her and take her to the queen.

Tooie, however, hadn't seemed to quite embrace the idea. He spun in place, trying to see the battlers who crowded around him, all of them clamoring excitedly. Everyone agreed with the idea of using the human men as bait to protect the women and the hive. One-Eleven really didn't understand how Tooie could resist that much pressure without a queen to support him, but for a surprisingly long time, he did.

~

Only a few blocks over, the Hunter listened to the battlers' plan. It hovered next to a building with its tendrils hanging in an alleyway used infrequently enough that only a few men wandered into its grasp. That was a good thing for now. They'd been noticing their fellows vanishing, sometimes from only dozens of feet away from them, and it could sense their terror, if not understand their words.

It could feel their anger as well, at the stealing of their females. The Hunter didn't really care about that, having its own plans for breaking into the hive, but it did care about this sudden idea of using bait. It had hoped they wouldn't think of that. The battlers couldn't see it, but they could figure out where it was if they saw its food eaten, and they could manage enough firepower to eliminate all of its tentacles if it wasn't careful. Worse, a truly lucky shot could eliminate *it*.

It looked at the men milling around the square. It wouldn't eat that great a concentration of food all at once, even if there weren't battle sylphs spreading out to watch for it. To do that would just make it rise and give it to the winds, which it didn't want. It was better to graze from the edges as it had always done, to eat them slowly and only glut on the hive when it was time to trust to the winds and go.

It watched the men starting to leave, not understanding what compelled them, but pleased to see it. If they traveled away from the hive, they would be easier to hunt, and if they spread out, they were less likely to even realize they were being hunted.

The Hunter looked toward the battlers, not concerned about them, and turned away, wandering off through the streets and going unnoticed as it picked up a man here, and there, and there . . .

CHAPTER SEVENTEEN

Feeling very much as though he didn't belong there and that everyone had to be staring at him—which of course, they were and he needed them to be—Devon stood on top of a crate next to the small, domed entrance to the underground complex and tried not to sound like an idiot while Airi did something with the air to make his voice project.

"I know none of you have any real reason to trust me," he said to them, sweating at the murmurs of agreement while hundreds of men glared at him, all of them angry and frustrated. "I can understand that. But whether any of us like it or not, what I'm telling you is the truth. The sylphs accidentally released some kind of predator into the city that they can't kill. That's why the battlers are taking all the women. They want to keep them safe, but they don't care if every last one of us mere menfolk gets killed."

"And you do?" one man shouted from the front ranks. He kept glaring at Zalia, who stood by Devon's feet.

"None of us want to be eaten," Devon raised his fists over the crowds, "and I don't want the battlers thinking that we're just going to die for their convenience!" A new murmuring started at that. "We can be safe in there," he shouted, pointing at the entrance to the pens. "The sylphs built a dome? We don't need them. We can go underground."

"You've got no proof there's a danger!" someone else shouted.

That started a roar of protest, some in agreement with the man, most—to Devon's relief—not.

"You're blind! You've seen the battlers take the women!"

"I saw a dozen people vanish from behind me," another shouted. "Fifty feet back they were and when I turned around they were gone. There was blood everywhere. I ran for my life!"

"I saw buildings pulled apart and that wasn't no battler who did it!"

"Every three or four streets, there's blood!"

I guess they don't need much convincing, Airi said.

No, Devon mused. They didn't. The whole city had an air of something wrong to it, and even in the short time he'd been here, he'd seen it. How much more obvious must it be to men who'd lived here their entire lives? Just standing here, he felt an itch between his shoulder blades and kept wondering if the men before him would start disappearing, or the buildings tear apart.

His mouth felt dry. "Get into the tunnels," he shouted anyway. "Bring as much food and water as you can find. Hurry!"

Men started moving, most of them carrying whatever food they still had, having brought it out of hiding like Zalia did once the battlers passed. Devon had no idea if it would be enough, and rather doubted it would, but that would have to wait. For now, they needed to get underground and hope the feeder pens would be deep enough without sylphs to seal the way in. He was sure there were a thousand logistical problems he wasn't thinking of, but he could only do one thing at a time.

"There are a lot of men still at that sylph hive," one old man pointed out to him as he passed, carrying a crate filled with live chickens. He looked withered and tired, his expression resigned at yet another disaster to deal with.

"I know," Devon assured him, clapping the man on the shoulder and urging him on toward the entrance. Getting in was slow going through such a small door, but no one was fighting yet. If the Hunter attacked, there'd be a panic and no one would survive.

He looked at Zalia, standing loyally at his side. "You should go inside."

She looked at him nervously. "I'm not leaving you."

"Zalia," he protested, much as he liked having her there. She made him feel good, but he didn't want her in danger just to make him feel better. She needed to go back to the hive and try to negotiate a truce with the battlers, before they decided to continue the insanity by doing something like breaking into the feeder pens and taking whatever food they did have, but he wouldn't send her until he found a way to do so that was safe. Despite how it was likely the best way, if not the only one, he couldn't bring himself to want a battle sylph to snatch her up and take her back. Besides, they seemed to feel they were done capturing all the women. None of the men had seen any for a while now.

She shook her head, her lips pressed together. "I'm the only woman here. It wouldn't be safe."

Devon hesitated, but only for a moment. Of course it wasn't safe. This wasn't the Valley. These men were frightened and angry, some could end up being violent, and any battler who came to her rescue would just drag her back to the hive. Even worse, if the battler was in a bad enough mood, he might decide to take out his anger on all of them.

"Okay," he agreed, reaching down to squeeze her hand, remembering again their intimacy with a warmth that was so much nicer than the heat of the day.

The men continued to file past, young, old, many of them bringing male children or infants with them. All of them looked frightened and as eager to get under cover as Devon. They kept looking over their shoulders at the clear sky and the spot between Devon's shoulder blades continued to itch.

I want to go underground, Airi whimpered.

"I know," he murmured, hopping down off the crate to Zalia's side when she looked inquiringly at him. He felt the same way.

Still, he stood there with Zalia and Airi, letting the men shuffle past. Maybe he was just deluding himself, but Devon felt that if he stayed there, everyone would see him and stay calm themselves. People need to see that someone is in charge when they're uncertain, Leon had told him. Devon didn't think he could be anything like Leon, but he could fake it, at least for now. He wasn't sure how he was supposed to keep them from panicking if they were attacked though. The best he could hope for was to keep them moving and pray it didn't happen.

He also stayed to take a mental tally of the amount of food coming in. There were a lot of men who didn't have anything and those who did didn't have nearly enough. Not to feed so many for long.

Devon looked toward the hive that loomed over the rest of the city, his mind churning away despite his rather honest desire for it to just stop. He had hundreds of men filing past him right now, all of them as safe as he could make them, but who knew how many men were still outside the hive, too angry to listen to the word spreading about the Hunter, or expecting they would be granted a place in the hive if they waited long enough.

Leaving them there would make it a lot more likely the rest of them would survive, he thought. There wasn't enough food for these men, let alone so many more. The battle sylphs had taken too much. It made sense to save only those he could, instead of risking mass starvation.

The only problem with that idea was that it was battler logic and Devon wouldn't do it. *Couldn't* do it. Devon closed his eyes and took a deep breath, slowly letting it out again.

"What is it?" Zalia asked. "Are we going inside now?"

Devon felt that same horrendous itching between his shoulder blades that screamed he was nothing but a target and an easy meal out here—he and both the females he loved the most. He hadn't wanted Zalia to go back with the battler to the hive, not with the risk of the creature stumbling right into the Hunter. He hadn't wanted to stay aboveground for the exact same reason. The way back was nothing more than a gauntlet now, filled with the blood of the dead and only an idiot or the truly desperate would risk it.

"No," he said at last, feeling Airi press against him while he looked into Zalia's wide black eyes. "We have something we need to do first."

~

One-Eleven floated over the crowds in weary contentment. The females were safe in the hive, if still a little upset about it, and the men were gone. It was just sylphs and women now, as it should be.

And camels, he thought to himself, passing a nervous-looking herd. He could hear goats as well, bleating somewhere among the stacks of food they'd liberated. Earth and air sylphs were working to sort the foodstuffs and take them to storage, and crates flew through the air or flowed along the ground as they were carried to their destinations.

He circled the women again, moving around and through his brothers. The women were upset and yelling to be let out, but they didn't really understand the situation. They'd calm down eventually, and of course, they'd be let out, once the Hunter was gone.

That was really the only part of this that bothered him. Every instinct he had said to kill the Hunter, but they couldn't find it. The only thing the elementals said they could do was wait for it to get hungry and leave in search of more food. It wasn't fair. He wanted to destroy it.

Maybe he should suggest killing all the men outside the hive, One-Eleven mused. Then the Hunter would leave sooner.

Yahe swept down beside him, his pattern tight with anticipation. *Tooie says you can go. Me, I'm heading straight to Kiala. It's been days since I've seen her. She's furious right now.*

Really? One-Eleven squealed. That meant he could go to Zalia, and once she was his master, he'd be able to feel her emotions like Yahe could Kiala, no matter how far apart they were. Even feeling her anger would be a gift.

Really, Yahe told him and flitted away, headed for the exit he'd need to get to his master. Other battlers were dispersing as well, though an unlucky few stayed hovering over the women, watching to make sure none of them were hurt or tried to do anything silly, such as leaving.

One-Eleven darted toward the apartment where he'd left Zalia, eager for her company and warmth. He'd hated to leave her so soon after he'd made love to her, but duty was inviolate. He'd spend as much time as he could with her now, and given a choice, he'd never leave her again.

He swept down to the apartment and in through the open window. As his pattern wasn't tied to hers yet, he didn't realize that Zalia wasn't there until he was in the room and didn't see her.

One-Eleven skidded to a halt, lightning flickering through him in confusion as he floated there and looked around. The bed was made and her clothes were gone. Uncertain, he moved forward, looking into the other room of the apartment and shifting to his human form to call her. "Zalia?" There was no answer, and somehow, the place felt abandoned. It made him nervous. "Zalia!"

Where would she go? Was she looking for him? One-Eleven turned and ran for the window, diving out and changing to a cloud as he did. The crowds at the gate. She must have gone to join them. Humans liked being around other humans, didn't they? She must have wanted company after her father was ejected from the hive.

She wasn't going to be mad at him about that, was she?

One-Eleven raced back to the exit, reviewing his memory of her pattern. He couldn't track her over distances yet, but he could certainly pick her out of a group if he was close enough, even if he couldn't see her. It would make searching the crowd easier.

He arrived only a minute later, swooping over the women while they ducked and screamed.

Hey! one of the battlers left to watch them shouted. *Don't scare them!*

Sorry, One-Eleven muttered, searching through the women with his vision and his senses, looking for Zalia's specific pattern. He'd learned it when he first saw her and becoming intimate with her only made him know it more thoroughly. There was no way it could be hidden from him, and she wasn't there.

With a flash of near panic that made the guarding battlers rumble, he turned and rushed back to the apartment, hoping he'd just missed her. He crashed through it, careless in his worry, but found nothing. Flitting out the window, he raced to the fountain that provided most of the drinking water, thinking she must be there. A lot of women were, most of them ex-concubines who were content to be in the hive, but Zalia had never been a concubine and they wouldn't have known her if she passed. Nor would the sylphs waiting there, since she didn't have One-Eleven's pattern in her.

Has anyone seen a woman named Zalia? he wailed, really starting to get frightened as he raced through the hive, heading for where the food was being stored and the kitchens set up. Nothing. He raced back along the outer wall, searching. *She's a beautiful woman. Has anyone seen her? I can't find her!*

Battlers swooped around him, drawn by his distress and the fear of a threat to a woman. *Where did you see her last?* one asked.

At the apartment where she'd been sleeping, he wailed. *Before the storm. We'd just made love.*

The battlers groaned, feeling his pain and fear. If Zalia had been harmed due to his inattention, he'd destroy whatever hurt her and then never forgive himself. He should have made her his master first, so that he'd have known she was in trouble. Had she been calling for him without any way for him to answer? The thought was horrible. His brothers started shouting to their hive mates, calling the battlers and even the elementals into the search. Only minutes later, he heard the call.

Come to the exit.

I was just there! he wailed, even as he raced there, skirting over buildings and around corners in his haste. She must have gone to the privy, she must have left for just a minute; when he found her he'd never let her go.

He raced back into the square, the women still milling around though they were mostly crying now instead of trying to get the old earth sylph at the closed wall to let them out. Half a dozen battlers floated before the gatekeeper and she nervously lifted her eyeless head toward One-Eleven.

Where is she? he gasped, casting his senses everywhere in search of Zalia's pattern.

A battler even older than One-Eleven looked at him, his own pattern sympathetic. *She let her out.*

One-Eleven was stunned silent for a moment. *What?*

The earth sylph. She let her out.

One-Eleven spun on the creature, one far more ancient than him but cringing now, afraid of what he would do. One-Eleven had no idea what he would do. Letting a woman outside when the Hunter was out there? What had she been thinking?

Why did you do it? he squealed, rushing right up in her face. She recoiled, her pattern quivering as though she wanted to turn invisible and run from him. Earth sylphs weren't as good at that as air and fire sylphs, and she'd never be able to hide her pattern from him. Not when he was this close and so utterly focused on her. *How could you let her out?*

The earth sylph held an arm up between them, as if that would help. *She told me you said to let them out. She used your name!*

One-Eleven was stunned speechless. The other battlers only watched, knowing it was his issue to deal with. He felt like he couldn't think. Why would Zalia even want to go outside? She knew what the Hunter was. Even if One-Eleven hadn't told her, those men she'd shown up with had seen the result of it firsthand.

The lightning flickering through the battler stopped for a moment. The men? Had she gone out with the men? Why would she do that?

She must have realized they'd be ejected from the hive, he realized in a flash of admiration. She figured out it was going to happen before the hive even reached the decision to do it. She would have gone with them out of misplaced loyalty. He had to respect her for that, but it was the wrong decision, so utterly wrong.

Wherever the men were was where she'd be, he thought. She'd be with the greatest target for the Hunter's hunger in this entire city. The terror of that sent the lightning crashing through him again. *Open the gate.*

The gatekeeper did so immediately, dilating the doorway open to show the wide corridor on the other side. Immediately, the women tried to push their way through the door, but the other battlers swooped down to press them back. One-Eleven darted through the gate and it closed behind him. The doorway at the other end opened just in time for him to shoot through.

The square on the other side was filled with angry and confused men. A lot of them were the men One-Eleven and his brothers had forced out, some so damaged from being feeders that they just stood there, or hunched to the ground shaking. Some were screaming in terror.

There were no women among them. One-Eleven flew upward so he could see all of them and be sure, but he didn't feel the pattern of any woman at all. Cursing, he flew higher, looking for more gatherings of men.

He saw them a good distance away, a crowd of them gathered in the place where the entrance to the feeder pens and the concubine harem was located. One-Eleven couldn't sense any women among them either, but he was too far away. It was still a good place to start looking and he flew forward, desperate to find her.

He passed within a dozen feet of the Hunter's tentacles, but of course, he never knew it.

~

The Hunter watched the battler pass by toward the other group of food. It knew what the creature was looking for, having heard his conversation, but it didn't care. The emotions of food were irrelevant.

It was feeling hungry, the human food not as nourishing in the long run as the sylphs it normally feasted on. It would have to glut and move sooner than it expected, but the food was thick on the ground, so long as it didn't alert the battler to its presence. It wouldn't, as long as the humans stayed distracted enough they didn't realize it was there. They could see it, but not well, and they still died so fast it was easy for the others to miss.

Keeping that in mind, it drifted along the edge of the crowd, the ends of a few of its thicker tentacles waving gently across the ground, along the farthest edge of the crowd, and grazed quietly on stragglers that were dead too quickly to be seen.

CHAPTER EIGHTEEN

Z alia stood next to Devon and watched the men and boys file past. Devon didn't seem to know it, but they drew strength from seeing him there, standing above them as if he were keeping guard and actually cared. Zalia wasn't so sure there would have been such an orderly procession—even knowing their lives were in danger—if someone hadn't finally stood up and taken charge. That's all they really needed; the emperor hadn't been much of a leader, but at least he'd been someone the rest of them could look to.

Now Devon stepped into that spot and Zalia was so proud of him she felt she must be glowing. She'd made love with him and she didn't feel dirty at all. After everything that had happened and all the confusion of the last few days, she felt free. Devon had taken her doubts into himself when he held her and when he asked her to marry him—that ultimate act of acceptance—she'd wanted so much to cry and understood that if she had, they would have been happy tears. She hadn't thought there was such a thing as happy tears outside the stories people told to entertain.

Men continued to pass, many of them glancing at her as they did, now that she was rare in Meridal, though none approached her. No one said much to Devon either, all of them likely too numb to even want to think beyond getting to safety. Devon reached up to gently touch her cheek and he smiled at her. His hair swirled abruptly into a look that made him seem almost shocked.

A moment later, Zalia actually saw another woman and blinked in amazement that she hadn't been snatched by the battlers, especially a woman like this. She was wrinkled and frail, her hair gray, and she was being carried by a man young enough to be her grandson.

Devon stared at the man carrying her instead, his eyes wide with sudden fear. Zalia gaped at him and looked at the man again. He had a battler's beauty. He walked up, carrying his woman, and stopped, looking critically at Devon. Devon shook, visibly forcing his fear back under control.

"What do you want?" he asked.

The battle sylph looked at him and then glanced at Zalia, his eyes quiet and thoughtful. Zalia couldn't find it in herself to be afraid of him—certainly she couldn't after One-Eleven—and she saw he wasn't quite as calm as he looked. He was as unsure of himself as Devon and she smiled at him. The battler nodded back at her a moment later.

"We're moving in," the battle sylph told Devon, turning back to him.

"Oh," Devon squeaked. "Okay."

A hint of a smile crossed the battler's lips and he continued on, joining the men filtering into the stairwell, not trying to push his way through. Zalia peeked at Devon, standing there with his hair sticking straight up, and giggled. "You're cute."

He shot her a wry look, his own mouth quirking with amusement now that the battler was gone. "Thanks."

Zalia ducked her head, still smiling. She didn't worry that she'd upset Devon, she found. She felt comfortable, and truly happy. They were all still in terrible danger, but that didn't affect how she felt. Her life was good.

Sand swirled behind Devon, forming into a floating face and hand as Airi pointed up into the air behind Zalia, her face rigid with terror. Startled, Zalia turned around.

The cloud of another battle sylph was heading straight for them, his lightning raging wildly inside him. He was still far enough away and high enough that the men hadn't noticed him, but he was closing fast. Shocked realization shot through Zalia, accompanied by a remembrance of passion that made her belly clench with sudden desire. It was One-Eleven, come to bring her back. She shot a look at Devon, who was only now turning to track his sylph's terror to the incoming battle sylph.

If One-Eleven realized that Devon had slept with her, he'd kill him.

Zalia backed away from her lover, not wanting to see him hurt, and his eyes locked on hers, wide with fear and joined understanding. She saw that he knew exactly the danger he was in, and in an instant, he reached toward her anyway, not wanting to let her go.

There was no time for an explanation and the terrible fear of an argument starting with him. Zalia bolted, running toward One-Eleven and waving her arms while she prayed Devon wouldn't follow her, or rather, that he wouldn't follow her in time. He would follow, she knew. Despite his terror of battle sylphs, despite how he'd logically needed her to go back to the hive anyway, he'd get his fear under control and come after her anyway, no matter the cost to himself. That left her only seconds to keep him safe.

She could only think of one way to guarantee that. "Over here!" she shouted, the men looking at her in confusion as she continued waving her arms. One-Eleven dived and she had an instant's vision of a lightning-streaked wall coming toward her, fronted by a pair of eyes formed by swirling ball lightning and teeth of electricity about to consume her. She flinched, hearing Devon shout behind her, and suddenly she was surrounded by darkness and being lifted upward, the sounds of the city and men muffled.

Zalia opened her eyes, not sure when she'd closed them. She was sitting on an oddly soft surface, surrounded by darkness. It was warm and the lightning she'd seen before was nowhere in sight. She couldn't see the walls all around her, but she felt the movement of their flight and her stomach lurched as One-Eleven turned, dropping down and moving forward with what felt like increasing speed.

"One-Eleven?" she whispered, though she couldn't imagine how he'd be able to talk to her in this form.

Apparently he either couldn't or chose not to. Zalia felt him wriggle around her and a tentacle made of what almost seemed to be solid black smoke came out of the wall toward her. She jerked back, but it pressed forward and caressed her cheek in a loving gesture.

Her stomach lurched again, flip-flopping as the sensation of rising came to her. Not sure what to do now or how she was going to get back to Devon, she huddled down, her arms around her knees, and felt the tentacle stroke her hair while One-Eleven took her away.

~

Devon gaped in horror and confusion as Zalia ran away from him, waving for the incoming battler to take her. He couldn't understand why. Hadn't she said she loved him?

She's protecting you, Airi told him. *The battler will kill you if he thinks you've taken her from him.*

Protecting? Going with a battle sylph to protect him? Devon's mind wailed at the idea of the woman he loved surrendering herself to his worst nightmare.

"No!" he shouted, intending to keep her with him no matter what it took, but the battler was already there. He swooped down, taking Zalia into his mantle, and arced upward again, men ducking to keep from being knocked over. He passed over Devon closely enough that he could have reached out and touched the creature. Devon scrabbled for his sword, drawing it, and the blade glistened as he swung it upward, just missing as the battler lifted out of reach. The creature didn't even acknowledge the swing and Airi cried against Devon's neck.

"What a dung heap," one old man in beggar's clothes groused. "Guess they figured out they missed one. Sorry about that, son."

"Yeah," another man added. "Real sorry."

Devon stared the way they'd gone, already vanished around the buildings. His fear was frozen inside him, deep underneath something else that was even stronger. "Don't be sorry," he muttered. "I'll get her back." He'd wanted her to go back to the hive and force the women there to fight against what was happening, but not if it meant her going with that monster. Not him.

Devon? Airi asked.

"Keep moving inside!" Devon shouted, pointing at the entrance to the stairwell. "Get everyone underground as fast as you can and shut the door!"

"Where are you going?" one man asked incredulously. "You can't seriously think they'll give her up."

"Oh yes I do," Devon growled and started up the road, striding as fast as he could in the intense heat. Airi hugged his neck, wildly ruffling his hair.

The men watched him go in amazement, though many nodded in agreement, and a few even followed, all of them understanding why he was going, if not how he ever hoped to succeed.

~

One-Eleven raced back toward the hive with the precious cargo he carried, so relieved he'd found her that he couldn't articulate it. Nothing else had mattered so much as finding her: not duty, not queen, not life. He felt her moving around inside him, her hands soft against his sides, and longed to tell her how he felt. There were no words though, just as there never were words when he was with her, and she couldn't hear his mental voice anyway. Not until she was made his master.

One-Eleven returned to the hive, but didn't swoop down to the entrance. Instead he lifted up, following a steady stream of sylphs carrying their own passengers to the palace directly overhead. There were a great many sylphs needing to be bound to their new female masters and only one way to do it. The bond had to be made in the presence of the queen, using her pattern. Now that he had Zalia back, One-Eleven wasn't going to risk waiting any longer.

He flew up to the palace, flanking a few air sylphs who could carry their own future masters and some battlers carrying the other elementals who couldn't, along with the women chosen to replace the men who used to own them. None of them looked as happy as One-Eleven felt, but he guessed the elemental sylphs didn't much care what gender their masters were. They were asexual after all.

One-Eleven darted around them, flitting up and onto the balcony that was being used as a landing zone for the newcomers. Yahe stood there, looking a bit put out while he watched them arrive and guarding against danger. He'd probably hoped to still be with Kiala, One-Eleven supposed, but didn't care. Sylphs needed new masters to feed from, now that the men were gone, and someone had to guard the queen, even if no one here was an actual threat to her. The Hunter certainly wasn't. Not even the elementals believed the Hunter could reach her this high in the air.

Shifting as he came in, One-Eleven landed in human form and caught Zalia before her momentum could tumble her to the floor. She crashed against him, staring up into his face with her eyes wide, her lips open and pursed, her hair tangling around her face. She looked so beautiful that he wanted to take her away and make love to her now. Five minutes, he promised himself with a grin.

"Come on," he told her, taking her hand in his own and running down the hall with her trailing behind him, fighting to keep her feet and match his pace. Her emotions were a riot of a thousand different feelings, all jammed up so much that they were hard for him to sort out. He was more interested in what she'd be feeling in a few minutes anyway, once she was his master.

The hall was half full of women newly bonded to elemental sylphs, all of them looking a bit dazed, their sylphs disconcerted. They moved out of the way of One-Eleven and Zalia and he ran with her into the presence of the queen.

~

Zalia didn't have time to catch her breath as One-Eleven rushed her down a hallway. He didn't even give her a chance to say anything, though she doubted that was because he was afraid she'd tell him no. She doubted he even realized what he'd done to her, or what he was doing now. He was just reacting in a way he thought right, and even now she could feel his lust flowing through her again. If he wanted, he could have her again, and she despaired inside a bit as she realized it. The way he made her feel turned her inside out and left her gasping, incomplete without him, even though she'd only minutes ago been with a man who'd said he loved her and whom she loved back. Still, when One-Eleven looked back over his shoulder at her, grinning so happily, her heart clenched, her wrist aching where he held it too tightly.

He towed her into a room made opulent with rich woods and silk cushions, tall windows filling the far wall and letting in the light, even as they showed a lethal drop down to the hive below. She was back in the floating palace, she realized in surprise. This was where Devon needed to be, negotiating with the queen to save them all.

The realization of that shocked away the lust building in her. There were more people in the room this time; women and sylphs both, since she doubted the men she saw were actually human. Zalia looked at the battler standing beside Eapha. He had his hand on her shoulder and was massaging her muscles.

Sylphs of every variety were bringing human women before the queen. Eapha didn't do anything and Zalia didn't see anything happening, but the battler beside her looked very focused, his hand never leaving his lover's shoulder, and after a moment the women would start or cry out, suddenly turning to the sylphs beside them with shock or amazement. None of them looked as if they really understood what was going on.

Zalia understood it. The women were being bound to the sylphs, without their understanding and therefore without their consent. They'd just been brought here and the queen wasn't even asking them if this was what they wanted. She only stood there, her eyes troubled, while her friends gathered behind her making jokes at the newcomers' expense.

One-Eleven looked over his shoulder at Zalia, his face flawlessly perfect and so handsome that even now her heart surged to have his attention on her. "Are you all right?" he asked. "It won't take more than a moment, promise. And it doesn't hurt at all."

Zalia's mouth went dry. She couldn't talk to him. He turned her so inside out it was all she could manage to have pushed him away the first few times they met. Now that he'd made love to her, her body ached for him, screaming with need. He smiled and that made the feeling a hundred times worse. Her body wanted him, wanting him on her and in her, moving against her with a slow languishment that would take her to heights mere humans could never reach. He would honor her and love her, and all she had to do was let it happen, as she'd let him making love to her happen. Just hang on and ride.

The woman and sylph before her stepped away, the queen's friends laughing at the girl's astonishment on suddenly being bound to a floating ball of fire. Zalia found herself staring right at Eapha, who didn't even bother to meet her eyes, looking disconnected from everything before her as she listened to her friends. Just hang on and ride.

That was exactly what this woman was doing and it was killing them all.

Before she could think about what she was doing, Zalia stepped forward and slapped Eapha right across the face.

If she'd been a man, she would have been dead in a heartbeat. Zalia realized that an instant after she struck, and almost panicked, which would have also gotten her killed. She was a woman though, she realized, and the battlers were working solely on instinct. They didn't know how to protect their queen from a woman.

Her friends did.

"Hey!" one woman behind Eapha shouted. Zalia hadn't been able to focus on the queen's friends much in her last visit, but she did recognize her as one who seemed to think that everything was a joke. That only infuriated Zalia further.

"Shut up!" Zalia shouted, pointing at the angry woman. She turned back to Eapha. "Do you know what's happening in this city because of you? Do you?"

The other woman stormed toward her, not willing to back off. Eapha was just staring, one hand to her cheek while the battler beside her stood with his hand still on her shoulder, watching Zalia and the other woman with a very calculating expression. The other battlers were frozen in shock, including One-Eleven.

"Don't you make anything her fault!" the woman yelled. "She shouldn't have to worry about some stinking city!"

"Then she shouldn't have given up being a slave!"

In the sudden silence, Eapha rubbed her cheek. "Kiala," she started to say.

"No!" Kiala snapped. "This bitch doesn't belong here! She has no right to accuse you!"

Zalia was livid. "I have every right," she breathed. "I was there when Leon brought her out of slavery. I was there when she gave her word she'd change things. I was there when she was made a queen and left the rest of us behind!"

Eapha turned white while Kiala sneered. "You have no right to talk to us at all. You don't know what we went through."

Actually, Zalia suspected she'd learned exactly what they went through with One-Eleven the other night. She didn't want to say so, not to this angry woman, not when she was so angry herself. One-Eleven stared at her, his eyes huge and his mouth hanging open, more like a startled little boy than the battle sylph he actually was. For once, he wasn't affecting what she felt, too shocked to do so. He continued to hold her arm, probably without thinking.

She turned back to Eapha, who still had a hand to her cheek. The battler with her continued to watch, his gaze on Eapha, and Zalia suddenly realized that, much as Kiala wanted her to shut up and leave them responsible for nothing, that battler wanted Zalia to say the things he apparently couldn't.

"We warned you about the creature that's hunting everyone in the city," Zalia said directly to Eapha, trying without success to shake One-Eleven's grip off her arm. He kept holding her, staring at the battler behind the queen in confusion. That one glanced back at One-Eleven once, only briefly, and his grip tightened to a burst of pain before he let go and stepped back. Zalia didn't really notice, though she had pause to consider it later, when she thought about the madwoman she'd become and its consequences.

"We warned you about it," she continued, "and you let them throw us out. Me? Fine, I don't care. But you threw out the ambassador sent by the man who saved you." Eapha flinched. "He came here to help and you ignored him."

"So?" Kiala started, but Eapha raised a hand, her face white. Kiala looked angry at that, but the battle sylph with Eapha glared at her and she quickly shut her mouth, the other friends of the queen surrounding her and urging her away. She only backed up a few feet and the room still felt crowded with so many people and sylphs in it.

"Since then," Zalia continued, inexorable, "the sylphs have made a hive, but not everyone's invited. The battle sylphs have kidnapped every single woman in the entire city and brought them to the hive *without* their husbands and sons, and they've thrown every single man out, even the ones who are masters." She gestured furiously at the women who were huddled behind her, all of them watching in fear. One-Eleven looked back at them as well, suddenly seeming guilty.

"Did you stop to wonder why so many people were coming to you?" she thundered. "Did you care? Did you wonder how many of them were actually *asked* if they wanted to be masters? I know I wasn't!"

One-Eleven gasped.

"I . . ." Eapha managed. "I . . ."

"Half this city has been left to die!" Zalia shouted, tears running down her cheeks as she realized that half included her father. "And just in case they manage to avoid the Hunter, the battlers guaranteed it by taking all the food! They left us nothing!"

"I didn't . . ."

"You should have!" Zalia screamed. "You're the queen! Stop being such a coward!" She pointed at the woman's friends. "Stop listening to them tell you you're useless! You can't afford to be! A *bad* queen will keep more people alive than these things!"

Everyone stared at her, standing there gasping now with tears running down her face, not knowing what to say anymore. The fury that had driven her was running out, leaving her drained and scared, wanting nothing more than to be with her father or Devon; just for someone to hold her. It was One-Eleven who sensed it and put his arms around her, warm and perfect. He didn't fill her with his lust this time and she was grateful for that. Zalia stared at Eapha, knowing she was going to feel so ashamed of herself once the anger fully wore off, part of her already wishing she could take it all back and just have stayed silent while the queen stared back at her, face pale, eyes wide. Her friends moved toward her, cooing that Zalia was wrong, that she was just bitter and she didn't understand them. All of them gave a dozen reasonable excuses for her to continue to do nothing, since then it meant that *they* would have to do nothing.

Eapha shrugged them off, her battler stepping between her and them once she raised her hand. She was trembling, her lips thin and tight, but she didn't meet Zalia's gaze with any less fear than Zalia was feeling herself.

"All right," she whispered.

CHAPTER NINETEEN

B y the time Devon reached the square in front of the hive, his fury had faded, replaced again by his more common-sense comprehension of how this got Zalia back into the hive just the way he'd wanted, as well as exactly what a battle sylph could do if he dared to confront him. He still kept going, his heart pounding as he prayed despite everything that he'd find Zalia outside waiting for him.

Not surprisingly, that didn't happen. There were a great deal of men there, even more so than before. Devon had thought that more of them would be headed underground, since there wasn't any way for them to get into the hive itself. It became obvious to him pretty quickly that none of these men had been here when he passed by the day before.

Oh, Devon, Airi mourned. *They're the masters. They've been turned out.*

Devon stood and stared, belatedly recognizing several of the men he'd seen in the hive by the fountain, singing or playing music for their air sylphs to dance to. There were no air sylphs with them now, no sylphs with any of the men who stood there. Some were yelling along with the rest of the men to be let in, others looked betrayed, and many were the numb, broken things who'd wandered aimlessly or huddled in doorways.

"Devon!"

Devon turned, seeing Xehm hurrying toward him through the crowd, dragging Gel along with him. The old man looked relieved to see him.

"I was afraid I wouldn't see you again, boy," Xehm said, smiling ruefully as he shook Devon's hand. "They threw us out."

Gel looked around them in a daze, his eyes wide with fear. "Where's Shasha?" he said. "Where is she?"

Xehm ignored his question, studying Devon. "Where's Zalia? She's still inside, isn't she?"

Devon swallowed and nodded. "Yes. She's safe." She was, after all. Right now, there was no safer place in Meridal, and she had work to do there, no matter what he thought of her rescuer. Realizing it hurt.

We could never get her out anyway, Airi mourned. *She loves you though. She'll remember that.*

Devon hoped that she could.

"We should go," he told the two men. "There's a place for us, in the underground feeder pens."

Gel stared at him abruptly, his eyes wide. "What?" he whimpered. "There's a monster down there. I saw it."

"I know," Devon soothed, kicking himself for forgetting where they had found the man. "The monster's not there anymore and it's a place we can go to keep safe from it. We need to tell these men about it and go now."

"But Shasha," Gel protested. "I can't leave Shasha."

"It's all right, son," Xehm soothed, putting an arm around the younger man. "We need to go."

"Go where?" the former feeder asked. "Shasha is all I have. She misses me."

Devon and Xehm looked at each other. Devon was sympathetic toward the broken man, but the space between his shoulder blades was starting to itch again. They had to go, with as many men as would come with them. He'd wonder about how he was going to feed them all later.

"Gel, Shasha isn't coming. We have to go."

Gel just shook his head. "She's coming. I know she's coming. Look." He turned toward the hive and pointed vaguely at it, his finger aimed nowhere near the darker stone of the gateway entrance.

As if he'd somehow taken on the powers of an earth elemental and done it himself, the stone rippled and ripped wide, revealing a tunnel more than fifteen feet long.

A half-dozen fire sylphs zipped out, all of them condensed into balls of floating flame, followed by water and earth elementals in a dozen different shapes. Devon didn't see the air elementals, but he felt the wind of their passage when they swept past him, spreading out through the crowd.

Shasha came last, stomping heavily out of the passageway despite her slight frame, her ruby eyes gleaming. Her entire stance exuded fury as she looked back at the opening she made and it closed in on itself, before any of the men could recover from their shock and try to get through. It sealed completely, with barely a mark showing from her efforts as she lumbered forward, grumbling under her breath.

Gel pulled free of Xehm and dashed toward her, skidding on his knees for the last few feet and into her arms, sobbing in his relief. Devon walked over to join them, a silent Xehm at his side. Throughout the crowd, the other elemental sylphs were finding their own masters, to the men's shouts of joy.

Shasha looked up at Devon, his face reflected in her eyes.

"I didn't think you were coming," he said to her.

"I was told I could pick my master when we were freed. I haven't changed my mind."

Devon looked toward the hive. "I still didn't think you were coming."

Shasha snorted derisively. "There is no queen to stop me."

Oh, Airi mourned. *This is a bad place, to have no queen.*

Somehow, Devon doubted Shasha meant the queen left. Eapha's indifference was worse than that. "Why not let us into the hive?" he asked her. It still was the safest place, though with a half dozen of each type of elemental, they might just be able to guarantee their survival in the feeder pens.

Shasha looked at him again. "The battlers would stop that."

Devon shuddered. "Right." He looked at the hive again, breathing a silent promise, which Airi echoed, that he wouldn't leave Zalia in there forever. When he could, he'd come for her. And he'd love her no matter what she did until he could.

"We should go," he said yet again, this time very softly.

The men moved, Xehm standing close beside Gel as the broken man rose, though Shasha was closer still. Wiping his eyes, the former feeder stood, lifting his head though his shoulders were still hunched, and froze. Shasha shot him a sudden look, her hand gripping his arm. "Gel?" she asked.

Gel was shaking, sweat pouring down his face, and his eyes wide. He started breathing in short, shallow gasps and Devon grabbed his shoulders, suddenly terrified himself. "Gel! What is it?" Gel was staring straight past him and Devon turned, looking behind himself and fully expecting in his growing terror to see people being devoured.

All he saw were men milling about, watching the sylphs reunite with their masters and try as they had all day to decide what to do next.

Devon turned back to Gel. "What is it?"

"Where is it?" Xehm added and Devon felt real terror.

I don't see anything, Airi wailed, cold against his neck. *I don't see anything!*

Gel raised his hand and pointed. Devon had been expecting the man to point past him, but Gel pointed vaguely to their right instead, toward the edge of the square. Devon looked that way, seeing absolutely nothing except more men moving around.

He looked back at Gel. "I don't see anything," he said. Gel closed his eyes and kept pointing as a tear trickled down his cheek.

Something flickered in Devon's peripheral vision and he looked back toward the edge of the square.

There were fewer men there.

It was one of the hardest things Devon had ever done, his terror was so strong, but he looked back at Gel, his gaze locked on the other man's as he tried to focus on nothing except the farthest edge of his peripheral vision. Wanting to panic and run so badly he could taste it, he forced himself to breathe and waited.

Something thick and as translucent as the finest stream of water swept across the edge of the crowd—a dozen somethings, a hundred. Tentacles, some thick as a man while others were thin as hairs, dangled along the edge of the crowd, picking off men so quickly and silently none of them realized it; none save the one man who'd survived seeing it before.

I can't see anything! Airi shrieked.

"Oh, gods," Devon groaned. "Oh, gods of us all!" He felt as though he was moving in slow motion, forcing himself to turn toward the Hunter. Straight on, he couldn't see it from this far away, not really, but he could see what it was doing as the crowd thinned and those still alive started to realize something was happening. Too slowly though, too slowly, and the battle sylphs were on the other side of ten feet of solid stone.

"It's here!" he screamed. "The Hunter is here! THERE!" He pointed toward the creature he couldn't quite see, unfocusing his eyes so that he could see the hint of it where it touched the ground, swirling the sand left by the storm. He kept his gaze there, afraid to look up.

The men around him moved. By now they knew they were being hunted, and like Devon, they'd been using their anger to overwhelm their fear. They heard his warning and moved in all directions, staring around in every direction for what they couldn't see.

Some of them stumbled right into it. Seen straight on, Devon gasped as they came apart, turning to a red mist that was sucked in and up so fast it was no wonder the first victims had died unremarked.

At least their deaths served to pinpoint the Hunter for the rest of them. "Run!" Devon screamed, even as men did all around him and Airi projected his voice so they could hear it even over their screams. "To the feeder pen entrance! Run!"

At last he turned and ran himself, hearing Xehm gasping at his side while Gel stumbled behind, Shasha at his side. The earth sylph was looking around in terror, not able to see even the tentacles his peripheral vision did.

Tentacles, he thought desperately. Tentacles hanging from the sky. He'd seen them before, in the clouds and in the sand, and thought they were imaginings. He'd *seen* them, and he tried very hard not to think about what he'd seen them attached to. All he could do was run, and hope it wasn't catching up, reaching toward them with those tentacles, reaching past the shadow that stretched behind him in order to take them. He couldn't even look back, for fear he would trip. Airi hugged his neck, sobbing.

The worst part of it was, he didn't know the way. The Hunter was between them and the road to the feeder pens. He'd just *walked* down that road and he didn't know how to get to the pens from here.

"This way," Xehm gasped, tugging on his arm and heading down a side street. Devon let the old man lead, Gel bringing up the rear with Shasha's firm grip on his wrist. Most of the men continued along the main road they'd just left, but at his shout, many followed them, wild-eyed with terror. All of them kept going, panting and sweating in the intense heat, their hearts pounding and their mouths dry, but none daring to stop.

They ran across the city, afraid at every turn and intersection, going as fast as they could through the piles of sand even as exhaustion slowed them to a walk, their legs shaking. It was only a few miles, but they couldn't keep running the entire way, Devon told himself. They had to save something in case the Hunter found them again.

Why had he left the safety of the pens? Devon wondered wildly. Was he crazy?

Of course he wasn't crazy. Even now, the thought of Zalia made his heart a little calmer and he was finally glad she'd been taken. She was safe; safe from death at least.

"How much farther?" he gasped.

"A mile from here if we went straight," Xehm panted. "I'm taking back roads."

"Good," Devon managed. The main roads had to be better feeding grounds for the thing, so long as they didn't get to the pens to find the Hunter floating right on top of it. He resolutely pushed that thought out of his mind and looked back at Gel. The man was in no shape for this and Shasha was carrying him, hurrying along after the rest of them. He still looked exhausted—small wonder since she had to feed from him to keep herself going.

"Thanks," Devon managed to gasp. "We wouldn't have escaped . . . without you."

The man stared at him, his eyes wide.

Devon turned around and kept going.

They reached the pens as the sun started to go down, them and a few dozen others, including all of the sylphs that rebelled with Shasha. Left without queen, hive, or battlers to protect them, they stuck close together, trusting human eyes to keep them safe. Devon didn't know if he could call that ironic.

His earlier thought that the Hunter would be waiting on top of the pens for them wasn't realized. Devon didn't know if any earlier arrivals hadn't thought of it or were just braver than him, but there were men at the little building that formed the entrance, the last of them moving their few remaining supplies down. Devon breathed a gasping sigh of relief, but he couldn't stop. He just kept looking around, trying to keep his vision unfocused and jumping at every trickle of sweat that slipped down past his eyes. Nothing. Thank all the gods there was nothing.

He hurried forward, the other men and sylphs following along. Airi still clung to his neck, the only cool spot on his entire body, and sobbed. In all the years he'd known her, even in the face of angry battle sylphs, he'd never seen her so frightened. He could only imagine how terrifying this was for her, and for him it was bad enough. He could at least see the thing, if only a little bit.

How could he see it? he wondered. It was much the same as looking at a heat haze, or one of the creatures that children's stories said could only be spotted from the corner of the eye. Usually those were the sort of monsters that hid underneath beds or in closets, waiting to devour children who weren't good. That's certainly what this creature seemed to be, though it definitely didn't care who it devoured. Even a human might not spot it coming until it was too late. Besides, seeing it wouldn't stop it.

Reaching the entrance to the pens, Devon pushed the door open and waved the others through. Most of them looked exhausted to the point they couldn't have gone any farther and he was glad they didn't have to. Shading his eyes and looking out over the square, he tried to spot the Hunter, but either the creature was somewhere else or he wasn't seeing it again.

The others were inside and Airi tugged at his hair, whimpering for him to come inside where it was safe. Devon did so, letting the door shut behind him. It was a good two inches thick, made out of well-balanced, sylph-shaped stone, but it wouldn't keep the Hunter out. Not when the hive walls were ten feet thick. Frowning, Devon looked at the stairwell that led downward into darkness. It was a little intimidating, but not nearly so much as thinking about what wandered around outside. Gel was on the stairs, leaning heavily on Shasha as she helped him down the steps. The man looked to be in shock again. Devon didn't blame him; he felt rather like he was in shock himself.

"Shasha?" he asked. The slim earth sylph looked up at him, her eyes expressionless. Devon tried not to wonder if she regretted leaving the safety of her hive now. Could she go back, or was she considered an outcast for leaving the way she did? To be treated like an outsider the way Airi was? Devon couldn't see that as something any sylph could feel easy with, and he hoped she wouldn't resent Gel for it. He doubted it; from what he'd seen of sylphs, their love was immediate and without reservation. It was only odd that more of them hadn't deserted the safety of the hive to reunite themselves with their male masters. Perhaps not all of them had a bond strong enough to make a sylph abandon their hive and queen and even their own chance of survival in order to be with their master.

He'd never asked Airi if she felt that strongly for him.

Isn't it obvious? Airi whispered into his mind.

Shasha looked between them for a moment, her eyes impassive as she sensed whatever it was she did between them. "Yes?" she rumbled after a moment.

Devon shook himself, one hand up into Airi's breeze. "Um, yes. Can you seal this entrance? Make it so we can get in and out if we have to, but the Hunter can't?"

Shasha's lips turned downward in a deliberate frown as she studied the door behind Devon, and the stone wall it sat in. "I'll think about it," she said at last.

"Thanks," Devon told her as she turned to her master again. "Wait." She looked at him again. "Can you get a message to your hive?" he asked.

She thought about it for a moment and then shook her head. "We were next to nothing and we left. Now we are nothing. They'll ignore anything we have to say."

Devon sighed. "I was afraid of that." *Next to nothing?* he asked Airi.

She swirled against his neck, playing with his hair again. It was a sure sign she was starting to feel safe again. *All of us except for the queen are expendable, but elementals are less important than healers and battlers in a hive,* she admitted. *We're just tools to keep the hive going. I like Solie for not being like that. She loves all of us.*

"Oh," Devon said. He hadn't realized that before. No wonder the elemental sylphs never had a problem with being bound to humans when they came through the gate. They'd all been slaves on the other side of it anyway.

They went down the long, twisting stairway, Devon's tension easing as the stone closed around them. They were safe down here, even if that safety was an illusion.

He'd have to see if the sylphs could repair the walkways and cages that the feeders used to live in. He certainly didn't intend for men to live in cages; but remade into something a little more humane, they'd provide more than enough room for everyone. Then it was just a matter of finding enough food and water to keep them alive. He didn't know how long they'd have to stay down here, but it would be a smart idea to plan for it to be a while. Airi said the Hunter would move on eventually, but he couldn't even wonder when that would be, or what other cities it would destroy when it did. How was he to even start to warn everyone?

They reached the bottom of the stairs, letting out into the corridor they'd been in before, only this time it was full of boys running excitedly, their fathers yelling for them not to go into the section with the broken feeder pens or else they'd break their fool necks. Most of the men seemed to have gone in the other direction, which was a way Devon hadn't seen, and they followed, making their way through a tight crowd of muttering men who nodded as they passed, many of them even stepping out of his way.

They know who led them here, Airi whispered to him and Devon found himself taking a deep, invigorating breath.

The hallway led into a series of guardrooms, men already claiming spots for their own or taking over small offices and sleeping rooms. Double doors lay broken ahead of them, and Devon walked into what he saw immediately was going to be the most popular living area in this place.

The double doors led into a massive, long room filled with cushions and curtain-covered alcoves. It looked opulent and comfortable, though he had to edge around a massive bloodstain right before the doors. The men were spreading out, claiming the little alcoves when they could. There was some arguing, but no fighting yet.

"This is a wonderful place," Xehm said, his eyes wide. "What is it for?"

Devon looked around at the scattered cushions. The whole place was done up in jewel tones and he could smell a faint scent of incense, even now. "I bet it's the concubine chambers." Xehm looked vaguely horrified, but Devon started forward, hoping to find an alcove that hadn't been taken. "It's better than a cage."

As they moved along, Gel walking at Shasha's side and looking much more comfortable in a room that likely didn't remind him of feeder pens, someone ran up. Devon barely recognized him as one of the men who'd first agreed to come to the pens. The man had brought a plethora of tools and useful items, more than anyone else managed, and he'd carried them all on his back. He'd even brought a pair of goats that the battlers somehow managed to miss.

"Come and see," he said excitedly, grabbing Devon's arm. "You won't believe it."

Devon looked at the others for a moment and then followed at the man's urging. Only Xehm looked interested enough to follow, though the old man didn't move so quickly and Devon had to slow down several times so he could keep up. He was tired himself and really wanted to find a place to lie down and rest for a while. That wasn't going to be happening anytime soon. Whether he wanted it or not, he had to be in charge, and right now, it was even more important that he *look* to be in charge. It was one of the lessons Leon had taught him back in the Valley, though Devon was a little amazed at how many of those lessons he actually remembered.

The man led him back out of the harem, excusing their way through the crowd until they reached a side corridor beyond the guardrooms that would have been easy to overlook. It seemed most people had, since it was empty when they went down it, coming to a door that was closed by way of a bar that swung down into a few outward jutting slots. The man, who Devon now remembered was named Blithori, swung the bar up and pulled the door open. Three steps led down into a room that was filled with shadows until Blithori lifted up a lantern he'd brought and lit it.

The chamber on the far side of the door was immense, almost as big as the harem, and filled with shelving. On the shelves, neatly stacked, were dried foodstuffs, from fish to grain to fruit and cheeses. Devon gaped at it, making a strangled sound.

Blithori grinned at him. "I guess they had to keep the food for the concubines somewhere."

And the battle sylphs hadn't known. Devon heard Xehm come up behind them and yelp in surprise even as Devon clapped a hand on Blithori's shoulder, grinning. "Good work, man. Really good work."

It looked as though they had a chance to survive this after all.

CHAPTER TWENTY

Eapha stood on the balcony outside her private chambers and looked down at the hive below. The sky was clear, the sandstorm long gone, but the height she was at gave a strange perspective she wasn't used to and there seemed to be a hazy miasma between her and the hive, something bulbous and almost textured, though she could see through it easily.

She just looked down at the hive, her fist tucked under her chin as she leaned on her elbow on the stone railing. It hurt a bit, but she didn't care.

Zalia was right about her. Wasn't she? Even after having agreed with the woman, even after having been screamed at about all the things she'd been thinking but never acted on, Eapha doubted herself. Kiala thought she was being stupid; if anyone was going to ruin the city, it would be an ex-concubine who'd lived in slavery since she was five. Besides, the city owed them nothing. Why would she want to help people who'd maintained the status quo that had kept her and all her friends in chains? That was Kiala's argument, the same as the rest of them. Eapha should be *ashamed* to think she should do anything.

Zalia disagreed, the same as Devon and definitely Leon. Devon and Leon certainly hadn't had anything to do with her being a slave and she could tell that Zalia hadn't either. The people who'd maintained Kiala's so hated status quo were all dead now and those left behind were just trying to stay alive themselves.

She'd thought she could just ignore any responsibility and let the sylphs be in charge.

"It's never worked that way."

Eapha turned, seeing Tooie standing in the doorway, leaning against the frame while he studied her, his face solemn.

"Can you read my mind now?"

He shook his head. "Not really. I just know how you think, and I've heard all the arguments the rest of the women have been making."

She turned around, leaning back against the railing. Both of them were trying so hard to look casual, though she felt anything but. Everything was tight inside of her and she could feel the tension in him. "You never said anything."

He shrugged. "It's not my place."

Eapha stared at him. "But . . . you're in charge."

He shook his head, his lip twisting. "No, I'm not. I'm lead battler, yes, but only as an extension of your authority. Without your support, I'm nothing. The queen is in charge. That's you."

"But I gave it up to you."

"Queens can't do that." He sighed and looked at his arm against the stone above his head. Grimacing, he lightly slammed his fist against it a few times. "I thought it could work, but . . . we don't . . . think that much. We just follow instincts. We don't think about what's best. I've tried, but I can't see it. That's what the queen is for."

Eapha felt her mouth go dry, remembering again Zalia screaming at her about what was happening on the surface. She never would have ordered that, would she? She'd thought it was an exaggeration—certainly Kiala had come to her afterward and told her it had to be—but Tooie was telling her it wasn't.

"You threw all the men out of the hive?" she asked. His expression was evidence enough. Her lip quivered. "All of them?" How exactly did he define *men*?

Tooie nodded, shifting a little uncomfortably. "The only males in the hive are battle sylphs."

He threw out the *babies*? The little children? She stared down at the hive again. The day before, there had been men gathered in the square before it. Now she could see through the miasma that the square was deserted. How many men had been trying to get back to their women? How many children wanted their mothers? How many needed their mothers' milk? Eapha suddenly felt ill and saw Tooie's recognition of it in how his chin jerked up, his eyes tightening.

"Why did you throw the men out?" Eapha asked him, afraid of the answer.

"Because men aren't part of the hive. They're other than us. They have no place here."

Eapha closed her eyes. That's what the people she hadn't wanted to listen to had been trying to tell her. Even Tooie had. Sylphs didn't think as human beings did.

"What," she asked him softly, "were you planning to do to ensure future generations of women without having any men around?"

He had no answer for her, she could see that. Eapha managed a laugh that was almost a sob and walked over to him, her arms outspread. Tooie pushed away from the wall to meet her and she hugged him, her face buried against his chest while his arms went around her.

"Why didn't you tell me any of this?" she whimpered.

He sighed. "Because you didn't want me to. Because you're the queen. You can do whatever you want."

"Including being a bad queen." She sniffled and pushed away from him, looking up at his face with a fear that she hadn't felt when she was first told she'd be queen. "I don't know that I can be a good queen," she admitted. "I might be really bad at it."

He smiled. "Maybe. I'll help."

Of course he would, but much as she loved him, she could see his limitations. Humans had them as well, but she had to hope she could get by her own, and find help. Leon did send that help, she reminded herself. Devon Chole must know something about how she could do this or Leon wouldn't have sent him.

"Kiala and the others are going to nag me terribly about this," she mourned instead.

He touched her cheek with the back of his hand. "You want them to stop? They will." She didn't ask how. Battlers had to obey their masters, but they had their own influences as well. She just wished a bit that Tooie used some of them before things got this bad, though that was only her blaming him for her own failure and she felt guilty to even think it. Now she had to figure out what to do on her own. Too much had gone wrong while she hid up here.

"Have you had any luck with the Hunter yet?" she asked.

"None."

"What do you do back where you came from?"

He shrugged, his face a grimace. "Usually wait it out. They leave eventually if there's nothing to eat."

They could do that, providing none of them ran out of food first. But how were they supposed to feed so many people? How was she supposed to round up the men and get them to safety while the Hunter was killing everyone? Eapha looked toward the edge of the balcony again, too far back to see the hive from where she stood but able to notice that the miasma she'd been looking at before had risen, now shimmering at the edge of the balcony. Lines like wisps in her vision shimmered above it, waving in the air.

"We have to start with the Hunter," she decided, wishing she didn't still feel so uncertain. Until it was gone though, nothing she tried to do would matter.

Tooie smiled and led her inside, closing the doors behind them to keep the dust out.

~

One-Eleven didn't know what to think anymore.

He'd gone after Zalia, rescued her from what surely would have been certain death and brought her straight to the queen to become his master. He'd have been able to keep her safe all of the time then, and love her as she deserved. It had been the most important thing in the world, only she slapped the queen and yelled at her and everyone was upset. Yahe was bellowing along the hive line, wanting to know what had his Kiala so infuriated.

One-Eleven couldn't answer him. He'd seen it, but he honestly didn't understand. Not this. Everything was going so well. They were organized and working together. The queen didn't have to bother with anything and One-Eleven's suggestions had merit. Sylphs *listened* to him. Only now the woman he loved most yelled at the queen for an idea *he'd* given. One-Eleven still didn't get what the problem with throwing out the men was. There was only so much food and it was vitally important to keep the females safe, everyone knew that.

He didn't want to try and explain that just now, since he doubted Zalia would be willing to listen. She was pacing around the room he'd brought her to, chewing on her nails and staring wildly around. Her emotions were a mess, angry and embarrassed and worried all at once. It didn't feel nice at all, not like the calm he'd sensed when he first saw her, bathing behind the stable in the predawn darkness.

He really wanted to regain that level of comfort with her, and banish her obvious distress. He focused, letting the lust he felt spread outward, blanketing her with the need he knew they both shared.

Zalia stopped and jerked her head around to look at him over her shoulder. "Don't do that!"

One-Eleven lost his focus and flinched, not liking the look in her eyes. "But I want you to be happy."

She stared at him for a moment, tense and rigid, and then exhaled loudly and slumped. "Don't do that," she repeated, more softly this time.

She looked away as he walked over and gently put his hands on her shoulders. "Why?" he whispered. "Don't you want to be happy too?"

"I was happy," he thought he heard her say. She stepped away, pulling free of him. It hurt. "I don't want you to force me to feel."

He really should have listened to Tooie, One-Eleven thought. Tooie had said to talk to her, get to know her. But oh no, he hadn't listened. He'd just gone for what he wanted and now he could feel the resentment in Zalia, resentment he had the sudden terror she'd been feeling the entire time, only hidden beneath the desire he'd given her.

None of this was happening the way it was supposed to. *Tooie!* he shouted in his mind, desperate for someone to tell him what to do, what he could say that would make everything better. *She hates me!*

Who hates you? Tooie responded, sounding distracted.

Zalia! She doesn't want me to make her feel happy!

Tooie snorted, already withdrawing his attention. *So don't do that. Talk to the woman.*

About what?

I don't know. About whatever she's interested in. Promise her the world. Think of something.

One-Eleven stared at Zalia, his hands twitching by his side with nervousness. She looked back at him, her hands crossed before her breasts, holding her opposing arms while she stood hunched forward slightly, closed in on herself. She felt stressed and afraid.

Much as he hated it, One-Eleven looked closer, actually examining the emotions of the woman before him. They were more complex than he would have expected, certainly more complex than anything he suspected he could feel himself. She was anxious and scared, worried and a bit angry. She had a desire to go somewhere and do something and felt a touch of embarrassment over her explosion at the queen earlier.

She liked him.

One-Eleven grabbed on to that, as fast and as hard as he could. She liked him, deep down where it wasn't being articulated. She genuinely did, or he suspected, with his newfound understanding, that he never would have been able to sleep with her. She didn't even regret that, not really. He felt in her instead a bit of uncertainty about it, as well as a strange, deeply buried sort of relief that it was over with. He'd somehow set her free, even if he wasn't quite sure how.

But she liked him. One-Eleven took a deep breath, his entire chest expanding, and let it out in a loud exhalation. Zalia studied him suspiciously and he smiled, lacing his hands behind his back. That made her more comfortable, he realized. It meant he wasn't about to grab her. He resolved not to, at least not until she wanted him again.

"Can we start over?" he asked. She blinked. He rose up onto his toes for a moment and dropped down again. "My name is One-Eleven. It's more of a designation than a name, but I haven't come up with one for myself yet. A real name, that is."

She shifted, her arms relaxing their tight grip a bit as some of the tension he felt in her eased into curiosity. "What do you mean? Why haven't you?"

He rocked onto his toes again, liking how her eyes tracked his movement. "I'm not really good at that. And I hoped that my master would come up with a name for me." Her eyes widened with a return to nervousness and he scratched his cheek, wanting to get her back to that calm again. Much as he hated it, she didn't want to think of herself as being his master right now. No one asked her if she wanted to be, he remembered her yelling. Well, right now did *not* strike him as a good time to start; even if it was the only thing his heart could see as mattering.

"No one back where I came from had names," he told her, "except the queen and her mates, of course. When I came here, some of the concubines gave us names in the harem. Like Tooie. I always really wanted one myself, except I didn't have any way of asking and no one thought to give me one."

"You want a name," she said slowly. Her arms were still around herself, but they'd dropped down lower, no longer so tense, and her shoulders were straighter, the muscles less tight. "From me."

"Well, yes. I figured it would be better for my master to name me since she—I mean you—would know me better than even I know myself. That's how it's supposed to work anyway." He looked at her hopefully, remembered her naked and wanton beneath him, and had to forcefully push the memory away before instinct made him drown her in lust again. It wasn't easy.

"I don't know you at all," she told him, and that hurt so much it crushed the desire he was feeling. "How am I supposed to name you?"

"But . . ." They knew each other intimately, he wanted to remind her. He'd tasted and touched every part of her body, but he knew already that wasn't what she'd meant. Tooie had told him to talk to her from that start. Sex didn't mean as much to her as it always had to him. If he wanted sex again, he had to give her what she wanted, whatever that was.

"I'd like to get to know you," he told her, "and you can get to know me. Then you'll be able to pick a name for me."

She thought about it. He felt her do it, felt her emotions swirling as she considered the perfection of it. Then her arms tightened again. "I don't know. I have someone." Her eyes lifted to look at him, dark and clear enough for him to see his misery and shock reflected in them. "I'm not looking for anyone else."

Find the bastard. Kill him. Rip his human heart out and crush it. He had to be human; no battler would have gone near One-Eleven's woman once he laid his hand on her. No other battler would have been stupid enough.

"I'll give you anything," he promised her, just as Tooie told him he should. "I'll always be there for you, always keep you safe. With me, you'll never have to be alone. I'll love you forever!"

Her face tightened with misery. "So will he."

No, he wouldn't. One-Eleven stepped forward, Zalia stiffening until he bent forward and kissed her as chastely as he could manage on the forehead. "I have to go think," he whispered. "But I promise you. I love you. I'll always love you and I'll never leave you." He turned and hurried out, before he could fully hear the protests she was starting up behind him, running toward one of the great windows left open in one wall of the room and diving out, immediately taking on his natural shape and arcing upward, heading up and over the floating palace toward the city. He knew where Zalia's man was, knew just who it had to be.

She'd love him. He'd win her slowly and surely like Tooie had suggested, convince her that loving him was the only thing for both of them.

Once there wasn't any competition to worry about.

∾

Zalia ran to the window after One-Eleven, screaming his name, though of course, he didn't answer. Since she wasn't his master, he didn't have to. That little conversation had actually been the most human and comfortable she'd had with him, letting her feel as if she could communicate with him and perhaps even be friends. She'd even relaxed enough to make the worst mistake of her entire life.

"What have I done?" she mourned.

≈

The men it had been planning to feed on were gone, retreating into some kind of hive of their own. The Hunter dragged its tentacles across the top of the main hive, considering its options. It had eaten a lot of them, and felt filled to the point of needing to hang on lest it rise too high, but it had wanted to be able to rely on them for a lot longer than this before it tried to leave. In all honesty, it was afraid to trust the winds to take it to a new food source, not after having been sucked out onto the ocean the last time. It was truly going to have to trust to the spirits of its kind to keep it safe, and it was afraid in a way that the worst storms of its home world had never been able to make it.

Ultimately, it had no choice. It had fuel for now, but not enough to feel safe giving in to the wind. The men had gone somewhere, but it wasn't sure where and it didn't have time to go looking for them. It had to get into this hive.

Carefully, it edged itself over to the floating palace and used all its strength to start raising its tentacles over the dome of its body, up toward the heavy building so conveniently waiting for it, careful not to touch any of the battle sylphs who periodically rushed in and out, just in case they got a warning off as they died. Straining from the effort it required to lift its tentacles so high, it searched for a way in.

CHAPTER TWENTY-ONE

The skies over Meridal were clear, the sun dropping toward the horizon and another night, though the air was still blisteringly hot. One-Eleven didn't notice, though of course, his kind rarely noted the temperature. He'd have to be a lot lower on energy to do so, and though he had no master to feed from at the moment, his energy levels were still high enough to do what he needed.

The men were easy to find. Just by crisscrossing the city, he would have located them once he came close enough to sense their emotions, but his feeder masters were with them and he could have tracked any of them across the world.

Their emotions led him to the harem. At first, he tried to dive down through the access ports that he'd used when the emperor ruled. The narrow tunnels were blocked, filled with solid stone. He went from one to the other, finding them all that way and turned in disgust to the entrance that humans used.

It was closed as well, though the stone that filled it felt different. One-Eleven wasn't an earth sylph by any means, but he could tell the difference between what was meant to be a wall and what was meant to be opened again.

He shifted to human and pounded on it, yelling along the hive line. *Let me in!* He'd find the man who had his Zalia's heart and destroy him. Then she'd be his. He didn't think of how Zalia would react to that or anything else. As usual, he was just caught up in instinct. Face the threat, destroy the threat. Nothing else mattered.

He pounded on the wall again and felt the stone start to shimmer underneath his fist. Grimly, he waited.

~

He'd found a flute in the storage room.

Actually, Airi had. There'd been a lot of supplies in there beyond the food: clothing that, of course, was for women, linens, games, and other musical instruments as well. Airi brought the flute to him while he and Xehm had still been doing a preliminary count of what was there, with Blithori's help. They'd also conscripted a scrawny young man named Glorki, who'd worked as a scribe before the emperor was overthrown. Devon already intended for Xehm to be in charge of the supply room, but the old man could neither read nor write. He'd need Glorki's help, as well as the half-dozen other men with stanchions who stood at the door. The last thing any of them needed was a riot to get control of the supplies.

Airi hovered over his shoulder, spinning the flute until it made an eerie, whistling noise. *Look look look look look,* she chanted excitedly, whirling it in front of his face.

It struck him as a good excuse to take a break, after everything he'd done already. Besides, as Leon told him once, just because he could do something, and even if he could do it better, it didn't mean he should. Xehm had it under control, as did his helpers and the men guarding the door. They looked content, in control of their own destinies. Right now, they didn't need him. Later, they would, but he wouldn't be any use if he was exhausted.

"Keep taking records," he told Xehm, clapping the older man on the shoulder. "It'll be good to know everything that's in here."

Xehm smiled at him. "We'll get it all sorted out," he promised.

Devon made his way out of the room, the guards letting him

through with their greetings and rough jokes. There were more men and boys in the hall outside, curious about what was happening, but everyone looked content to wait. They were men with a purpose now, not just refugees, and they'd found the food supplies before anyone had time to get really hungry. Devon didn't like to think about what the atmosphere in the pens would have been like if they'd started to become desperate. If they had, the six men on the door likely wouldn't have been enough.

Devon made his way through the crowd, offering reassurances that the food would be available and they wouldn't hold it back from anyone. There were some questions about when and just what was available, as well as how long they'd be down here, but he noticed that no one asked about the women. That would come in time, he suspected, once the shock and fear wore off. Devon wasn't looking forward to dealing with their anger when it did.

This flute is pretty, Airi said hopefully, still floating it through the air over his head. It was, as well as being larger than the one Devon had left behind in the hive, but he suspected he could manage to play it. Letting her continue to carry it, he looked back toward the arch that led into the feeder pens. Strange noises came from there as their small group of sylphs worked to turn the feeder pens into something that a human being would actually want to live in. Given that so many of the men down here were ex-feeders, Devon hoped that the results would be healing for them. From the look of the feeders he saw crowded around the entrance and watching, he suspected it just might be. He left them to it, too tired to even consider checking on their progress. They could do it without his supervision. Right now he needed sleep, food, a bath, and some time with his own sylph. For the moment, only three of those things were really possible, since he didn't see a bath happening anytime soon, and despite his own weariness and hunger, he knew which of the three was most important to him.

"Let's play you a song," he murmured and felt Airi's joy as she cheered in his mind and swooped with the flute into the harem.

As he'd figured, most of the alcoves were taken, many of which seemed to be inhabited by men who'd brought their sons along. Devon looked down the length of the room and could only see two alcoves with their curtains still pulled back and empty. They were on either side of an obviously claimed alcove, where a man sat against one of the jambs of the doorway, his foot up on the other jamb opposite him, his face obscured as he looked into the alcove. The alcoves to either side didn't have belongings set down to mark their ownership, but Devon recognized Gel sitting outside one of the alcoves just beyond. Airi dancing above him, still spinning her flute in distracted happiness, Devon made his way through the crowd to join the man.

"Hey," he said to Gel, crouching down. "How are you feeling now?"

The former feeder looked up at him, really making eye contact as he reached up to scratch his neck. "Shasha says this is the safest place now. I don't want to leave."

"I guess it is," Devon smiled, "and you don't have to." He gestured at the empty alcove beside him. "Has anyone taken this one?"

Gel slowly looked at the alcove and finally shook his head. "No one wanted it."

"I guess it's mine then." Even when the feeder pens were converted, Devon doubted they'd be terribly comfortable, not unless they spread all these cushions around. At least now no one would say he was taking advantage of his new supposed authority, not with the alcove going unclaimed for this long. He sat down cross-legged in front of it and held up his hands. "Give it over, okay?"

Immediately, Airi dropped the flute into his palms, squealing. Devon tested the holes, checking the balance as he thought about what he could play. Because the flute was larger than his, it likely had a deeper tone. It felt more suited to a somber piece, or perhaps that was just the way he felt after everything that had happened. Zalia taken, seeing the Hunter . . . What was he supposed to do now? Hide until it went away? Tell the battle sylphs he could see the thing and have them laugh at him? Or use him to hunt it? He, go to a battler deliberately? Unbidden, he remembered Heyou, who'd forced him into fatherhood and then into what was essentially exile. He couldn't go back, and didn't want to either, not now that he'd found Zalia; except she'd been taken by a battler, who could make her feel ecstasies no human man could match. How was he supposed to compete? How was he supposed to do anything?

He put the flute to his mouth and blew, his lip vibrating as a song that was mournful and slow came out of him, detailing his sorrow and helplessness. Airi settled down, her emotions shifting to match his sadness, even as she was happy that he played for her. Gel stared at him, his mouth hanging open, while men nearby lifted their heads to listen.

Devon played an aria of doubt. They couldn't stay here forever, not here. Nor could they just expect the Hunter to go away as the sylphs obviously did. It would only go somewhere else and kill someone else, and there was no guarantee it wouldn't come back. Meanwhile, the very foundation of their society was torn apart, families broken, and everyone was hiding and wondering, not knowing how their loved ones were.

His fingers danced rapidly over the holes of the flute, changing the tune as he swirled down the scales. The Hunter would destroy them all; break them if it couldn't devour them. The sylphs couldn't see it, but humans could. Devon's memory of the monster was haunting and horrible, a series of notes as low as the flute could go before climbing up to the highest in discordant triumph. The battle sylphs couldn't kill it because they couldn't see it. Men could, if they got close enough and lucky enough and it didn't eat them first. He had to tell them.

Sudden terror made him lose his mouth position and the flute fell silent. Devon lowered it, wishing beyond anything that Zalia was there with him, just so he could lay his head on her breast and not worry about the world for a while.

That was beautiful, Airi said.

"It was."

The comment came from beside him. Devon turned to see the man who'd been sitting in the doorway of his alcove, next to the empty one Devon had claimed. He was the man Devon had seen carrying an ancient woman into the hive, and Devon froze in terror at the sight of him while Airi squeaked above. Now he knew why the alcoves on either side of the creature had been left unclaimed.

The battle sylph regarded him evenly for a moment before he looked up at the ceiling of the harem. He studied it for a moment and turned back to Devon again. "She liked your music. Play for her until I get back." He leaned into the alcove, whispering something Devon couldn't even pretend to hear, and finally stood and walked away. Men scrambled to clear his path as he left the harem.

Do we have to live next to a battle sylph? Airi complained.

Devon couldn't answer her, too busy trying to get his lungs to take in air again after the shock. Battle sylphs. He just couldn't handle battle sylphs, not at all.

Still, something niggled at him. "Shasha said that the elemental sylphs weren't listened to," he said. "Right?"

Usually, Airi agreed.

"But battle sylphs are?"

I think so. The ones who can blow the most stuff up usually are anyway.

So that battle sylph could take word to the others about how men could see the Hunter. Devon had an image of being surrounded by the creatures, leading them into battle, and nearly fainted.

A low whine sounded from the alcove the battler had been guarding, rising to a cry of despair and loneliness. Startled, Devon got up and walked over to see the woman the battler had carried in lying on the cushions, her face creased with distress. It was hard to imagine the ancient woman with the beautiful battle sylph, but it was obviously happening. She looked around desperately for the creature, her withered face damp with tears as she tried to push herself up and failed.

Even if it hadn't been a battle sylph who told him to play for her, Devon couldn't leave anyone like that. Dropping to his knees, he brought the flute up to his lips again and resumed playing.

This time he didn't play of his own sorrow, not wanting to think about it. Instead he played a song about Zalia, and how deeply he loved her. The song nearly danced as it twirled through the air, forming an aria that sent Airi swirling up to the ceiling and had the old woman smiling by the end of it, her head bobbing nearly in tune. Again, men fell quiet in order to listen, while boys ran up and down excitedly, a few dancing in place, just being happy.

For the moment, it was enough.

～

Haru headed up to the surface, following Shasha's summons. He'd hardly needed it. He'd felt the angry battle sylph up on the surface and recognized him. One-Eleven. Ignorant, immature, always thinking he was entitled but otherwise not thinking at all. Old though, older and larger than Haru by far.

Haru went up the stairs as Shasha opened the way for him, climbing the curving stairs and feeling the other battler's anger growing. He'd been denied what he wanted and he was going to punish the one he felt to be responsible for it. Haru didn't know who that someone was, but he wasn't going to let there be any killings in this new little hive of his. Not so long as he was guarding it.

The last of the rock that blocked the stairwell parted, melting back into the original walls, and he saw One-Eleven step forward. One-Eleven started when he saw the other battler and Haru moved, forcing him to back up into the sunlight again. The sun was starting to go down but the sky was still clear, oddly empty without flying sylphs in it. Haru almost hesitated before leaving the safety of the stairwell, but he had no choice. The Hunter would kill him or it wouldn't. The door was already closing behind him to make sure neither it nor One-Eleven got into the hive.

"Hey," he protested, trying to step past Haru. "I need to get in there!"

Haru planted a palm on his chest and shoved him back. Surprised, One-Eleven stumbled away and looked at him, stunned.

"What do you want?" Haru asked, though he already knew. He could feel the anger in the other sylph. He wanted to kill, and in all the years Haru knew him, One-Eleven wasn't known to be subtle. He hadn't even been usable as a guard, given how many men he killed for the slightest infraction. He'd worked solely in the human fields, reaping grain and guarding against anything that might try to taste the harvest.

One-Eleven glared at him. "That ambassador. The pale man who came here. I'm going to kill him. He took my woman from me!"

Of course it was him. Of course One-Eleven wanted to kill him. The one man who had the little hive behind Haru functioning and safe with a real leader. Who was currently sitting right beside Fareeda so she wouldn't be alone. The irony of it all was immense, but even if it had been some other man One-Eleven was after, Haru wouldn't have handed him over. The rules in this hive were unstated, but that didn't make them any less obvious. Men weren't expendable here. Haru had accepted that when he came, which made his response to the other sylph the only one he could give.

He hit him, punching One-Eleven so hard that he fell back with a yelp, landing on his back on the stone of the square. Haru immediately went to his natural shape and attacked. For all his immaturity, One-Eleven was still the 111th battle sylph to be brought to Meridal when the last was numbered 702, and he was older than Haru by hundreds of years.

That age made him fast. Despite not expecting the attack, he shifted to his own natural form and was airborne before Haru could reach him. Haru swept up after him, closing as fast as he could and lashing out with his tentacles. He didn't want to kill his hive mate, just drive him away, and he used nonlethal attacks, hoping that One-Eleven would do the same. Otherwise, this could get fatal really fast.

This hive is sacrosanct, Haru told him. *You can't kill anyone here!*

One-Eleven dodged around his attack, lashing out with his own tentacles and scoring painfully across Haru's back. *This isn't a hive!* he protested. *It's full of nothing but men! They're worthless!*

They grappled, Haru still lashing out with as many tentacles as he could form, biting as well when he got the chance. One-Eleven roared, wincing back from the attacks, and then yanked away, shooting upward. Haru followed, grabbing the trailing end of One-Eleven's mantle and being pulled along.

Just leave! Haru shouted. *I want you to leave!*

No! I'm going to kill him!

They arced high over the city, the streets empty below them and the main hive rising above, with the queen's palace floating overhead. Neither of them could see the Hunter that hovered between the two structures, watching them, and neither went within range of it, which would be within range of the queen's dwelling as well. This was a fight between them alone.

The queen gave leave to do whatever we wanted!

Haru slammed a tentacle against One-Eleven's side, the other grunting before he whipped his own across the smaller sylph's back. It hurt, but he couldn't both put up a shield and continue his own attack. One-Eleven hit him again and Haru realized he'd have to. Battle sylphs usually fought each other in groups, attacking other hives en masse. One-Eleven was too old for Haru to fight one-on-one; he would just take Haru apart. Haru brought up his shields, losing his grip in the process, and was knocked away.

I'm allowed to do this, One-Eleven snarled.

The queen never gave you permission to do murder.

The two battlers circled each other, glaring. Haru hurt, more than he'd thought he would. One-Eleven had hit him a lot harder than he'd realized. In the backs of their minds, the hive line was screaming, battlers roaring and rising at the anger both of them felt.

What's going on? Tooie shouted. He appeared at the edge of the palace, rocketing straight toward them, a half-dozen other battle sylphs at the edge of his mantle. *Why are you fighting?* He sounded furious.

One-Eleven turned toward him, the lightning inside his cloud body raging. He was big enough that all of them together might not have been able to take him, but his tone was slightly more polite, recognizing Tooie's ascendancy with the queen. *He won't let me in his so-called hive.*

Tooie slowed, his eyes swirling. He looked at Haru. *Hive?*

Haru wearily looked back at Tooie, not wanting to fight his own brothers but prepared to. *The queen gave me leave to take Fareeda where I felt she would be safest. Devon Chole has made a hive for the men. I brought her there. One-Eleven wants to kill him.*

He took my master from me! One-Eleven shouted. *Once he's dead, she'll love me!*

Tooie's angry emotions suddenly felt tired and Haru had to wonder just how worn out the lead battler was with all of them. He'd watched him try to council the queen, only to be ignored. He'd watched him try to lead on his own and had to agree it wasn't working. If it had, Haru wouldn't have had the need to take Fareeda away. Only these humans seemed to have the ability to succeed regardless of gender. The other battlers hovered around him, watching curiously.

I think, Tooie said at last, *that the queen will be asking for this Devon Chole at some point.*

But! One-Eleven protested.

He lives, Tooie told him. *I'm giving the order. He is to stay alive. None of us touch him, not unless the queen herself commands it, and I for one pray she doesn't.*

One-Eleven reared above him, his hate aura flaring. He was larger than Tooie, but the other battlers reared up as well to match, Haru with them, and even though he still might have won, One-Eleven pulled back. *It's not fair! She's mine! You can't say he's more important than me!*

Tooie snarled at him. *If you can't even manage to name yourself, you don't get to say who's most important. I told you to talk to the woman. You think you'll win her by killing any man she likes? You're an idiot!*

One-Eleven shrank into himself, still outraged. *What would you do if it was the queen? What if she decided she loved someone else?*

I'd let her go, and grieve. Leave the human alone. Tooie turned away from him and looked at Haru. *You're hurt. A healer should see you.*

Haru pulled back. He could feel Fareeda in the back of his mind, missing him and stressed by his absence. *I won't leave this hive.*

Fine. Just don't treat your brothers as enemies.

Haru bowed in acknowledgment, his mantle aching. He would heal, but it would take time. He would have lost this battle if Tooie hadn't come, he realized. Shamed, he returned to the hive, calling on Shasha to let him in. All he wanted was to see Fareeda, and this Devon Chole, and reassure himself that the man was worth all of this.

Tooie turned to One-Eleven. *Don't fight anymore.*

One-Eleven focused angry eyes on him, his mouth gaping with lightning. *What am I supposed to do? I want her to be mine!*

Tooie sighed, turning away with Yahe and the others. The queen was calling along the hive line, asking inexpertly what was happening. He just wanted to get back to her, and remind her of this man Devon Chole, who'd gathered hundreds of men and given them a place to survive. He could feel them gathered under the ground, and while many of them were unhappy and angered, they were overall more content than the women still panicking in the main hive.

I keep telling you, One-Eleven, Tooie said. *Talk to her. Be her friend before you try to be her lover. Be someone she can rely on for once.*

He led the way back, trusting One-Eleven to at least obey him about not killing anyone, the other battlers of the Circle flanking him as he arced high over the palace to enter through one of the skylights.

One-Eleven watched them go, Tooie and the others entering the palace while Haru limped back into the hive below them. He hovered in midair, staring after them all.

But I don't know what to say, he whispered.

CHAPTER TWENTY-TWO

Cautiously, the Hunter watched the two battlers fight, not liking it. Its tentacles were largely expendable if they decided to start tossing energy blasts around, but they were flying fairly high, much higher than they did when they looked for it. It would be disastrous if they hit its actual body with one, or stumbled into it and realized what it was. It could only feed with its tentacles, not its gas bag, and it couldn't raise its tentacles quickly enough to protect itself. Already it had spent much of the afternoon raising even the lightest of them to reach the palace. They clung to the underside as it watched the fight, waiting.

Its patience was rewarded as more battlers came out and the fight ended. It waited until all of them were gone, even the last straggler returning to the palace, before it started its work again, feeling patiently along the underside of the palace for all the myriad ways there were to get inside.

~

Fareeda liked the music. Even if Airi hadn't told him, still dancing over his head, Devon could see the woman's distant gaze start to focus, her head bobbing in achingly slow counterpoint to his rhythm. He tried to gauge that, to judge what she liked, and found himself playing a slow, soft waltz. She closed her eyes at that and smiled.

He finished the song. He was tired and needed some sleep and food before the men invariably started coming to him for advice and orders, but he felt his music was really making a connection with the old woman and he liked to see her happy. It looked as though it had been a very long time since she was. He changed to another waltz, one his father first tried to teach him on the fiddle and he'd adapted for the flute. Sitting up, Fareeda swayed to the music, humming so softly that he couldn't hear it.

Someone else could. "She's singing," a voice breathed.

Devon looked over his shoulder and the playing faltered in fear as he saw the battler had returned, looking no different than when he left, except now an expression of wonder was on his face. One hand pressed to his belly, he ignored Devon's fear as he waved with the other hand for him to continue. "Keep playing. Please."

Devon swallowed and did so, fighting to keep the music as even and clear as it had been. He squeaked a few times, but Fareeda didn't seem to mind, still swaying and humming as she smiled up at the battler. His own answering smile was beatific as he dropped to his knees with what Devon could almost have thought was a wince and started to sing himself, softly in time to the music.

Come to bed, beloved one,
It's time to rest, for day is done.
Night lifts up her weary head
And calls for all to come to bed.

Fareeda smiled at him, her wrinkled, spotted old hand reaching toward his. To Devon's amazement, she sang the next lines of the song, her words more mouthed than spoken, but there.

No, it's barely dark, it's time to play,
Gone is the blinding light of day.

While dark is when the world's alive.
A time for ecstasy to thrive.

The battler's eyes were huge, his hand trembling as he touched the old woman's. Battle sylphs loved, Devon reminded himself. For all their faults and dangers, they loved, and he grieved for Zalia, who he hoped couldn't love one back.

The battler sang again, his words choked and nearly as inaudible as hers. No one but Devon and Airi even realized what was happening, her length pressed against his back again.

It's dark, my head is growing thick,
I must sleep or else be sick.
I crave your warmth right by my side.
Head on breast and hand on thigh.

Fareeda sighed, lifting the battler's hand to press against her cheek, and finished the song.

When put like that, I can't say no.
To bed with you for now I'll go,
And when at last you are asleep,
I'll be there still. The night can keep.

Turning, she hesitated, her eyes glazing over, but not as badly as before. The music had woken something in her that had been asleep a very long time. Still, she turned and shuffled farther back into the alcove, apparently intending to follow the words of the song in deed as well. The battle sylph shot Devon a glance so filled with gratitude that it made him nervous, and followed after her, closing the curtain behind them.

Devon let the flute drop into his lap.

What just happened? Airi asked.

"I think we made a friend," Devon said, and resisted the urge to throw up as a result of it.

～

Zalia wasn't sure what she was supposed to do now. She wanted to get off this floating island and back to Devon, but there was no one she was sure she could ask to take her to the surface and, she had to admit, she was afraid to leave the safety of the palace. She did see a battler in the hall outside the room she was in and considered asking him to carry her, but he was with Kiala, and the last thing she wanted to do was face that woman again.

Zalia had no idea if anything she'd said to the queen made any difference. She'd just been too angry to keep her mouth shut. Now she felt she couldn't leave, that she had a responsibility to help the queen. Devon had hoped at most that she'd be able to return to the hive and talk to the women there, not that she would be brought right to the queen herself. Regardless, Zalia had no real idea what she could actually do. It was Devon who was the ambassador, and even he doubted his ability to do what he'd been sent for. Zalia had no reservations that he could do it, but she was hardly in a position to share her opinion with him just now.

She was also afraid of what One-Eleven was doing and flinched every time she heard an explosion outside. He was after Devon, she was sure of it, or at least after what he thought was his competition. He might not know it was Devon she cared about, or where the man was if he did. The very last thing Zalia wanted to do was risk leading the battle sylph to her lover.

It was almost strange; after having been a virgin just a short time ago, she'd had sex now with two different men, but only considered one of them her lover. She'd always have a connection to One-Eleven, she supposed, given how he'd been her first and how, if nothing else, he'd opened her up to the idea of actually being intimate and how the world would hardly end as a result of it. What would Ilaja think of her now? she wondered. Likely, Ilaja wasn't thinking of her at all. She was probably in the hive, perhaps with a battle sylph deciding that she would make the perfect master. Zalia wasn't quite sure if she wished Ilaja luck with that or not. Certainly the opinion toward women and a woman's virtue was going to change in Meridal. Granted, with all of the other changes going on right now, it was possible that no one would even notice. She sighed. Given how there were likely not going to be any men in the city at all if Eapha didn't stop waffling, no one would care. She just hoped that Devon really was safe in the feeder pens the way he thought.

She wished she was with him.

It was night out, the sun having vanished with its usual speed and the temperature already dropping. Shivering, Zalia went over to the wide windows that had been left open after One-Eleven dived through them. Outside, the city was eerily dark, the ground and buildings below her shadowed and the sky filled with more stars than she had ever seen before. Zalia looked at them for a moment, but she was restless and the night was only growing colder. Quietly, she closed the windows and latched them, thinking that if One-Eleven wanted to get back in, he'd have to find another way.

She didn't notice threads as fine as human hairs wavering below the edge of the window, tentacles, thicker across than she was, climbing slowly up behind them.

What was she supposed to do now? Sleep here? Find a place to bathe? Her stomach rumbled, but she had no food to eat. She'd just been left here and she wasn't even sure if she could leave the room.

As if they'd known what she was feeling—and of course they probably had—a knock came at the door. Zalia gaped at it for a moment, thinking that it was One-Eleven, but she already knew he wasn't the sort to knock. "Who is it?" she asked.

"Tooie," came the answer. "The queen's battler."

Oh. Suddenly nervous, she went to open the door. The battle sylph she'd seen standing behind the queen while she was yelling at her—the one who'd seemed to support what she'd been saying—smiled at her. He was just as stomach-tighteningly beautiful as One-Eleven, but he didn't look at her with desire. His smile was kind, his eyes reassuring.

"The queen would like to see you."

Zalia gaped at her. "Me? I didn't think—"

"That she'd want anything to do with you after your last conversation?" His smile broadened. "You didn't say anything to her that she didn't want to hear."

"She wanted me yelling at her?"

Tooie shook his head. "Not really. But she did need someone to tell her what she'd been feeling herself was right."

Zalia was surprised by that. "But . . . if she wanted to hear it, why wasn't she doing anything?" Realizing that the battler was probably disposed to be on his queen's side, she flushed.

Tooie's smile didn't change. "It's been hard for her, when you consider the opinions of her friends. You should know, being queen makes her empathic. She could feel their scorn and ridicule."

Thinking of Kiala, Zalia flushed. That woman was hard to deal with. It must have been even harder for someone who could feel whatever she did. Tooie grinned, reading her emotions, and turned sideways, gesturing for her to precede him out the door.

Zalia went nervously, not sure what her reception would be like. It was different than before though. This time, the queen was sitting at a battered harvest table in one corner of the kitchens, one obviously meant for the palace's onetime servants to use, and there was no sign of the women who'd been lounging around her before. Sylphs worked in the kitchen, most of them looking like girls made of mist or earth, water or fire as they cleaned and started the preparations for the next day. Eapha was sitting alone, nibbling from a tray of cheeses, bread, fruit, and smoked fish. Suddenly, Zalia was famished.

The queen looked up at her, so achingly beautiful herself it was no wonder she was taken for the harems. "You're hungry," she said. "Have some."

"Oh, no," Zalia stammered, suddenly shy around her. "I couldn't."

The queen gave her a slightly exasperated look. "I can feel how hungry you are. Just have some, there's more than enough to share."

Zalia sank into a chair across from her while Tooie went to sit by his lover. She took some of the bread. It tasted wonderful.

"You really can feel what I do?"

Eapha nodded. She looked tired. "It's something about being queen. If sylphs are around, I can feel anyone's emotions, the same way they do. I just don't understand them as well."

And obviously she couldn't feel what was happening on the ground below either, or Zalia couldn't imagine Eapha ever having allowed what happened. Still, she looked at her resentfully and saw the woman flinch. Tooie frowned.

"Why did you want to see me?"

The queen studied her for a moment, her mouth moving slowly around a bite of cheese before she swallowed it. "I'm not sure," she admitted. "I guess I just wanted to talk to you without everyone around. You've put me in quite a spot."

"That's not my fault," Zalia blurted.

"It's not my fault either," Eapha reminded her. "I haven't had control of any of this. I just fell into it."

As a slave and concubine, she certainly hadn't had any control. At least it hadn't been Zalia who'd been given the queenhood. Zalia didn't want to feel sympathetic toward Eapha though, even as she found herself liking the woman, now that she wasn't lounging around with her friends waiting for the world to take care of itself. Zalia could see the intelligence in her eyes now, and with it, the fear. Given the attitudes of her erstwhile friends, suddenly Zalia could understand why she herself was sitting here.

"When I was brought here," Zalia said slowly, "Devon was getting all of the men into the feeder pens. We're pretty sure they'll be safe there, providing the food holds out."

Eapha's eyes lit up at that. "Really?" She turned to Tooie, looking up at him. "How much food do we have?"

"Not enough for that many people, not with the crops destroyed by the storm."

Eapha looked at him with despair. Zalia felt much the same way. Devon hadn't given up though, frightened though he was. Eapha looked over the table, with its trays of food that was more than she could eat by herself, and suddenly reached across it, grabbing up a strip of smoked fish.

"There's fish in the sea to eat, isn't there?" she demanded.

"Yes," Tooie said slowly, "but the Hunter could eat any fishermen sent out. They might not make it back."

Eapha looked at him. "So send water sylphs. If they're underwater they should be safe from it, shouldn't they? They can drive the fish back here for battlers to catch."

"But to get them there . . ."

"Dig a tunnel," Eapha told him, her eyes bright with inspiration. "We have hundreds of earth sylphs with nothing to do. Dig a tunnel to the feeder pens as well. We'll live underground until that thing starves."

Tooie's eyes gleamed, staring at his queen with his body stiff with pride and barely contained motion. He never would have thought of that, Zalia thought. She wouldn't have either, would she? How could she? Only one woman could order all of the sylphs to action after all. Now all of the sylphs in the room stared at her, taut with excitement. Eapha seemed to draw strength from it, straightening in her chair with a flush on her face.

"That's actually brilliant."

Both of them turned toward the doorway. Kiala stood there dressed in a sleeping gown, her long hair braided down her back. She had a frown on her face, a line between her brows, as she regarded them both. Zalia tensed, but the other woman only seemed interested in getting a snack. She came over and gathered some of the cheeses and breads, not speaking as she studied her friend and shook her head. Eapha just watched her, tense and uncertain. "I didn't think you were that smart, Eapha," Kiala sniffed at last and left, taking her plate of cheese with her.

Both women watched her go, as did Tooie, his eyebrows raised. "Jealous woman," he said at last.

Zalia sagged, glad to have avoided another fight. Beside her, Eapha sagged as well, obviously thinking the same thing.

Eapha dragged her hand through her hair. "In the morning," she decided. "Tell everyone we'll start in the morning." She looked at the tray of food and sighed. "In the morning," she said again and helped herself to a piece of marbled cheese, indicating that Zalia do so as well. Zalia did so, gratefully, and they sat in silence while the battle sylph watched, all of them thinking about the day ahead.

CHAPTER TWENTY-THREE

Word spread, news traveling about the conversation between the two women and what was decided as a result.

Even though she wasn't part of the hive, Airi heard what was going to happen from Shasha and spun excitedly in place. Half seen through a gap in his curtain, the battle sylph didn't move due to his pain, other than to look out at them, but the rest of the sylphs rose up in excitement. Loyal to their masters or not, none of them had wanted to leave the hive and all the safety and comfort it brought.

Devon was asleep, curled up in his alcove, even as Gel was asleep in his own. Airi met Shasha's eyes, which gleamed in the light of the few fire sylphs, and both of them went to relay the news. Airi didn't know what Shasha was going to say to her damaged master, but she knew what she would say to hers.

Devon, she called, blowing her gentle winds on him to ruffle his hair. He mumbled and pulled his thin blanket up higher over himself. It was still a bit cool underground, even with all the human bodies sleeping in the former harem. *Devon, wake up. I have the best news.*

Devon started awake, his eyes heavy with exhaustion. It had been a long time since he'd had any really proper sleep, Airi thought guiltily, but he needed to know this. "Is Zalia back?" he slurred.

No. It's almost as good as that. The queen has spoken. The hive is to dig a tunnel to us. We'll all be reunited.

Devon took a moment to absorb that and sat up slowly, studying her. "Are you serious?"

Yes. Shasha says the head battler told them all. She even has a way for us to collect food without being exposed to the Hunter. We'll be safe from it.

Devon gaped at her. "When did this happen?" He hadn't formed a good opinion of the queen, Airi remembered, and she felt his disbelief. Uncertain, she sent a query to Shasha, who relayed it to her sisters in the hive and brought back an amused answer a few minutes later.

Zalia convinced her, she said, surprised herself.

"Zalia?"

Airi ruffled his hair straight up and giggled, amazed at the story. *Apparently, she yelled at her. The queen listened.*

Devon slumped back on his elbows, gaping at her with his mouth open. "She . . ." He threw back his head and laughed. "I guess I really didn't need to come at all, did I?"

He was laughing, but Airi felt what was running through his heart. *You had to come,* she said slowly, wanting him to feel better about himself. *Zalia would never have been taken to the queen if not for you.*

"She would have been taken," Devon said bitterly. "That battler's wanted her since before we met."

Yes, but without you, she wouldn't have known what to say. She plucked at his shirt with her wind until he looked at her. *And most of these men would have died on the surface when the Hunter attacked the square in front of the hive.*

Devon thought about it and exhaled loudly. "I guess so. Still, it doesn't feel like I did anything. Hiding in the ground isn't very glamorous. Better than dying though."

Airi giggled. Devon had never seen himself as a hero. Despite his successes, he'd always felt he accomplished far less than he did. *Why are you supposed to do it yourself? We've always been a team, haven't we?* She flicked his nose and he jerked his head up, but he was smiling.

"I guess we better start thinking about what to do next," he said. "We have food here, but it still needs to be rationed, and we have a lot of people who have reason to be angry with the battlers. I doubt the battle sylphs are so keen on the queen's change of heart either." He shuddered at the reminder of battle sylphs, as did Airi. She extended her awareness toward the battler in the next alcove, but despite the excitement, he was asleep. He'd been hurt badly when he left. She didn't know precisely why and didn't want to. He'd been benign to them and he'd be able to go back to the hive and get healed once the tunnel connecting them opened up. She could hear Shasha discussing the logistics of it. A day it would take them, if all of the earth sylphs worked together. They sounded eager. Then Devon yawned and she turned her full attention back to him.

You need to sleep, she told him. *You're worn out.*

"I know," he mumbled, yawning again. "But there's so much to get ready."

It can wait. None of the humans know about this. The queen said nothing was to happen until morning. You can sleep, and then you'll be able to do useful things.

"I guess you're right," he said, lying back on the cushions with only a little reluctance, his body already turning back to sleep.

And you'll be able to see Zalia again! Airi added happily. Immediately, Devon's eyes shot open and his weariness burned away on a surge of adrenaline.

Oops, she said, berating herself as she realized how far away sleep was from her master now.

∽

Zalia and Eapha didn't say much. Neither of them knew each other very well and both were tired. Instead, they sat together, nibbling at the food until the trays were empty, ignoring any future need to ration in a moment of camaraderie. For Zalia, it had been the best food she'd ever had in her life, though she never remembered how it tasted afterward.

Eventually, she'd gone back to the room where One-Eleven left her, and fell across her bed. She was asleep immediately.

She didn't know how long she stayed that way, but she woke up to warmth and the feel of a bare shoulder under her cheek. Dazed and comfortable, she felt the smooth skin under her face while a hand tenderly stroked her hair, softly enough that it might not have been what woke her.

Her hand was across his stomach, just lax, and her toes brushed against his leg. She was warm and content and sleepy, but she knew this wasn't Devon. Zalia sighed, not sure how to deal with this. She didn't want to break anyone's heart tonight. All she really wanted to do was get some sleep, in this wonderful bed with a full stomach for one of the first times in her life. Tomorrow would be overwhelming with the work to get the men and women back together and she wasn't going to be exempt from it. Eapha hadn't said she was needed, but Zalia had the feeling the queen wanted another woman around who was on her side.

One-Eleven's hand slowed, cupping the back of her head as he leaned over to press his lips against her forehead. Zalia kept her eyes mostly closed, barely able to see the curve of his chest in the darkness as she lay there. What had he done? she wondered. Would he honestly have come back and tried to act as though nothing was wrong if he'd killed Devon?

"I didn't know when you'd be back," she said at last, not able to keep silent. "You didn't . . . hurt anyone did you?"

His hand resumed stroking her hair. "No." Did his voice sound bitter?

Zalia opened her eyes and twisted her head around so that she could see his face. It was vaguely luminescent in the light of the moon coming through the window. "You said you had to think."

"Yeah." He breathed out, the motion of his chest dropping her down in the mattress and unintentionally closer to him. She didn't feel shy about it; how could she, given what they'd done together? But she didn't feel desire either. He was doing nothing to affect her feelings this time, and, she thought with amusement, having more success with her than he would have otherwise. He looked vulnerable for once, and real. "I really messed up getting you to love me."

Zalia thought about that for a moment and sighed, rolling away from him and onto her back. He let her, his arm straightening out so that it was under her neck. She adjusted a bit and rested her head on it, staring up at the indistinct shadows of the ceiling. "You can't make someone love you."

"Yes, I understand that. I mean, Tooie told me, but I didn't listen. Not until now."

He looked at her and his expression was so hopeful her heart nearly broke. He was so beautiful, and so sincere, and so utterly, amorally dangerous.

"What do you want from me?" she asked quietly.

"Everything," he whispered. "Just everything."

She sat up and slid her legs over the side of the bed, sitting with her back to him and staring at her hands. "I can't give you everything. I don't know that I can give you anything."

Zalia heard him sit up behind her, imagined him reaching out toward her, perhaps hesitantly. On some level, she might have felt powerful to have such control over him, if only she hadn't been so miserable. She loved Devon, but when she was here with One-Eleven . . . she saw such *potential* between them, yet didn't, and was afraid of all of it. If only she hadn't met one of them—only she couldn't believe that and didn't want to. Both of them had changed her life so much. Devon's gentleness, One-Eleven's passion, Devon's sweet lovemaking, One-Eleven's control. She closed her eyes and his hand rested on her shoulder from behind.

"You don't have to," he promised her. "I was thinking . . . I'll prove myself to you. I'll be there for you. No matter what, I'll be there. You're first to me, before anything. I swear it. Nothing else matters, not even you loving me back."

Zalia turned her head to look at him, her mouth opening for all the words she couldn't say. She couldn't think what to say, not at all. Language deserted her. One-Eleven just looked back at her, with his perfect, beautiful eyes she could lose herself in so easily and his flawless body that spoke to the woman inside her, the one that had so recently discovered such a desperate need to be touched. She could go to him now and the ecstasy would be more than any human man would ever be able to provide. He'd always be young and he'd always love her, and she would always be in control of him. She'd lose none of her freedom, not to a creature who had to obey her every whim. She'd always be wanted, no matter how she aged or who she became, and she'd always be safe, because he would kill to defend her.

She just wasn't sure that was what she wanted.

What about having children? She'd never really let herself think about them, but it was there. Devon had told her when he described his life that he'd been used by a battler to father a child for the creature's lover, and then told to leave. She could have a child the same way with One-Eleven, but did she want that? Did she want her children to have a battle sylph as a father? Did she even want to think about such things right now? She knew she didn't, not with everything that was to happen in the morning. Already it was horribly late and she was too tired for philosophical thought or even the desires of her own heart.

"I need to sleep," she said at last and lay again on the bed, her back to him. One-Eleven didn't leave; she suspected he wouldn't unless she directly ordered him to, and there was no compunction yet between them for him to obey. He might not. She didn't really care anyway. She just closed her eyes and was asleep in seconds, even though she'd thought she'd be awake a long time yet.

One-Eleven lay beside her, not needing to sleep though he was weaker than he liked, the masters he'd thrown aside for her not available for him to feed on anymore. He'd be all right until she changed her mind, as long as he didn't stress himself too much. He hoped she changed her mind. She had to, or else he'd go mad.

The battle sylph stroked her hair gently with his hand, careful not to wake her. Awake, she was filled with doubts and conflicting desires that tried to pull her away from him. Asleep, he could pretend she was his the way he wanted her to be, and take whatever comfort from that he could. It wasn't much, but it had to be enough. He was what he was. He loved her and would always love her, and nothing would change that. Instinct was too strong and always would be.

One-Eleven sighed and settled down to share her rest, if not her dreams, while invisible wisps as thin as a woman's hair drifted up across the closed windows all around them.

~

Despite Airi's efforts to get him to sleep, Devon stayed awake long past when he should have, thinking.

They were going to survive this, they really were. Between the hive and this place, as well as all the food stored here, they'd have enough to outlast the Hunter. Not that they'd even have to anymore. With the human ability to *see* the monster, the battle sylphs would be able to destroy it. It wouldn't be easy to approach them, but Devon wasn't so much of a coward that he wouldn't say anything, and if he had to, he'd prove it to them. The Hunter would be dead by the day's end and everyone would be able to reunite with their families. The stupidity of the last few days wouldn't be repeated.

It amazed him how much difference a single woman could make, though he supposed it shouldn't, given how he'd seen Solie take on her responsibilities and how she ran the Valley. Eapha wasn't Solie though, and Meridal was a very different kind of world. He'd have to help her, he thought with an exhalation of breath. This was what Leon had sent him for, and if he had to ask Airi to carry him back up to that floating palace and force his way into her throne room through a hundred battle sylphs, he would. He'd probably piss himself a few times, but he'd do it. He'd grown too, he supposed. There were hundreds of men safe now because he'd stopped letting himself get crippled by his own doubts. He was trained for this. He'd do it and stop letting himself think he couldn't. He'd just do it and let the doubts bother him later, after it was done. He knew it wouldn't be that easy, but if he pretended it was, maybe in the long run it would be.

Devon sighed, lying there in the darkness of his little alcove on top of a pile of cushions that had been used by concubines and battlers for purposes he did *not* want to think about, and listened to the sounds of the men and boys all around him. It was mostly quiet, nearly everyone asleep, but the sounds were still there. The muttering, the snoring, and sometimes the weeping. He tried not to listen to it. If it had been him, he wouldn't have wanted anyone paying attention to his grief.

In the morning, he'd be able to tell them all that they'd be reunited with their women again, that there would be a passageway linking them, and that the Hunter would soon be dead. He'd probably have a hundred volunteers to lead the battlers after the thing.

Most of all, he'd see Zalia again. Despite everything else, he kept coming back to that fact. She'd done so much more than he'd dreamed he'd ever be able to, and he was so proud of her. More, he missed her. He hadn't yet told her father that they were betrothed.

He was waiting for Zalia to be with him in order to do that, and to make sure that she hadn't chosen a battle sylph instead.

Devon closed his eyes, forcing himself to think positively, to imagine the best happening and ignore his doubts. Tomorrow. Everything would wait until tomorrow.

Eventually, he slept.

~

The sylphs were talking, planning the process of joining the two hives into one, and the Hunter listened.

It didn't matter to it what they did, not really. It would be in the main hive soon anyway. If they'd had the passageway they talked about made already, some of the food would flee down it and it could only reach so far after them, but they didn't have it dug yet. They'd start come the morning, but that would be too late.

With a final, massive effort, it heaved up a tentacle high enough to latch on to the side of the palace and heard the air sylphs who held it complain in confusion about the sudden extra weight. They weren't inventive thinkers, so it didn't worry about them guessing what was going on, but there wasn't much time to waste. It didn't have the strength to hold its tentacles over its head for long and it needed to get this done before it used up too much of its food stores.

Using the one heavy tentacle as a brace, it reached up with more tentacles, anchoring them on to the palace and using them to hold itself as it wormed its way inside, digging deep in search of its target. It would like to suck the entire palace clean and get the queen, causing complete chaos in the hive, but it would settle for its most immediate target—the air sylphs who kept the hundreds of tons of rock from plunging down on the egg-like hive below.

CHAPTER TWENTY-FOUR

There were three air sylphs holding up the palace. In actuality, there were twelve who took turns teaming up to support it, but at the moment there were only three, nestled in chambers created for them at different points underneath the palace. Not able to see each other, they still chattered endlessly, holding the palace in place with experienced ease while they talked about the day to come, inadvertently telling the Hunter outside exactly what was happening among the hives. Old and powerful, they were happy where they were, even as they talked about finishing their shifts and returning to their masters, as well as what the hives would be like with the passageway connecting them.

Since they weren't aware of it, none of them talked about how humans would help the battle sylphs destroy the Hunter.

The Hunter carefully reached in, stretching with tendrils only a few inches wide and worming them along the vents that pockmarked the underside of the palace. It reached the air sylph on the westernmost side of the palace first, dangling down out of a crack in the stone above her as she talked about her master's various ambitions. The tentacle hesitated a moment, shrugging itself to get a bit more length into the crack, and dropped down right into the center of her.

She died instantly, the energy that formed her pattern immediately breaking down and sucking up into the tentacle, racing along its length to feed the main body. Her hive mates didn't even feel her death, though they did feel the absence of her power and screamed as the entire palace suddenly lurched to one side. They scrambled to right it and hold it up as the Hunter grabbed a better hold and forced more of itself in, now that the edge was closer to it. Invigorated by the taste of the sylph, it went hunting for her sisters.

～

Eapha pitched off the bed and onto the floor when the palace lurched. Startled out of a sound sleep, she screeched in surprise, followed by a yelp of pain that turned into a wail of terror as she slid across the suddenly angled floor toward the wall, the bed and everything else in the room scraping uncontrollably after her.

Tooie rolled off the bed after her, putting himself between her and the sliding bed and bracing his feet against it as it continued to slide forward. Raking his fingers against the floor for leverage, he kicked outward and the bed flew backward up the slope, smashing into the cabinet and vanity that were trying to come after it. An instant later, the entire collection exploded as he destroyed it and put up a shield around both of them. Bits of wood scattered against it and flew past.

The floor abruptly righted itself, throwing Eapha back against Tooie as it settled, not quite as level as before, but much better than the sudden slope it had become.

Thanks to Tooie's proximity, Eapha could feel the emotions of everyone close by in the palace. Terror, horror, rage, and the roaring of the battlers as they rose to defend against a threat she couldn't immediately identify.

"What's going on?" she shouted, so he could hear her over the thunderous noise.

Tooie hadn't joined them, his head cocked to one side while he listened. "One of the air sylphs is gone," he told her.

"Gone?" she shrilled, suddenly terrified. Where? How? None of them would ever abandon a duty. It was too ingrained in them, even without orders.

The floor dropped out from under them, Eapha suddenly too breathless to scream as it dropped no less than five feet before it stopped again, the palace trembling as if it were a live thing as frightened as her.

"Another air sylph is gone!" Tooie shouted. His own terror was tempered by his growing rage as he grabbed her arm, somehow getting to his feet and pulling her up as well. Eapha clung to him, afraid of the floor dropping away again, or of the entire palace falling. How many sylphs were supposed to be holding it up right now? She couldn't remember. Where did they *go*?

They weren't gone, they were dead. The epiphany hit her with perfect clarity, bringing with it a calmness she was pretty sure would turn back into uncontrollable terror in a heartbeat if she let it. Tooie stared at her, picking up on her emotions but not understanding them. Of course he wouldn't, she thought. He wasn't an intuitive thinker. The whole reason she had to be the queen was because the sylphs weren't shrewd, only she'd been so stupid and convinced of her own inadequacy that she hadn't let herself *be* the queen until it was too late, and it definitely was too late.

"Get me out of here," she told her battler, her voice clear even over the screaming of the women in the palace and that endless, growing roar of almost seven hundred battle sylphs all rising at once. "No matter what, get me out of here."

So she could salvage this, if there was anything left to salvage once it was over. She knew what was happening, even if Tooie didn't, and she knew he didn't. The confusion in him was obvious to her, along with the absolute trust he had in her to understand what was happening and figure out how to deal with it. Eapha hoped he was right in his faith, but like Devon only a few hours before, though in far more desperate circumstances, she put her doubts aside for the needs of the moment, the first of which was her own survival.

Tooie grabbed her up in his arms, holding her against his chest for a moment before he shifted to his cloud form and darted outside, Eapha cushioned on blackness that surrounded her as she felt him arch up, heading into the sky above the palace.

"I need to see!" she told him.

He shifted a bit, the part of his belly closest to her eyes turning translucent. Eapha stared down, feeling vertigo swamp over her as she looked down through the darkness at the palace, lurching and trembling in place. Below it, the hive was a rounded shape covered even more than the rest of the night-darkened city by the palace's shadow, and from the main gate and every suddenly opened vent, battle sylphs rose, lifting in a cloud of black rage she couldn't see save where it was sparked with lightning, rising to defend against the impossible.

The Hunter? Tooie asked her.

Eapha nodded slowly, though she thought he couldn't see, until a tendril formed inside the space where she lay to wipe her cheek of tears. "Yes," she whispered. She almost imagined she could see it right against the palace, looming like the jellyfish she remembered from the harbor waters when she played on the docks during her childhood, before she was a slave. Only no jellyfish was ever this large and it was only shadows she saw.

Why is it doing this? he asked. *Hunters only ever attack along the ground. How is it even doing this?* Battle sylphs were swarming, circling the palace and firing off blasts of energy that exploded in midair or on the ground, doing nothing.

Eapha looked down at the palace, floating above the hive, right where the sylphs moved it when the palace was first made, and knew exactly what it was after.

~

Zalia went off the bed with a shriek the same way that Eapha had, the bed itself flipping over and landing on her. Luckily, it was mostly straw, cushioning her from bruises even as she yelped, caught under it. The floor sloped farther and it rolled off her, skidding down to the far wall. The lamp she'd left burning by the bed rolled after it and shattered, catching fire, and Zalia pressed her hands against the floor, desperate not to go rolling right after it.

One-Eleven grabbed her arm, yanking her up onto her feet as the floor releveled itself with a lurch. Zalia clung to him, utterly terrified. "What's happening?" she gasped.

One-Eleven stared toward the window, where already she could see the lightning flashes of battle sylphs in their natural form. "We're under attack."

He sounded almost gleeful at the thought. "By what?" Zalia gasped, though of course, there was only one thing she could think of that would be attacking them now.

The floor dropped under them. Zalia screamed, but One-Eleven kept both his own feet and hers as it stopped again five feet lower down. Zalia felt like throwing up, but he looked at her, his eyes gleaming. "We're going to go and kill it," he told her. "Stay here, you'll be safe."

Safe? she wanted to scream. How could she possibly be safe here? She could hear other women screaming, barely audible above the roaring of the battlers, and grabbed his shirt. "You have to get me out of here!"

"Why?" he asked. "I might miss the fighting."

She stared at him, suddenly cold. "You're going to leave me? But you promised!"

The battler roaring grew louder, the storm outside the window larger and closer. She was hearing explosions as well, horrifically close. If the palace didn't fall first, they could destroy the building themselves. "One-Eleven!" She should have named him; then she could have ordered him to get her out. Instead she had to rely on his inhuman sensibilities.

"I'll be back," he assured her, pulling her hands free. Ducking in, he kissed her as if he were just going to the gladiator ring for some pretend sport, and turned, diving through the window, changing shape as he went.

"One-Eleven!" she screamed, running after him and leaning out, heedless of the broken glass that cut into her hands. He was already gone, roaring with exhilaration and rage as he joined the others. He'd left her, he really had. Zalia looked down at her hands, lifting them to see the cuts on her palms. The sight of them just made her sad. For everything he'd said and all the things he'd promised, One-Eleven didn't put her first, not even as a friend. He didn't even put her high enough to rescue her before he ran off to be the hero.

How long would the palace stay up? One-Eleven's trust in it could get her killed. Zalia looked down at the darkened hive, the growing fire behind her demanding that she get moving, and froze.

Tendrils, some as thin as her own hair but others as thick as her finger, and in one case her arm, were crawling up the side of the palace, waving in the air. They were next to invisible, so translucent she could see through them, but their edges gleamed in the firelight. Zalia sucked in her breath, knowing there was no use in screaming for One-Eleven, but damn him, why didn't he wait just one more minute? And then she turned and ran. Fleeing past the fire that used to be the bed she'd been sleeping in, she ran out into the hall, already filling with women who'd either been abandoned by their own battlers or were still trying to find them.

~

Devon woke to the sound of every sylph in the men's hive screaming.

He lurched to his feet, stumbling almost drunkenly out of the alcove. He had no idea what time it was. The harem was still dark, men turning up the wicks on lanterns to provide more light. Then a fire sylph flared and he had to duck his head, his arm up to protect his stinging eyes.

"Airi!"

The palace is under attack, she told him, her terror beating in his own chest. *The battlers are rising!*

Devon spun in terror, looking toward his neighbor's alcove in fear of seeing the creature leap out, destroying everything in his way as he went to the fight. Instead, he saw the battle sylph lying on his side just inside it, one hand holding the curtain open as he looked out at them, lifting his head to regard Devon. All the spit in Devon's mouth immediately dried up.

The battle sylph slowly blinked at him. He should talk to him, Devon knew. He should warn him about the Hunter, that humans could see it. He swallowed, working moisture back into his mouth.

The battle sylph stared at him and winced, moving one hand toward his rib cage.

"Are you hurt?" Devon asked instead, surprised.

The battle sylph sighed. "Yes. I can't rise." He glanced at the woman sleeping behind him. "I wouldn't leave her anyway." He sighed again and looked back at Devon, his eyes so intent that the man's breath caught again. "You know something. I can feel it."

Behind Devon, he could hear Gel crying, Shasha trying to comfort him. Xehm was coming toward them from where he'd bedded down for the night, fearfully asking for an explanation of what was happening. Other men were coming closer as well, braving the battler in search of news, even those with sylphs who could tell them what was happening. All of them were staring at him, and Devon took a deep, terrified breath.

"I can see the Hunter," he said. "All humans can," he added belatedly, feeling stupid.

The battler's eyebrows shot up. "What?" He sounded as if he felt as stupid as Devon. Certainly his expression was now one of shock. Xehm arrived at Devon's side, the old man looking up at him in confusion.

We saw it, Airi told him, her voice as clear to the battler as it was to Devon. He looked at her. *I mean, my master saw it.*

"We all did," Devon admitted, suddenly weary beyond belief and not sure the creature would even believe him.

He did. He stared at Devon, his mouth hanging open in a surprise that would have been comical if Devon wasn't so afraid. "You can . . ." The battler closed his eyes and groaned, trying to sit up farther and wincing before he sank back down. "You have to tell them," he said.

"Me?" Devon squeaked. Wasn't it enough that he'd forced himself to tell this one?

The battler looked at him with irritation. "You think too little of yourself, human. Tell them. Go to one of the battlers up there and scream it into his face, if you can get him to stop for you long enough."

"Why can't you tell them?" Devon asked. "I know you can talk mind to mind."

It was Airi who answered. *They've risen, Devon. They won't hear anything he sends to them through the roaring.*

The battler nodded. "I can't warn them and even if I got to the surface, I'd be running the risk of getting caught up in their rage. I can't leave Fareeda. I promised her and the queen gave me leave. You have to go."

Devon closed his eyes, feeling cold and terrified. "Gods . . ."

Xehm put a hand on his shoulder and Devon looked over at the old man, whose face was pale and lined. "It has to be someone who can do it," he said and paused before adding, "My daughter is out there."

That was really all that mattered. Devon nodded shortly, surrounded on all sides by men he'd led down here to try and save their lives, men who were afraid that the women who'd been stolen to keep them safe were now in greater danger. He thought for a moment that he'd never get through them, but they parted for him, humans and sylphs alike, and left him a pathway out.

"Right," he muttered, squared himself, and ran down it, Airi at his back.

~

The battle sylphs were rising. All over the city, they rose, taking to the air and their natural shapes as they roared in rage, the hatred consuming them. Their queen was in danger, the floating palace she lived on wavering in the air, held up now by only one desperately laboring air sylph. None of them could see what was attacking. They could only see the palace itself shaking, dropping a dozen or more feet before stopping and listing increasingly to one side even while it tried to stay in the air. Below it, the dome of the hive stretched, clean and untouched by anything in the early dawn light except the shadow of the palace above it.

They saw nothing else.

Because of that, they attacked randomly and the ground all around the hive exploded, rock erupting everywhere as they turned the buildings to rubble, the sound of it echoing even through the thick walls of the hive. They sent explosions through the air as well, creating shockwaves that carried waves of dust outward from the center hive, filling the streets as surely as the earlier storm had. The Hunter was untouched by it all, clinging to the side of the floating palace to keep itself from being blown away by the unnatural winds, or worse, getting caught in one of those explosions. Its body was higher than any of the detonations and they wouldn't target the palace itself. Even in their madness, they wouldn't do that, not so long as the queen was at risk.

As the battlers continued to throw their energy everywhere, hoping desperately to catch *something*, the Hunter readjusted its grip and delved deeper into the palace's underbelly, searching for that last air sylph.

Eapha looked down at it all, half-blinded by the dust, and coughing, held in Tooie's mantle as she felt him tremble with the need to attack. She just dug her fingers into his body, afraid that if she let go, he'd dive into that madness, for it was madness. She felt near total insanity from the battle sylphs as they tried to defend against something that couldn't be fought, and as their madness grew, they forgot the most important things.

Eapha didn't. She couldn't hear anything other than the roar of the battle sylphs or feel more than their swamping hate auras, but she knew she hadn't been the only one in the palace.

"Save the women!" she screamed, her voice almost hoarse from dust but her mental cry as loud as Tooie could project it. The voice of a queen who couldn't be denied. *Save the women in the palace!*

Hearing her cry, everywhere around the palace, battle sylphs dived, heading for entrances, some of them dying unheeded when they flew straight into the Hunter's tentacles, and with a hum of satisfaction, the Hunter speared into the final air sylph's chamber and found its prize.

CHAPTER TWENTY-FIVE

The palace fell.

Zalia screamed, her stomach rising as she was suddenly weight-less, everything in her pressing upward as the floor beneath her fell.

Then the battlers were there, streaking into the hallway where the women were, coming through windows that they smashed open, the lightning inside them roiling faster than the most violent of storms. They snatched the women up and Zalia was caught with them, surrounded by warm blackness. The feeling that she was fall-ing down was replaced by an even more sickening one of racing forward while darting side to side, as though avoiding a great many things, until suddenly they looped up in a steady arc. Finally, they leveled off and immediately began to drop again. The drop wasn't so abrupt this time and slowed nearly to a stop before the darkness around her changed, turning into a tall, beautiful man holding her in the middle of a street where other women wept in the arms of other beautiful men.

"Are you all right?" One-Eleven asked her.

Zalia stared at him, her lungs only just starting to work again, and then looked over his shoulder and forgot how to breathe again.

The palace fell onto the hive, the pointed bottom of it slamming into it like a hammer against a glass jar. The sound of it hitting the stone of the hive punched her like a wave, so loud it hurt, and the side of the dome where the palace hit crumbled wide open.

"Oh gods," Zalia whispered, though she wasn't sure if she said the words aloud.

Still holding her by her arms, One-Eleven stared back over his shoulder at the devastation, his grip tightening until it began to hurt. The roar of the battle sylphs changed with the breach in the hive and after a moment, Zalia realized that she was hearing screams from that direction, coming from inside the hive. She shouldn't have heard them over the battle sylphs, except there were so many people screaming.

"What's happening!" she shouted at One-Eleven. He didn't seem to hear her, still staring. The other battlers who'd rescued the women were rising, very few of them staying with their women unless they were ordered to. Zalia saw Kiala, her feet dangling off the ground as she kept her arms around Yahe's neck, desperately clinging to him while he tried to get her to let go. "One-Eleven!"

He looked at her, his eyes glazed and wild.

"Zalia!"

Hearing the voice behind her, Zalia turned, the air whooshing out of her and back in as she started to breathe again. Devon was running toward her, his face frantic and his hair sticking out in all directions.

"Devon!" she shouted and One-Eleven yanked her to him, his grip suddenly possessive as he hissed at the man.

Devon skidded to a halt so fast that it was as though he'd run into a wall. He stared at One-Eleven, his face ashen white and his mouth a terrified little O. Zalia thought for a moment that he'd run, and she pulled herself free of One-Eleven's embrace, taking a step toward him. In that moment, Devon swallowed and managed to find his voice.

"I can see the Hunter," he said.

Both of them stared at him, Zalia standing in front of One-Eleven and feeling almost as confused as she was sure One-Eleven was.

One-Eleven's face twisted. "That's stupid."

"It's not," Devon whispered, his voice so low Zalia wasn't sure she heard it over the roaring of the battle sylphs. "I can see it."

Zalia turned back toward One-Eleven, staring up into his beautiful face and not knowing what to think. The other battle sylphs were continuing their roar, a note of desperation in it now as they hurled explosions at the area around the mouth of the gaping hole into the open hive. Even the sound of it shattering didn't dampen the echoes of the screams inside, shrieks of pain that had nothing to do with the damage caused by the broken stone. Women were being devoured inside the hive, Zalia knew it. She still couldn't see any Hunter, just streaks of dust blown by the winds of the explosions that could have been massive swinging ropes if she let herself believe it.

Just like what she'd seen reaching up to her window at the palace, right before it fell.

"One-Eleven," she started to say.

He didn't hear her, or perhaps chose not to. "You're a liar!' he shouted at Devon. "You just want *her*!"

"No!" Devon gasped. "I mean yes. I mean—"

"Go away," the battler snarled. "Coward. You're just a coward. You're nothing but fear. Go away. I'll show you what real heroes do."

He leaned forward and kissed Zalia, firm and hard on the mouth. She gasped, rising up on her toes as his kiss overwhelmed her despite herself with promise and something more. Something like madness.

"We battlers will stop the Hunter," he whispered to her, pulling his mouth away. "We have it now. That coward just doesn't have the courage to do it."

What did he mean? Zalia wondered, suddenly terrified. There was something final in his tone, and proud, and utterly insane, as irrational as the roar of the battle sylphs was becoming.

"Don't go!" Kiala was shouting at her battle sylph, her arms still locked around his neck. "I'm ordering you not to go! Don't go!" Yahe looked crazed, trembling as he held his master, his eyes turned toward the three of them.

Don't go where? Zalia wondered, staring up at One-Eleven, seeing something in his eyes that suddenly made her wish that she had agreed to become his master. Only that, she understood, would have been enough for her to stop what was about to come. Now it was too late to stop him at all.

One-Eleven gave Devon a look that could only have been triumph and kissed Zalia again. A moment later he was in the air, shifting to his cloud form as he raced to join the mass cloud that was forming in the air next to the hive, so dense that nothing could be seen through it. Dozens of battlers were joining it, hundreds, until the only ones that remained on the ground seemed to be those with screaming women hanging on to them. Knocked to the ground by the force of One-Eleven's departure, Zalia stared up at them in confusion, her reeling mind not understanding, or not wanting to understand, for when it started, she wasn't actually surprised.

The battle sylphs started to dive at the entrance to the hive, throwing themselves not into it, but at the invisible creature they knew was there. Dozens of them at a time, they fed it with their own bodies, drawing it away from the women and sylphs inside the only way they could. Zalia barely realized she was screaming, knowing that One-Eleven was in that suicidal cloud, perhaps even already dead, and there was nothing she could do to stop it.

"By the gods," Devon groaned behind her. "Why didn't you listen to me? Why didn't you damn well listen?" A moment later, he grabbed Zalia, manhandling her roughly to her feet, and pulled her against him. "Look!" he shouted. "Look at it!"

She looked, watching as battle sylphs died at the gaping hole into the hive, screaming and vanishing in sparks of energy. They shrieked in agony as they died, but still more dived to replace the ones gone, suiciding en masse.

"Not there!" Devon shouted, grabbing her chin and forcing her gaze up. "LOOK AT IT!"

Zalia looked and suddenly she saw. Above the cloud, above where the palace used to be, there floated a flattened oval shape, hundreds of tentacles hanging from its body, all of it so faint that it could have just been dust if he hadn't told her it was there, if Devon hadn't forced her to look. The Hunter hung over its feeding ground, devouring the battle sylphs who sacrificed themselves on its tentacles so willingly, none of them able to see its actual body as it floated safe above them.

"Oh gods," she whispered. It was nearly a hundred feet across, obvious to her now and horrible.

"I have to stop it," Devon whispered. "Airi, I have to stop it and I need you to help me. Zalia, if I don't, you have to tell them where it is, what it is."

"How?" she gasped, turning to face him as he let her go and drew his sword, the first time she'd seen him even touch it though it had always been at his side. "How can you stop it?" Then he lifted into the air, carried by his air sylph, and she knew what he was going to do. "NO!" she screamed, though she couldn't stop him any more than she could have stopped One-Eleven.

All she could do was watch.

~

Devon realized just as Zalia did what the battle sylphs were doing and why. It was utter insanity, but how much saner was what he was considering? He had no choice. They wouldn't listen to him; it took all the courage he'd been able to gather to go up to Zalia's battle sylph and try to talk to him. Now they were all insane and he felt like he had no courage left.

Why are we doing this? Airi shrieked, her terror beating at him as she carried him awkwardly up and over the buildings of the city, fighting to lift him above the battle sylphs and the Hunter. *This is battler work!*

"There aren't going to be any battlers left in a few minutes," Devon told her, clutching his sword hilt with sweaty hands as he tried not to look down. Airi did her best to carry him, but as always, the ride was rough. He desperately hung on to the sword.

Why us? she wailed.

Because there was no one else. Because he had to. Because if he stopped to think about it, he'd take Zalia and her father and run, and he'd never be able to live with himself. Of course, if he got Airi hurt, he'd definitely never be able to live with himself. There was just no other way up to the body of the Hunter. All he could do was pray he was right and that it was vulnerable there.

"Go right," he told Airi, knowing she couldn't see anything ahead of them except dying battlers flickering into oblivion in mid-air. She jerked them both to the right, making Devon want to vomit but keeping them clear of a massively thick tentacle that swung almost lazily, impacting against three battle sylphs who flashed and were gone, leaving only faintly glowing afterimages being sucked up the tentacle toward the body. Devon was still terrified, but he grieved for the battlers. They were sacrificing themselves for no good reason. The best they could hope for was to feed the Hunter enough that it would leave. They wouldn't destroy it, only themselves.

"Go up," he directed, his voice thick.

I'm trying, Airi sobbed, hauling them both upward, but still forward. She couldn't just lift him and had to settle for circling upward, using the winds as much as she could. It seemed agonizingly slow, though they moved quickly enough.

"Left!" he screamed and she rushed that way, a tentacle lashing through where they'd just been.

I hate this, I hate this, I hate this.

"I'll play an entire symphony for you after this," Devon promised. "I will." His gorge rose and he almost vomited. "And I'll never ask you to carry me anywhere ever again."

You better not! Just kill the thing so I can put you down and cry!

"Move right!" he shouted.

~

The Hunter fed lazily, gorging itself on the creatures so willing to feed it. Their energy filled it, pushing the gas production in its main body to maximum. It would feast on these creatures and the rest of the hive once they were gone. Then it would give itself to the winds. There was even more food in the hive than it had hoped for and it wasn't worried anymore. It could cross that ocean with this much to fuel it. The underground hive would escape, but that didn't matter. If the winds ever brought it back, it would have more food waiting for it.

The battle sylphs threw themselves at it, a nice delicacy that it savored. They truly were stupid creatures, given to instinct so much that they never even considered attacking except where it did damage. So they hurled themselves at its feeding tentacles and it savored their taste, enjoying itself as it always did when it managed to breech a hive.

For all its thousand eyes, it almost didn't see the human and the air sylph. It didn't see them at all at first, hidden as they were by the battlers, but it did spot them once they finally got clear of the cloud and continued climbing, rising to get above it. It paid attention to them then, never having seen such a thing, and listened. It couldn't understand what the human said, but it could understand the sylph and listened to what she was saying with growing horror.

A moment later, it turned its attention away from the hive completely, abandoning its meal.

≈

The battle sylphs hurled themselves without thought at the Hunter's tentacles. They were hatched to protect, to keep the hive safe, and the hive was in danger. Abandoning it wasn't even an option and the shrieks of their brothers as they died in agony didn't get through their maddened determination. Caught in a fugue of insanity, they threw themselves at it more and more, knowing only that Hunters ate until sated, and if it had to be sated, it would be on them, not their hive or their queen.

It was a shock to many of them when the last of the battlers to hurl themselves down just raced through the entrance to the hive instead of dying. Inside, there was rubble everywhere from the devastation and blood, but no bodies. The Hunter had swept away any living thing it touched.

Alive along with the rest of the few survivors, One-Eleven gaped around himself and then started to roar in triumph, echoed by the others. The Hunter was gone, they'd driven it out!

It's not over yet! Tooie shouted to all of them.

They turned, looking back up through the gaping wound in the side of the hive. One-Eleven stared with the others, not sure what he was supposed to be looking at yet, until he saw the last thing he would have expected. The human that Haru hadn't let him kill earlier was being carried by that foreign air sylph through the sky, both of them darting around in all directions as though they were trying to avoid something.

Hadn't the human claimed something about being able to see the Hunter? One-Eleven wondered with a sudden uncertainty.

～

When Eapha saw the palace crash into the hive, making a jagged hole fifty feet wide in the thick stone, she was horrified. When she saw the battle sylphs start to make their suicide run, her horror only increased. If she stopped them, everyone inside the hive would die. If she didn't, the battlers would die instead.

Everything happened so fast she couldn't even think, let alone tell Tooie what order to relay. Then she saw the human floating through the air and thought at first that he was coming up to where Tooie held her above the ground, only he wasn't taking a direct route. He was darting back and forth, dodging awkwardly around swirling lines of dust and smoke that were almost like tentacles.

They were *exactly* like tentacles. "I can see it!" she shouted, startling Tooie. "I can see it!" Hundreds of tentacles, barely visible, all of them trying to lift up toward the man but most too heavy as he continued to rise. All of them were pulling away from the hive, straining toward him.

Send the battlers in, she thought, but couldn't. There were so few left where there had been hundreds before and they couldn't see the Hunter. Devon could. If they went in, if they got in his way, if they *hurt* him . . .

"Tell the battlers to hold their explosions," she told Tooie, peering down from his embrace at the battle. "Tell them to let that man through. They have to keep him alive!"

Let him through what? Tooie wondered, but he obeyed and far below her, the battle sylphs obeyed as well.

~

"Left!" Devon shouted, seeing a tentacle swinging toward him. He was nearly at the level of the underside of the Hunter and it was so close it filled his vision, clearer and easier to see up close. It was still translucent, but obvious enough this close that he easily saw its tentacles lashing toward him. The tips dangled far below, apparently too heavy to lift, but the midsections were high enough to reach him.

Sobbing, Airi lifted him over the tentacle coming his way, Devon raising his feet high to avoid it. Immediately, another swung toward him from the other direction. "Down!" he screamed and Airi dropped, almost landing him in a mass of thinner tendrils below before his next scream stopped her. He didn't like to go down, there were more tentacles there, but he had to get close. It knew he was there, he had no doubt about that.

The battlers knew something was up as well and they swarmed around him, staring at him with their terrifying ball lightning eyes. Devon saw one blunder into a tentacle and vanish immediately, his energy sucked into the length of it. The other battlers roared, having seen him disappear, and attacked that spot, two of them falling into the same trap and being devoured as well.

The tentacles stopped when they drew in energy. Devon didn't know if it was intentional or involuntary, but he screamed for Airi to go up and she lifted him, gaining another fifty feet and carrying him over a feeding tentacle that had been impassible a moment before. He was able to see the edge of the Hunter's rounded body now, only a few dozen feet away. The sides of it were smooth, faintly patterned and completely clear of tentacles. They all came out of it from its underside.

I can't do this, Airi wailed. *I'm too tired!*

Be tired later, he wanted to tell her. He was terrified himself and really wanted to go home. Someone far braver than he was should be the one doing this.

A battle sylph swept up to them, eyes swirling, and Airi shrieked, nearly dropping him. Devon shrieked as well, at the proximity of the thing and at how he'd never reach the ground if Airi dropped him now. The entire air beneath him was a mass of crisscrossing tentacles and the battlers had already lost a half dozen of their survivors to it. More tentacles waved all around them, the Hunter lifting its smaller, lighter ones as fast as it could. They had to get out of their reach while they still could, but Devon could only stare at the battle sylph hovering before him. It was huge, even bigger than Mace back home, which meant it was old and powerful, though even the youngest of them could turn both him and Airi into an ash too fine for the Hunter to taste.

Some older battlers were skilled enough at shape-shifting to form a human voice in their cloud form. This was one of them. "So you *can* see it," the creature hissed.

Zalia's lover. Devon nearly wet himself and Airi pressed close, whimpering at the appearance of her master's rival. The battler glared and Devon tried to speak, but he couldn't get anything out.

One-Eleven moved closer, lightning teeth frighteningly large in its massive head. "Why you, you pathetic coward? You're nothing."

Devon swallowed, trying to talk. If One-Eleven would listen, he could point him at the Hunter's head. He could destroy it in a heartbeat. It had to be vulnerable. The Hunter wouldn't be trying to kill him so much if it weren't. One-Eleven could kill it and Devon could just go and find a place to collapse.

"Are you trying to impress Zalia?" One-Eleven went on. "She's picked me. Not you . . . me! You think you can change that by pretending to be brave? No one here thinks you have any courage."

Devon tended to agree with that. He licked his lips, forcing himself to speak. He could feel how tired Airi was getting and she couldn't keep this up for much longer. "I just want to keep everyone safe."

"I don't care what the queen ordered, that's a battle sylph's job!"

Behind the battler, who was between Devon and Airi and the Hunter, a tentacle only as thick as a human arm managed to lift itself up high enough, the curve of its middle rising up beside its bulbous body bag while the rest of its length hung below. Trembling from the strain, it lashed out, heading straight for them.

"AIRI! LOOK OUT!"

Airi screamed, not knowing which way to go.

Up, he tried to say, pointing at it, knowing she couldn't move fast enough. One-Eleven gave him a look of pure disgust. "The queen gave her order," he said, spitting the words.

Then he placed himself between Devon's pointing arm and the Hunter.

Devon saw the tentacle hit him. One-Eleven grunted, shifting to human form, perhaps involuntarily, and Devon saw the pain on his face as the tentacle sank into him, or perhaps he sank into it, growing transparent until he was as hard to see as his killer, his eyes still locked on his rival's before they closed and he faded entirely, becoming just a flicker of energy running up the length of the tentacle.

The tentacle stopped, hesitating as it fed, and Devon managed to get out his order. "Up! Airi, take us up!"

She did, howling, and the tentacle moved again, lashing below Devon's hanging feet as they rose to where even the finest of the monster's tentacles couldn't reach. The whole body started to move, the Hunter giving up on catching him. Instead its tentacles lashed out below, ignoring any battlers still around as it grabbed for buildings, wrapping the ends around them and digging in as it used them to pull itself away, trying to flee. Battle sylphs howled at the sight of the tops of buildings exploding, trenches suddenly appearing in the stone, and whether by luck or desperation, they started to attack the buildings. Stone exploded, leaving the Hunter nothing to grab on to as it hung there.

It started to roll over instead, trying to turn its vulnerable back away from him and get its tentacles in the way. Carried by his air sylph, Devon rose above it, seeing those tentacles swirling under it, his mouth dry and his hands covered in sweat so that he had to let go of his sword with first one and then the other to dry them off on his shirt. He had no idea what would happen next, but he knew what he had to say.

"Let me go," he told Airi.

What? she gasped. *You'll fall!*

Yes, he thought, but only he would. Airi would be safe. He didn't know how long she'd last without his energy, but surely they'd get her back to the Valley in time. Surely Eapha would be willing to give her that much.

"Drop me!" he shouted.

She wailed and did, unable to disobey. Devon fell straight toward the Hunter, unable to breathe as he braced himself, afraid he'd be absorbed the same as One-Eleven the second he touched it, but hoping that the steel of his sword, pointing downward, wouldn't.

He hit it hard, his breath whooshing out of him and his feet slipping on a surface that was smooth and somehow slimy. His sword, however, plunged hilt deep into the Hunter, and he was lucky that he couldn't inhale as foul gasses suddenly poured out of it.

The Hunter shrieked, its scream echoing in Devon's head and into the minds of everyone there, human or sylph. Stunned by it, Devon could only hold on to the hilt of his sword with both hands, feeling the monster pulse underneath him.

He'd landed off center on it, on the slope of its side. After a moment, he started to slide, his sword blade slicing through the monster as easily as it would pass through water, leaving a great tearing rent in the side of the creature that poisonous air rushed out of as it continued to scream, now dropping in altitude as Devon continued sliding, reaching the bottom edge of its body in seconds and slipping right off the edge. Still clinging to his sword, he fell.

The battle sylphs still couldn't see the Hunter, but they did see Devon sliding along it and they saw the distortion of the gasses escaping from it into the air. The first energy wave one of them threw hit the creature dead center and it exploded. The force of that sent everyone in the air tumbling and hit Devon like a wall. He fell, unconscious, which meant he didn't know it when, a few seconds later, a battle sylph caught him just before he reached the ground.

EPILOGUE

Zalia walked down the hallway, her hands clasped together before her. She was dressed in a beautiful blue gown found in the closet of her new room, but she didn't feel beautiful. She wasn't sure what she did feel but she knew there was a whole morass of feelings inside of her that she'd have to deal with someday.

One-Eleven was dead. She knew that from Airi, who'd seen it and turned herself solid so she could tell Zalia. He'd died to protect Devon long enough to kill the Hunter and Zalia didn't know what she thought about that, or about the queen who'd ordered him to do it. He didn't really feel dead to her, not yet. She suspected it would be very painful once he did.

The building she walked through was light and airy, with big windows to let in the cooling breezes of attendant air sylphs, much like the palace that fell out of the sky, though this one was firmly attached to the ground. It also wasn't inside the ruined hive. No one wanted to stay there, so the light that came through the windows was natural.

Zalia went up to one door. She'd been there several times before, but Devon had been sleeping each time. There was no guard outside, so she tapped once and peeked in, just in case he was still asleep.

Devon was sitting up in the bed against the pillows, his hair spiking as she saw him.

"How are you feeling?" she asked, coming in and walking over to sit on the side of his bed.

Devon smiled at her, the sight of it making her heart skip a beat, even as his hair suddenly flattened out again to either side. "Better." That was good. He'd been healed by a healer sylph, but it had still been very close. Zalia heard the healer say that if he'd actually inhaled any of the gasses that came out of the Hunter, he would have been dead even before the battler caught him. Tears welled up in her eyes and Devon looked alarmed. "Hey, I'm okay, really."

"I know," she said, wiping her tears away. He was, he really was. And if he ever risked himself like that again, she'd kill him.

For now, she leaned down and kissed him instead. It was good. He felt alive and strong and loving underneath her lips and she moved her mouth upward to kiss his nose and cheeks and eyelids, grateful only that he was alive, and loved her.

"I told my father we're going to be married," she whispered to him.

He smiled. "What was his reaction?"

"What do you think? He was ecstatic." She blushed. "I didn't tell him we were already practicing the good parts."

"Probably a good idea," he admitted.

Though she had other things in mind that she'd rather be doing with him, Zalia sat back. "The queen sent me to get you if you're feeling up to it."

He looked a little dubious. "How's she doing?"

"Feeling guilty. Determined to make things better." Zalia shrugged. "I think she's doing a lot better than I would in the same situation. She does want to see you though."

Devon sighed and got up. "I guess we better go then, or I'll never get out of this bed."

Zalia blushed at that and also when he started to take his night-clothes off; but she didn't leave, instead watching without shame as he stripped and put on the clothes that had been left for him. Devon grinned at her, but he didn't protest as she kept him company until he was dressed. Then she led him down the plainly decorated halls toward the dining hall that Eapha was using as her throne room.

"How many people do they think died?" Devon asked as they walked. Airi was still playing with his hair and it looked as though he'd slept on half of it.

"No one's sure yet," Zalia told him. "A lot. Not nearly as many as would have if you hadn't saved us." She paused. "We've lost about eighty percent of our battle sylphs."

Devon stopped there and looked at her. She suspected he wouldn't ever get over his terror of them, but he appeared to be as disturbed by those numbers as she was. "That's . . ."

"Scary," she finished for him. She'd sat in on some of the meetings they'd had while Devon was recovering, at Eapha's invitation. There were fewer than a hundred and fifty battle sylphs in Meridal now and there was real concern that one of their desert neighbors might decide to invade if they didn't do something. "They're going to reopen the gates to get more. It'll take a long time to get our numbers up."

Devon sighed. "Here's hoping another Hunter doesn't come through."

"They're going to be careful, and have human guards on them as well as battlers."

"Right. Solie will have to be warned, so she can do the same thing."

They walked on, their hands somehow ending up entwined as they made their way. It was only down a flight of stairs and across a few halls to the dining room and Zalia felt Devon's hand tighten in hers as the battler on guard outside the door looked at him. Devon's hair neatly rearranged itself.

The battler didn't say a word, instead pulling the door open. Devon hesitated for a moment and then hurried through, Zalia trotting at his side. They'd just crossed the threshold when he stopped again.

They might have lost most of their battlers, but the majority of those who survived seemed to be in the queen's throne room and Devon looked at them with something like despair before he steeled himself, preparing to walk forward anyway. Zalia's heart ached for him.

The battle sylphs, however, looked back at Devon, and all of them started to step away, leaving first an open area around the man and then the entire room as they went out through other doorways or changed shape to fly out the window. In moments, the room was clear of them, save the lead battler standing by the chair at the other end where his queen sat. He leaned down and kissed Eapha's cheek before straightening. With a nod at Devon, he left.

Devon gaped, alone with the queen of a hive save for a few human women and elemental sylphs. "What the—?"

Zalia smiled at him, though she hadn't known they were going to do that. "I think that's their way of saying thank you," she told him and watched him shake his head in disbelief.

~

Devon stared after the departed battle sylphs, feeling his fear drain away. He hadn't thought they'd do that. He hadn't thought they'd acknowledge him at all, let alone leave him with their queen.

Eapha laughed, rising up from the chair and coming toward him, her hands outstretched. "Don't worry about them. Tooie says they trust that you of all people won't hurt me."

Devon stared at her, bemused, as she took his hands and squeezed them. "Okay, I guess."

She laughed. "Well, considering you probably don't want one of them draping a medal around your neck, staying away from you is probably the next best thing." Her smile faded. "Can you forgive me for being a fool?"

Devon looked at her, forgetting about the battlers as he studied the woman. She'd aged since he saw her last, though he supposed he had as well. She carried a heavier burden than he did. If she'd only listened to him . . . He pushed the thought away, knowing she was as empathic as Solie and felt whatever he did. She was queen. She needed his help a lot more than his condemnation, and she was listening now.

"I can, Your Majesty."

She smiled again, her face beautiful. "Come on then, have some lunch with me and we'll discuss what the ambassador of Sylph Valley can do to help Meridal." The hint of dimples showed on her cheeks. "I suspect it will be a lot."

Devon smiled at her. "Yes, Your Majesty."

Eapha smiled as Devon and Zalia left again. She was glad to have him with her, though there was time enough for him to recover. He'd been through a lot, and he'd go through a lot more helping her turn her hive into a real kingdom again. For now, she could give him a few more days to get his feet under him.

She returned to her chair as she sensed the battlers filtering back into the room. She hadn't asked any of them to leave the way they had and she was touched by the gesture. It was the best reward they could give to Devon, she supposed. It was more than recognizing they didn't want to frighten him. They were showing they trusted him.

The chair was hard and still a bit uncomfortable under her, despite the cushioning. She supposed she'd have to get used to it. She couldn't look very regal sitting on a pillow on the floor, after all, though she'd keep a few in her private quarters.

Over by the window, Kiala sighed, and Eapha felt her exasperation, her surety that Eapha looked stupid sitting on a chair and was only putting on airs. As if she were selfishly pretending to be more special or important than anyone else, including, she saw now, Kiala herself.

Eapha's hands tightened on the arms of her chair, her heart suddenly pounding but her voice firm. "Stop it," she said, not turning to look at the other woman. "Stop it right now, Kiala."

"What?" Kiala said.

"Say a single word about what you're thinking and I will banish you from Meridal, do you understand me?"

Kiala's shock was absolute, as was that of the other survivors of the Circle. Not all of them had made it through that horrible night. Even fewer of their battle sylphs had and most of them were grieving, though that didn't stop their surprise now. Finally, Eapha allowed herself to turn and glare at all of them, even as Tooie walked back up behind her chair, his pride in her overwhelming.

"Kiala. I am the queen of Meridal. Accept it or get out. That goes for all of you."

Kiala stared back at her, her eyes huge, and finally gave a short, stilted nod of agreement. Eapha turned back around in her chair, her heart still pounding, her stomach feeling ill, and the shock and condemnation—and even the admiration—of her friends ringing in her mind. She felt the happiness and relief of the sylphs at her words too, and for their sake, for the moment, that would have to be enough.

"We have a lot to do today," she said. "Let's get to it."

⁓

Life in Meridal changed, but in some ways it went on the same as it always had before the hives. The entire city was a hive in the sylphs' minds, but to the humans who lived there, it was home, now without battle-sylph law being enforced. Zalia suspected that the quality of life was going to go up quite a bit, at least for the people who'd been poor, such as her old neighbors in the hovels outside the city. They had homes themselves now, empty buildings granted to them by the queen. After all, there were certainly enough of them sitting vacant. Eapha had started deeding them out, and if anyone didn't like the rules she came up with, she did still have over a hundred battle sylphs to protect her, as well as one determined man with a single air sylph and a lot of training in how a society should be set up.

Zalia smiled a bit as she stepped up onto the patio where she'd once worked, looking around. She hadn't been back since One-Eleven bullied her old employer and it was bittersweet to see it again. It would also be the last time, she told herself. Just as, earlier in the day, going to the hovel where she'd once lived had been her last visit there. They were part of the life she used to have and she just needed to say good-bye.

She was going to go back to the stable where she'd met One-Eleven next.

There were a number of customers in the restaurant; the survivors of the Hunter were determined to get on with life as if nothing had ever happened. Zalia couldn't really blame them and turned to go.

"You! You're still alive!"

Zalia turned back around to see Ilaja standing in the door to the kitchens, her hands on her hips as she stared at Zalia, her face already turning down into a frown. She'd been taken to the women's hive, Zalia thought. What had it been like for her? Zalia had no idea if Ilaja was made into a battle-sylph master there as One-Eleven tried to do with her, but if Ilaja had, her battler hadn't survived and she was back here, as bitter as always.

"I'm alive," Zalia said, just to say something. "I'm glad you are."
Ilaja sniffed, stomping toward her. "Don't think Orlil will be glad to see you," she retorted.

"Zalia!"

Both women turned to see Orlil coming out of the kitchens, mopping sweat off his forehead. He smiled at her winningly enough while the customers were listening, but when he reached her side, his voice dropped. Ilaja backed away a few steps, looking smug but also as though she didn't want his attention on her by mistake.

"You little whore," he snapped. "I heard that your battler got killed. Well, I'm going to make your life a nightmare now."

Zalia looked at him, studying the man who'd once held her life in his hands and made her so miserable. Any fear she'd had for him was long gone.

"Zalia." Zalia turned, smiling at the voice as Orlil blanched, seeing Devon walk up. His looks were unmistakable and there wasn't anyone in Meridal who didn't know what he'd done or that he now had the ear of the queen. Certainly there wasn't a man surviving in the city who hadn't seen him lead them all to safety in the men's hive. Zalia beamed at him, loving his timing even as his hair started spiking in all directions again. Seeing power of a sort very different from a battler, Orlil began stammering greetings.

"Devon," Zalia murmured, kissing his cheek. "Orlil was just telling me how he's going to make my life horrid again, since I don't have a battler to protect me." Orlil started sputtering.

"Oh?" Devon looked down at Orlil, amused. "She has all of them, just as she does"—he pointed at Ilaja—"and everyone else here. We're bringing in new laws, about fair treatment and fair wages. The battlers will be enforcing them." He smiled at Orlil, who looked as though he was going to go into shock, and nodded at Ilaja, who gaped at them both with all the bitterness washed off her face. She blinked at him and stared at Zalia, who nodded and saw the first light of hope she'd ever seen in her appear on the woman's face.

"Have a nice day," Devon told Orlil, probably just to rub it in, and turned away, taking Zalia by the hand and leading her with him. They strolled down the street, enjoying the day before the sun got too hot. A battle sylph on patrol saw them and turned down a side street to take the long way around.

Devon sighed happily as his hair started rearranging itself again. "It's a beautiful day."

"It is," Zalia murmured, laying her head on his shoulder and feeling her hair get tangled together with his. "I think for the first time ever, it really is."

They walked on.

THE END

ACKNOWLEDGMENTS

To Francois Bergogne, because I promised him a long time ago that I would.

To Michelle Grajkowski, for helping me get these books out to the world.

To Amazon, for deciding to take me under their wing.

About the Author

Kevin Daly Photography

L. J. McDonald is a fresh new voice in fantasy romance. Her first book, *The Battle Sylph*, was published by Dorchester in 2010 and named one of the top-five romance novels by *Library Journal* that year. She quickly followed her debut with two sequels: *The Shattered Sylph* and *Queen of the Sylphs*. McDonald earned a degree in anthropology from the University of Victoria and joined the Canadian Air Force in 2002. She currently lives in Embrun, Ontario.